Whitehorse Peak

P.G. BADZEY

For Siobhan
For her faith and encouragement, no matter what else got in the way.

Novels by P.G. Badzey

The Grey Rider Series

Whitehorse Peak
Eye of Truth
Helm of Shadows
Assassin Prince

CONTENTS

ACKNOWLEDGMENTS

"The author wishes to acknowledge the following people for their invaluable assistance in making this first novel come to life: Dora Badzey, for providing the editing expertise garnered in over 30 years of teaching English and Literature; the good people at Wavecloud for the fantastic cover art; Gene Badzey, for his meticulous proofreading skills; Veronica Badzey, whose professional background in typesetting and publishing saved this author's sanity, and C. Dale Brittain, for her friendship and patient, expert advice. Thank you all and God Bless."

Song of the Grey Riders

Seven they are, the Riders Grey,
who come to serve the Holy Way.
Seven they are of varied flight,
on winged steeds of dark midnight.
The Riders Grey, the warriors brave,
who seek to stem the Evil Wave:
One with sword from dwarves of old
and one fair maiden with hair of gold.
To aid the ones who follow the Three
comes another of the Silver Tree.
One with hawk of sharpened claw,
one forest guide of Christian law.
One small and swift, silent and light;
another the same with magic bright.
North they go to face Cold Fire
to battle the dragon and quench her ire.
When ogre's rage meets its end,
then does their true quest begin.

In tower cold and cavern deep,
the Diamond Eye they now must seek.
For good or evil all must choose
or choosing none, their lives to lose.
When gold to red at passage end,
then halfling toy upward must send.
Golden sorrow, heart's true Love,
pray to God in Heaven above.
That she may see, and all may learn,
what Truthful Eye cannot discern.

Holy relic, giver of life,
meant for tresses of carpenter's wife.

Ancient Evil, Good to slay,
seeks to thwart the Holy Way.
Relic's might of love is wrought,
so evil's will avails it naught.
One Dark Rider fights seven of Grey,
yet Queenly Crown shall win the day.
Seven they were, from varied flight,
on winged steeds of dark midnight.
Seven they were, the Riders Grey,
who came to serve the Holy Way.

MAPS

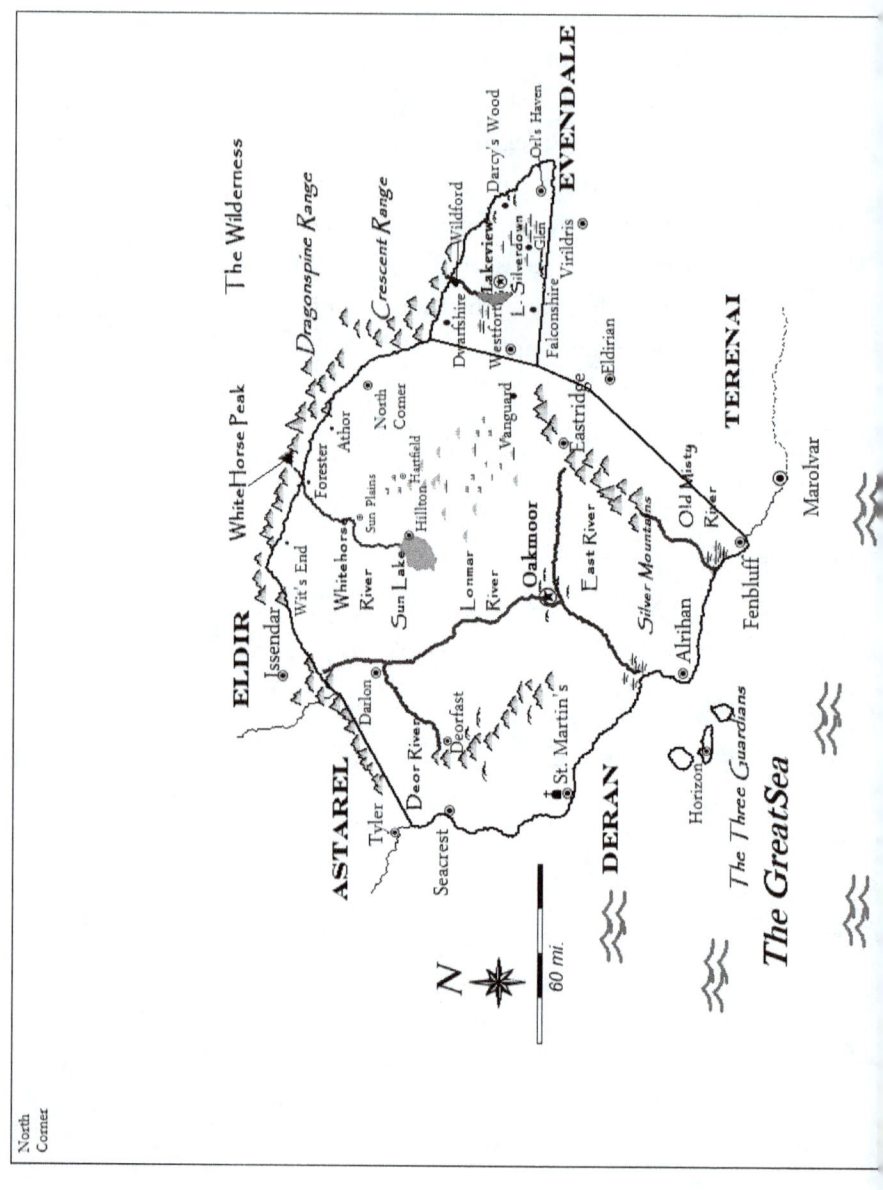

Chapter One- Fire in the Forest

When the birds stopped singing, Dar Cabot knew something was wrong.

He frowned, reached back over his shoulder with a gloved hand and drew an arrow from the quiver. Nothing stirred.

Still, he waited, eyes roaming the forest. Something caught his attention. A trail of footprints marched ahead of him over the soft earth.

Someone small and heavy...

He knelt. Two arrows whizzed overhead and thudded into a tree next to him. He dropped to the ground and rolled, holding his bow and arrow close. He counted to three, then scrambled up. Another arrow zipped past and he took cover behind another tree.

Heart pounding, he waited, feeling the metallic taste of adrenaline in his mouth. Something rustled in the bushes to his right, about thirty feet away. He peered around the tree.

Two stocky, bandy-legged creatures with simian features and short horns stalked out of the underbrush, yellow eyes glaring in his direction. They held curved bows with arrows at the ready.

Goblins! This close to town...

Dar loosed his arrow, catching one archer in the chest. The goblin jerked backwards and thumped into the moist earth, to lie still.

The remaining archer fired at Dar. The shaft hummed past. Dar slipped around the tree, hearing the rush of booted feet on the pine needles. He dropped his bow, reaching for the sword strapped on his back. He released the buckle and drew the blade, dropping belt and scabbard on the ground.

The goblin leaped around the tree at him, saber and dirk stabbing.

Dar turned aside the sword and kicked the dirk-hand away. He swung at the goblin's head. The goblin ducked and stabbed at him again, but he dodged and thrust. Steel rang on steel.

The goblin broke away and stalked left, carving small circles in the air with his weapons. Suddenly, he jerked a foot upward, kicking earth and leaves in Dar's face.

Dar crouched. A blade whistled over his head. The dirk came next and he parried it, then thrust upward. The sword-point ripped through leather and mail and the goblin went limp.

Dar jerked his weapon free and whirled, spinning low to the ground, heart pounding.

A bird chirped from its perch on an aspen tree and a few insects scuttled away in the undergrowth. Still he waited, eyes scanning every shadow. A squirrel poked a curious nose out of a large hole in the side of a nearby oak, beady eyes watching Dar. It took a tentative step, then raced out on a branch.

Dar sighed and relaxed. A slight breeze caressed his face and he used the corner of his tunic to wipe off the sweat.

He shrugged off his backpack and pulled out a waterskin. The water felt cool, washing the dryness from his mouth and throat. He held up a hand. It wasn't shaking now.

All that training really does work… I have changed.

He remembered the jesting comments from some of the townspeople and knew *they* didn't consider him to be any different.

"Oh look, there goes the man who's going to protect us from Evil Wilderness Things," Alex the carter had remarked before he left. His apprentice guffawed behind him.

"Fought any dragons lately, Dar?"

He didn't really blame them. Free-lance mercenaries were people who came and went from his home town of Forester, larger-than-life figures with exotic tales and more exotic magic. They weren't local boys who'd once been toddlers wandering around in diapers. Most thought "taking the free-lance" was the pastime of idiots: years of training for a chance to get killed at an early age.

He pulled out a tiny gold medallion on a chain from between his shirt and armor. The insignia of a rose below a mace winked back at him in the sunlight, above the inscription "Servus Sancta Kira".

One day, all this will help me find you...

He eyed the dead goblins, pursing his lip. *Speaking of finding out things...*

He stood and wiped his blade on a goblin's cloak, then replaced his weapons. He turned the body over.

Monkey-like features stared up at the sky, eyes lifeless. Small, dark horns protruded from a shock of bristly black hair and the jaws hung open, revealing yellowed but sharp fangs.

Dar shook his head, feeling a faint sickness in his stomach. He had seen death before on training missions with his mentor but he still felt an emptiness, nausea and pity, even for a creature of Darkness.

He inspected the other dead goblin, looking over the armor, boots, and weapons, searching for something that could identify them. Their black, studded leather armor held no symbols or markings.

Dar frowned. Goblins prided themselves on identification with their blood-clan.

Are they loners? Bandits? And what in the world are they doing this close to town?

He knew goblins hated humans, but they also tended to shun large settlements like Forester. He straightened and looked out at the quiet forest with narrowed eyes, then down at the place where he had seen the first goblin. Judging from the broken twigs, bootprints, and scuffed rocks in their wake, their trail would be easy to follow. Dar could see why these creatures were better suited to underground warrens.

He stood for a moment, debating with himself whether to find out where they came from or go back to town. He really should be getting back.

He shrugged. *What the hell, why not? This should be good information back in town if I can find out what's going on. There's got to be a reason for this.*

Dar fitted another arrow to his bow. With a wary eye on the forest around him, he stalked through the woods, following the tracks.

***

Gorlak crouched under the bush, still as a stone, waiting for the two tall

3

young men to pass. Their voices rang out as they strolled the narrow path, hefting their heavy wood axe. Late afternoon sunlight streamed down through maples and aspens.

Gorlak's eyes locked on them and he flexed his fingers over his saber handle.

Damned Ghai-zhal. Think they own the world, do they?

He gauged his chances of getting off a thrown weapon into the back of one of the men, but the other might escape and alert others.

The two humans continued on. When the *Ghai-zhal* were out of earshot, Gorlak faded back into the shadows. The dimness cast by the towering trees made him feel hidden and safe. Large ferns and bushes clustered near the trunks, providing plenty of dark places.

He remained a moment, watching them stride towards the huts and houses clustered together in a clearing farther down the path. A few trees stood between the structures, providing some measure of shade. Behind many of the buildings, Gorlak spied blocky kilns of red brick.

He whispered a curse, squinting against the sunlight that washed the village square. Full daylight hurt his eyes.

He saw two smiling young women greet the men. Gorlak caught fragments of their speech. Humana was very different from his own tongue, but he could understand some of the words.

"...should see what little Kala brought home this time... "

A trio of laughing children pursued a dog between two huts, casting up a cloud of dust that drifted down around the men and women. A small boy ran up to one of the women and held onto her leg. Gorlak spat on the ground.

He slipped back through the trees towards the hill. On the way, he passed three others of his band crouched in the bushes with spears and crossbows ready. They glared at the village and its occupants. Gorlak saw eagerness in their eyes, but they wouldn't dare attack without an order. He would slit their throats.

Picking his way through the trees and undergrowth, he emerged at the top of the hill. Lady Aalre waited with a guard detail among a thick stand of doriff trees. Despite their relatively short height, doriff trees provided good cover and shade with widespread branches and plentiful leaves. If it weren't for the thrice-cursed sunlight, Gorlak might have liked the place.

His eyes alighted on the woman and his throat tightened.

Lady Aalre was one of the *Urmum*, or Elder Children—an elf, born in sunlight and clean air of the forests. She stood slightly shorter than the human women in the village but moved with far more grace. A green dress clung to her lithe, supple figure. A slit in the side of the hem revealed a smooth leg and a doeskin boot. Golden hair cascaded down her shoulders, framing a delicate, heart-shaped face and bright amber eyes. She fingered a silver wand in her belt, looking down through the thick foliage at the village.

By contrast, Gorlak was a *Za'arak*, known to other races as a goblin. He wore the garb of a warrior, a leather jerkin reinforced with metal plates protecting his vitals. Two daggers and a hand-axe hung at his belt, complementing the saber on his back. He stood only about four and a half feet tall, a foot shorter than Aalre.

Gorlak suppressed the urge to growl. Next to the dwarves, goblins detested elves the most of any creature that lived on Damora.

His eyes alighted on the round medallion resting against Aalre's dress, between her breasts. It depicted a fanged, horned visage leering out from a background of pink, purple and red. Gorlak's chieftains and the *Ghai-zhal* sworn to the cult of Ja'al wore similar ones, showing their dedication to the Manipulator Church, worshippers of things of Shadow and Evil.

His eyes narrowed. That symbol meant he and she should be allies. His lip curled in disdain.

He accepted his allegiance to the Ja'al for the wealth and power they promised. She, on the other hand, had abandoned the faith of Verian, elven god of the forests, and taken the side of the Shadow. Gorlak did not know why nor did he care. In his eyes, she was a betrayer and not to be trusted.

She seemed only a disgustingly innocent and sweet elven maiden when she first appeared as their commander. More than forty goblin fighters lurked there in the forest with her, yet Gorlak knew she could kill a third of them by herself and escape the others easily if she so wished.

Gorlak approached and bowed low, every muscle in his body tight.

"Great Lady," he growled, his tongue pronouncing the words in Humana with difficulty. She insisted on using that vile tongue of the *Ghai-zhal*, partly because she didn't speak much Za'Arak and none of the goblins in her platoon spoke the Elder Tongue.

Aalre tossed a vagrant lock of honey blonde hair from her face and smiled sweetly down at him. "Ah, my faithful Gorlak! How did your scouting fare?"

He straightened. "We have counted all the *Ghai*- ...humans in the village. There are score and eight. Seven whelps. No soldiers. Only one old woman. She looks like mage."

Aalre smirked. "Of course there are no soldiers! Westhaven is an artist's community and the nearest town is at least a day away. They consider it an escape from civilization to be out here, relying on their small size and unimportance to protect them. After all, they have nothing here that anyone could want."

She raised an eyebrow at Gorlak. He snorted and she laughed softly, a merry, silvery sound he had learned to fear.

"Fools," he said, raising a finger to scratch at a scar on his face.

Without turning her head, she addressed the other goblin leaders. "Team Sergeants, Strike Teams One and Two, prepare for the main assault. Team Three will split and circle north and south. Attack at your convenience, but be certain everyone is in position first. Make it fast and make it thorough. After all targets have been eliminated, Search Teams One and Two will get to work."

She glided up to a doriff tree and examined a low-hanging leaf, shredding the soft leaf with her fingernails. No one moved. Gorlak could feel the tension in the air.

"I do not need to remind you of the penalty for failure," she said, "Lord Halkith will be most *disappointed* in a shoddy job. If we are to succeed, no one on the borderlands must know why we are here. Understood?"

The goblins bowed and left in a rustle of underbrush.

Gorlak exchanged a glance with Sergeant Avkar, who shrugged. Lord Halkith, their liege and a High Priest of the Ja'al, made it quite plain that obedience to Aalre was the same as obedience to him.

But that was not bad. If it got Gorlak and his cohorts what they wanted, so much the better. Working for Halkith meant conquest, wealth, food, slaves, and easy living.

Gorlak stood next to Lady Aalre in the forest gloom and watched with her, avoiding looking directly at the sunny areas. His duty was to keep the scouts next to the Lady, in case they were needed for emergencies.

Black-armored goblins filtered through the trees downslope, two lines of them curving to the right and left. In a short while, Lord Halkith's plan would be set in motion.

Those fools will never know what hit them...

***

Dar paused, leaning against a wide-boled spruce. The sun drifted ever lower in the sky and now he was closer to the hamlet of Westhaven than Forester. He began to wonder if it this nothing more than a wild hootling chase on the trail of a pair of lost free-booter goblins.

He sized up the terrain. He remembered the little hollow off to his left and the jumble of rocks next to it.

He clambered over the boulders and hunkered down on the earth under the wide leaves of a tanrin bush. A few birds flitted in the branches of a maple overhead. Sir Tan had trained him in areas such as this.

The thought of his teacher and mentor brought back a memory from two months ago and he grinned.

"Why are you doing this?" Sir Tan had asked him suddenly in the middle of archery practice.

Dar sighed. Sir Tanner Collins had a way of doing that, taking Dar off guard so that he would forget what he was doing. Dar thought he himself pretty good at catching people unawares, but Tan was a master.

"Doing what?" Dar had asked, lowering his bow.

"This," Tan said, waving at him and his equipment, then at the forest. "All this training. Why?"

Dar ran a hand through his hair. "Er... well, to protect the people of the Realms, serve my God and His Church..."

"No! No, no, no," Tan shook his head, irritated. "Not what it said in the books. What's *your* reason?"

"Oh, that," said Dar, waving a hand, "Well, I just like to kill things and take their money. And I can meet women."

Tan pressed his lips together and fixed him with his one good eye. Dar's return grin faded. He was going to be running five miles with a fifty-pound pack if he didn't watch his step.

He sighed and looked at the forest floor, then into Tan's eye. "I want to see people raising their children without fear, right here in Forester. No more burned caravans. No more school-kids vanishing in the night, no more lost trappers or miners in the forest. I seem to have a talent for guiding and tracking and I'm needed here."

Sir Tan grunted his approval. He scratched his face next to his eyepatch. "That's more like it. All I want is the truth from you, boy. Be honest with yourself and remember why you're training."

The old knight put a boot on a nearby rock. "I didn't pick you out of twenty candidates to hear my own words right back at me. You've got to make up your own mind. Yes, I know you have something on your mind concerning your grandparents, but only you and I and a few other people know about them and what they were looking for. Family quests aside, you've got to think on what's right, find out the truth of why it's right, and then *do* it."

"Sir Tan, you sound like a paladin."

"Aye!" the old knight exclaimed, punching him in the arm. "And if you've any sense, you'll think like one. A paladin is a holy warrior sworn to uphold the laws of God and never back down to evil. Don't forget your own Lord Nolan here in Forester, or King Philip in Oakmoor. They're paladins and fine ones at that."

"Well," Dar said, rubbing his arm, "That isn't going to help me right now. What use is this training and my talents if I can't help anyone?"

Tan gave an explosive sigh and shook his head. "Don't be so damn impatient! People find out about those who take the free-lance, whether they're scouts or healers or warriors or mages or whatever. Believe me, you'll get your chance. Now let me see you put that arrow in the center of the target this time, not the tree trunk..."

That conversation had seemed so long ago, but in reality, he had "graduated" at Eastertide, only three weeks past.

He made sure nothing waited for him out in the brush, then continued tracking. The goblin footprints took a meandering path through another hollow. He followed, leaping over rocks when he had to, alternating between watching the forest and checking the earth. After skirting the edge of a brambly thicket, he came to the edge of a shaded clearing and slowed.

More tracks joined the ones he followed— a lot more.

His eyes ranged all around the open area under the towering pines. Two, four, ten...

A pass around the edge of the clearing revealed a large number of tracks heading northwest.

Dar touched the bootprints in the earth. Two goblins he could handle, but this? He stopped counting at thirty-five. He saw evidence of at least that many goblins here, probably more, judging by individual tracks and other signs of their passage.

This close to town.

He wiped sweat from his brow. *At least thirty-five or forty... Holy Mary, that's four attack teams...*

He looked up at the woods. A bird flitted across the branches, but the rest of the forest looked peaceful.

Was this a search party? An ambush for one of Forester's patrols? Or worse, preparation for an attack on a caravan or a village?

He knew what the forces of Darkness could do. People traveling the northern border of the kingdom of Deran used Forester as a crossroads, a resting place and a small trading center. Dar grew up hearing his father's dire warnings about children who dared to venture out beyond the city limits after dark. Sometimes, even wily trappers and strong woodsmen vanished without a trace.

He straightened. Finding the other tracks made up his mind for him. News of this had to get back to the town guard. They wouldn't be able to move until the next morning and would take a day to get there, but he had to tell them what he had found. This had to be investigated.

He turned south-east, towards Forester. It was getting late in the afternoon.

A faint odor reached his nostrils. He sniffed the air and stopped. His brow furrowed and he looked to the northwest.

A thin column of smoke snaked up into the blue sky. He estimated the distance to be about another five miles, through rough terrain.

A hollow feeling started in his stomach. That was near Westhaven.

Steady now. They burn brush out there once in a while. Not so unusual to see smoke in the forest.

He stood for a moment, watching the tendril of grey grow thicker against the blue sky. The tight spot in his innards constricted more. His nervousness increased the more he gazed at the smoke. With one more look at the woods, he took off at a loping run through the patchwork of sunlit forest towards Forester.

Chapter Two- All Quiet on the Frontier

Finally.

Eric Indidarc leaned on his spear and stood still for a moment to catch his breath. After an entire day of hiking from the last village—a place aptly named Wit's End— he looked upon the town of Forester.

A packed dirt road stretched ahead of him to meet the wide, open gates of a walled fort about a mile away. The late afternoon sunlight washed a reddish glow over a scattering of homes and a hundred-yard deep expanse of cleared ground ringing the walls. People trudged down the path towards the fort or the houses, carrying bundles or pushing handcarts. In the fields, others carried baskets or herded animals towards shelters.

In all, Eric guessed about forty or so structures occupied the area around the fort, the majority of them as close as possible without encroaching on the cleared area. Each farm covered about eight or nine acres, the borders clearly marked with stone walls or wooden fences. The homes and the town reminded Eric of chicks clustered next to a mother hen.

Thin rivulets of now-cooling sweat ran down his body under the chainmail and tunic. Eric ran a hand through his short-cropped blond hair, examining the fort's defenses. A bath would be nice.

Twin gate towers, twenty feet high, framed a single steel gate and portcullis. No moat encircled the walls, but the cleared space around the fort looked daunting enough. Archer's holes glared down from the walls.

With that field of fire, attackers won't last long.

He estimated the town within the confines of the walls to be about two miles across in the shape of an odd, seven-sided polygon.

He turned to his traveling companion. "Not exactly a metropolis, Buck."

A tall, rangy human tramped up the small rise next to him and stood huffing for a few seconds. Sandy collar-length hair was tied at nape of his neck. A longsword and dagger hung from a wide leather belt and the tip of a short bow protruded over one shoulder. Chain mail covered his broad-shouldered, slouchy-looking frame. The edge of a round metal shield peeked out from behind his backpack, reflecting the dying sunlight.

"I just hope there's a tavern worthy of the name," Buckminster Bydecy answered. "And a few women to help pass the time."

He stamped his scuffed boots and beat the dust from his cloak. Grey eyes roamed over the scene below.

Eric chuckled. "Well, I'm sure there's a tavern at least. Come on. It'll be dark in an hour and I hear they button up these frontier towns as soon as the sun goes down."

"The farms are a little small, aren't they? I mean, you'd need a lot more land to feed a town of this size, wouldn't you?"

"City boy, aren't you? Magical augmentation is common nowadays. Wizards use spells to increase the yield per acre."

Buck shrugged. "If you say so. Let's get in before I fall over from thirst."

They trudged down the main road, passing between several properties. Chickens scattered at their approach. A tall, thin farmer straightened from filling his wheelbarrow, dark eyes curious. He mopped his brow with a handkerchief, watching until they had passed by.

Closer to the town, Eric noticed more details. His eyebrows rose.

The tall trees he noted earlier were seven in number, placed where the walls formed an angle.

That's why the place has such an odd shape.

Whoever built the town used the biggest, sturdiest trees in the area as his wall-towers. Ladders went up the sides of the trees to huge wooden platforms. Eric spied a few helmeted figures in armor carrying bows, moving about among the leafy branches. The gleaming point of a ballista bolt poked out from under the leaves of the nearest tree.

Three guards in neat red and blue livery stopped them at the gate and asked them their business.

"Just passing through," replied Eric with a smile.

The weathered-looking, bearded sergeant sized them up with a piercing gaze and a grunt. "More free-lances? Well, you'll find there's a few rules here. No magic, no fighting, no public drunkenness, and no molesting the townspeople. There's a list of town laws outside each tavern. You can read, can't you, elf-boy?"

Eric stifled his irritation. "Of course I can read, Sergeant," he replied. "And don't worry. We really *are* just passing through."

Buck gave the guards a broad smile and followed Eric inside.

When the guards were out of earshot, Buck shook his head. "*Can we read?* Where the hell has *he* been? All free-lances can read. It's one of the first things you learn. And weren't you trained by a wizard?"

Eric shrugged, then smiled and clapped his companion on the shoulder. "Yes, I was. And I'm only half of an "elf-boy" anyway, my mother's half, but I'm too tired right now to make an issue of it. Let's find that tavern."

The pair continued down the street. Short wooden buildings lined the road, painted signs declaring their purpose: here a seamstress, there a blacksmith, there the general store. A gang of dusty children darted in and out of hiding places among the barrels and boxes piled up in an alley, yelling and laughing at each other. An elderly couple ambled down the street on their left, the woman leaning on the man's arm for support.

Eric glimpsed a church steeple behind a row of houses. He smiled to himself, remembering the reaction of the pastor in Wit's End when Eric joined the congregation. Though uncommon, some elves and dwarves had taken the New Faith. In large cities, it didn't even cause comment, but in small towns it was rather rare— and Wit's End was small.

At the end of the main road through the center of the town, he saw the manor house, just beyond what looked like a carved fountain and an open courtyard. He was surprised to see neat homes with well-tended gardens and iron fences along side streets.

Big enough to be safe and small enough to be comfortable. The perfect place to get started. No one knows me here and no one from father's 'business' would bother with it.

"There!" said Buck, pointing and picking up his pace. Eric followed him towards a one-story structure with grimy windows. A wide, peaked roof shaded the front of the building. Two old men sat in battered chairs on the wooden porch, grey smoke from their pipes curling upward in the afternoon air or wafting into the rough pine boards of the wall behind them. A weathered sign swung in the light breeze, decorated with the faded figures of a man and a bear wrestling. Eric squinted to read the words: "The Pit".

He and Buck stopped by a wooden board next to the entrance. True to the gate-sergeant's word, a parchment declared the local strictures and rules. He also read notices of employment, items for sale, and a few writs of warrant for criminals-at-large.

Buck perused all the papers carefully, even the writs of warrant. Eric looked at him sidelong.

"So what do the rules say about those women you were looking for?" he asked.

Buck started. "Oh, uh, well...bawdy houses are illegal here." He gave another homespun grin. "Damn law. I'll have to wait until the next town."

Eric gave him a cheerful smile. "Don't get your hopes up. I saw a law just like it in Wit's End. That's probably a local version of a royal edict."

Buck's face darkened and he muttered something vulgar about prudes and what they could do with their laws. Eric laughed and walked in past him.

His eyes adjusted to the musty, dimly-lit interior of The Pit. It looked a little grubby, but not unpleasant. Rather, it had the air of a well-used living room in need of a good cleaning. A large fireplace dominated the left wall. Two pitted shields hung over the mantle. One bore the symbol of a cracked skull and the other of two crossed spears.

Eric's eyes widened a little. Capturing goblin tribal shields was a neat trick.

Directly opposite the front door, a huge bar stretched almost the entire length of the back wall. It was so large it took three bartenders to keep things running. Long shelves slouched against the wall behind the bar, crowded with bottles, pots, and drinking vessels, looking as if they would collapse any minute. A door hung halfway open on each side of the bar.

Eric stepped to the side to get out of the doorway, sensing Buck moving aside with him. Three burly humans headed past them towards the bar, clad in homespun brown clothes and smelling of fresh-cut wood.

Booths occupied the right side of the room. A few lanterns hung from hooks in the high ceiling beams, providing a little light for the patrons in the booths. Tables and chairs crowded together in the great open space between the booths on the right and the fireplace on the left.

Hung the lanterns high enough, Eric mused. *Wouldn't want an errant fist in a brawl to start a fire.*

Behind the bar, a glass ball emitted enough light to illuminate the whole room. Eric's senses tingled as he detected magic.

He waved a hand and whispered a small word. In his eyes, the ball showed a faint blue glow. He noted a similar light on the dagger at one barkeep's belt, on an axe strapped to the back of a bearded dwarf at the bar, and on the ring on a finger of an elegant-looking lady in a booth, accompanied by four swarthy and shifty-eyed guards in dark leather armor. No less than three swords, two suits of armor, and another ring glowed in his sight, all property of a group of three women in another booth.

Eric pursed his lip.

Merchants, caravan guards, dwarves and few elves swirled around the tables and bar. They carried their drinks to tables or took seats in the booths. Sprinkled among them were more mundane-looking people, probably shopkeepers or the like. Three slim, golden-haired young women in faded but neat blue dresses darted from one area to the next, carrying steaming platters of food or trays crowded with frothy mugs.

What we need is a guide, Eric thought, trying to pick out an empty table. *Someone who knows the area.*

A male halfling sauntered in, dark-haired and wearing brown trousers tucked into black boots. Black eyes glittered as he looked around the room in undisguised appreciation, eyeing the magical light over the bar with interest. A broadsword hilt hung at his hip and a leather jerkin protected his upper body. His head came up about as high as Eric's stomach.

Eric watched him. The halfling Republic of Evendale shared a border with both Deran and the Elven Empire of Terenai, to the south.

The halfling stopped at a table to speak to a young man hunched over a flagon. The human waved at the chair across from him. The halfling vaulted into a seat and began a conversation.

Eric blinked. He hadn't noticed the human before, but he might be someone of interest. He looked the part of a free-lance: broad-shouldered and wiry, he wore a dark brown tunic over chainmail armor and a handaxe hung at his belt. A camouflage cloak draped his shoulders and Eric spied the hilt of a sword over the man's left shoulder.

Eric nudged Buck. "Look."

Buck finished paying a barmaid for an ale. He took a long sip from his tankard. "What?" he asked.

"See the halfling? He might be a possibility. The guy he's talking to might be a local."

Buck took another swallow and smiled, giving the tankard an admiring look. "Now that's an ale!"

Eric cleared his throat.

Buck sighed and watched the pair in question. "There are a lot of people in here. How can you tell who's the local?"

Eric pointed. "Watch all the caravaners. They're checking out everything, especially the magic light behind the bar. The halfling's doing the same thing. The human isn't. He's been in here before, and I'd guess frequently. We should watch them for a while."

Buck cast a glance at the other people in the room, then back at the pair at the table. "I'm tired of standing. Let's go talk to them."

Eric reached out to stop him but missed.

Oh well, he sighed, following Buck to the table.

"These seats taken?" Buck asked.

The human and halfling looked up, startled.

The human overcame his surprise first. "Go right ahead. There'll be few enough of them soon."

"Great!" said Buck. He grabbed a chair, turned it backwards and draped himself over it.

Eric rested his spear against the back of another chair and slipped into it. "Thanks. I'm Eric Indidarc and this is Buck Bydecy."

The human's dark brown eyes met Eric's. "Dar Cabot of Forester. This is Connor Lomin of Oakmoor. He's...an agent."

Eric nodded. Dar *was* a local, and this Connor person was a newcomer, from the Deranese capitol.

The halfling was quite the traveler if he had gone to the big city and then to this small town. And an agent? In many societies, it meant "spy", "bounty hunter", or "investigator". In others, it was the same as a thief.

Buck drained his mug. He thumped the vessel down on the table with a satisfied grin.

"That'll cut the dust just fine," he declared.

Dar saluted him with his own mug. "Best ale on the borderlands."

Connor's eyes measured Eric and Buck. He looked into his own mug. "Traveled far?"

Eric exchanged a look with Buck, then shrugged. "I'm not sure how far Buck has traveled. I almost fell over him on the road about five miles out of Wit's End. Saved his bacon from a bunch of wolves."

Buck gave a hearty chuckle. "Saved my bacon? I seem to remember tossing my food to them to give us enough time to climb the tree."

"Really? And I suppose it was someone else's spear that got one of them before it could bite your hand off."

"You're a warrior, Mister Bydecy?" Dar asked.

Buck grinned. "Trained in Tyler, Astarel at Joko Roundtree's Academy. And it's just Buck." He turned to look for a waitress.

Dar nodded. "And you Mister Indidarc? Your people are adept at magic."

How polite. No country bumpkin this.

Eric grinned at him. "It's just Eric. And yes, I have Elder blood, but only from my mother's side. I'm a mage and I was trained as a scout too."

"Interesting last name." Eric could feel Dar's eyes watching him carefully.

"Yes," Eric kept his grin. "Many branches of that family in the Kingdoms."

Dar's eyes remained hooded. "So, a scout and a wizard. How long did you study? You must have been in school for decades."

Eric laughed. "No, it just seemed like it. I'm sure my professors thought I was going to stay that long."

Connor looked at him. "You didn't say how long you were in school."

"No, I didn't," Eric replied, "It was about three years after my apprenticeship."

"Passing through?" Dar asked.

"Maybe," Buck said, taking another tankard of ale from a serving girl's tray and handing her a silver coin, "We were hoping to find some work here. Maybe caravan outriders or bodyguards for travelers."

Connor and Dar exchanged a look. "Good," said Connor after another sip from his mug. "We were just talking about the same thing."

"Any luck?" Eric asked. "I'm sure you've seen other freelancers."

Dar shrugged. "Sure, but nothing came of it. Most of those groups have a couple of years under their belt. In the words of a woman I talked to "No offense, but the assignments you're likely to get would just be boring for me. The ones I'm likely to get would be deadly for you." She's right."

Buck snorted. "Sure she is."

Eric shook his head. "I agree with Dar. Veterans don't take neophytes into their ranks. The more seasoned go out into the wilderness for weeks or months at a time. We'll just slow them down or worse, get them all killed."

Connor nodded at Dar. "But you were telling me about some strange goings-on around here lately."

"Really?" Eric rested his arms on the table.

Dar frowned, letting his reserve slip enough to look worried and frustrated. He ran a hand through his dark brown hair. "I was out in the forest this morning when two goblins tried to puncture my head with arrows. Later, I noticed smoke coming from north-by-northwest. There's a couple of hamlets and villages out there."

Eric nodded. "And you think something's wrong."

Dar scratched his chin. "I'm not sure. They burn brush out there to reduce the fire danger, especially close to the communities. But they usually do that a couple of months from now, closer to summer. Besides, I found tracks of a lot more goblins farther on. That could be just a small tribe passing through or it could mean trouble. I told the city guards anyway and they said they'd investigate, but they won't be able to do anything until tomorrow."

"But you're still worried," Eric persisted.

Dar's brow furrowed. "I don't know. It could be nothing, but bad things have happened out here before. People have disappeared out in the forest. Forester has actually been attacked a time or two, usually by some wild tribe from the Wilderness. You can smell those coming a fortnight away."

Connor took another drink. "If I'm going to be employable, I have to get familiar with the area. If we help you go make sure this Westhaven place is okay, would you be willing to guide us around?"

Dar looked thoughtful.

Eric nodded. "We might be able to team up as a group. Should be valuable to someone."

Dar agreed. "All right. Now, the formalities."

He reached under his tunic and pulled out a small metal plate on a chain. The others produced similar items themselves.

They exchanged them. Eric read the inscription on the first. "Buckminster Horatio Bydecy, certified in military sciences. Blank-shield and free-lance. Authorized by Joko Roundtree, Director, Steel Wind Academy, Tyler, Astarel."

He handed it over to Dar and read the next one. Connor's instructor wasn't familiar, but he had heard of the Black Ferret Guild and it was a legitimate, credible institute. He handed it back and looked at Dar's.

Eric stared at Dar.

"You trained with Tanner Collins?" they both asked at the same time.

Connor and Buck started laughing.

Dar grinned. "I guess he gets around. When did he give you this?"

"Three years ago, before I started mage training."

Dar shrugged. "I guess it happens." He handed the plate back. "Have you heard from him lately?"

Eric shook his head. "After he finished training me, he headed north to Eldir, I think."

"I still don't see why we have to do this," Buck muttered, replacing his own plate.

"I'm sure you were told why," Eric said. "It's to make sure we don't have a pretender in the ranks, someone who would betray us. It also helps identify people. If you had trained with the Black Skull Academy of Torosc, I don't think we'd be forming a group with you."

Dar nodded. "All right. Done. Let's leave in the morning. But dinner first. The Pit has great meals."

Buck beamed and waved to a waitress. The woman stopped next to their table. "What can I... Oh, hi Dar!"

Dar Cabot looked up at the barmaid and grinned. "Hi, Elaine. Guys, this is Elaine Ward. Elaine, these are Buck, Eric and Connor."

Eric met Elaine's clear blue eyes. A delicate oval face looked back at him, framed by wavy hair the color of wheat.

"You get to see a lot of Dar then," he noted.

19

Elaine put a hand on Dar's shoulder and gave them all a confidential look. "A lot more than is healthy for most people."

Dar grinned wider.

She continued. "I went to school with this brush-tramp. Beat him up a few times for playing pranks on me. Can you believe he dropped an overripe eggplant on my head from the top of the general store? He's been hanging around the Pit these days, looking for free-lances, as if he were some kind of hero or something."

Dar shrugged. "I have trouble making people believe me sometimes."

Elaine's eyes were amused. Eric smiled. "And I thought he was here to see you. That would have been understandable. Now I'm disappointed in him."

"Who? Dar?" Elaine looked surprised. "Hell, we went to school together..." She and Dar looked at each other for a moment, then made faces.

"Absolutely not," they said in unison.

The group chuckled. "His loss then," said Eric. She smiled and blushed.

Buck drained his tankard and held it up to Elaine. "Another ale," he said. She nodded, eyes twinkling. "Anything for the rest of you?"

Eric ordered a cup of wine and she left.

Nice town, thought Eric, watching her blue skirt swish around slim legs as she walked to the bar.

"So, you want to take a look out in the forest tomorrow?" prompted Connor.

Dar nodded, leaning back in his chair. "Where are you guys staying?"

Buck shrugged. "We don't have a place. Any ideas?"

"There's an inn attached to this tavern. It's called the Woodsman," Dar said. He indicated one of the doors by the bar. "If you go out through there, you'll see a courtyard and a low building. It costs one silver disk a night if you want a room all to yourself or five copper gits if you want the common room. Meals not included."

Elaine returned with their drinks. "Supper is served in half an hour," she said, giving them a once-over, "So if you want some, you'd better go get cleaned up."

Buck's eyes widened as she departed.

20

Dar chuckled. "Do it. She's a tough one, I'm telling you. She likes you or she wouldn't have mentioned anything."

Connor hopped off his chair. "I'll meet you all back here in half an hour then."

***

Eric and Buck decided to cut costs by teaming up on a room. They arrived together at the tavern, looking less dusty. Dar and Connor awaited them at a table.

They ordered a meal of venison stew, bread, and cheese.

Dar grinned at the way the other three devoured the food. "Glad you like it."

Connor popped the last piece of bread into his mouth. "My people are experts at this sort of thing."

Eric chuckled, then elbowed Buck. "Another ale? That's your forth one already."

The warrior drained the rest of his mug. Despite having eaten a meal while drinking, his eyes looked a little glassy. "I can liquor my hold, um, hold my liquor."

Eric shook his head. Carrying him to the room was going to be a chore.

A strong alto rang out behind them. "I've heard enough! Let go of me!"

Eric turned. Two women stood near a table with a human male, as tall as Buck, and an unshaven halfling.

The women both had similar facial features and golden hair with a hint of red. Each stood a little shorter than Dar.

One squared off against the human and halfling, hands on her hips. A single braid laid against her back, ending just under the shoulder blades. A sky-blue tunic covered the metallic glint of scale mail and two short swords hung at her belt. She had a trim, athletic build.

The other woman's hair lay softly on her shoulders. A pair of daggers glittered against the navy blue of her blouse, and dark boots peeked out under the hem of her black skirt. She looked to be the younger of the two.

Eric saw their eyes. *The older one has violet eyes, the younger one amber. Probably some elven blood.*

The younger woman looked around the room, then turned back to her companion. "Please, Brandi, you're making a scene. I'm sure we misunderstood what James meant."

Brandawyn shook her head, never taking her eyes off the two men in front of her. "I've heard enough, Megan."

The tall man before them laughed, smoothing shoulder-length brown hair. He wore scale mail as well and carried a sword over his back like Dar.

"Really? Well, that's not what you said out there in the forest, along the trail. Seemed like you needed our help then. I think you owe us."

Brandawyn's violet eyes narrowed. The tall man smirked. Eric felt his irritation rising. He knew this kind of person: arrogant, smug and more than ready to use intimidation to get his wishes. A bully.

He looked at his new companions. Dar's jaw set in a firm line and Buck tried to focus on the scene before him.

Eric realized with a start that Connor had disappeared.

The tall human reached out and grabbed Brandawyn's arm. "No more debate, wench."

With a circular motion of her hand and arm, the woman broke his hold and took a quick step back. "The name's Brandawyn, not "wench", you idiot."

"Now, now," the unshaven halfling stepped forward and held up a hand. Eric had the impression of a scorpion.

Where the hell is Connor? Is he in on this?

"Megan is right", the halfling said. "James, it's obvious we need to explain the whole thing again, but not while disturbing these other folk. We should take this outside where the fresh air will clear our heads." The halfling's mouth curved in a smile. His green eyes bored into the two women.

Eric stood. Dar rose and with surprising suddenness, stepped up next to Brandawyn.

Quick, thought Eric, getting his spear and stepping off at an angle from the confrontation.

"I heard the lady say she wasn't interested. That should be enough for any man," Dar said. He smiled, keeping his eyes on James.

Megan gave a little jump of surprise.

James looked at Dar as if he had just discovered a bug in his ale. "And

22

who the hell are you?"

Eric spoke up. "He's trouble to you, friend. All of us are. Why don't you cut your losses and get out while you can?"

He heard a movement next to him. Buck stood, weaving a little and trying to look dangerous. He put a hand to the hilt of his sword. Eric hoped he didn't draw it. Fighting with blades was probably a worse offense than brawling in this town and Eric wasn't sure of Buck's skills when inebriated.

The halfling looked annoyed. "I don't recall asking for a debate on this," he said in a tight voice.

Dar's grinned. "Well, you're getting one," he answered, "I don't know where you come from, friend, but in Forester, the word 'no' has only one meaning."

Brandawyn gave Dar a piercing look. "Thank you for the help, whomever you are, but we have the situation well in hand."

James stepped closer to her and Dar, face screwed up in anger. "I'm giving you one chance, runt. This isn't your affair, so get out of here while you can still walk!"

Dar pointed at him. "Close your mouth or I'll close it for you."

James' face darkened in rage and he lunged forward. Dar and Brandi dodged.

Dar stepped in as James went past and slammed an elbow into his back, propelling him into a table. The table overturned, scattering its outraged patrons and showering beer over everyone in the vicinity.

Wait your chance, thought Eric, his heart beating faster. *Try to solve this without bloodshed.*

James picked himself up. He wiped beer from his armor, murder glowing in his eyes.

"You're going to be very sorry you did that, friend," he growled. His voice rang out in the now-quiet room.

Dar looked very pleased. "Then let the games begin."

James stepped in and swung twice. Dar ducked the first one and weaved out of the way of the second. He shifted his weight, then punched straight forward. His fist slammed into James's chin. The taller man reeled, then fell in a heap.

Nicely done. Eric moved to the fallen warrior in a heartbeat, spear planted

23

on the wood floor, a boot on James' head. He scanned the crowd.

If Connor and that other halfling are in it together, it could be a trap.

He remembered his sister's admonition: *Trust freelances after you've been with them a while. Otherwise, be wary.*

He heard the hiss of drawn steel and raised his spear.

The unshaven halfling stood in front of a tall table, sword drawn and glittering against the shadows. Purple fire danced along the blade. People scrambled to get away.

Magic weapon, Eric thought in amazement. *Why didn't I see it?*

"That's quite enough of this brawling," the halfling said. "Brandawyn, Megan, I'll thank you to accompany me outside to continue our discussion."

Then he went rigid.

The tip of a broadsword blade poked out from the jumble of chairs and tables behind him and laid itself under his neck. Connor Lomin's head popped up over the halfling's right shoulder.

"I wouldn't," he said.

Wild frustration crossed the unshaven halfling's face for a split second, then he relaxed. A slow smile spread over his blunt features and he sheathed his weapon. He held both hands out before him, palms out, and Connor quickly stepped in front of him, sword unwavering.

"Okay everyone," Eric said, seizing the moment. "Show's over."

He reached into his belt purse with his free hand and held up two silver disks.

"Looks like we need some help hauling garbage. Who wants to earn a little money?"

A stocky, graying woodsman stepped up. "I'll do it for nothing." Behind him, two young bearded men nodded and followed.

"Then consider this a tip," Eric said, clasping the coins into the man's hand.

A loud commotion at the entrance drew his eyes away. Five soldiers in red-and-blue livery strode in. Armored in dull, serviceable scale mail, they stopped in the center of the common room and held their spears at the ready. A heartbeat later, another guard with twin crossed axes on the sleeve of his tunic stepped in, longsword in hand. He spared a disgusted look at James, sprawled on the floor, then eyed the assemblage.

"Getting a little boisterous, are we?" he asked in a rough voice.

Dar grinned. "Hi, Sergeant Roldan."

The sergeant turned to him, frowning. Then he shook his head and sheathed his weapon. "Dar Cabot? All right. Explain."

Dar described the altercation, soliciting comments from the crowd. Eric turned his attention to James, still unconscious under his boot. He tapped the human in the head with the butt of his spear. When he didn't respond, Eric lifted his foot off and motioned to the woodsmen.

The trio hauled James to the door like a sack of meal, dragging his feet behind him. Three town guards strode at his heels, escorting the glowering halfling. Eric smiled at him and waved, receiving a bitter look in return.

That man has some problems. He felt cheerful, glad that the incident had been resolved without getting blood on the floor.

Sergeant Roldan and Dar continued their conversation, the soldier's eyes flickering over at Dar's newfound companions.

"Everyone okay?" asked a voice from Eric's side.

Connor Lomin perched on the table like a boy, his legs swinging over the edge.

Eric nodded with a smile, setting his spear against a nearby chair. "Thanks to you. Nice work. I didn't see you at all."

Connor inclined his head in a mock bow. "Compliment accepted. Looks like everyone is fine for now, except for Buck."

Buck stood in the middle of the room, looking around at the crowd, the guards, and the lights. He tried to follow the discussion between the sergeant and Dar but couldn't keep up with the questions, instead contributing a "Right! That's just how it happened" at odd moments.

Eric chuckled, then noticed Megan and Brandi standing off by themselves in a heated but whispered argument. The younger woman gestured at Eric and his companions, but her friend (*relative?* wondered Eric) shook her head.

Sergeant Roldan's interview ended and he departed, making notes on a slateboard as he did so.

"No problems," Dar said as he approached, "There were plenty of witnesses to the whole thing. They fined the halfling and that James fellow and used some of the money to pay for the broken furniture."

Buck weaved over and sat with them. He lifted an ale tankard from a nearby table and drained it. Megan and Brandi still stood apart but stopped talking when Dar rejoined his companions.

Megan stepped forward, smiling and extending her hand. "We appreciate the help. I'm Megan Alenar and this is my older sister Brandawyn." It was a brilliant smile.

Dar smiled back and held her hand. "Glad to help, —"

Brandawyn stepped up and took Megan's arm. "Yes, it was very timely. Now, if you'll excuse us..." She turned to go.

Megan jerked her arm free. "Brandi! Don't be so rude! They only did it to help. I think we at least owe them some courtesy."

Brandi looked exasperated. "Right. They're just helping. This is exactly how it started the last time, if you recall correctly, and see where that ended up?"

Megan stamped her foot. "That's no reason to pass it off like it was nothing."

Brandi mouth set in a firm line. "We could have handled it."

"Who were those guys anyway?" Connor interrupted. He looked up at the sisters, still swinging his legs.

Megan blinked, noticing him for the first time. Brandi shrugged.

"We met them on the road from Athor. We were jumped by a group of about seven men, armed with clubs and nets. James and Kili helped us fight them off. Kili thought they were Viper slavers."

Eric gave a low whistle. To hear of Vipers this far north of their home bases in Jered was not unusual, but...

"Vipers," growled Buck. "I've fought them before."

The others looked at him in surprise.

"You've fought *Vipers* before?" asked Eric. Sure, they were thugs, but Vipers also had a reputation for toughness and smarts.

Buck burped and nodded. "Damned snakes. Always getting into the henhouse at Uncle Roger's farm. Showed them a thing or two."

Megan grinned and even Brandi got a little smile on her face. Eric shook his head, then turned back to the women. "I suppose James thought you owed it to them since they helped you?"

"He and Kili made it clear that we needed their 'protection' and that refusing could be hazardous," Brandi said, "I took exception to that."

"You know," said Connor, bracing his hands on the table and leaning forward, "they could have been in on it with the guys who jumped you."

Everyone digested that statement silently.

Megan looked worried. "He could be right, Brandi. They just drove them off. No one was killed in the fight."

Brandi's eyes narrowed.

"Well, you're free of them now." Dar pulled up a few chairs for them and sat next to Megan. "Did you ride in this afternoon?"

Megan slipped into the chair and looped a vagrant hair over her ear. "No, actually. We don't own horses. We were with the last caravan that came in today, but we left at noontime so we could get a room at one of the inns ahead of the crowd. It was a big caravan. We were about four miles from town when we ran into the ambush."

"So, you're caravan guards?" asked Connor.

Megan looked at Brandi. "Well, big sister?"

Brandi looked at the men, then sighed and straightened in her seat. "You're right. Yes, we were hoping to find employment here, maybe for the town guard or one of the local merchants. And I was wrong not to thank you all for your help. You're not like James and Kili, I can see that. I'm a free-lance battle medic and Megan is a mage. We traveled here from Terenai after finishing our studies."

Dar slapped his knee. "I've been looking for novice free-lances for weeks, ever since Easter-time. All I could find were the veterans who didn't want to have a new guy tagging along, getting underfoot. My luck is changing."

Eric shifted in his seat. "Do you think you could take us to the place where you were attacked? There's probably a bounty on slavers, especially Vipers."

Brandi waved a hand. "It was outside of town, near the roadside, but those guys are long gone by now, I'm sure of it."

Dar frowned. "But only four miles away? That's close. Did you tell the city guards?"

Brandi nodded. "One of the sergeants sent a runner to the manor when I told our story at the gate. James and Kili took off to find a tavern and we ended up here. That's when Kili told us about his little business proposition."

"Business proposition?" Connor leaned back on his hands.

Megan and her sister exchanged a glance.

Eric sat in a nearby chair and looked up at the sisters. "Is that what all of you were arguing about? It must have been some business."

Megan sighed. "They said they had been hired to hunt down a gang of bandits near here, something about a raided caravan near Forester. We started to get suspicious when they wouldn't mention which lord or magistrate hired them. I remembered checking the notices on the board and there was nothing about any bandit raid. Brandi and I agreed something wasn't right and we turned them down. That's when James started to get pushy."

Eric nodded. "Where were you supposed to start your search? Maybe we can all take a look for ourselves."

Megan shrugged. "They said the bandits had built a small hamlet and would be hiding out there. It was a place called Westhaven."

Dar sat bolt upright, eyes wide. "Westhaven?"

"Mister Cabot?" Eric asked.

Dar leaned on the table. "Westhaven isn't a bandit hideout, it's a little village out in the wilderness, only twenty people or so. That's near the spot where the goblins attacked me and where I found the other tracks. And smoke was coming from that direction."

The two women looked blank and Eric explained about Dar's encounter earlier in the day.

"We were planning to go out tomorrow and investigate," he finished. "Westhaven is about a day and a half walk for most people. We could probably be there in a day."

"What do you think happened?" asked Megan.

Dar rubbed his hands together, brow furrowed. "I don't know. Could be that one of the huts caught fire or the goblins were part of a foraging party that burned a house. Then again, they really could be burning brush, though with the rains last week, I doubt it. This business with James and Kili makes me really nervous. It can't be a coincidence."

"What's in this Westhaven that they could want?" Connor asked. "Goblins don't attack villages for fun. That sounds more like Kaftu or ogres."

Dar frowned. "Westhaven is known for its pottery in these parts, but that's about it."

The group just stared at him. "Pottery?" asked Megan.

"Yes." Dar looked around the common room, bustling and active again, as if there hadn't been a brawl ten minutes earlier.

He pointed at a crock sitting on a shelf behind the bar. It was a light cream color, with dark black zig-zags framing figures of miners in a cavern. "That's one of them right there. The merchants and traders who come through here say they're quite good and sell very well. The designs are kind of strange sometimes. A woman named Clarissa is a retired sage and the de-facto mayor of the place. Her pieces are expensive."

They sat in silence for a while, hearing only the sounds of the tavern around them. Three workmen shouldered past their table, laughing and clapping each other on the back.

Elaine glided over to their table bearing a tray. She put a hand on her hip.

"Well," she said, "It seems like trouble just follows you everywhere, Dar."

Dar raised his hands. "Trouble? Hey, I wasn't doing anything, just sitting here talking to my friends here when that James guy..."

The serving girl's eyes narrowed. "You said that a lot in school too."

Dar gave Elaine a sturdy but gentle push. She dodged aside and made a threatening motion with the tray.

Eric offered her a couple of silver pieces. "Don't let this boor trouble you, miss. Would you bring a couple of wines for the ladies?"

Her eyes twinkled at him. "Certainly, Mister Indidarc."

Brandi looked amused. "Thank you, Eric."

He smiled at her. Despite her suspicious demeanor, she was quite pretty.

Megan cocked her head to one side. "How far away did you say Westhaven is?"

Connor hopped on a chair from the edge of the table. "I thought you'd never ask. Dar, Eric, what do you say we include Brandi and Megan? James and Kili were up to something and I'll bet my underpants it's connected to Westhaven somehow."

Dar's eyebrows rose. "I hope you win the bet."

That drew chuckles from the others. "We'll leave in the morning, then," Dar continued, drawing his handaxe and laying it on the table. "This is the Dragonspine Range. This beerstain over here is Forester..."

Chapter Three- Westhaven

Connor Lomin scanned the forest for signs of movement. The trunk of a fallen tree leaned on a stump next to him, providing a shelf over his head and plenty of shadows. To his left, a thin pathway strewn with fallen leaves wound through the forest. A few birds chirped in the trees above him and he heard the occasional rustle of a small animal in the underbrush.

He held a short bow in his hand, an arrow nocked. The familiar weight of his pack rested against his upper back.

His eyes flickered over the quiet woods one more time. The late afternoon sunshine fired golden light through the boughs above onto trees of varying shades. Flowering shrubs, multicolored mosses and ferns grew among spruce and aspens. Between gaps in the trees, Connor could see the white-capped mountains ahead and to the right.

He turned his head at the sound of voices.

Buck sauntered down the pathway, seemingly unaffected by last night's encounters with the ale tankards. Behind him, Eric walked next to the Alenar sisters, using his spear as a staff. Megan explained something to Eric, moving her hands in gestures as she did so. Brandi kept her eyes up and a bow and arrow ready in one hand.

Connor shook his head. *As quiet as a dwarven bachelor party.*

With all that metal armor clanking away and Megan holding a seminar, it was a wonder half the creatures in the region hadn't jumped on them.

He supposed Dar's knowledge of the area kept them out of trouble.

Guiding them with almost military precision, Dar planned their route through the forest. More than once, Connor had thought they were going the wrong way only to find they had just skirted a dark hollow or avoided a dead-end trail.

Dar had also suggested Connor range out to the sides of the narrow pathway, a proposition he greeted with enthusiasm.

He grinned. Humans and half-elves were notoriously oblivious to smaller beings. He took great pleasure in making his companions jump by falling into step behind them and tapping them on the back. If the group were composed only of elves or gnomes, he would never have gotten away with it. Gnomes were a crossbreed themselves, a mixture of halfling and dwarf, and very sly.

Connor looked across the pathway through the trees. Dar Cabot stood next to a large maple. He waved. Connor saluted back, then slipped through the undergrowth up a hill and over to the other side. He stopped to rest next to a large boulder, keeping a close eye on his companions on the trail. Dar fell into step next to Brandi.

This is a good way to make a new start, he mused. *This far away from Glen, maybe the past can stay there.*

He felt an all-too-familiar knot in his stomach at the memories and took a deep breath.

"There's nothing you could have done," Farfan, the town healer, had told him, hand on his shoulder in sympathy. "We don't even know where the disease came from. Fortunately, it's burned itself out and we're safe. I'm sorry for your loss."

Dar halted and held up a hand, breaking Connor's reverie. Irritated at himself for losing focus, Connor rejoined the others.

"What is it?" he asked, walking up to his companions.

"I smell wood smoke," Dar said, his brow wrinkled in thought. "And something else."

He looked worried. Connor stared at the forest, his senses on full alert now. Maybe there was something to Dar's fears about the large group of goblins.

"Well, don't they have fireplaces?" asked Buck. "You told us we'd be coming up on Westhaven about this time anyway."

Dar shook his head and nocked an arrow. "The smell is too intense for our distance to Westhaven. It's a couple of hundred yards ahead, just over the rise. The road curves to the right a little so you can't see the buildings from here. Besides, there's something else."

Brandi sniffed the air. "It does seem a little different than burning wood."

"What's our next step?" Eric asked.

Dar pursed his lip, eyes looking off at something none of the others could see. "Go slower, for one thing. That hill up ahead has a good field of view. I've always been able to see Westhaven from there. We'll go off the trail and have a look. You hide out at the base of the rise and wait until the all-clear."

He nodded at Connor. "You want to take the right flank?"

Connor nodded. Dar picked his way up the hill and the halfling followed, about twenty yards to the right.

Connor stopped behind a large spruce. Now he understood what was making Dar nervous, a sweet scent hidden in the aroma of burning pine and maple. His heartbeat quickened as he recognized the smell.

Oh no. Not that...

For some reason, his eyes found those of Brandi and Megan. They also recognized the smell.

They've seen this before too...

He peered around the spruce.

Dar crept up to the top of the hill. He slid up next to a tree and peeked around it. He froze. He backed downslope, his bow held ready in front of him and eyes darting around.

Connor followed Dar, a feeling of dread tightening his innards. He knew that smell. In Glen, during the epidemic that had killed so many, they had burned the bodies.

Dar looked as pale as death when they rejoined the group.

"What's wrong?" asked Megan in alarm.

Dar shook his head, eyes wide with shock. "All of them...they're..." He leaned against a tree trunk for support, then he shook himself.

"Follow me," he turned back towards the trail. "Stay in a group and for God's sake, no noise!"

They followed Dar up the hill, stepping among the leaves and twigs with exaggerated care. At the top, they hid behind trees.

The slope dipped down before them. A wide clearing held a collection of short buildings surrounded on all sides by trees.

Very short buildings, Connor realized. In fact, they were even too short for halflings. Lazy tendrils of smoke curled up from the remnants of homes. Dark figures lay in the spaces between the ruins, several of them sprouting shafts. As Connor watched, small furry creatures crawled over the dark shapes and black ravens alighted on the ground nearby.

Dar looked pale, his eyes haunted and anguished. Eric pulled at his sleeve and motioned for the others to follow. He led them out of sight of the ruined village.

"We've got to know what happened," Eric whispered. "I say we send Connor down there to see."

Brandi frowned. "Why don't we all go down together?"

Megan, her face still pale, shook her head. "Whoever—whatever did this might still be around. Connor is so quiet, they'd never know he was there."

She turned to Connor. Her eyes were wide, scared, but honest. "We wouldn't ask you if it wasn't necessary. Will you go?"

He felt all eyes upon him and shrugged despite his increasing pulse rate. "Sure. What do you want me to do?"

"No," said Dar, shaking his head. "I should be the one to go. I should have done something yesterday, when I saw the tracks... I should have..." His voice broke and faded.

Megan put a hand on his shoulder. "Should have what? Gone ahead to the village? Gotten yourself killed? Dar Cabot, I don't know you very well, but you're not a fool."

"I should have done something!"

"You did do something," Brandi interjected. "You went for help but it was too late already. I'll bet everyone was dead by the time you saw the smoke. Now help us out. You're the local. Tell Connor what to do."

Dar swallowed, then nodded. "The brush ends about fifty feet from the nearest building on this side. Look for any survivors and see if anyone else is still around. There's a big thicket of blackberry on the far side. It's large enough to hide an ogre, so keep your eyes open."

Eric tapped Connor on the shoulder. "If we don't hear from you in a five-hundred count, we're coming in after you."

Connor tested his bowstring, trying to hide the fact that his hands shook.

"Better make it seven hundred. I want to take it slow."

He slipped into the brush and trees, heading for a stand of aspens. Soon, he forgot about the others behind him. He reduced his task to watching the burned town and trying to select the path of least visibility. He reached the aspens and stood motionless between two of the larger ones.

He watched the remnants of the town, looking for movement. Seeing none, he watched the edges of the forest, paying particular attention to the blackberry thicket. Flies buzzed in the spring air.

He worked his way down a slope, ducking behind shrubs and tree trunks. Every time he stopped, he waited for a different number of heartbeats before moving again.

He was now close enough to make out the sizes of the bodies. Most were adult humans but he noted a few children. His mouth set in a grim line, remembering his own home town.

He cast his eyes around the village, trying to glean more information from the scene: a short and decisive fight to be sure.

Probably took the poor folk by surprise, he thought, shaking his head. Many of the dead looked as if they were heading back towards the village center when they were struck down.

He bit his lip, trying to remember his training classes back in Glen. *Taken by surprise, no survivors and herded to a kill zone. Organized and well-planned.*

He let out a slow breath and moved closer, trying to make for the nearest burned structure. Suddenly, he froze, heart pounding. A stocky armored figure lay about ten feet away, almost hidden in a clump of ferns.

The figure remained motionless. After a few moments, he slipped closer.

It was a goblin. Half-monkey features stared up at the sky, sightless eyes unblinking. A large burn mark scored its chest above the heart, flies clustered on it. A clawed hand still gripped a short, curved sword. Stubby dark horns poked out from a shock of bristly hair atop a narrow skull.

Connor drew back. He had seen enough. He sneaked back to the others, stopping several times to stand motionless next to vegetation to watch for movement in the forest.

The group was making preparations to come in after him when he rejoined them.

They whirled when he spoke, weapons at the ready.

"I'm back. It's okay," he said, keeping a wary eye on Brandi's twin swords. Some of this crowd were on edge like a hair-trigger crossbow and he didn't want to end up losing an arm.

Megan breathed a sigh of relief. "Good. We were starting to worry. What's going on down there?"

Connor related what he had seen and heard.

Dar put his face in his hands but Brandi took his hand and squeezed it. "Dar, you can't bring them back by blaming yourself."

Megan swallowed. "Why would goblins wipe out a village that specializes in pottery?" she asked with a nervous look towards Westhaven.

Connor nodded. There had to be a reason.

Eric shook his head. "Desperation? Maybe someone put them up to it on pain of death? A vendetta maybe?"

"You didn't see any live goblins?" asked Brandi. Connor shook his head.

"Well, what now?" asked Buck.

Dar put his hands down. "We investigate," he said firmly. Jaw muscles clenched and eyes hard, he led the way down into the village and they followed, spreading out to cover the entire area. A cautious search revealed no goblins so they turned their attention to the remnants of the village.

As they combed through the wreckage, Connor felt a growing anger. He had seen some of the dead from his vantage point and knew it was going to be bad, but this?

Old women, children, babies: no one had escaped. He inspected six bodies himself, all of whom had either been shot with arrows, stabbed or clubbed.

Finally, he stood up in disgust from the ruins of the biggest hut. The monkey-bastards had made a mess of everything, burning what they did not break and throwing debris in all directions.

He turned at the sound of Brandi and Megan approaching.

Brandi's jaw was tight and Megan's eyes were shiny with tears. Even as they came up to him, Megan brushed at her eyes.

"Well?" asked Brandi. Connor heard a furious tone beneath the controlled voice. He watched her for a moment before answering. She stared back, violet eyes smoldering.

"Nothing yet," he said, turning back to the junk so she couldn't see his own tears of anger. "I was going to start clearing away the stuff here and look on the floor for anything special. Sometimes people hide stuff in covered pits under the floor."

Megan's lip trembled but she spoke with a clear voice. "The same for us. We found—one little boy had a knife in his hand," she swallowed and continued, "He was trying to defend his mom. They just shot them with arrows. He was so little, Connor. And the babies! Why did they kill the babies? They couldn't hurt anyone..." Her voice broke and she stopped.

Connor's anger started to return again. *When I find those sons of...*

A voice came from behind him. "Probably did them a favor."

He turned to see Buck striding forward, a goblin helmet in his hand.

Brandi shot him a furious look. "And what's that supposed to mean?"

Buck shrugged. "They kill the adults and leave the kids, what happens then? Mighty Oaks, the wolves out here would have them in two seconds."

Brandi's jaw tensed. "If you think these people deserved to be murdered—"

Buck gave one of his disarming, homespun smiles. "Didn't say they did. Just pointed out that they didn't suffer much this way."

For a moment, Connor thought Brandi would say something harsh, but instead, she looked down at the ground and nodded. When she looked up again, her eyes glistened.

"It's little enough to be thankful for, I'll give you that. At least we're here to give them a proper burial."

All this talk of death...

Connor stood and smacked Buck in the ribs. "Help me move these beams. I'm going to give the floor a once-over."

Buck shrugged. Between the two of them and the Alenars, they managed to wrestle away most of the burned wood and smashed furniture. They tossed the scraps aside, revealing a worn, faded rug covered in ashes. Connor inspected the entire area. The last two huts he had searched turned up nothing out of the ordinary.

He lifted up the rug and began inspecting the dirt floor underneath it.

Aha!

There: a seam in the dirt, a straight line where Nature couldn't have made one. He pulled out a knife and worked the seam until he uncovered an area about one-foot square.

Buck, Megan and Brandi crouched down next to him. "What's that?"

"A floor pit, just like I was hoping," said Connor, absorbed in examining the seam. "Whose house did you say this was?"

"It was Clarissa's."

Dar and Eric had joined them. Dar held a child's toy wagon in white-knuckled hands, the plaything's surface sooty and scarred.

Connor remembered he was a local.

Probably knew them all by name.

"I found a floor pit," he said, hoping his discovery would take Dar's mind off the carnage.

"Do you know what she might have been hiding?" Megan asked.

"It doesn't make much difference now," Buck said. "Open it and find out."

Eric held up a hand. "If it was valuable enough, she may have put a trap on either the lid or the inside."

Connor shot a glance at him. That was very devious thinking. Devious enough for a thief maybe.

The halfling turned back to the seam, probing under it with his knife. He looked for trip wires or odd symbols carved into the earth. He shook his head.

"No traps that I can see. Buck, give me a hand."

The top of the floor pit was heavy, and with good reason. It was made of solid stone with a layer of earth to make it look like the rest of the ground.

Connor looked inside. Something oblong-shaped lay in the dirt of the shallow hole, shrouded in cloth. He pulled it out and sat.

It was a bowl, broad and about two of his hands in diameter.

What the hell? he thought. *Why go to all this trouble to hide a bowl?*

He looked inside, but it was empty. Turning it in his hands, he chewed his lip. Along the outside surface, crooked line in deepest indigo meandered in a jagged, uneven pattern on a cream-colored background. A small star marked in blue glimmered next to one of the largest spikes in the pattern.

Connor scratched his head.

"That's it?" asked Buck, getting on his hands and knees and sticking his head in the hole.

"Yes," said Connor.

Dar crouched next to him and asked for the bowl. He turned it over and over in his hands, brow furrowed in concentration.

"Familiar?" asked Megan, her hand out.

He shook his head and gave it to her. "I don't know. It's Clarissa's style, but I've never seen this particular design. Maybe it's just *like* one of her other ones and nothing more." The puzzled look remained.

Eric let out an explosive breath. "Well, we should pack it up and head back to Forester, Dar. It's getting dark."

The scout shook his head. "We'll never make it. I had planned on staying in the village overnight— when it was still intact. Now we'll have to use a tree-house near here. Sir Tan and I built it while I was still training. It should be big enough to hold all of us. In the morning, Eric and I can track the attackers to find out which direction they came from."

"Why not just stay down here?" asked Connor, frowning. "We can make a defensible hut out of some of these places."

Dar looked around at the ruined town, eyes distracted. "There are worse things out here at night than goblins."

"And after you've found the goblins, then what?" Connor persisted. Watching Dar's eyes, he knew the answer, but wanted the others to hear it.

Dar looked straight ahead. "I go after them."

Everyone exchanged glances.

"Dar," Brandi said. "How many did you say there were? Forty-plus? You can't take them all by yourself."

The scout picked up his bow and tested the string, not speaking, then let his hand fall down by his side. Birds chirped in the trees, oblivious to the wreckage of Westhaven.

Dar turned around. "Look," he said, "If we find where they are and then go back to get the guards, then what? Goblins are canny and they can hear Lord Nolan's troops coming miles away. Then they just pull up stakes and head off for some other rock to hide under."

"You want us to help you," Megan said.

"Whoa!" said Buck, holding up his hands. "No one said anything about taking on a goblin tribe. I say we go back to town, let the guards know what happened, and bring them back here."

Brandi turned to him, face set. "I have to agree with Dar. These people were innocents, slaughtered for some unknown purpose. We can't let their slayers get away. We have to find out why they were killed."

Buck stepped back, his lazy eyes suddenly sharp. "Justice? Yeah, I've seen my fill of "justice" in my life. I'm out here to be a mercenary, not an avenging paladin. I want to see some money out of this."

Dar slung his bow over his back and stared at him for a while, then sighed. "You don't have to come if you don't want to. I have to do this for myself and for these people. I owe it to them."

Eric picked up his spear and clapped Dar on the shoulder. "Well, I'm in this with you."

Megan and Brandi nodded. "We're with you, too, Dar."

The four looked at Connor.

He shrugged. "Hey, I'm not doing anything right now anyway. Let's go."

Eric turned to Buck. "Yes or no?"

Buck hesitated. "I don't want to get involved."

Brandi gave an exasperated sigh. "You're already involved."

Connor looked up at him. "You know, the baron of Forester would probably give a good bounty to whoever captured the ones who did this. Quite a bit of money in that."

Buck looked down at him, silent for a while.

"Okay," he said. "But if I end up getting killed, I'll turn into a ghost and haunt the rest of you forever."

Eric chuckled. "You'll be doing a lot of traveling then, because by the time you die, we'll be crotchety old farts, scattered all over the known world."

The others grinned, the tension broken.

Connor looked up. The sky changed to a deepening grey off to the east and the fiery sky of sunset was just visible behind the trees away to the west. He stood, brushing off his trousers.

Dar looked up at Megan. She smiled at him and his grim demeanor softened.

He tried to smile back. "The treehouse isn't far. We should get there long before it's dark. But first we've got to see to burying the people. Brandi, I'm going to need your help. Maybe you could say a blessing over them."

Brandi smiled. Connor had never seen her smile before. It gave her a startling, brilliant beauty, warm and kind. "We'll do it together, Dar..."

***

"This was a great idea," said Buck, leaning back against the trunk of the great oak with a sigh. He took another pull from his wineskin.

Dar gave a half-bow from where he dangled his legs over the edge of the treehouse platform. "Thank you, Mister Bydecy. All we're missing is the music and we'll have our own tavern."

Connor watched the two. Dar's wry sense of humor returned after a warm dinner, a private talk with Brandi and the relative safety of the treehouse. He wondered if Christian healers studied counseling as well as medicine.

After leaving the scene of the massacre, Dar located the correct tree in a grove of oaks. A ladder hidden on one side faced another oak not five feet away. About twenty feet up their tree, a wide, square platform surrounded the trunk. Joists and braces fastened to living boughs and branches held it secure and sturdy.

I have to meet this Tanner Collins fellow, Connor thought.

Dar and Eric then constructed a firepit on top of the platform using rocks and earth. Not an outdoorsman, Connor wouldn't have thought it possible to make a fire on top of a wooden platform without burning the whole thing to ashes.

He watched Megan swing her legs off the edge of the platform. Her dark boots contrasting with the skin of her calves, peeking out from under the hem of her dress. Her upturned face regarded the trees around her, amber eyes intent and faraway, the firelight behind her casting a pale glow on her cheeks.

Though she was half-elven, her face reminded him of Janey. He looked away.

At least I don't have dreams about it anymore.

He felt footsteps and a light thud next to him. Brandi sat between him and Megan, handing her sister a wineskin. Megan smiled up at her and accepted it.

"You know, Meg," Brandi said, "It's actually pretty out here. There are so many stars."

Megan took a drink and nodded, looking up at the sky. Kaliri, the larger moon, floated in the shimmering starfield, a thin sliver of light, while the golden orb of Diometrius glowed high above and more to the north.

"Very pretty," said Megan. "Reminds you of Mil-Tereth a little, doesn't it?"

Brandi considered this. "A little, but those mountains sure make a difference."

So, they were in the Elven capital. Interesting.

Connor watched the sisters. One could learn quite a bit just by listening.

Eric Indidarc slipped up next to Brandi and swung his legs over the edge. "Evening, ladies."

She nodded at him, eyes twinkling. "Mister Indidarc."

He favored them both with a cheery smile. "Enjoying the view?"

Brandi pursed her lips, but Connor could see a smile lurking behind them. "It's pretty dark out there, Eric," she said. "There's not much to see of the forest."

Eric gestured grandly. "But look up above: that's the best part. God Himself lights the sky with a million lamps for us."

"Are you a poet, too?" Megan asked with a coy look.

"I suppose so," said Eric, keeping his grin. "I've learned a few skills in my day." The firelight cast red-gold shadows on his narrow, handsome face.

Connor remained silent. No telling what might become important in the future.

Eric favors his elven side, thought Connor. *It's obvious that he's half-human, though, with his build and height.*

"Speaking of God," Brandi asked Eric, "which one do you follow?"

"Why, the one True God, of course. Isn't it obvious from my saintly behavior?" answered Eric in pretend shock, placing a hand on his chest.

He looked up her and winked. "On second thought, don't answer that. But I am Christian, just like you and Dar. You have an insignia on the left shoulder of your tunic. Let's see, Saint Raphael's Order?"

"Yes," Brandi answered, "and Megan is in Saint Terenil's."

Eric gave a wistful look at Brandi's emblem. "I was studying so much I didn't have time to inquire. Most orders require preliminary service work before accepting candidates and I didn't have time for that either."

Megan tipped her head to the side. "You said you had some magical arts training. What school did you go to?"

He hesitated, looking out at the forest. "Well, I was tutored."

Both Megan and Brandi stared at him. Connor knew why. Only the wealthiest of merchants and lords could afford to have their sons tutored by a mage.

"By whom?" Megan asked.

Eric squirmed a little. "Er...my father."

"Who was..."

Eric looked resigned. "Melinor Indidarc."

Connor felt satisfied. His earlier suspicions from their meeting in the tavern were justified. He had studied espionage, not sorcery, but even he knew the name of Melinor Indidarc, Wizard of the North and a King's Baron of Deran. Stories of his exploits and his awesome arsenal of magic were legion. And this was his son?

He couldn't hold himself back from the conversation. "Wait a minute, Eric. Melinor is full human. So was his wife. Besides, everyone knows he has only two children, Emily and Brendan."

Eric grinned. "I'm adopted. Melinor... found me about seven years ago."

Megan gasped. "You know the White Demon, Saren DeMey!"

Eric's grin widened. "Oh, you mean the Senior Brat? Yes, I know her. She was Melinor's ward until she took the free-lance. We spent a lot of time together at Melinor's home. She's like a sister to me. I was at her wedding."

Connor had heard of Saren DeMey, a half-daemon found by Melinor as an infant and raised to follow his Christian religion. She had married recently, to Terenil DeMey, an officer in the Deranese military, amid a swirl of rumors about her role in foiling a plot against King Phillip. She and her husband were now Earl and Countess of Tallemar, a suburb of Oakmoor.

Brandi looked stunned. "This is incredible. How did Melinor find you?"

Eric sighed. "Well, actually..."

Buck's voice rang out behind them. "Hey! By the Mighty Oaks!"

The trio turned around to see him standing up on the platform, fumbling for his sword. His eyes darted around the dark branches above him.

"What's wrong?" asked Megan, following his eyes into the shadows overhead.

"I saw a flying lizard," said Buck, getting his sword out and nearly stepping in the fire in the process. "Or a dragon."

"Here in the tree?" asked Brandi. She held her hand out, then spoke a short word. Her eyes glowed light blue.

"Nothing," she said. "Nothing evil at least. Are you sure?"

"Yeah," said Buck, still eyeing the leaves overhead. "It flew over the fire, just above my head. It was a little one, not even as long as my sword."

Eric moved his hands together, then apart. A trio of tiny lights sprang up and he motioned towards the area Buck indicated. The lights swirled off into the darkness, illuminating the limbs and branches. Connor saw nothing crouching there.

Connor stood and moved into the shadows, heat-sensitive vision looking for any sign of a creature in the leaves.

Dar stood with the others for a moment, waiting in the silence, then shook his head. "I don't see or hear anything. Maybe it was a bat."

"It was not a bat!" said Buck, sounding a trifle indignant. "I know a dragon when I see one."

Eric pursed his lip. "And how many have you seen?"

Buck shot a black look at him, then resumed his survey of the tree. "Enough. Just keep watching. It might come back."

"What do you think?" Megan asked Dar.

He shrugged. "There are all kinds of creatures in the Wilderness. The odds are small for a dragon, though."

"Maybe it's one of the good dragons," breathed Megan. Her eyes shone with wonder and anticipation.

Connor remained in the shadows. Some dragons were good and some evil. However, without knowing, it was best to treat all such things with extreme caution. Dragons were dangerous, even the small ones.

Dar took one more look up above. "Any of you Elder Children see anything up there? How about you, Connor?"

Only the chirp of crickets broke the silence. Brandi, Megan and Eric shook their heads.

"Nothing," Connor said. He still had the eerie feeling he was being watched.

Dar shrugged. "Well, whatever it was, it decided the neighborhood was crowded. I say we sleep in turns so someone is awake at all times."

"Do you think that's going to help if something can fly up here to get us?" Buck muttered. "I'll sleep like a baby now."

Dar gave him a wry look. "Yes and some creatures can climb ladders. I'd rather be safe and look a fool than actually *be* a fool and a meal besides."

Connor chuckled. "In that case, I volunteer for dawn watch."

Chapter Four- Into the Breach

He was old: far older than most of the creatures of this forest and older even that the elves in their mighty empire far to the south.

He watched as his spy soared on the thermals above, then turned his gaze down at the forest below.

Who were they? A group of six including two women and one halfling.

He was reminded of the prophecy and the Song but withheld judgment. He had seen similar groups before in this place, seeking adventure in the wilderness, on a mission for a local lord or merely seeking fortune. A little more than half of them never returned.

Still, those predicted by the Song had not arrived.

His spy drifted off again over the forest, tracking them. He shifted his magic focus, looking through the spy's eyes. He watched the group traveling with care through the woods and noted their caution and attentiveness.

He sighed. Through their conversation, he now knew about the massacre at the village. He grieved for the innocents caught in a deadly game. Yet with the patience of his kind, he knew the Victory of the Light was already won. All that remained was choosing whether to be on the winning side.

Of course, if he had been there, the people in the town would still live and their slayers would be charred bits in the green forest. But even he could not prevent that which he did not know about.

Could these six complete the prophecy?

His spy whirled in a circle, signaling he was at the limit of his range. He recalled the creature and it flew back towards him.

A while later, he stretched out an arm and his spy landed on his wrist, trilling a question.

"No, little one," he replied. "Not yet. We will watch and wait. Remember, there were others before, but they were only concerned with themselves, with riches and glory. If these are the ones, it will be obvious. They will be different."

Donnervassilianelikilandra smiled to himself. Time would tell...

***

Maybe there is something to this tracking stuff, thought Buck, looking down into a dark hole in the earth.

Following the goblins was easier than either Dar or Eric had anticipated. That large a group, as Dar put it, could be 'tracked by a blind drunk'. The trail led northwards from Forester, farther into the wilderness.

When they finally found the goblin hideaway, Dar almost fell into it by accident. The group paused at the edge of a large clearing to catch their breath that afternoon and Dar went ahead into the forest, impatient at any delay. He returned a few minutes later, nursing a stubbed toe and motioning them all to silence.

He led them to a hillside, its flanks cut through by rain-paths and covered with brush and doriff trees. He went past the hill and up the far side to the relatively flat top. There, a hole in the ground gaped up at them, hidden behind the trees and surrounded by a collection of large rocks. About twenty feet wide, it sported a rusted iron ladder on one side.

Eric looked at him and raised an eyebrow.

"How do you know this isn't some abandoned mine?" he asked in a low voice.

Dar pointed to the opposite side of the shaft. Buck jumped in surprise and heard a muffled gasp from Megan. A neat pile of skulls gleamed in the shade.

"That's a warning that this place is occupied. Besides," whispered Dar, "their tracks lead right up to this area. There's no sign of them going past it. I think it's here."

46

Buck's mouth felt as dry as paper.

The group crowded around the entrance. Buck looked down again, straining to see any sign of trap or ambush.

Too damn dark. And it smells of rotting leaves.

Buck felt the short hairs on his neck prickle. What if the goblins had set traps? What if it just led into a giant chamber filled with warriors? For that matter, what was to say they weren't out here in the forest, watching and setting up an ambush?

He stared at patches of shadow among the golden-lit forest floor. A spring insect flitted past his ear. He strained his hearing for something out of the ordinary.

Eric raised his hands in a helpless gesture and shook his head. He stepped away and motioned for everyone to follow him.

"I can't see any better than you can," he said, eyes darting towards the pit.

Buck frowned. "Can't you Elven people see in the dark or something like that?"

"There's too much sunlight here, even in the shade," Brandi answered. "Bright light makes it almost impossible."

"Well then," said Connor, sounding impatient, "Let's get underground."

"Are you volunteering to take the point?" asked Eric, amused. Connor gave him a withering look.

"Actually," said Megan, "We need a strong fighter in front with good armor."

Buck almost didn't catch the significance of that remark. He found everyone looking at him.

"Oh, no you don't," he said, holding up his hands. "I'll need every bit of that 'good armor' if I go down first. I can't see and I can't climb with a torch in one hand and a sword in the other. I'll get clobbered by the first thing that sees me down there."

Brandi measured him, then nodded. "He's right. I'll do it."

Buck looked at her in surprise. "Really?"

Why would she go into obvious danger in his place? She barely knew him.

"Yes, really. Unless you have a better idea?" Though apprehensive, her eyes sparked with a flash of irritation.

Careful here, Buck thought. *This one doesn't like to be second-guessed.*

"No, I don't," he said, giving her a broad smile. "Actually, I'll follow you down if you need someone to watch your back. I'll have a torch ready to go."

All I have to do is make sure nothing gnaws me to death before I can scream loud enough to deafen it.

The group followed Brandi over to the hole. She took a sword in one hand and set her feet on the ladder rungs.

Dar took his place in line. "Don't worry Brandi," he reassured her, "We'll be right behind you."

Buck's heartbeat accelerated as he followed her down the ladder.

All right, stop acting like a fishwife before a storm. This is what you trained for. Make Dad proud.

He took out a torch and searched for his tinderbox, letting out a breath at the same time. *Remember the training. Remember the wind and the wheel.*

***

Well, this is nice, thought Buck what seemed like hours later. *We've been walking for ages and the only things we've found are glow-in-the-dark mold and a few cat-sized rats.*

He sniffed the stale, moist air, heavy with the odor of earth and decomposing vegetable matter.

And I think I've caught a cold.

He held up his torch a little higher, trying to see beyond Dar and Eric. The group had asked him to pick up the tail end of the formation when everyone had entered that first silent, blocky chamber. He agreed, partly to avoid argument and partly to ensure he didn't get the first spear in the neck.

Somewhere up front, he knew, Connor scouted the earthy, root-choked tunnel. Then came Dar and Eric, casting a more critical eye on the floors and walls, followed by the Alenar sisters and Buck. Eric and Dar assured the others that the goblins had come this way.

Buck stifled an urge to sneeze, then forgot about it when Eric's hand shot up. He hoped it was something interesting. So far, this 'adventurous' lifestyle could be best described as cold, damp, boring and nerve-wracking all at once.

The group formed a knot in the passage, huddling together as Connor sneaked back to them.

Connor's face was an odd mixture of excitement and fear. "I've found the entrance to their lair."

"How are you sure?" asked Megan pointedly.

Connor shot a furtive glance over his shoulder, then looked at the two women. "Well, there's a couple of..." His voice trailed off.

Megan frowned. "A couple of what?" she whispered back.

Connor looked uncomfortable. "Well, bodies."

Brandi shook her head, exasperated. "We just saw a lot of those. We can handle it. Lead on."

The halfling gave them an odd look, then shrugged. "Fine. Keep quiet."

The group wended their way through the tunnel, turning left where the path sloped downward. It leveled off and became taller and wider.

Eric's hand went up again and Buck tried to crowd forward, holding up his torch to allow more light. Brandi gasped.

Two bodies were pinned to the side of the earthen passageway by spears. One was an old woman and the other a boy of about twelve. Both were very dead. Buck's stomach lurched, but he gritted his teeth and took a deep breath. The tunnels seemed to close in on both him and his little flickering light in the darkness.

Get used to this, Bucko. Goblins don't place much value on life. The dark earth around them was stained even darker. Both corpses had been mutilated and the boy was missing a leg.

Probably used it in the cookpot. Got to make sure I don't end up there either.

He was surprised to discover he was sweating.

"Animals!" Eric hissed, eyes burning. "What kind of beasts..." His question trailed off.

Connor looked grim and Dar was as pale as a ghost.

Brandi took a slow breath. "Be at peace, Eric. These people are gone now," she said in a remarkably calm voice, "Where they've gone, there is no pain, no war."

She bowed her head and the other Christians in the party did likewise. Buck looked at Connor and shrugged.

Brandi whispered something and made a motion over the bodies. Dar looked for a long moment at them, then nodded curtly and led them into the passage.

As he passed, Buck took a handful of earth and sprinkled it on the old woman and the boy.

As Nature sows, so it collects again, he offered. *By the Sacred Grove and the Nine Circles of the Moons, I bid you safe passage to the River of Forgetfulness, Old One and Young One. The Earth Mother welcomes you.*

And I will kick some goblin chieftain in the teeth for this, he added as he followed the others. *And I'm going to tell him exactly why I'm doing it.*

The passage narrowed again, then came to a crossroads. After a brief discussion, they decided to send Connor down the left-hand path to investigate. If they didn't hear from him in five hundred counts, they would go in after him.

The halfling returned soon. "There's a chamber on this side with firelight inside," he said, putting an arrow to his bow. "I count at least ten goblins."

"That's a few," Buck noted, watching the others for reactions.

"We can handle them," said Eric. He hefted his spear in his hand, then gave a smile not mirrored in his eyes. "Justice for Westhaven."

Buck almost jumped. The transformation from joking, laughing Eric to lethal, venomous Eric happened a little too fast to suit him.

Who are these people?

They advanced down the left path, slowing to a creep when the opening to the chamber came in view. Buck extinguished his torch, leaving them with only the flickering light from the chamber. He swallowed and hoped they would get inside fast.

At Connor's signal, they burst into the room.

A fire blazed in a pit in the center of the roughly rectangular area. An iron rod, braced by two swords rammed into the rocky earth, held the carcass of some unknown animal.

Eleven stocky figures whirled in surprise at the commotion. In a matter of seconds, they scooped up weapons and spread out in an arc formation. Horned simian faces with glowing yellow eyes glared back at Buck and his companions. Many of the goblins wore coats of leather reinforced with metal studs and some carried wooden shields. A single dark passageway, about eight feet tall, gaped behind the assembled goblins.

Buck took two steps over to his right, keeping his bow at the ready.

Connor stepped in front of Dar and held forth his hand, palm outward.

He yammered at the goblins in a strange, monosyllabic tongue.

Buck's eyebrows rose. *A man of hidden talents, this Mister Lomin.*

The biggest of the goblins swaggered forward. He sported a ridged helmet with what looked like a couple of dried ears dangling from one side. Where the others in his group wore leather jackets, he had a shirt of metal plates sewn on a leather jerkin. He placed his gnarled hands, one of them missing a finger, on the hilts of his two short swords and sized up the group. He threw back his head and gave a barking laugh, then replied with a monologue of his own. The other goblins began grinning.

Connor's eyebrows rose in mild amusement. "Just so you'll know," he said, directing his words back at his companions, "I told him we were looking for the ones responsible for the Westhaven massacre. I said we had evidence they were goblins from this tribe."

"And the answer?" asked Megan.

"Loosely translated," Connor answered, "he told us to go have sex with our parents."

"At least we have parents from our own species," shot back Dar before a heartbeat passed.

Either the goblins could sense his tone or they could understand Humana. Their faces contorted with rage and they charged.

Nice going, Cabot!

Buck's heart leaped in his throat and he levered an arrow at the first goblin he saw. He dropped his bow without waiting to see the effect and drew his sword. Two goblins came at him screaming. The first had a curved sword and the second wielded a large battle axe.

Buck parried a sword strike, then swung at the axe-wielder. Both opponents skipped aside. Buck slipped his shield onto his arm.

He heard shouts and clanging of metal all around him, but had only eyes for his opponents. His mind screamed that this was all happening too fast.

Remember the wind and the trees. Bend, don't break.

The goblins split apart, one on each side. Buck darted forward, slashing. With the first ring of his sword on his opponent's weapon, his mind became still and calm.

Just like the practice yard.

The goblin moved back under his attack and stumbled. The other jumped in to help, raining blows at Buck with more gusto than accuracy. Buck parried each sword strike, then slammed his shield up into the goblin's blade. He followed that up with a clumsy but powerful kick. His boot struck the goblin in the arm. The sword flew up and out of the way. Buck thrust, running his enemy through. He tugged the blade free and whirled, not even taking the time to revel in his first kill.

The second goblin swung an axe. Buck jerked his foot out of the way more by instinct than anything else and barely missed getting his leg chopped off. The blade banged into the stone floor and the goblin raised it for another strike. Buck stepped to the side, striking diagonally across the plane of his enemy's weapon. The axe veered off course and slammed into the floor with a ringing clang and a flare of yellow sparks. The goblin lurched to the side. Buck swung a hard backhand, sweeping the goblin's head off in a single stroke.

He spun again, looking for other opponents.

Megan stood to his left, wary eyes sweeping the room. She held her staff with white-knuckled hands, but a dead goblin lay at her feet. A rip in her blouse at the waist showed a thin, bloody line along the bottom of her ribs.

Brandi stood with Eric, a total of five goblins dead in front of them. Even as he watched, Eric sheathed his sword and went to jerk his spear from a fallen warrior's chest. Brandi wiped a sword blade on one goblin's cloak and shot an irritated glance at Dar.

Buck gave a soundless whistle. *Five between Eric and Brandi?*

Brandi strode over to Dar. "Nice going. Do you always snap like that? I was hoping to get through this without a fight."

Dar looked both grim and somewhat weary. "I'm sorry. I said it without thinking. But honestly, Brandi, I don't think they would have given up."

The irritated look in Brandi's eyes softened. "Well, you may be right. They didn't look disposed to surrender. At least they had a chance to give up and decided to fight instead, not like the people in Westhaven."

Dars eyes were hard. "Not like Westhaven."

Connor stepped over his dead opponents, watching the only other exit, "It's a sure bet all this racket is going to rouse *somebody*."

Eric nodded. "I hear you. Let's keep an eye on the passage. Why don't you guys see if these rat-eaters had anything useful on them?"

Buck blinked. Under national laws, any booty taken while on an assignment or mission was theirs to keep. Subject to tax, of course, but maybe...

Buck quickly began pulling belt purses off the bodies.

Hmm...a dozen silver disks here, about twenty copper gits...ah! A few bits of peridot and garnet...

He emptied all of it into his purse and continued on with his search.

Someone behind him cleared her throat.

Megan stood with her hands on her hips and a delicate eyebrow arched in question. "And just what do you think you're doing?"

"Er..." Buck thought fast. "Um, I was going to start a reserve fund. You know, for a rainy day."

Megan gave him a dazzling smile. "Really? How sweet of you to think of our welfare! And very wise, too."

He looked at her in surprise.

"In that case," she continued, holding out her hand, "We certainly don't want to load down one of our best fighters with all that treasure, do we? I'll hold it for you."

Troll crap...

"Uh..." he hesitated, stalling. Maybe if he distracted her somehow...

"Now!" she said in a tone so commanding that he froze in astonishment.

She raised her eyebrows. He handed over all the money, then made a face at her retreating back as she went to join the others.

Boy, for such a dainty-looking wench, she acts like a drill sergeant. He eyed her, then shook his head. It was going to be really hard to get ahead in life with this crowd.

He retrieved his bow and went to join the others at the open doorway across the room. Eric's brow furrowed as he peered down the tunnel.

"I don't get it. If someone made that much noise in *my* house, I'd sure as hell try to find out what happened, at the very least."

Connor gestured at the opening, "We aren't going to do anything standing here. Let's move."

Buck re-ignited his torch and held it in his shield hand, trying not to let the flame get too close. He wished for a solid metal shield instead of his metal-reinforced wooden one.

Move they did, creeping along as fast as they dared. They weren't sure about goblin tactics, but an ambush was almost a certainty.

In spite of their caution, they were almost caught off-guard. Arriving at a crossroads, they re-grouped to discuss the best direction. Without warning, the wall in front of them rippled.

Seven goblins burst out from behind a stone-colored curtain and charged. Buck clawed for his sword.

Eric had just enough time to raise his spear before a javelin hit him in the left shoulder, snapping against his armor. Buck clanged aside a sword blow and saw Connor almost disappear under a flurry of clubs to his right.

Without thinking, he stepped forward to help Connor and attacked. He split the helm of one goblin and broke another's spear. From the corner of his eye, he could see Dar's bastard sword flashing in the torchlight as he swung it in a deadly arc. There were two metallic clangs accompanied by short screams.

More goblins joined the attack and he was in the midst of it, trying to block a myriad of blows with his shield and still hit something goblinize with his blade in between dodging. He heard Brandi yelling something, but couldn't even place her location.

He turned, seeing a fat goblin raise a mace over its head to strike at him. It stopped in amazement at a spear that suddenly appeared in its chest, then toppled backwards.

Eric was screaming something at him, Buck realized.

"Back, you idiot!" Eric's shoulder was bloody and he had a cut over one eye. "Back to the first chamber!"

Buck blinked, then began moving backwards, knocking clubs and swords aside as he beat a fighting retreat. Eric's longsword and Brandi's twin blades flashed next to him. Buck slammed aside a spear thrust, then whipped his blade down, breaking the shaft.

Wind and the wheel. He clung to his training. *Hold to the wind, Bucko. Bend, don't break.*

They reached the first chamber. He stood shoulder to shoulder with his companions in the room and managed to score two more kills, just missing getting a spear in the eye. He lost count of how many hits he took, but his chainmail armor and shield held up under the onslaught.

How many more? he wondered, gasping for breath.

"Fire in the hole!" rang out Megan's voice from behind him.

A glittering bottle-shaped object sailed over his head, a tongue of flame fluttering from one end. With a crash of glass, it broke on the stone floor right in the middle of the goblins. A pool of fire erupted and he recoiled from the heat.

Goblins shrieked in agony and several of them dropped into writhing, flaming heaps on the ground. Two managed to stagger back down the passageway, their armor afire. There was a double twang from next to him and arrows appeared in the backs of the walking torches. They dropped.

Buck sheathed his sword and readied his bow. Connor leaned against the wall next to him, aiming an arrow down the passage. The halfling's face was taut with pain and several nasty cuts bled down the side of his face.

"What was that?" asked Dar.

"Fireburst formula," whispered Megan. "A concoction I learned to make at the university."

The corridor was silent now, occupied only by goblin bodies, a few of them burning brightly. No more warriors came forward to assail them from the passageway.

Oaks and mistletoe, they stink!

Weariness hit Buck full force and he leaned against the cool stone next to the doorway. His hands shook so badly he could barely hold an arrow to the bowstring.

Connor tapped him on the hip. His eyes were tired and a bit glassy. "Thanks," he said.

Buck nodded and tried to smile. "Just get them for me when it's your turn." He was sure he sounded like an idiot.

Dar walked up next to them, no longer the avenging angel, but now just shocked and pale. "Where the hell did they come from? There must have been dozens of them!"

"Probably set up the ambush when they heard the first fight," said Megan. Her eyes darted around the passageway and their chamber. She leaned on her staff.

Brandi took a deep breath and brushed a vagrant lock of hair from her forehead. The red-gold was a little redder than Buck had remembered, probably with blood from a nick in the head or from her enemies. Buck tried to figure out how many he had seen her kill in the passageway and lost count at about five.

"We got the tar kicked out of us," she said, replacing her swords in their scabbards.

Dar took his place at the passage next to Connor. "But that's about fifteen less to murder innocent villagers."

Buck couldn't believe his ears. "Yeah, but how many more are there? Are we going to fight an entire tribe? There could be hundreds. I say we go back now, before we get ourselves killed."

Dar gaped at him. "What are you talking about?"

Connor wiped at the blood on his face. "We almost went down the path of no-return there. I don't know if you've noticed, but we're kind of beat up and we haven't even gotten past their first guardrooms yet."

Dar shook his head. "No! We can't give up now. We're in their lair. We know they're the ones who did it."

Brandi nodded. "Now that we have evidence, we have to finish what we've started."

Buck felt the situation slipping away from him. "But what good is that going to do if we're dead? We don't stand a chance."

Eric stepped next to him. "I think you're giving them a bit too much credit. That was a pretty hard fight and we're still standing. How many of them are dead now? More than thirty, I'd say. That should give them something to think about."

Connor and Buck exchanged glances. The halfling shook his head and winced.

Megan and Brandi walked to Dar's side. He gave them a grateful smile.

"Look, Buck, Connor," he said, eyes earnest. "This isn't going to be easy. We knew that going in. But there's something going on and we've got to find out what happened at Westhaven."

Megan's eyes were sad. "Didn't what we saw at the entrance make any difference to you? Or at the village? I know you felt something."

Buck lowered his gaze and scuffed a rock with his boot. "Well, I did. But I feel like living too."

Brandi stepped forward and took his hand and Connor's. "I know we don't share the same faith," she said, "but I know that evil is not tolerated by druids any more than it is by Christians. And do you want to have to do the job again later? If we leave now, there's a chance they'll just run away."

Connor leaned against the wall, weariness showing on his face. Buck guessed the pop on the head from that goblin club was taking its toll. Finally, the halfling sighed.

"She's right. We've got to finish the job." he murmured. "I don't know how, but we've got it to do. Otherwise, we'll end up repeating this whole exercise."

Buck looked at all of them, then nodded.

At least Old One and Little One can go back to the earth in peace now, thought Buck. *They have been avenged.*

Dar came up to him and clapped him on the shoulder. "I won't forget this, Buck. You too, Connor. I owe you."

Brandi turned her attention to the others in the party. She shook her head. "It looks like we're going to have to patch ourselves up a bit if we're going to go any farther."

Dar looked back at her, then gave her a crooked smile. "Really? I feel pretty good. Why don't you guys just wait here while I go get the goblin chieftain?"

She made a face at him, then knelt down next to Connor. Taking her backpack off, she rummaged around and came up with a jar of something that looked like it had been scraped from the bottom of an ale barrel. She produced some bandages and bound up the cuts on Connor's arm and leg, then applied some of the ointment to his forehead. Already, an egg-sized lump had appeared there.

Brandi sat back, then looked him in the eyes. "Look at me, Connor."

The halfling tried to focus on her. She shook her head and frowned. "Not good. He may have a concussion."

"First, I'll make sure everyone else is in something resembling good condition," she said. "Then I'll take care of Mister Lomin."

Her hands were gentle and skilled for someone who had been hacking her way through goblin helmets only minutes earlier. Buck discovered several bruises and cuts on his right hand, left arm, and left ear. When she had finished treating him, he didn't feel like taking on a fortress, but the pain had subsided and he wasn't as tired.

He watched her minister to her sister's wounds, which were very slight, and Dar's and Eric's, which weren't. He sniffed at the ointment on his wounds and was surprised to find an invigorating, pleasant scent.

Good stuff. I'll have to get some of my own.

His curiosity increased when Brandi returned to Connor's side. He had seen Druid Anthan heal someone a long time ago in the grove near his hometown, but he sensed this was somehow different.

Brandi closed her eyes and placed on hand on Connor's head and the other over his heart. A pale yellow glow started from her hands and spread to Connor, shining brightest where she touched him. Buck had an uncanny feeling Brandi was connected to Something *outside* herself.

After a couple of heartbeats, the glow disappeared. Brandi smiled and opened her eyes. Connor sat up in wonder, feeling his head.

Buck's eyes widened. Brandi was a battle medic for sure and her abilities included healing magic, a rare gift.

He shivered. Religion always made him nervous.

Megan put a hand on her sister's head and smiled down at her. For an instant, Buck saw a tiny hint of a closeness and sisterly affection that made him feel warm—and lonely.

He shook his head. *I must be getting soft. None of that stuff matters. It's all over at the first reincarnation anyway.*

He poked Dar in the shoulder. "Which doorway you want to watch?"

Chapter Five- Brandawyn

He looked out at the dark forest with narrowed, cat-like golden eyes. Absently, he stroked his white beard and regarded the wooded hills.

Rustling in the brush attracted his attention. Four giant wolves crept out of the forest near him, their eyes glowing red with a hateful intelligence. Each stood as tall as a man at the shoulder and horned ridges of bone ran down their spines. Nostrils flared as they searched the wind.

He raised an eyebrow and watched them. They would find his scent and, if they had any brains at all, would leave without violence. If they did not, he would burn them to ashes.

The fell wolves picked up his scent. The largest whined to the others. One barked, then the quartet loped away from him, north and east, deeper into the wilderness.

Wise.

He turned back to his observation of the hill below. Nothing moved here without his knowledge.

He sighed. His spy had again seen the freelance sell-swords. They were like so many other groups he had seen over the long years: energetic, youthful, naive, and spirited. In this case, he believed, their hearts were also good.

Donnervassilianelikilandra stepped off the flat rock and picked up his walking staff, strolling towards the rocky outcropping near his vantage point.

The evil groups he didn't mourn so much, except for the fact that they

59

chose Darkness, a pale perversion of the wonder and glory of serving the Light. Ones like these, now, eager to right wrongs—for these he felt the most sympathy and the most empathy.

His thoughts winged away to his kin and he felt a temporary nervousness and fear. How did they fare? Were they unharmed?

He took a deep breath and calmed himself. For one as old as he, patience was a way of life. He knew that after all deeds are brought to light, evil garners its own reward in this life and the next. Those who waited and acted prudently could thwart it through decisive action at the right time.

He looked back at the hill, thinking of the group. Were these the ones, chosen since the dying days of a fallen Empire? Were these the ones who would bring justice to the lands, the ones who would answer the prophecy with their own sacrifice?

If they were, they could help his kinfolk and release him from the promise.

He determined not to worry about it. He wasn't the Creator of All, and the Creator of All kept His own counsel.

A fluttering sound in the branches made him turn his head and smile. A small winged lizard flew down to him and landed on his arm with a chirp. He smiled and patted it on the head. It curled a barbed tail around his wrist.

We will keep an eye on our freelancers, he thought to the creature, which trilled in response. *If it is really they who answer the Song, then maybe the cycle will come to an end and at last the prophecy fulfilled.*

He released his companion to fly up into the air, the raised his hands over his head.

With a word, he transformed, feeling his own wings spread out behind him.

***

What's taking them so long? Brandi wondered.

She peeked over her shoulder. The others crouched in front of a door. The light from Buck's torch flickered against the tunnel walls. A drop of perspiration ran down the side of her face.

She turned back to her sentry duty. She glanced left and right down a wide, musty passageway, leading off into murky darkness.

Only more roughly-hacked stone met her eyes, broken by a few patches of mold. Far off in the depths of the tunnels, she heard echoes of shouts and running feet.

Eric stood to her left, a goblin spear cradled in his arm.

"You'd think it wouldn't take quite so many people pick a lock on a door," she whispered to him. "We've given them the slip for now, but we'll have more guards here any minute."

Despite the tension, Eric raised an amused eyebrow. "Would you rather have the others here with us?"

"Point taken," she answered. The turnoff only allowed two people to walk abreast. The last thing she and Eric needed was a congregation at their end of the passage.

The group hid in a short tunnel that turned off from a long, wide passage they had dubbed "Main Street". Behind them, Connor, Dar, Megan and Buck worked on a locked door.

Correction. Connor is working on it. The others are "supervising".

She wished they would hurry up. If this door didn't lead to somewhere clear of goblins, they were going to have to keep moving down "Main Street". No one liked that idea. They needed to rest.

How did they get here, anyway? It seemed like such a confused jumble. After healing Connor, they sneaked through the tunnels, feeling their way along, trying to figure out where the goblin leader hid. That strategy was quickly replaced by one of survival, as more goblins got wind of their presence and began a systematic sweep of the complex.

The companions had been running for the last hour, it seemed. It started with another ambush: this time in an empty chamber. Two groups of attackers boiled up out of separate passageways. The companions survived that encounter more by luck than by skill. Eric used his spear to trip up one warrior into his fellows and Dar had killed two on the other side with well-placed arrows. Then, before they even had a chance to catch their breath, drums boomed in the distance. They raced off through another tunnel.

Fortunately, they weren't lost. Connor kept a map, updating it as they stopped for the all-too-brief rests. He also kept a tally of how many warriors they killed or drove off. Despite encouraging results from the tally, the map brought into stark reality the gravity of their situation. All routes to the entrance went through areas likely occupied by goblins. Without any idea of the size of the enemy force, they had no way of knowing whether there were two goblins left or two hundred.

Maybe Buck was right. Maybe we should have gone back to town to get help. Lord, was I too insistent on us staying here to find the leaders? Will I be the cause of our deaths because I was too rigid?

Megan's voice floated back to them. "He's got it. Let's go."

With one last look down "Main Street", Eric and Brandi turned and rejoined the group. Ahead, Buck and Dar braced themselves against the door, swords ready. Connor and Megan stood behind them, hands gripping weapons. Brandi put an arrow to her bowstring and tried to ignore the dry feeling in her mouth.

Does anyone ever get used to this?

At a signal from Dar, the lead warriors burst through the door and the others charged in after them.

A room full of boxes, barrels, and weapons racks greeted them. Brandi sighed with relief, then peeked down the passage behind them and closed the door, re-locking it from their side.

"Your turn, Buck," she said, replacing her bow and arrow. "Be careful."

Buck gave her a sour look, but went to the door anyway, crouching next to the latch. He leaned against the wall and put his head up to the keyhole, looking bored.

Brandi hid a smile. Since the second ambush, the group now posted a guard on each exit. Buck and Dar, in particular, manfully put up with it, although from their groans and pithy looks she could tell they detested it.

"Now what?" asked Dar, looking around the chamber. Racks stood against the opposite wall and an assortment of boxes lay in orderly stacks between the door and the racks.

Brandi had learned about goblin society in the academy. They thrived on organization. She was willing to bet someone in the complex (probably the leader) had a listing of the contents of every container.

"Well," said Megan, putting a finger to her lips, "we might find something worthwhile here, like arrows or food. I say we start with the crates. There's some spears and swords in the racks and the barrels probably have water and stuff like that."

They opened all the boxes. The results yielded only sacks of grain, dried meat of suspicious origin, various bags of roots and tubers, some shovels and other mining equipment, and dry goods.

Brandi glanced at Buck to make sure he wasn't daydreaming, then turned back to her box of cloth.

She wondered about him. Druids and those who followed their precepts made her uneasy with their unpredictability. They followed strict rules sometimes and then made radical changes without warning. Only one thing was certain: if the natural world was threatened, they were sure to take action.

Brandi had heard stories of how druids had turned into adversaries when they had determined that "too many good works" were being done. In the view of the Old Faith, "too much good" was as bad as "too much evil".

She frowned and chided herself as she sifted through the bolts of textiles. *I shouldn't be judging Buck by the actions of some of his faith-brethren. Someone else can easily condemn me for acts of so-called 'Christians'.*

A hiss from the door halted her musings. Buck waved at them. "Lights out! Someone's coming!"

Dar and Megan snuffed their torches. Heat outlines of Brandi's companions shone in the darkness. Varying grades of temperature marked the boxes and stone walls. The sullen, residual glow of a torch-tip inscribed an arc as her sister laid it down.

Muttering sounds wafted back towards them from the door. Buck straightened and stepped back, hand on his sword.

Brandi listened, straining to pick up the words. *Wish I would have paid more attention in class when we were studying Goblin.*

"...check in here. They head this way last time we see them."

Brandi's heart pounded in her chest. She slipped her bow off her back and laid an arrow to it. She turned to the others and pointed at the door, then made a "come-hither" motion with her finger. They took cover behind containers, weapons ready.

More muttering from the door.

"...locked. Must get key."

She was sure they could hear her breathing. She licked dry lips.

A louder voice now. "Fool! Chorg has key. Ghai-zhal do not. How can they get in there without key? We waste time."

Clattering boots rang out, receding into the distance. Still she waited, her hand in the air. Seven heartbeats passed, then ten, then twenty. She let out a long easy breath and nodded to her sister. Several clacks echoed in the room and torchlight flared again.

Buck and Dar blinked in the light and Brandi had to look away for a split second.

Megan stepped towards the back of the room, torch in her hand. "I thought they would come in for sure." She jammed the flaming brand in a ring set in the wall.

Dar nodded. His squared, even features looked shadowed and eerie in the torchlight. "Then we'd be finished. There's only one exit."

"Are we ready to go yet?" Connor asked.

"Yes," Brandi answered. "We've searched all the boxes already."

"This one too?"

"Yes."

He nodded. "How about the bottom?"

Brandi watched him, confused. He hopped into the box, which came up to his shoulder, then knelt and tapped the bottom with his fist.

It sounded hollow.

"False bottom," he noted with a twinkle in his eye.

Brandi felt her face growing warm. "Er, yes. I guess I missed that."

They pried up one of the bottom boards of the container and extracted a small bag. Connor picked it up by the drawstrings and laid it on the ground.

Eric used his spearpoint to cut the strings.

"Why are you being so careful? It's only a little bag," asked Dar next to her. He held a wineskin and fumbled with the stopper as he spoke.

"Sometimes people put little surprises in containers," Connor answered without taking his eyes off the bag. "A pretty scorpion, a magical trap...could be anything."

Connor worked the bag open with his dagger. Several fistfuls of shiny silver coins, a silver bracelet with graceful enameled patterns, a small brass key, and three grape-sized, pale blue gems winked at them in the light from Buck's torch.

"Wow! Are those sapphires?" exclaimed Dar.

Megan picked up the stones and smiled. "No. Aquamarines. Good ones, though."

The ranger nodded, taking a swig from the wineskin.

"What are you drinking?" Brandi asked, knowing it was probably something other than water.

"Beer," Dar announced with a satisfied look, "One of the barrels was full of it. I took out one of their wineskins and filled it up." He took another mouthful.

Brandi sighed. "I should have known. Be glad it isn't poisoned."

Dar stopped with his cheeks bulging.

Brandi had to smile at that. "Don't worry. I don't think goblins would poison their own beer. They'd make the bait a lot more tempting, like putting it in whisky or spirits or something like that. But I wouldn't advise sampling anything in goblin tunnels. You never know."

Dar swallowed and nodded.

"Now what?" asked Eric.

She gave the room a once-over. "Check the weapons and take a rest for a while. Then we get out of here and hope we can get to either the leader or an exit soon."

"And we should check for secret doors," Megan interjected.

Brandi gave an exasperated sigh. Megan tilted her head to one side, eyebrows raised. Brandi knew that look.

"Sure. That'll be fun." said Dar. "I don't have enough cobwebs in my hair from all the other fruitless searches. We've done this in every room, Megan, and not one *secret passageway* to show for it."

Megan glared at him.

"Besides," he continued, "There's got to be a way to the leader of this crowd out there in the passages somewhere, and we're getting closer. I can feel it."

"Are you sure it isn't the goblin beer?" Eric asked.

Dar considered this, then brightened. "Could be," he replied, taking another pull.

Megan stamped her foot. "We'll waste a lot more time if we just stand here debating. Besides, who do you think hid that little treasure trove in a false bottom of a common box? Someone who is rather important, maybe even a chieftain. If you were him, wouldn't you want to be near your storeroom, just to make sure your men didn't snoop around looking for little stashes of treasure? Like the one we just found? And what is the key for?"

The others exchanged looks.

Megan took their silence to mean agreement. "Good. Brandi, Eric, let's see what we can find." She turned and strode off towards one wall.

Connor rolled his eyes and went to join Buck at the door. Eric took off to inspect one of the other walls.

Brandi stepped behind the weapon racks. "Let's make it fast, Megan," she said over her shoulder. "I think we're going to have a mutiny if we don't."

Brandi looked for the usual tell-tale signs: cracks in the wall that were a little too straight, discolored stones, particularly worn sections of flooring.

She finished her search and sighed. Nothing.

Megan gave a little cry of triumph. "Here!"

The others rushed over. She pointed at a flat stone with a worn spot in the center.

"It looks like a pressure release mechanism," postulated Connor, his eyes sparkling with interest.

"I told you I had a feeling," said Dar with an arch look at Brandi.

Brandi eyed her sister, who turned away to hide a smile. *One of these days, someone is going to swat him in the head. Probably me.*

Connor checked the stone, running his gloved hands over the surface. Finally, he took out his sword and pushed the stone with the pommel.

The stone slid in and to the side to reveal a metal plate with a keyhole.

Connor held out his hand for the key. "Now if only this is a real door and not a trap."

He examined the lock, then slipped the key inside and turned it. The section of the wall swung back with a faint hiss, revealing a dark slot in the stone just wide enough for one person at a time.

They crept into a passageway that led straight ahead to a curving wall. The curve ended in a square wooden door.

Connor waited there. Dar tapped his ear and pointed at the door. Connor wiped the area around the handle and laid his head on the crack between the door and the wall.

Seconds passed. Brandi tried to not to breathe, readying her bow.

Finally, Connor looked up at them and nodded. He moved his mouth and pointed at Dar.

Brandi made a face. *What did that...? Oh! Someone speaking. Someone like Dar, a human.*

She breathed a silent prayer to Saint Michael and then the front line of Buck and Dar surged forward. The door swung open.

She lined up her sights on the first target she saw, a large female goblin in chainmail armor. She and four other goblins whirled, grabbing for weapons. Brandi saw a door on the left, a couple of bunk beds, and a curtain on the right. The table and chairs in the center could make maneuvering difficult.

A sixth goblin, larger than the others, spat out a guttural curse and snatched a battle axe from the top of a table. A powerfully built brute, he towered over Connor and wore a helmet decorated with parts of a human skull. Twelve goblin eyes reflected yellow in the torchlight, making them all seem like devils from some alien world.

A human man in dark purple trousers and a deep red tunic caught her attention. He sidestepped behind the goblins.

"Hold!" Brandi commanded in Humana, hoping her voice wasn't shaking as much as her hands. "Under the authority of King Philip and Queen Ahlana of Deran, I place the leadership of this outpost under arrest for the murder of the citizens of Westhaven."

The goblins looked puzzled but brought their weapons to ready position. The human gave a rakish smile, showing even teeth in a handsome face. Bright blue eyes regarded her.

"And whom do I have the honor of addressing?" he asked.

Brandi blinked. An attack, a growled order to the goblins— maybe. Even maniacal laughter would have been expected. But civil conversation?

"Er...Brandawyn Alenar," she replied, feeling a bit silly at the formality.

The man in purple and red nodded and straightened to his full height. A silver dagger in his belt glittered in the torchlight and he held a slim metal wand in his other hand. She saw a sundered moon emblem in the center of his tunic and wondered at its meaning.

He smoothed a neat black mustache with one hand. "High greeting then, Brandawyn Alenar," he replied. "I am Faedan Delphin. Upon what evidence do you place your charge of murder?"

Brandi's eyes narrowed. What game was he playing? "We have bodies of goblins from this tribe at the crime scene, arrows that match those used by the ones here, and the bodies of two villagers at the entrance to this complex."

"Convincing evidence indeed. However, as you can see, I am not a goblin. Therefore, I am not one of those charged with the murders, am I?"

Brandi frowned. *He's stalling. Trying to get us all tangled up mentally while he maneuvers for an opening.*

He had to be the ringleader of the operation, but he had a point. How could they link him to Westhaven?

Before she could reply, Connor spoke to the goblins in their yammering tongue. They began to mutter and cast vicious glances at the human. Brandi smiled. She knew what Connor had told them.

"What did you say?" Dar whispered.

Connor shrugged, still holding his own arrow on target. "I told them their leader said he wasn't one of them and that he wasn't guilty of the attack on the human tribe. I informed them that they would therefore be taken in to prison while he would be set free. Just translating."

The muttering among the goblin troops increased. The leader spoke to Faedan in a long, rolling sentence and the human shot back a terse, almost monosyllabic response. The leader turned back towards the companions, glowering now.

"That wasn't very nice," he said with a tight smile. "You've made them agitated."

"Killing women and children isn't nice either," Dar shot back. "But I guess it's all you can do anyway, since you can't fight against real warriors. Typical incompetent pretend-wizard."

Faedan turned white with fury. He screamed an order, pointing at Brandi and her friends.

Both sides exploded into action. Brandi sensed Eric on her right. Her arrow and his spear slammed into one of the charging goblins, throwing the creature off his feet.

Faedan spoke a different word now, one that made Brandi's hair tingle. Three glowing darts sizzled out at them, one heading for her and two at Megan. Brandi tried to twist out of the way, but the missile altered course with terrifying accuracy and hit her just below the left breast. She gasped at the searing pain, dropping her bow. She heard Megan scream.

With a supreme effort, Brandi quelled the impulse to turn and instead drew her swords.

There was a soft word from behind her and she felt a wave of cottony energy flow past. She shook her head, focusing just in time to see a goblin's eyes roll back in his head. He crashed to the floor in a metallic rattle.

Megan's alive and that's her calling card.

All of the remaining goblin guards snored away on the floor. Now only the leader and Faedan stood before them. The chieftain crouched in front of Buck and Dar, battle axe raised and fangs bared in a snarl.

Faedan nodded, a thin smile on his lips. "Well-played, Brandawyn Alenar of Deran and companions. You have passed the test. We will allow you join our company now."

Brandi wasn't sure she had heard right. "What?"

"We have been watching you. Do you think I would let you get this far without a reason? You have proven yourselves to be quite capable. The Dark Rider could use ones such as you. Join us and you will rule in the New Vision. Refuse and you will fall in the wave of power that follows."

"Oh sure," Dar retorted. "We really want to join up with this Stark Rider or whatever the hell his name is. That's why just busted up an entire company of his troops."

"Give up," Eric added. "We outnumber you."

Faedan's eyes took on a faraway look. "My life is as nothing compared to the power that awaits me."

Brandi lowered her blades just a fraction.

Faedan pointed at Eric and spoke a short word. A ball of light sprang up in front of Eric's face. With a cry of pain, he staggered backward, holding his spear on guard. The sphere followed him like a living thing. The goblin leader screamed and charged at Buck and Dar.

Brandi lunged forward.

Faedan dodged her first sword strike and blocked the second with his wand. The silvery rod spun out of his hand into a corner.

Faedan thrust both hands out and hissed another magic word. Brandi ducked, more from reflex than anything else. A filmy web of greyish strands soared over her head. It caught Dar, Buck and the goblin chieftain where they exchanged teeth-rattling blows. The strands enveloped them, turning them into a struggling, ash-colored mass of webs.

God, how many tricks does he have?!

Brandi stepped forward, desperate to end it. She faked a thrust, then cut in with her other blade. The mage ignored the feint, correctly dodged the second attack, then, just as she had expected, slashed at her with his dagger. She blocked it with one sword and thrust with the other. The point of her blade sank into his midsection. He gasped and staggered back.

She lowered her blades. "Surrender now?" she asked. "We've had enough killing."

Faedan turned and stumbled to the curtain— right to Connor Lomin.

How the halfling got there so quickly and so quietly, Brandi didn't know. Faedan dodged Connor with surprising nimbleness and cut to his left. Almost too fast for her eyes to follow, Connor skipped aside and thrust his sword to the hilt in the man's side. Faedan gurgled and dropped.

"Brandi!"

She whirled to see Eric, blinking from the aftereffects of the globe of light, a struggling mass of webs, and her wounded sister.

Megan struggled to disentangle herself from a fallen chair. "Quick Bran!" she managed with a grimace, "We've got to get Buck and Dar out of the webs before they suffocate."

Brandi and Connor ran over to the grey pile, hacking with their swords until the two men could stagger free. Together, they and Megan managed to clear the sticky strands away from their mouths and noses.

"Thanks!" gasped Dar when he could speak, clawing the webs from his face. "I don't know how much longer I could have held my breath."

"And you don't have to worry about old Stoneface in there," Buck added, "Dar ran him through just before the webs hit."

Megan leaned on the table and Brandi went to her. "Are you okay?"

Her sister shook her head. "I caught two fire darts. Hurts like hell."

Brandi peeled away burnt fabric from her sister's side and whistled. Two bleeding burn marks, each the size of an acorn, were below Megan's left lung and just next to her navel.

"Is it bad?"

Brandi sighed. *First, I hack up enemies, then I heal friends.*

70

She smiled and flipped a lock of her sister's hair with her forefinger.

"No problem at all," she said. "Just remember you weak little wizards can't take as much punishment as us mighty warriors."

Megan grinned. "I'll try to keep it in mind."

"Now relax and don't wiggle," Brandi said, seating her in one of the few unbroken chairs. She put one hand on each of Megan's injuries and took a deep breath.

She let it out, relaxing into a familiar trance and feeling a familiar warmth seep through her. She felt Power building up. It tingled in her brain and then coursed through every fiber of her body, steady and comforting. She focused on Megan.

In her mind's eye, she pictured Megan's wounds, then imagined them knitting together with healthy new flesh. She felt a lightning-quick surge of heat and energy.

Brandi opened her eyes to see Megan examining healed, unscarred skin through the holes in her clothing. The younger Alenar smiled and kissed Brandi on the cheek.

"Thank you, sister dear."

"Don't mention it."

Now if only you'd stay out of the way of battles, she added mentally. *How the hell can I keep an eye on you if you're always in the thick of things?*

"Ahem!"

Brandi turned to see Eric regarding her. "And what about you, miss? You got hit by one of those little firedarts too."

Brandi inspected her armor. Two chain links in her armor had blown off and another was deformed. She poked a finger in the hole in her tunic underneath it.

Sore, but not bleeding. The armor helped.

She smiled. "It doesn't hurt much. Besides, I don't have enough strength for another healing right now. I'll have to get some rest first."

Eric frowned. He looked deep into her eyes for a second and then sighed. "Okay, but don't push yourself to the edge, understand? We need you, and not just for the healing skills."

Part of her wanted to retort that she was fine, that she could take care of herself. Something in his demeanor made her stop. Shamed at her short temper, she turned away.

He cares, that's why he's asking. Be thankful he's also a mage. Most warriors don't understand how spellcasting drains a person.

"Well," noted Megan, "these goblins aren't going to sleep forever. Let's make sure they can't take us out from behind." She started pulling rope from her shoulder bag.

Buck looked at her for a moment, then shrugged and drew his dagger. He moved towards one of the sleeping figures.

Eric stopped him. "What are you doing?"

Buck blinked, confused. "Uh, I'm making sure they can't sneak up on us. One strike and—"

"No!" interrupted Eric, shaking his head. "That's murder. Let's just tie them up instead."

"So they can get free and sneak up on us?" asked Connor with an irritated look.

"I won't be party to an assassination!" Eric shot back. His eyes flared with anger— and something else.

Brandi wondered. Eric looked almost panicked.

She stepped forward. "Eric is right. If we kill them like Buck says, we'll be just like them. They have less chance to live than the people of Westhaven did. At least the villagers were awake."

Buck and Connor exchanged glances. Connor nodded, looking chastised. Buck shrugged, replacing his weapon. Eric relaxed.

Trussing up the goblins took a short amount of time. They also emptied every belt purse they could find. Megan got the little silver wand, which had survived Brandi's sword with no ill effects.

Bran sighed. She hadn't told Megan, but if those two firedarts had hit her over the heart or in the head, her younger sister would have needed a pine box, not a healing spell. It was better knowing the wand was in Meg's hands anyway.

Eric slipped up next to her, back to his cheerful self. "Now, what do you suppose was so important behind that curtain?"

His short-cropped blond hair glowed almost golden. A thin line of perspiration ran down one cheek from his hairline and he brushed at it. Without realizing it, she stared at the way the torchlight glittered in his violet eyes.

No! Stop it! You can't afford any entanglements, she reminded herself.

She shook her head and stepped towards the cloth barrier. "I'm not sure. Connor, didn't you check it out after you killed Faedan?"

"Yes," he replied. "There's a couple of sacks, a chest and a door we might want to check out. I think he was heading for an escape."

She turned and raised an eyebrow at Eric as she walked to the curtain. "Well? Are we all going to stand here? This might be our way out too."

Chapter Six- Ghoul's Kiss

Gorlak lifted up the goblin trooper's head, then dropped it to the stone floor with a thump. He surveyed the rest of the carnage in the intersection, snout wrinkled in disgust. Corpses of guards formed dark, cold lumps on the darker, colder floor.

Fifteen in the first room, five in the corridor, three at the first intersection, then six, seven and now six again. Whoever was in Outpost One was tearing it to pieces despite the careful ambushes. The body-count approached the total for the outpost.

True, the dead were goblin regulars, not elite warriors of his strike team, but still, to eliminate that many?

A goblin trotted up to him and saluted, placing a fist to his forehead.

"Sergeant, I try to deliver message to Mage Delphin."

"Try?" Gorlak felt his anger mounting. "What means try? He is in his chamber, or in passages finding invaders."

The goblin looked nervous. "He is dead."

Gorlak started. "Dead? How?"

"Ghai-zhal," said another voice behind him. Gorlak turned, drawing his saber.

A group of Outpost One regulars trotted up to him and saluted. The oldest in the group leaned his spear against the passage wall. He removed his helmet, decorated with a string of human teeth.

"Group of Ghai-zhal in tunnels," Tooth-Helm said, "Have mages. Kill

74

Faedan and still running in outpost. Kill Grand Sergeant Chorg too."

Gorlak gritted his teeth. *How did this happen?*

"They are soldiers?" he asked.

"Do not have uniforms. Another patrol saw them for a short time but lost them in tunnels. They think there are some Urmum too."

A cold chill ran down Gorlak's spine — Elves, like Aalre, and maybe mages. This looked worse and worse.

How did they find out about the village so fast? Or were they just wanderers who stumbled on Outpost One and decided to pillage?

He knew when he was out of his element.

"We go," he announced. He replaced his saber and swung a crossbow off his back. He began loading it, speaking as he did so.

"Corporal, you in charge here. Find Ghai-zhal and Urmum, kill them. When this is done, send runner to Outpost Two. The Lady and I are waiting there."

Tooth-helm Corporal blanched. "Me? In charge? There only one team left, Sergeant. We only ten. We not fight humans and Urmum mages. What about the priests? What if they—"

Gorlak glared at him. "Priests take care of selves. We not in charge of them. They here by Lord Halkith's orders. You find intruders."

Sergeant Gorlak turned to his squad. They followed him towards the exit without enthusiasm. He didn't blame them.

***

"My lord Halkith."

Captain Kalar Cintos, Courier of the Ja'al High Command, bowed in obeisance even though his every muscle rebelled against it.

A tall, brown-haired man turned away from a map on the wall. Black plate armor glowed beneath the man's multi-colored robes. An ebony mace hung from his hip, marked with red runes on the handle.

He nodded at Kalar. "What news do you bring from the High Council?"

Kalar couldn't suppress a smirk. "The High Ones wish to know what progress you make in assisting their ally, the Dark Rider. They hear tales that all is well on the Borderlands and that King Phillip's subjects are at peace. This is not what the Council had in mind when they sent you here."

Blue eyes met Kalar's. The courier defied his gaze for a moment, then looked down.

With a swish of his robes, Halkith stepped over to an oak side table carved into a claw holding a platter. He selected a parchment from the pile on top, his hand resting for a second on a crystal decanter filled with a dark blue liquid. He eased himself into a comfortable, padded chair. A pair of spears hung on the wall behind the chairs next to a battle standard embroidered with two crossed hammers over a mountain peak.

The banner of the Obsidian Company, 3rd Division of Khal-Rinduth, thought Kalar. *Ostentatious. Perfect for a pompous ass like Halkith.*

Kalar kept his eyes on the priest as Halkith inspected his parchment. "If I recall correctly," Halkith said in a mild tone, "I requested supplies for my forces a month ago and only received it just yesterday. In addition, we had twenty defective bows in the last shipment of weapons. The goblins need every advantage they can get. I remind you that many of the rabble here on the frontier are armed."

Kalar kept his expression neutral. He knew the Council was aware of all this. Moreover, Halkith, by all accounts, lost his temper at times, even with emissaries from his superiors.

"The Council indicated that you have ample troops to conduct the proper foraging maneuvers in the area for both supplies and weaponry," he noted.

Halkith frowned, laying the parchment on the glass top of a dragon-carved table in front of him. "Conduct a major foraging campaign? And rouse the garrison at Forester? Maybe in Hillton too? The Council is highly optimistic."

"Perhaps," countered Kalar, "But resources are needed elsewhere and the High Ones are confident in your ability to carry out your mission. Considering the consequences of failure, of course."

Halkith nodded and stood. "Hmm. Of course."

A knock sounded at the door.

Halkith frowned again. "Enter."

A large goblin in chainmail slunk in and bowed from the waist, eyes downcast. The crossed arrows insignia on one sleeve identified him as one of Halkith's chieftains.

"I thought," said Halkith, rising and sweeping across the room like a dark ghost, "I said I was not to be disturbed."

The goblin straightened but kept his eyes averted.

"Great Canon say to tell news of search teams. Say to bring word immediately. We have news."

Halkith raised an eyebrow. "I did say that, didn't I? You are correct in alerting me. Continue."

"We receive message from Strike Team Four of Skullcrusher Tribe. They attack village at Westhaven, kill all. They find no pottery of black and white with blue star. They returned to Base One." The goblin dared to look up.

"I see," mused Halkith. "No pottery?" He turned towards a wall map next to a bed of dark wood layered with embroidered cushions.

"None, mighty Sword of the Ja'al."

Kalar waited for a long minute while Halkith mulled over the goblin's news and examined the map. If Halkith's ideas about Westhaven and its crafty sage-woman were right, the Ja'al *and* the Dark Rider would have the key to conquest in the Northern nations...

If...

Halkith turned around. "Go and tell the other tribes to remain hidden. Only mild raiding on the edges of the wilderness. We don't want to alert that idiot Hanford in Forester or his pet bitch."

The goblin bowed his way out.

Kalar pursed his lip, watching the oval door swing shut. It slammed shut and a thin line of blue light sizzled around the edge.

One of the hazards of being a Ja'al courier. At least the pay is good.

He turned back to Halkith. "Problems?"

"Minor ones," said Halkith a wave of his hand. "If Clarissa has sold the pottery already, then it's in one of the nearby towns by now. I don't want to arouse any suspicions just yet, so our spies will have to do some more investigating."

Kalar considered before offering his next question. "Are you certain Clarissa's pottery holds the key to all this? After all, it's literally been over a thousand years."

Halkith smiled, eyes cold. "Oh, I'm sure all right. When we find the components of the map and recover the Darkwings, we'll be able to take over this entire county in a week."

***

Careful, boy, Dar Cabot warned himself, peeking around the corner.

The door behind the curtain in Faedan's room was, of course, locked. Connor took several minutes to worry it open, revealing another tunnel that sloped downward and stretched ahead for a great distance. Dar and Connor went ahead of the group to investigate.

The flickering flame of Buck's torch shone on the walls behind him, giving just enough light for Dar to see. He looked at the tunnel with interest, smooth to the touch and worn with age. It was very different from the roughly hewn passages and chambers they had seen before. Briefly, he wondered how the goblin complex fit in with this. Had the goblins stumbled upon it and just decided to use it? Where did it lead?

His pulse quickened. This was what he had heard of in the stories: long-lost caverns of a long-lost race, hidden for centuries and concealing treasures and dangers beyond his wildest dreams.

Dar remembered curling up with his siblings in front of a warm fireplace in his parents' house, listening to his father's stories of Sir Tan, Kyla the White, Brendan Hallmoor, and the Black Stag.

Dar's brother showed only passing interest in the stories about people who tramped around in crumbling ruins, searching for dusty relics no one else cared about. To Dar, it was an amazing, fascinating world.

Dar waited and watched for any signs of danger, then followed Connor.

Why had the goblins attacked? Were they searching for the hidden bowl that Connor had found? If so, what in God's name did they want with *pottery*? Gold, jewels, or magic swords he could understand, but pottery?

How did this Faedan fellow fit in? What had he meant by the "new vision"? And who was the "Dark Rider"?

A rounded square of light peeked at him from the next turn. Connor stopped and put up his hand, and Dar mimicked him. He heard footsteps behind him cease.

"Why don't you scamper up there and see what's going on?" Dar whispered to Connor. "Careful of traps, of course."

Connor saluted. "Scampering as ordered, Mister Cabot."

Dar grinned. He was starting to like Connor, and all the rest of them. Despite their awkward beginning in the tavern and the grim discovery at Westhaven, they worked together well. Sure, he hadn't known what to expect, but Connor, Eric and the sisters were easy to deal with and good people. The only one he wasn't sure of was Buck.

A hand landed on his shoulder and he turned his head. Megan stood next to him.

"Connor had better be careful. There's a few warding and trapping spells that could burn him to ashes in a second."

He could smell dirt and perspiration on her, but also a spicy-sweet scent that made his heart beat a little faster. He turned back to the passageway, trying to focus.

"I'm sure he knows. Connor knows quite a bit," he said, shifting his weight. "I also have a feeling Mister Lomin isn't telling us everything."

Megan smiled. "Do you expect him to divulge his life's story? For all he knows, we could be Vipers ourselves, or Ja'al cultists, or worse."

Dar looked at her, then back down the passage. "We are worse. We're free-lances."

She shook her head, eyes dancing, then returned to the main group.

Connor returned a few seconds later. "No traps near the entrance that I can see. It's a room about thirty feet square with an altar about twenty feet straight ahead of the opening with a few statues on both sides. There's some really disgusting artwork on the walls, but I don't see anyone."

Altar? Dar felt a sense of warning tingling in his head. Didn't Sir Tan warn him about altars?

Brandi looked grim when they told her.

"We'll have to tread very cautiously," she warned. "If it's what I think it is, we may just want to bypass the whole thing."

Dar eyed the interior of the chamber when he got to the entrance. Lurid depictions of some kinds of religious rites decorated the walls. Four sculpted replicas of wicked-looking creatures lurked next to a red and purple stone altar. Eight stone hands gripped flickering torches at the walls.

"Ja'al chapel," said Brandi in a choked voice.

Dar felt a chill run up his spine and he shuddered.

The Ja'al, the Manipulator Cult, dedicated their nefarious efforts to a number of vile deities and other, alien beings. They made no secret of their hatred of Christians as well as those who followed the forest god of the elves, Verian, or the halfling deity Irial, or the dwarf-god Kurental.

Dar averted his eyes from the artwork, feeling his stomach give a slow, queasy roll.

Holy...! I knew the Ja'al were into fertility rites and tortures and that kind of stuff, but this is grotesque!

He took a deep breath. *Okay, so this was where Faedan was heading... but why?*

Connor nodded to him, his jawline tensed. Dar stepped inside, his heart pounding and nerves as taut as his bowstring.

They moved along the walls, expecting an attack from behind the altar, next to the statues, even from the torch-holders, but nothing happened.

Dar felt another chill. A motion caught his eye and he jerked his head to the left, but nothing was there. He stifled a sudden urge to run.

Brandi and Megan stood behind him, tight-lipped. Eric turned in a slow circle next to them, bow at the ready, eyes narrowed, face pale, and body tense. Only Buck didn't seem to be affected very much at all, looking a little confused.

He broke the silence. "Looks like the bats have flown the cave."

"Not quite," noted an unfamiliar baritone.

Dar felt cold. The companions whirled.

Three man-sized shapes glowed in the rock wall next to the entrance. As Dar watched in horror, three humans flowed out of the granite: one short, stocky and bearded, the other two tall and clean-shaven. They wore steel breastplates covered by tunics of a riotous mix of clashing colors. Flails and hammers hung at their metal-studded leather belts.

The bearded man smiled, his grey eyes roaming over them. He flicked his cloak over one shoulder.

"Welcome to the chapel of the Ja'al. What are you doing here?"

Wonderful, thought Dar. *My first mission and I'm about to get plastered all over a Ja'al temple. Why didn't I listen to my mother?*

He brought up his bow, keeping the arrow tip pointed at the stocky cleric with the beard and mustache. He waited, not answering the Ja'al's challenge.

"I repeat," their adversary said, over the chuckles of his companions, "Are you deaf or are you going to tell us what you're doing here in my chapel?"

Brandi's voice echoed in the cold chamber.

"We are from the Kingdom of Deran. Are you the leader of the goblin tribe in these caverns?"

The short cleric joined his companions with a hearty guffaw. He stepped forward. The mind-numbing pink, red, and purple patterns on his tunic took on an almost hypnotic effect. He drew his wicked-looking flail and began to whirl it. A circlet with a screaming demon-face glittered in the torchlight against his dark black hair.

"And if I say yes, warrior-girl-child? What then? Arrest me in the name of your king?" His eyes widened in a look of mock fear.

"Yes," came Brandi's instant reply, "You are outnumbered. Lay down your weapons and surrender."

The priest stopped whirling his flail, catching the head in his gloved hand with a slap. He pursed his lip and made a clucking sound, shaking his head.

"I don't think so." He waved a hand behind him.

A rock wall covered the only exit from the chamber.

Dar gaped. *That's impossible.*

He knelt to present a smaller target. One of the lesser clerics laughed.

"Right, little man. Kneel before your betters."

A red irritation started in Dar's head. This was the kind of arrogant punk he hated: someone who thought of everyone else as inferior. He took a breath to calm himself, stifling the acid retort poised on his lips.

Remember what happened the last time you let your mouth move before your brain could get started. Let Brandi have a chance to do it her way.

The other underpriest began twirling his own flail, the metal head winking in the torchlight with a steely flash. "Shall we take them, Canon Derrig?"

The chief Ja'al cleric held up his hand, an indulgent expression on his face. "No, Eltor, not yet. We should extend them the same courtesy as they offered us."

Lord, if you can hear us in this place, give us a sign.

The Ja'al canon smiled almost kindly. "You may surrender now. I remind you, warrior-girl, that your feeble Christian magic will not work, despite all the brainwashing your priests gave you. The Mighty Ones of the Ja'al hold sway here, not your puny church and puny god."

That's it. They're insulting God.

"The magic might not work here. But this still does."

He let fly at Derrig.

The enemy leader jerked as the arrow splintered on his armor in a flare of red light.

Both sides exploded into action.

A hail of arrows darted out at the clerics, catching one of the underpriests in the leg and the other in the upper arm. Dar's second shot broke on the rock wall behind the Ja'al leader.

Three glowing darts howled over his shoulder, detonating on the cult priest's plated mail. He cursed and staggered backward.

The Ja'al named Eltor jerked an arrow out of his upper arm and raised a hand at the party, muttering vicious-sounding words. Suddenly, Dar felt a vise-like grip of some unseen force tighten around him. His limbs felt like lead.

Jesus! Holding spell! He struggled and felt something snap. He was free.

Without pausing to ponder, he drew his sword. Eltor shouted in triumph and charged, his flail spinning. Dar barely managed to block it and staggered back.

Behind Eltor, the other underpriest charged off to attack Dar's friends. Meanwhile, Derrig thrust forward a fist and barked a strange word. A small, silvery globule shot out and wiggled through the air past Dar. He heard a scream from behind him.

Red anger swam before his eyes again. *Not Megan!*

He slashed at his opponent's head, not caring when the man blocked it. He reversed direction and cut downward.

His blade sliced into Eltor's leg armor and the flesh beneath. The cleric screamed and staggered backward. He growled a curse, limping. Blood ran down his greave. Dar tried to follow up but the cleric whipped out his hammer and held it before him on guard.

Damn.

Dar leapt forward and they exchanged a flurry of blows. He received a hearty whack on the left shoulder, but when they disengaged to catch a breath he was satisfied to see Eltor bleeding from a cut on his calf and right shoulder.

Eltor's eyes narrowed. He stepped back a pace and began another chant. Dar remembered the silvery globule and charged forward.

It wasn't a spell but a decoy. Dar twisted to avoid the flail head as it whirred in at his face. A sudden shock jerked his head to the side and he tumbled, trying to turn his fall into a roll instead. He popped up into a kneeling position, lights bursting behind his eyes, and thrust his sword before him in guard position.

The deadly flail head slammed into Dar's blade with a ringing clang. His head aching, Dar lurched to his feet and lashed forward in a kick, catching Eltor in the midsection.

The cleric let out a whoof of air and stumbled backward, landing on his backside and then rolling to a half-prone position.

Dar tried to regain his balance. Around him, the ringing of blades and shouts echoed in the chapel, but he kept his eyes on Eltor. Dar's friends would have to take care of themselves.

Eltor whipped his handsome face up to stare at Dar in fury. He dragged himself to his feet and spread out the fingers of his left hand, beginning a chant.

Dar felt the air around him begin to tighten with energy.

This one's for real.

He lunged forward and thrust. Still chanting, Eltor parried his blade downward, just as Dar had hoped he would. He went with the deflection, whipping his sword around and over, turning it into a powerful downward arc.

His blade split the cleric's head in two down to the chin.

Dar staggered and jerked his weapon free as Eltor folded in a clatter of weapons and armor. A wave of dizziness and nausea overcame him, not all from his head wound. He heard a shout and turned, grabbing for his hand axe.

Canon Derrig staggered against the rock wall. Two arrows sprouted from his armor, a cut made a red line on his face, and blood ran down his side. The last Ja'al underpriest lay in a pool of blood near Dar's friends.

"Misbegotten whores!" the Ja'al leader screamed in impotent fury. Spittle flecked the front of his robes. "Foul, filth-eating scum! I will have vengeance!"

With a shout, he took a single step backwards into the rock wall and passed through as if it was air.

Dar was too tired to be amazed. He dropped to his knees.

Thank you, God.

After a century or two, it seemed, a child-sized pair of boots appeared in front of his eyes, soon followed by a concerned halfling face.

"You okay?"

"Yeah," croaked Dar, "Just great."

"You're a numbskull. Come on. I'll help you over to the others."

I wish my skull was numb, Dar decided. *That way I wouldn't feel these little dwarves hammering on it.*

Connor helped him over to where Brandi knelt in front of Megan, lying motionless on the grey stones.

Brandi looked up at them, her eyes grim. Dar's heart skipped a beat.

"She's paralyzed."

Dar felt the world spin and he sat down.

Paralyzed... What are we going to do now?

Eric asked the question in all their minds. "What was the magic? Is it curable?"

Brandi slapped a hand down on the stone floor. "The damned thing's called Ghoul's Kiss. I learned about it in the seminary. It's a dark magic and I don't have a counterspell."

Megan's eyes were still open, wide and frightened. She smiled at Dar. He slid over to her on the floor, ignoring a wave of pain that clouded his vision for a moment. He reached out and took her hand.

"Well, looks like you found a way to get some rest before we finish this thing, eh?"

Megan's eyes filled with tears. "Yes. Clever of me, don't you think? But as Brandi can tell you guys, you're all still in trouble. My mouth isn't paralyzed."

Dar chuckled with the others. Even Brandi's worried face relaxed.

Dar felt the side of his head and winced as the colored lights washed across his vision again. *Great. A bump the size of a goose egg. Wonder if it's a concussion like Connor's...*

"What happened to the rest of you?" he asked to take their minds off Megan's plight.

Eric looked sour. "I seem to be a magnet for those damned little light balls. That idiot over there hit me with one of them just after I plugged him with an arrow." He indicated the prone figure of the second undercleric. "Good thing Brandi was there. She kept him busy until I could see again."

Brandi, taken aback by the compliment, blushed. Dar winced at another wave of pain in his head.

Brandi noticed and came over to sit next to him. "Looks like you took quite a pop."

Dar waved her off. "I'll be fine," he lied.

She pursed her lip, then slid over next to him.

Dar sighed. Though he was glad for her ministrations, he also knew she needed her strength. He opened his mouth to protest.

An elegant eyebrow arced over violet eyes. Dar closed his mouth again. He had seen a similar look on his mother's face.

Brandi's gentle fingers probed under his hair. Dar closed his eyes and let her do her job. To take his mind off the possible prognosis, he spoke to the others. "It's a wonder the leader didn't just take us apart with spells from back there."

"He couldn't," Brandi said, moving his hair out of the way, "Every time he looked like he was going to cast a spell, Connor or Buck shot him."

Brandi's fingers found a sore spot and Dar winced. He opened one eye to look at Buck.

"Busy boys, weren't you?" he asked. Brandi reached into her hip bag for something and he closed his eyes again.

He heard Buck's voice. "Well...Brandi had the other guy under control, so I stepped back and helped Connor out."

Brandi spread some kind of sweet-sour-smelling material on Dar's bump, then wound a cloth around his head.

Dar opened his eyes. He probed his head. It felt a little bit better and the bump had receded somewhat, but it was still sore. At least the dizziness was subsiding.

"Well, you should have seen the fight I had with my guy."

Eric clapped his hands together, then hugged himself, shivering. "Yes, well, I'd love to reminisce and trade battle stories, but this isn't a really good place to do it. No pun intended."

Dar put his hand on his head. "Please. I'm in enough pain already."

Brandi shook her head, eyes worried. "We can't go anywhere until that doorway is clear."

Connor strode over to the blocked-off exit and waved a hand towards it. "What's this thing?"

"Another spell, called Stonecurtain," said Brandi. "Someday, after I've had enough training, I'll be able to make one myself. I wouldn't touch that thing right now, but don't worry. It isn't permanent. We just have to wait until it wears off."

Connor looked irritated. "You mean we just sit here and play at dice until it goes away? I don't know if you've looked around lately, but this isn't the card tables at the Pit."

Something tickled at the back of Dar's mind and he began to feel annoyed. "Hey, Connor. That's enough. She's knows what she's talking about."

Connor gave him a black look, but returned to wait with them. Dar was surprised at Connor and at himself. *What's bothering him? And why am I so irritable?*

Even Eric looked edgy. He paced back and forth in front of the altar, trying not to look at the wall paintings or the statues. Occasionally, he shot a glance at the stone curtain that blocked the way out.

Buck sat on the steps, sharpening his sword. Finally, after about twenty strokes of the whetstone, he looked up at Eric, eyes glittering.

"Quit pacing. It won't go away any faster."

"Right."

Eric turned and stood facing the doorway, then began pacing again.

"He said," began Connor, "stop..."

"Connor!" said Brandi, her eyes flashing. "Leave him alone."

He turned on her. "Who asked for your opinion?"

Brandi opened her mouth to say something, then thought better of it and turned away.

There was that tickle. Dar's head hurt and the tickle really bothered him. He concentrated on the quarrel, his irritation increasing.

"Shut up, all of you," he barked. "Arguing about it isn't going to help anything."

Buck stood, sword in hand. His eyes were dead grey, like stone. He nodded. "Right. Arguing isn't going to help. Let's settle this like men."

Dar felt the tickling again, but his rising anger submerged it. *What the hell was wrong with Buck? Why is he so touchy?*

"You're going to point a sword at me?" he asked.

Buck took a step forward, but a shout from Brandi held him.

"Stop! Stop it! All of you!" She stood over her sister, fists clenched. "What's the matter with you? Have you taken leave of your senses?"

Busybody, thought Dar, a red haze swimming in front of his eyes now. *She needs to be taught a lesson.*

Brandi's eyes suddenly fixed on something behind Dar and she froze. "Oh my God! Look at the altar!"

The party turned as one.

It glowed with a faint, reddish-purple light. The red veins in the rock pulsed like a vile heartbeat.

They stood in shock for a moment.

"Buck!" he called, picking up Megan by the shoulders, "Help me with her!"

Their quarrel forgotten, Buck helped him carry her back towards the curtain. The others scrambled back with them and they stood as close to the exit as they dared, weapons pointed at the altar.

Dar looked around the chamber. There had to be another way out.

"That explains it," said Brandi. She looked grim.

"What does?" asked Connor, looking all around him.

"The altar. That explains our behavior. The altar apparently has some evil spirit of vigilance in it. It's been working on our minds, trying to get us to fight among ourselves and kill each other off."

"Can they do that?" asked Connor in amazement.

"And worse."

Dar shuddered.

"What can we do against it?" asked Megan.

Dar looked down at her.

She's been helpless during the entire exchange. Poor thing. We almost chopped each other up and she had to lay there and watch it. If that was me in her place, I'd be raving mad by now.

Connor looked at the walls, then at Eric. "Can't you use some kind of magic to make it stop?"

Eric looked at Brandi. "I don't think I'm strong enough to do that. I've only heard of wizards and high clerics being able to destroy enchanted altars."

Brandi shook her head. "We don't need magic, we need prayer. Buck, I know that druidical followers have some kind of mind-centering chant. Why don't you start reciting it?"

"We," she nodded at Eric, Dar and Megan, "are going to pray."

This is weird, Dar thought, hearing the murmured Druid chant mingling with the Our Father. *I'll bet there aren't too many people who've heard these two prayers together.*

Sure enough, if he concentrated on the words, the feathery sensation and the attendant short temper subsided and disappeared. He looked up at Brandi and smiled.

"Amen..."

There was a long silence.

"Good call," he said. The altar still flickered, but it didn't seem quite so malevolent. "Now all we need is for the Stonecurtain to wear off. Do you suppose praying did anything?"

They looked at the wall. The stone curtain remained.

Brandi sighed. "The prayer has repelled the presence in the altar. As long as we keep our minds off it and how anxious we are to get out here, we should be okay. I know for certain the Stonecurtain will wear off."

We hope.

They found that the mental tickle returned if they let their minds wander, so Brandi, to everyone's surprise, took a tiny ivory flute out of her backpack and began to play.

Dar began to hum along. He refrained from singing. Elaine had accused him of trying to make her deaf after an attempt at carrying a tune in church.

Brandi's good. And Megan has a beautiful voice.

Brandi had just finished playing "Moon over the Mountain" when Eric called out.

"Hey! The curtain! Thank God!"

The entrance stood open and empty. Brandi sighed with relief and put away her flute.

"Well," said Eric, "Now what? We're just back in the frying pan."

Brandi shook her head. "There's only about ten soldiers left, from Connor's count and the records we found in Faedan Delphin's treasure trove."

She strode over to the dead Ja'al clerics and came back bearing their insignias.

"With these, we should be able to convince the goblins that they've lost."

"And if they don't believe us?" asked Connor.

Brandi readied her bow and put an arrow to it. "We'll convince them."

"Without their leaders they have no central commanders," Eric agreed. "Besides, if we go slow and careful, we might not see any of them."

"Well, we're dead if we stay here, so let's go," Dar said. "Buck and I will carry Megan and play rear guard. You guys clear the way. If you get in trouble, one of us will guard her while the other one helps you smack around some monkey-soldiers."

He knelt down next to Megan. "Ready for a ride?"

She rolled her eyes. "As if I could protest. At least pile the seat cushions on my left side. And I like my drinks cold."

He chuckled and helped Buck pick her up. Holding her just under the shoulders, he rested her head against his chest. Connor waved a hand for them to follow and the group moved forward.

"Just relax," Dar told Megan. "Only a few goblins left and I wouldn't bet on their chances against your sister. We'll take it nice and slow out of here and be back to Forester soon. Then we'll have you put back together in no time."

Chapter Seven- Agents of Their Lordships

Buck Bydecy laid back on the rough planks and sighed, resting his head on his backpack. He smiled, listening to the gentle lapping of water, bird songs and the occasional buzz of an insect.

Why didn't we think of this before?

He rolled on his side and looked up at Dar, guiding their makeshift raft with a long pole.

"You know," he offered, "even though you're a brush tramp instead of a real warrior, I have to hand it to you. You come up with some of the best ideas I've heard yet."

Dar grinned down at him. He adjusted his head bandage with one hand and turned his eyes down river. "Thank you, I think. We already had the wood from the tree platform and some rope. All we needed was some poles."

Buck lounged back. Now that he had finished his turn at steering, it was time to relax. He appropriated Dar's wineskin of goblin beer.

Back in Faedan's room after escaping the Ja'al chapel, Dar pointed out that the quickest way back to Forester was by water. The Whitehorse River flowed past only a couple of miles away from the goblin stronghold. Going overland would be slow and would leave them vulnerable to attack, especially considering their exhaustion. Even with Megan on a travois, Eric and Dar estimated that it would take almost three days march. With a raft, they would get to town in a matter of hours.

That decision made, they took the time to loot Delphin's treasure. They packed away silver and copper coins, loose gemstones and silver jewelry. They headed for the entrance to the complex, hiding in dirty hallways and empty chambers, listening for sounds of goblin patrols. They had to hide twice from roving guards, but their luck held and they left without being noticed.

They hoisted Megan up out of the entrance tunnel with ropes and great care. The light of early morning surprised them as it broke out over the trees. Buck found it hard to believe an entire day had passed, but Connor assured him it had.

They tramped back to the tree house, dismantled the platform and dragged it to the river. Some planks from the tree house also made a convenient litter to transport Megan. When they reached the full, rushing waters of the Whitehorse River, Dar, Eric and Connor made some modifications to their raft.

Buck took a drink. Connor demonstrated a hidden skill on this little sailing expedition: navigation. He proved quite adept at determining depth, course and current. Using yet another map, he estimated their arrival in Forester to take place late that afternoon.

As if summoned by his thoughts, a small halfling figure thumped down next to him and Buck gave him space.

Connor smiled at him, holding out his hand. "You going to keep that beer for yourself the entire trip?"

Buck looked at Dar's wineskin, at Connor, then shrugged and handed it over.

Connor tasted it and swirled it around in his mouth, then swallowed and made a face. "Not what I'd order."

"It's all the bar has right now. Once we get back to the Pit, we can get the good stuff."

The halfling nodded. "I think a bath and a five-course meal would do the trick right about now. Comforts of home. Speaking of home, how is life in Astarel?"

Buck nodded. "In the winter it's colder. Tyler is not as bad, since it's near the ocean, but the storms get nasty. Lots of wind."

Connor leaned back on his hands. "You grew up there?"

Buck sat up. "Went to an academy and everything. My dad owns a small general store in the south of the city."

"Your friends there too?"

Buck kept his expression neutral. "Most of them."

Connor changed the subject. "You and Eric were attacked by wolves on the road from Wit's End. Kind of funny, isn't it? Wolves usually don't attack people by campfires."

Buck opened his mouth, then closed it. They didn't. Come to think of it, that particular bunch seemed a little more aggressive than usual. They hadn't been deterred by Eric's torch or the campfire. He heard of several other incidents while in Wit's End. Strange times, the townspeople said, and strange goings-on in the Wilderness. Even the fur trappers and miners started to look to other parts of the country for their livelihoods.

He closed his eyes and lay down again. He enjoyed the silence, feeling the gentle rocking of the raft. The errant wind brought him scents of the wet forest and the sun's warmth made him feel relaxed and drowsy.

Connor's questions turned his mind to home.

I thought I could at least trust one of my friends, someone I grew up with. Bad idea. Best to trust to your own skills, Mother Nature and the luck of the dice.

Trust. It all came down to that anyway. The Christians and Irial and Verian and Kurental believed in trust. They were fools to depend on their gods of love and kindness and valor to take care of them.

He half-dreamed of his home in Tyler. He remembered sitting at the side of a sloping, hilly road, looking out over the GreatSea. In his mind's eye, he saw his father's face, and Joko Roundtree, his academy teacher—and Derek.

Buck rolled over on his side and opened his eyes. The willows and oaks of the shoreline slipped past and his train of thought turned morose.

Now I can't see Dad, or Jack, or Summer again, not after what went on. And all for a stupid bunch of gems that couldn't even buy a good warhorse.

He sighed. Well, there was a way out, but it was a slim chance at best. An heirloom from family legends could clear his name. It dated to the old days of the Esten Empire and his grand-dad's stories convinced him it was what he needed. He knew what it looked like and that it was somewhere along the border of Deran and the Wilderness. Unfortunately, it would be like looking for an onyx in a pile of coal.

However, he now belonged to a group. With the others to provide their own strength and talents, he could bide his time and look for clues. Maybe they would help him in his quest—if he told them.

He mulled this over. There was a chance he could bring them into his confidence. They had stood by him in battle and helped him when he needed it, so far. Maybe he should tell them about Derek's betrayal and the Bydecy family legend.

Maybe they would all throw in with him and start searching the wilderness for a magical crystal no bigger than a gold piece.

Sure. And I'll find a winged horse to ride someday.

A motion near him made him look up. Brandi gave him a quick, wan smile then returned to guiding the raft with the pole.

She looks worried. If it was my sister, I might be a little worried too.

Eric joined Dar next to the still form of Megan and Buck felt a pang of pity.

Poor kid. So young, and paralyzed. What a shame. But, those are the breaks. And as Dad always said, "them's that make their own breaks don't get broken".

They had all discussed the possibility of treating Megan. They needed to find someone with experience and healing skills of sufficient power. Dar insisted that the priest of his local church had the required level of skill and might be able to help. However, Buck and the others all knew there were no guarantees. If the priest couldn't help, it would leave the group minus a mage and probably Brandi as well.

Buck frowned, his pity diminishing as he contemplated how much it was going to cost them. A free-lance healer from a caravan would charge quite a bit if Dar's pastor couldn't help. And even members of a faith were expected to give substantial offerings.

Buck stood, trying not to rock their makeshift barge. A trio of dragonflies whipped past in the breeze. With a wet winter, it was going to be a great spring, if the bugs were any evidence. He swatted at a blood-biter hovering around his head.

Nature as it should be, he reflected. No one trying to break it down or alter it or 'civilize' it in any way. Pure and simple, like a Druid grove.

Now *that* would come in handy if he needed his own healing done. If there was a grove nearby, the druids there would help him, for a fee, of course.

He sneaked a look at Brandi, which was becoming one of his favorite pastimes. Her gaze flitted along the shoreline, taut lines around her jaw and eyes.

He let his eyes roam over her figure once, then looked away.

They came around a bend and she called out.

"There! The landing!"

"I see it," Dar said. Connor stood and took the pole from her. Together, Dar and Connor guided the raft towards a wood platform jutting out into the river. Beyond the landing, a pair of squat buildings stood out in marked contrast to the thick foliage. A faintly visible path stretched into the forest behind them.

"How far to town from here?" Brandi asked.

"Only a couple of miles. It won't be long."

Dar, Eric, and Connor beached the raft on the grassy, weedy shore. They lifted Megan off, then tied the watercraft to a nearby tree and set off towards the buildings. Buck pulled Megan's travois off the raft and they placed her on it.

As the companions approached the buildings, two men in homespun, dun-colored clothing emerged. One of them called a greeting to Dar.

Dar waved back at him, then spoke over his shoulder. "That's Ervin, an old classmate of mine. This is a staging area for harvesting the trees sent downriver by lumbering parties in the Wilderness."

The companions trudged up to the cabin and set Megan down. Ervin whistled when told of the nature of Megan's injury, then shuddered and crossed himself when Connor mentioned the Ja'al.

"I want nothing to do with them foul ones, you can bet on that," he said as they left, "Best of luck to you, Dar. Hope Father Ander can do something for her. Road is clear beyond to the town. We'll be heading back ourselves soon."

"We can make the outer gate before nightfall," Dar noted as they marched along.

"Great," said Brandi, her eyes locked on the road ahead, as if by concentrating she could make them all move faster. "Do you know Father Ander well?"

"Yes," he said, adjusting his grip on the travois handles. "He's been around forever. Baptized me and my brother and Lord Nolan's kids."

Eric winked. "Well, I hope the sacrament took effect with the baron's kids at least."

Buck considered adding a comment of his own but, seeing the anxiety on Brandi's face, decided against it.

It was not long until the walls of Forester loomed up between the pines and oaks. They shuffled down the main road, the strain of the last day pressing down on them. They passed between several houses. A thin woman hanging out her washing paused in her work. She watched them as they passed by, one hand on her hip, the other brushing a lock of hair out of her face.

Probably doesn't get to see many sell-swords brought home on their shields.

Buck's mood brightened a little as they approached the gate and the tree-towers. A lord who used trees in his town walls couldn't be all bad, Christian or not.

They passed through the gates. The gate sergeant stopped them but Dar held a quick discussion and the soldier waved them through with a glance at Megan.

Dar led them down the main street and left at the second intersection. Passers-by stared and a few even called out to him, but he only waved and answered that he would explain later.

On the right side of the dusty road, he stopped at the church, a one-story building with a short, cross-topped tower in the front. "Saint Anne's" proclaimed a sign next to the front door. They stepped up a walkway of spotless paving stones, lifted Megan off the travois and laid her next to the door. Stained glass windows mirrored back their grubby faces in the shadows of the awning. Someone had applied a fresh coat of paint to the walls and colorful flowerbeds blossomed under the windows.

"Wait here," Dar said, taking a deep breath, "I'll see if Father Ander is around."

He disappeared around one side of the church.

Buck slouched against the wall, watching the people nearby. An old man stopped his slow amble down the street to lean on the frame of a well. He began stoking his pipe. Three lumberjacks passed by and eyed them but continued on without comment. A woman with flour on her apron came out of a shop and wiped her hands on a towel, lips pursed.

Buck felt a little uneasy at the scrutiny. He always thought he would march into town as a hero, not slink in as part of a beaten-up, worn-out bunch of vagabonds.

Footsteps crunched behind them and he turned to see Dar stride up with a grey-haired human in tow. A dark grey cassock fluttered around his slim frame as he approached. Animated, bright blue eyes darted this way and that. His face, long and morose-looking, creased with a gentle smile.

"This is Father Ander," Dar began, but the priest held up a hand and nodded at the group.

"Time for introductions later," he said in a deep and velvety voice. Buck imagined he had the attention of everyone when he spoke at services.

The priest knelt down next to Megan. "Hello, young lady. Had a bit of a run-in with the Ja'al, I see."

Megan bit her lip, a tear starting in her eye. "Yes, Father. I can't feel anything but my head. Can you help?"

The cleric smoothed her hair. "You have nothing to worry about."

A huge wave of tension ebbed out of the group, especially Brandi, who smiled and raised her eyes heavenward, lips moving in a silent "thank you".

Buck cut in. "I don't know how much this is going to cost, Priest Ander, but we don't have much money."

Brandi shot him a furious look, but Ander chuckled. "I'm sure we can arrange something," he said with a wave of his hand.

Buck saw Brandi's face and Dar's warning glance and refrained from asking what the arrangements were going to be.

Damned if I'm going into poverty because Megan can't dodge fast enough, he thought. *It's going to take time and money to find the Bydecy heirloom.*

Ander looked at Dar. "What happened?"

Dar started to explain about Westhaven, but when he got to the part about the ruined village, the priest interrupted with a shocked look.

"What? Westhaven?"

Dar filled him in on the details and Ander stared at the ground, disbelieving. The priest looked up at them, eyes burning. "His Lordship will want to see you. After I am finished with your friend, you must go to the manor. For now, bring her inside."

***

Nolan Hanford sighed, looking out the great window of his hall at the afternoon sky, scattered with puffy white clouds. There was supposed to be rain in the next few days.

Rain I can handle. Rumors of trouble in Westhaven, that's another matter, even if it's only bandits hijacking a shipment of pottery or a run of red fever. It takes effort to get someone out there, especially at the start of the trading season.

He turned around, facing down the hall. Fourteen banners hung high on the walls, each representing a tribe or gang he or his sires had defeated to wrest control of this freehold near the Wilderness. Nolan leaned on his throne. He laid his hand on the blue-and-red insignia on the cushioned back of his wife's chair, feeling the worn spot where her head rested.

Against the left and right walls stood glass cases holding drinking vessels, a couple of decanters and an assortment of what Nolan liked to call his wife's "collections"— knickknacks, really, ranging from unusually shaped stones to a wand that could send out a paralyzing beam of energy. It was all wizardly business anyway, and Nolan Hanford left that department up to Ellen.

The arched double doors at the other end of the hall swung open, breaking his reverie. Colin Parker marched in, longsword swinging at his side. He bowed.

"The freelancers are here, milord. Shall I send them in?"

Nolan brushed a hand through his brown locks, only just now starting to show signs of grey. "Yes, Colin. Is Lady Ellen finished with Timmy and Alice's lessons?"

Colin straightened. "I am not sure, milord. Did you want her to meet them as well?"

"Only if she has the time." It was blessing to get the children to sit still long enough.

Colin bowed again and left.

Nolan waited, hoping that the freelances would at least be direct about whatever was going on in Westhaven.

Colin swung the doors open again, admitting six persons. "His Lordship, Nolan Richard Hanford, Baron of Forester and Knight of Saint Michael."

Colin slipped out as the new arrivals bowed.

The baron took a few moments to inspect the group. *Two humans, three with Elder blood and one halfling. And unless I miss my guess, the shorter, wiry one is Stephen Cabot's boy.*

Nolan didn't recognize the other human—sandy-haired and rangy, wearing warrior's gear. Eyes, calm almost to the point of boredom, swept the hall, lingered on a troll standard near the window.

Nolan took in the two half-elven women so alike in appearance they had to be related. The older wore the garb of a warrior while the younger stared in fascination at the chandelier above. Nolan hid a smile. Most wizards and mages appreciated his chandelier, a silver structure with four crystal doves pointing in each of the cardinal directions, the birds' heads lit from within by arcane light.

Nolan would wonder later why he used Soulsight on the third half-elf, a blond fellow. But his scan showed nothing. There was something about the way that he stood after entering. The man was tall for his kind, almost as tall as Cabot.

Nolan turned his eyes to the halfling and realized that he had been sizing up Nolan in the span of those few short seconds when he himself was reviewing the group.

A trained spy, or I'll eat an ogre's helmet.

Nolan gestured at the room. "Welcome to the Manor House of Forester."

The halfling and the tall human looked a little surprised.

One of the men stepped forward a pace and bowed. "Allow me to introduce us, milord. I am Dar Cabot, and—"

"You're Stephen Cabot's son," Nolan interjected with a smile.

Dar smiled back. "I wasn't sure you would recognize me, Your Lordship."

Nolan chuckled. "How could I forget you? You fished my son Timmy out of the Whitehorse River when he was about three years old. How are your parents?"

"They are doing well, milord," answered Dar. "Father is the chief clerk for the Count of Hillton."

"For Marcel DeGrance? My sympathies to your father. I'm sure he has found the finances in a lovely state of disarray."

This brought smiles from the rest of the group.

"Dar, introduce me to your friends." Nolan turned and sat.

Before Dar could say anything, the sandy-haired human stepped forward and proclaimed, "And I? I am Buck, Buck Bydecy of Astarel."

Nolan coughed into his hand. *He sounds like he's waiting for the roar of the crowd.*

Instead, he nodded. "Welcome to Forester, Mister Bydecy."

Dar next introduced the women as Brandawyn and Megan Alenar. He didn't mention a hometown.

"And," continued Dar, "these are Connor Lomin of Oakmoor and Eric Indidarc, also of Oakmoor."

"Did I hear the name of Indidarc?" chimed a feminine voice from the hallway entrance.

Nolan stood as his wife closed the double doors behind her. "Freelancers, I present my lady wife, Ellen Monica Hanford, Baroness of Forester and Wizard of Saint Terenil's Order."

Dar elbowed Buck and bowed. The others followed suit. Ellen's dark ebony skin, oval face, bright eyes and slim figure caused just about everyone to stop and stare.

Ellen gave them all her friendliest smile, black eyes passing over them. She ascended the dais and slipped into the seat next to her husband.

She kissed him and brushed at her dark, short curls. "The children are playing in the garden now. We've got a few minutes of peace. Next time, milord, it is your turn for the lesson."

He nodded. "Done, milady. I was just getting acquainted with our visitors. They said they had news from Westhaven, although I'm not sure of the nature of the news just yet." He repeated the introductions for his wife.

Ellen smiled at them. "Welcome. It is good to see you again, Mister Cabot. Any news from Westhaven is gratefully accepted since we haven't heard from them in three weeks, which is about a week too late. But first, I'd like to speak to Mister Indidarc."

Eric bowed, his face calm.

Ellen leaned forward a little. "Are you in any way related to Melinor Indidarc?"

Eric looked relieved. "Yes, milady. Adopted son."

"Why so nervous?" asked Ellen.

Eric shrugged. "People usually don't believe me. Then I have to endure an interrogation as I explain how Dad found me an orphan and raised me. And yes, I know Saren DeMey quite well. We were raised as brother and sister."

"Ah." Ellen sat back.

Nolan pursed his lip, watching her expression. She said nothing further. He made a mental note to talk to her later.

She nodded to Nolan. "Please continue, milord."

"Certainly, milady. Now, what did you find out about Westhaven? Clarissa is reclusive sometimes, I'll admit, but usually someone from the hamlet comes into town for something. Not a peep in over twenty days."

Dar Cabot cleared his throat and looked at the others. They stared at the floor. Nolan felt a sudden dread.

"Milord, Westhaven has been destroyed."

Nolan's heart skipped a beat. He wasn't sure he had heard right. "Destroyed?"

Buck spoke up. "Goblin attack group, over forty of them. We tracked them back to their lair."

Nolan met Ellen's eyes.

My God...

He remembered the villagers and set his jaw. There was a long pause.

"Any survivors?" He was surprised at the calmness in his voice, even though he couldn't hide the coldness.

Dar shook his head, eyes distant. "None, milord. All dead, even the children. Homes burned to the ground. I... I suspected something the day before yesterday when I was out in the woods and saw smoke... I reported it."

He gave a deep sigh. "Two goblins attacked me and I tracked them... there was evidence of others... I should have..."

Ellen cut him off, her eyes and voice hollow. "Should have gone to get yourself killed? Nonsense. Then how would anyone know? You did right in coming back to tell the guards. Besides, if you saw smoke, it was already over by the time you noticed. It was only our slowness that prevented you from going out to Westhaven with a full patrol in the first place."

Nolan remembered the report. Colin was even now assembling a squad to go out and check the area just to be sure. He would have to recall them now.

Competing emotions swarmed through him. Sullen, bitter pain hit him in the midsection. Brutal anger rose to the surface. He took a deep breath and let it out again.

Nolan closed his eyes for a moment, remembering Clarissa's sly wink and the solid, firm handshake of Dyrin, her right-hand man, also a potter. He crossed himself and said a quick prayer for the dead.

He opened his eyes again. "Were the bodies properly buried?"

Brandawyn nodded. "I am a Scholastic Novice of Saint Raphael's Order, milord. I cannot hold burial services but I did recite the Psalm over their graves. They did not meet God without someone to pray for them."

Nolan realized his whole body was tensed and he relaxed. "I thank you for that, Miss Alenar."

Ellen wiped tears from her eyes. "Do you have any idea about the motive?" she asked.

She knew all the children by name.

Connor scratched his head. "They were looking for something. All the homes were ransacked and there had been a lot of digging. We searched around when we got there and found a bowl hidden in a buried strongbox. My guess is that the goblins didn't find it because they were a little too eager to destroy the house."

"A bowl?" Nolan blinked and looked at his wife.

Megan pulled a small sack out of her shoulder bag. "It was in the home of the mayor. We weren't sure why this Clarissa person hid it," Megan offered, "but Dar seemed to recognize it and we thought it might be important."

She stepped forward and handed the sack to Nolan. He opened it, pulled out a clay bowl wrapped in cloth. He unwound the wrapping.

A zigzag design in black meandered over the tan-colored clay surface. The bowl was rimmed at the base and mouth in deep forest green. A small blue star hovered next to the biggest zigzag. He turned it over.

Looks like...yes. One of Clarissa's.

He brushed a finger over the sage's red symbol as Ellen looked over his shoulder. Ellen took the bowl from him.

"Go on," he directed the group.

Connor shrugged. "There's not that much else to tell. We—I mean, Eric and Dar—tracked them back to their lair about three miles away in rough country. We went in and tried to apprehend the goblins. They didn't want to be apprehended, so now there aren't many of them left."

"You had evidence it was that particular tribe?"

Buck nodded. "They had pinned two of the villagers up against the wall next to their entranceway, with spears. We also found arrows in Westhaven that matched the ones used by the soldiers in the lair. It was them all right."

Nolan steadied his resurgent anger. *Pin my people up against the wall like bugs on an exhibit, will you?*

"And the location of the goblin base?" he asked in an even voice.

Brandawyn answered. "We have a map if your Lordship would care to look. There was a chieftain in charge, but he was being directed by a mage, and both of *them* were commanded by a Ja'al cleric. I would say we managed to kill about forty or fifty of the warriors, plus the mage, goblin chieftain, and two Ja'al acolytes. The head priest escaped."

The Ja'al... Great, he thought. *Not only do I have to worry about marauders, but I have to watch my back from now on, trying to figure out where those cutthroats are going to strike next.*

One thing was sure. This wasn't just wanton banditry, not with the Ja'al at work. How he was going to break this news to the townsfolk of Forester, he had no idea.

Later will I grieve for you. Justice first.

Ellen inspected the bowl.

"Milady?"

She looked up, brow furrowed. "Milord, this looks, well, familiar. I know I've seen one of these patterns before, with this same set of colors."

"Any idea where?"

She shook her head and stood up. "Somewhere here in the manor house. I'll get the servants together and see if we can come up with something."

He nodded. "As you wish. Mister Cabot and his friends will join me in examining the map in the meantime."

With a distracted wave of her hand, she floated out of the room, not even noticing the bows of the freelancers as she left. Nolan shook his head.

Despite the grim situation, he was amazed at his wife's ability to mentally "leave" and still not trip over the furniture.

He went to a side table and pulled out a thick scroll. He unrolled it on the table as the freelancers crowded around. A detailed topographical map of the area around Forester showed altitudes, gradients, typical foliage, and known underground areas.

"Well?" he asked, eyeing the young people.

Dar and Eric gave him a pretty good idea of the location of the goblin hideout.

They will make good rangers someday, if they survive.

Brandawyn described the Ja'al chapel. Nolan watched their reactions, noting the way that everyone except Bydecy squirmed a little. He sympathized. He had been in a few Ja'al temples.

Dar produced a few rolls of parchment he said were outpost records. Nolan unrolled the first and raised an eyebrow. It turned out to be a military accounting of the goblin outpost. He glanced at the numbers on Connor Lomin's tally sheet.

Well, not bad at all. I doubt if more than eight goblins survived...

Dar and Eric finished their briefing.

Nolan pointed to two locations on the larger map, each about five miles from the first outpost. "When I was policing the region about three years ago, these were abandoned dwarven mines. There were goblins in one and kobolds in the other. The one you just returned from should have been clear. These others should be also, but I'm beginning to wonder."

He stood in silence for a while, finger tapping the parchment.

"Well," he declared, "we have a definite lead on this Ja'al situation. You say there was a chief cleric in charge?"

Megan Alenar nodded, looking wistful. "Yes, milord. He was. And he was quite, um, capable."

The doors to the hall opened and Ellen swept in, carrying a vase in one hand and the mysterious bowl in the other.

"Look, milord," she said, beaming. "One of the maids found this in a guest room. I knew I had seen this before." She offered the pottery to him.

Nolan took the vase and bowl and compared them. In contrast to the pot's asymmetrical jagged line running around its middle and the blue star, the vase had a wavy line in medium blue running down its length, surmounted by a black star at the top end. Nolan saw a tiny figure of a black, winged horse next to the star at the top. At the bottom of the wavy line, an arrowhead pointed down. There were two identical designs, on opposite sides of the vase.

The Baron nodded. He remembered this one. Clarissa had given it to him and his wife only last year, for their wedding anniversary. He also remembered the expression on the old sage's face when she presented it to him.

"Keep it well, milord," the wispy-haired old woman had said with a strange glint in her eye.

Nolan had looked at her. "Of course, Clarissa. We always keep our gifts well, especially yours. Why do you say that?"

Clarissa's eyes became distant. "When they come, milord, you will know what to do. Until then, I cannot say more, to protect what must be. I will inform you when the time is right."

Unable to bring up the subject with her again, he forgot about it over time, dismissing it as yet another one of her cryptic pronouncements.

He brought his thoughts back to the matter at hand and related the story of Clarissa and the vase.

Ellen raised an eyebrow at him. "I never heard this one."

"It didn't seem significant at the time. I quite literally forgot about it."

"Could it mean something, milord?" ventured Eric.

Ellen answered for Nolan. "It might be or it might not. Clarissa was retired, but a scholar of some renown. She knew obscure facts about the Esten Empire even though it fell over a thousand years ago. She kept talking about some wave of dark or mist of shadows but we could never understand what she was saying. Clarissa was a sweet old lady but, at times, she could get very mystical. And no one knew where she came from or where she got her knowledge. I sometimes got the impression she was trying to warn us."

Ellen made a helpless gesture.

Nolan shook his head. "Well, wily old sages or no, we have to get to the bottom of this Ja'al problem. We will commission you as our officers."

He rang a small bell at the side of his chair and waited until Colin Parker entered. He whispered his intentions and Colin nodded, taking up a scrollboard and quill from a side table. Nolan walked up to the dais and turned to face the freelancers, Ellen joining him at his side. He reached around to the back of the throne and drew his longsword from a scabbard behind the backrest.

"Dar Cabot and company," he announced, raising the sword over them, "Step forward."

They looked a little confused but complied anyway.

"In the name of the Barony of Forester and its people," Ellen intoned, "County of Hillton, Kingdom of Deran, we hereby commission the assembled blank shield free-lances to find the perpetrators of the massacre at Westhaven and to execute justice upon them. Of military rank we designate each of them to be corporals brevet, to be obeyed by lesser ranks in every command for the duration of this contract. This we declare on this sixteenth day of Aprilis in the one thousand and eighty fourth year following the fall of the Esten Empire."

Nolan continued. "The goals of your mission are to find the leader of the Ja'al forces and bring him or her to Forester to be tried for the crime against the people of Westhaven. For completion of this duty, you will be paid five hundred gold pieces. Any treasures beyond this brought into Forester shall be yours to keep, subject to one-half the standard city tax. Lieutenant Sir Colin Parker is our witness and we will all sign our names as testimony."

He looked at Dar and his companions. "Is this agreed by all parties?"

A jumbled chorus of agreement answered him.

"Now," he asked, lowering the sword, "is there anything else you need before you set out again?"

Dar looked at Brandi, who nodded. "There is one thing, milord. We got the tar kicked out of us down there and if it weren't for the grace of God, some of us would be dead. We need another healer. We need to post notices here and in the outlying towns looking for someone to help."

The baron nodded. "I will send couriers out to Athor, Wit's End, Hillton, and Sun Plains immediately with an advertisement for a healer cleric, preferably a recent graduate with some experience. The notices should be posted before nightfall. It may be some time to get a response, but then again, this is springtime and everything starts moving faster in the spring, free-lances especially. If someone arrives while you are gone, we will ask them to remain here until you return."

Dar reached for his belt purse but Nolan waved him off. "You are in my employ now, Corporal Cabot. This cost will be paid by the Barony. Now, I'd like you out in the forest the day after tomorrow at the latest."

Ellen smiled. "Godspeed to you. Our prayers are with you."

And may you find the bastards who killed my people, finished Nolan in his mind.

Chapter Eight- Secrets

...Four, five, six... she counted, peeking around the corner of the alley next to the Forester General Store. A group of people—two humans, three Elvenbloods and a halfling—passed down the main street and headed towards one of the intersections.

She waited in the cool dark in the shade of the store.

Should be easy. Amateur free-lances. The easiest three hundred crowns we've earned yet.

She smiled to herself and fingered a long knife at her belt. Satisfy the customer - do the job and do it quickly.

Tonight, she decided.

She slid back into the shadows.

***

"Come on in everyone," announced Dar with a grand sweeping gesture. "Find a spot on the floor somewhere and make yourselves at home."

Brandi Alenar followed him in and looked around the interior of the house. Directly across from the front door, a counter sat under a small glass window. The window, framed by grey drapes, looked out into a tiny garden and the back door of another house beyond it. Cupboards bracketed the counter. A large washing bowl was on a table in the center of the entrance room. Four sturdy wooden chairs stood next to the table, complemented by an additional pair to the right beside a small round table. A red and blue rug lay under the round table and three oil lamps hung on hooks set in the walls.

Doors on the right and left hinted at rooms beyond. Next to the right-side door, near the rightmost cupboard, a brick fireplace hunkered down like a dark, rocky dwarf. The floor was of smooth, burnished wood. Next to the entry door, a large glass window with white curtains looked out on the street outside the house.

"You actually own this?" Brandi asked, looking at a padded divan next to the entry.

Dar grinned. He knew the windows and curtains would elicit a comment. Glass windows, while not rare, were uncommon enough to be noticed.

"My parents owned it when we all lived here, before they moved to Hillton. It was a little crowded with three boys and two parents, but we did all right. My dad said I could keep the place if I wanted to."

Megan entered, looking all around the room. "Neat and tidy for a bachelor's home," she noted, placing her backpack in a corner and brushing a lock of hair out of her eyes.

"Thank you, thank you," said Dar, bowing.

Buck and Eric came in next.

"Not very big, is it?" asked the rangy warrior.

"Just right, actually," piped up Connor, scooting around him.

"There are only three rooms but one of them is for storage," Dar explained as the others set their packs and weapons down on the floor. "My brother and I had this common area here and my parents had the room through the door to the right."

He strode over to the door he had just mentioned and opened it. "Megan and Brandi can have the bedroom."

Brandi looked at him askance, eyes twinkling. "Worried about improprieties?"

He couldn't resist. "Well, you know, with my reputation with the ladies and all that, two women in my home..."

She gave him a disapproving look, trying not to smile.

Dar chuckled. "Well, actually, even though the townspeople know me, we've given the rumor-mongers plenty of ammunition by bringing you here already. No need to give them anything else. Freelancers do have a sort of reputation, you know."

Megan laughed and pushed Brandi towards the bedroom. "Move, sister dear. I want to get cleaned up."

Dar clapped his hands together and walked into the kitchen area. "You can all relax while I throw together a little dinner."

Now where did I leave that ale?

Connor winked at Buck. "Do we need to get Father Ander as a precaution?"

Dar pointed at him. "You, sir, don't have to eat at all."

That kind of threat often struck fear of starvation into the hearts of halflings, because, to a halfling, missing one meal *was* starvation.

Eric brushed off his clothing, smoothing the tunic over his armor. "Well, gentlemen, I have a different plan for tonight. I am heading out to the Pit. There is a young lady there requiring my attention." He bent over his backpack.

Dar blinked and turned in surprise. "Really? And who might that be?"

With a flourish, Eric produced a wooden comb from his backpack. "The fair Elaine. I intend to find out more about her."

Eric and Elaine? Dar remembered their mutual attraction.

"Good luck in the arena, warrior," he said.

Eric stopped in midstroke. "Is something wrong with her?"

"No."

"So?"

"I guess she'll always be Elaine the Pain to me. I know what she's like, or what she *can* be like. But don't let that stop you. I don't know you that well and you might be a good match."

Eric pondered this, then nodded. "We'll see." He finished combing his hair and resettled his sword, turning to face the others.

"There now. How do I look?"

Connor smiled. "Like a ruffian. A neatly combed ruffian, but a ruffian nonetheless."

Eric winked. "Thanks. Don't wait up for me."

The door to Megan and Brandi's room opened just as the front door closed behind him. Megan, looking less grubby and more lively, swept into the room, a friendly smile on her face. Dar forced himself to stop staring and turned back to the kitchen.

"Well, what's for dinner?" she asked.

"Smoked pheasant stew. Who's asking?"

"The assistant cook," she answered, pinching his arm and reaching into the nearest cupboard. She produced another knife. "Scoot over." Soon, she was busy chopping vegetables.

He stole a look at her, watching the soft lines of her face as she sliced carrots. With an inward sigh, he forced himself to pay attention to the meal.

Free-lances formed groups quickly and broke up just as quickly when a task was done. He had to admit he really didn't know very much about her or her plans for her future. One thing was sure, she was pretty enough to stop a charging giant in its tracks.

And he knew he liked her immensely.

The door to his parents' old room opened again and he looked over his shoulder. Brandi glided into the main room, brushing her hair. She had taken it out of its braid and it was obvious now that she was Megan's sister.

Wow! They could both stop a charging giant.

"Where's Eric?" she asked.

Connor hopped up on the kitchen counter and began ransacking a cupboard. "Went to the Pit."

Brandi's eyebrow arched upward. "Really? Can't stand the company or the food?"

Buck's languid voice sounded out from somewhere behind Dar. "Let's just say he was going to sample someone else's cooking."

Connor guffawed. Brandi looked perplexed, then shrugged.

The halfling turned to Buck, a bottle in his hand and grinning wickedly. "I found the ale."

Dar snatched it from the halfling's hand. "That's where it is! Thanks for finding it. It's for dinner and it's the last bottle." He placed the container on the table and turned back to the counter.

"Oh," said Connor, looking chagrined. He hopped off the counter and headed back towards Buck.

There was silence for a while, broken only by the sound of knives and a mockingbird from the garden outside.

"Put it back if you want any dinner," said Megan, not even looking up from her task.

Dar heard Connor's muttered curse and the sound of a bottle being set back on the table.

***

Megan leaned back in one of the chairs, impressed. "Amazing. A bachelor who can cook."

Dar turned a darker shade of tan. "Well, I had good teachers. My parents taught me before they left for Hillton."

"So," Megan said, pouring the last of the ale for herself, "Brandi and I saw a small jewelry box in the bedroom. It doesn't look like something a man would have."

Dar shifted in his seat and tried not to meet her eyes. "It isn't. It's my mother's. I'm hanging on to it."

Buck snorted. "What are you, a banker?"

Dar gave him a pitying look. "No, she wanted me to have it because it has something from my grandparents."

Brandi leaned back on the divan. "Really? Can we see it?"

He fidgeted. "Well, it's no big deal. It's only a keepsake. My grandmother used to have it and..."

Megan nodded.

Dar sighed. "Oh, all right."

He stood and disappeared into the bedroom for a minute, then returned carrying a flat, carved wooden box. A field of flowers and a unicorn decorated the top.

"My grandparents were freelancer sell-swords, like we are," he said, sitting down again and opening the box. "My grandfather was a scout, a Ranger Protector, and my grandmother a mage, like you, Megan."

Connor raised his eyebrows at Buck but held his peace. Dar held up a slim dagger. Megan leaned across the table in wonder.

A silver handle chased in gold glittered in the lantern-light. Silver bands and a few turquoise gems decorated a leather scabbard.

Megan reached for it. "May I?" she whispered.

Dar hesitated, then handed it to her. She drew the blade and tapped it against a steel dinner plates, eliciting a clear ringing sound.

Brandi whistled. "They must have been some freelancers. That's solid silver. Are they around? We might be able to get some pointers from them, if you haven't already."

Dar looked down at the table and sighed. "They disappeared when I was ten."

The others looked at him in surprise.

Megan put a hand on his. "You don't have to talk about this if you don't want to."

Dar shrugged, then looked up into her eyes. "Actually, I've been arguing with myself whether to tell all of you or not. Hardly anyone knows about this, but we've been through battle together and I'm never going to be able to do this on my own."

He leaned his forearms on the tabletop. "I don't know if any of you might have guessed this, but there's a reason I've stayed here in Forester instead of going off to the bigger cities. My grandfather and grandmother were both in the Order of the Falcon and traveled all over the borderlands of Deran before getting married and settling down. They helped Lord Nolan's father clear out some of the forestland north of here when Lord Kelvin took over rule of the barony about forty-seven years ago. Then they helped Nolan after Lord Kelvin died."

He sat back. "They set up a small trading post before my mother was born, in a small town called Wit's End."

Buck scratched his head. "Gordo's Trading Post is the only store in Wit's End. Gordo doesn't look like one of your relatives."

"Well, he isn't," Dar replied. "Gordo built another one on the same spot. Kaftu destroyed the original store during a raid and my grandparents barely escaped with their lives. They came to Forester and found out that soldiers had met a similar band in the forest and fought them off. More importantly, they captured one. Grandpa Robert spoke the Kaftu language so he got to interrogate the prisoner. He found out that the attackers were a search party, looking for something called the Helm of Shadows. It was said the Helm could transport multiple persons great distances in the blink of an eye."

"I don't know why they didn't just get jobs here in Forester and bide their time. Instead, they decided that since the store was gone, the Helm was their chance to rebuild their lives. I guess grandfather had a good idea of where it was hidden or they wouldn't even have considered it. They dusted off their gear, practiced their skills with the town guards for a while, then left. They never came back."

Megan's eyes were soft. "Then what are *you* trying to do? Find the Helm?"

Dar shook his head. "Not really, though I've considered it. I just want to find out what happened to grandma and grandpa. I don't know if they're alive or dead or imprisoned or lost or what. If nothing else, my mother has been wondering and fretting for ten years now. I think she deserves peace."

Brandi looked up at the ceiling. "Let's see — ten years. And they were how old when they left? In their late fifties? They might still be alive."

"They could also be anywhere," Connor pointed out. "They might not even have started here, in this barony. Deran is a big country."

Megan's eyes met Dar's. He found himself unable to look away. "But a scout has many ways to track, right Dar?" she asked, "If he gets good enough, maybe the best in the land, tracking a fifteen-year-old trail would be possible. Maybe not the actual tracks in the dirt, but the trail could be discovered by logic and research."

He sighed. "That's why I chose this career: To honor grandpa and to find them. I've wanted to do this since I was a boy. I still remember grandpa teaching me how to string a bow and grandma taking me for walks in the woods. I just want to know."

Megan only smiled back.

Connor gave a low whistle. "Good luck. I don't know how long we'll all be staying together after this mission, but you've got your work cut out for you."

They sat in silence for a while. Megan and Brandi exchanged a significant glance.

"We should, you know," said Megan.

Brandi set her mouth in a stubborn line. The men looked at them, mystified.

Megan gave an exasperated sigh.

Brandi looked down at the tabletop. "We can't rely on anyone but ourselves, you know that," she said. "You know what happened before."

"I don't know if you've noticed, Bran, but we're already relying on these men. I think they've proved themselves."

The two stared at each other for a while. Connor, Buck and Dar held very still.

Brandi nodded. "You're right. We've got to start trusting somebody."

Megan took a deep breath. "We're from Torosc," she said.

Dar's mouth suddenly dried up and his stomach felt like he had swallowed a rock. It couldn't be. These women were so kind and honest and good. They couldn't be from Torosc. Beautiful Megan and lovely Brandawyn... from Torosc?

Connor turned a piercing eye to the two sisters. "Well, you don't look like the usual crowd from that place," he said, "You're not half-daemons or trolls. And we haven't seen you sacrificing any infants or young maidens lately, unless you've been very discreet about it."

Buck's hand strayed toward his sword hilt. "Then what are you doing here? Spies maybe? How much did they pay you?"

Brandi's face flushed in anger. "No, not spies!" she flared. "Saint Andyn, would we tell you this if we were spies?"

She turned to her sister. "Megan, I knew this was a mistake."

"Why didn't you explain this to us before?" asked Dar, eyes locked on Megan.

"Look at your reactions!" retorted Brandi in disgust.

"Brandi, please," Megan put a hand on her sister's arm and fixed the men with her gaze. Her voice was firm and unyielding. "Anyone from Torosc is immediately suspected in the northern kingdoms. We thought it best not to say anything until we were sure of people's loyalties."

"If you had come clean with it in the beginning—" began Connor.

"As if any of us have come clean with our pasts yet!" Brandi looked disgusted and, thought Dar, a bit embarrassed.

She was right, he decided. "Connor, she's got a point," he said. "Let's give them a chance."

Brandi's angry gaze held them for a second, then she looked very sad. "I'm sorry I'm so angry. I know you have been raised to think that anyone from the 'Republic' only has insurrection or murder on their minds, but there are good people there, despite the government. It's just that life there was so horrid and we're judged the moment we tell anyone. It wears on you."

After another pause, Brandi sighed and continued.

"Our parents were Christians, just like us. That's a death sentence in Torosc. Everyone's required to either follow Gariil, goddess of chance and luck, or one of the evil gods. Our parents pretended Gariil because followers of that faith are so unpredictable no one would suspect odd behavior."

Dar nodded. A Gariil worshipper's religious expression could be just about anything. Even priests of Gariil were made by simply claiming the title. Because of this and the uncanny reputation of Gariilites to turn a profit, the Dark Churches left them alone. One of the oldest religions on the planet, Gariil had many adherents.

Brandi forged on, as if she would lose heart by pausing. "Our Uncle Stephen and Aunt Daphne, my dad's brother and sister, also lived in the town because they were attached to a military unit nearby. They were both exceptional fighters and got drafted by the Army in their teens. In addition, Stephen is a wizard."

"How long did they keep up the deception?" Dar asked.

Brandi took a deep breath. "Longer than most. They moved around quite a bit and were very good at hiding anything related to the Church. Others weren't so lucky."

Megan looked up with dead eyes. "We saw a lot of our friends disappear, most times old people or little children. The Ja'al clerics would parade a statue of Gudarta or Arachnia down the street, stop at your home and tell you that you had just been "honored" as the next "Chosen of Ja'al". Or the Vardish would just kidnap you in the middle of the night and sacrifice you to the god of death. There was nothing you could do."

Brandi shuddered. "They would take the Chosen into one of the temples and you'd never see them again. Sometimes, they would sacrifice them right in the village square and force everyone to watch. They'd burn them alive, or feed them to a dragon, or tear them to pieces in a frenzy..."

She shut her eyes, tears streaming down her smooth cheeks.

Oh God, Dar thought. *I had no idea.*

Brandi's eyes held fury when she opened them again. "Dad and Mom finally decided to escape. A local wizard noticed Megan and one of the generals pressured Stephen to put her up as a concubine. Even though our aunt and uncle were officers, they couldn't refuse a direct order."

"You too," interjected Megan, wiping her eyes. "They noticed all the young girls in the towns. The priests had you picked for a temple guard the moment you touched a sword."

Brandi nodded. "Somehow, the Ja'al found out about our plans. Aunt Daphne and Uncle Stephen heard from their sources that there was going to be a raid at the house and fetched us from school instead. We tried to get them to take us to Mom and Dad, but Daphne wouldn't let us. We hid out to the forest on the edge of town while Stephen went back to get them."

Connor cleared his throat. "I assume they were captured."

Megan looked up, eyes shiny and hollow. A single tear traced a path down her cheek. "No. My father and mother promised each other they would fight rather than be used as a blood sacrifice. By the time Stephen got to them, the house was on fire and both of them were dead."

She stopped, then managed to choke out, "We didn't even get a chance to say good-bye."

Dar reached forward and took her hand. She squeezed it in return, staring straight ahead.

Brandi brushed at her eyes, sniffed and smoothed her hair back from her face. "Our aunt and uncle took us to a military outpost, miles to the north, telling the soldiers they were on a training exercise with new recruits. The sergeant there had suspicions, I'm sure, but he couldn't argue with a captain and a major, so he let us stay the night. In the morning, we made it to a seaport in one of the coastal provinces and hired a fishing vessel to take us to the next port. We did his all the way to Gorostol, then met a family friend who helped us get to Terenai. We finally ended up in Eleth-Anor."

"And you stayed there until now," continued Dar softly.

Megan nodded, wiping her face with one of the table-napkins, her composure returning. "Yes. We had some very rough times for a while. Our aunt and uncle had to move constantly because Torosc sent assassins out after them. About four years ago, they disappeared for two whole years. We ran out of food and money. We were so poor. I learned how to make some simple potions so I stayed at our little hut on the top of a building, trying to make do with what we had."

"I'm so sorry." Dar finally managed, "But why didn't you ask for help? I know the elves would have helped you. The church of Verian has aid societies for the poor."

Megan's mouth quirked in a sad smile. "The agents of Torosc are very clever and very familiar with their enemies. They knew we'd try to ask for help from a local temple or church, so they laid in wait and almost got us once while we were on our way to Eleth-Anor. It was a very bad fight. Some of the people in the temple were killed and injured. We couldn't risk that anymore, so we decided to lay low. We didn't realize how long it would take. "A couple of months" turned into two years."

Brandi finished the tale. "Our aunt and uncle finally got free of the assassins and somehow got them off their trail. They came back to us and gave us clothes and food and money. Things got better after that. We moved to one of the suburbs and got a house. They worked for the city guard and managed to pay for our education for the next twelve years, at the academies."

Brandi stared at some unknown spot on the floor. "That's our history. Wonderful, isn't it?"

An awkward silence ensued.

What do I say?

Finally, Buck said, "And how did you end up here?"

Megan traced a whorl on the tabletop. "We stayed in Eleth-Anor until about a year after I graduated. We ended up in Alrihan, in southern Deran. The Christian seminary in Eleth-Anor was very hard to get into and Brandi wanted to become a battle medic. Our aunt and uncle stayed in Terenai because they were finally offered positions in the Imperial Intelligence Service. The elves had been watching them and were finally convinced they weren't spies so they were quite the hot commodity."

Brandi frowned. "A few years ago, they told us they had a new and special assignment involving Torosc. Uncle Stephen told us it would be better if we went up north for a while, started working on assignments and establishing ourselves as blank-shields. They said they would come for us when the time was right. It was strange. They usually weren't that secretive."

She exchanged a glance with her sister.

That stone in Dar's stomach began to sink farther. He was just starting to like Megan and her sister. Now it seemed these mysterious relatives could come along and break up their group on a moment's notice.

He picked up a couple of dishes and turned towards the kitchen. This was exactly the kind of internal conflict he didn't need. He certainly didn't want to lose allies and friends just when he had filled them in on his family secret.

The timing was all wrong.

He heard Connor's voice. "So, this means they could take you away any time."

"Basically, yes," said Megan, "But they might come tomorrow or a year from now. Remember the last time the left us. A short while turned into many months. And they might show up to say that they didn't find anything or that what they're looking for is too difficult for us to take right now. Or they might hire you guys as well to get some extra help. I just don't know. We both decided we were going to do what we thought was right and not just sit around waiting for them."

Dar set the dishes on the counter and turned to watch them.

He wondered. How much did he know about any of them? Briefly, he considered insisting on hearing all their stories, even Connor and Buck, but decided against it. Forcing them might make them lie to cover up something. Waiting was better.

In everything there is a season.

"I'm sorry we doubted you, Megan, Brandi," he said. "I should have known from your behavior you weren't the enemy. It was wrong."

Megan looked at him with that same, sad smile but a grateful look in her eyes. "That's okay. I'm just glad all of you are willing to give us a chance. Since we left Terenai, the only family we've had have been our friends, and that's what we thought Kili and James were."

Connor came over to her and hopped up on the table. "I don't blame you for not talking. They lied to you. I would probably be just as wary."

"You're very different from Kili and James," Megan replied, "I'm hoping we can be real friends with all of you."

Dar smiled. "I think that can be arranged. How about helping clean up the kitchen, friend?"

***

"Dar."

Dar stirred in his dream. Misty shadows flitted just out of the range of his vision. *It must be Buck. So help me, if he wakes me up, I'll smack him in the...*

"You are all in great danger."

"Danger?" Dar said out loud, suddenly feeling the hardwood of his living room floor beneath him. He blinked and wiped his eyes.

He sat up under his blankets, hand on the hilt of his sword. Eric stirred next to him.

When did Eric get in? he thought. *Oh, that's right, we let him in. It was pretty late. We told him all about Megan and Brandi. He took it in stride.*

He shook his head, remembering the dream. He remained still, trying to sift out the sounds of steady breathing from the forms of Buck, Connor and Eric.

He heard a whisper of sound from outside the house.

It might be a rat. He tried to decide whether to tell anyone else. His dream lingered in his mind.

He decided.

"Hey Buck," he whispered. *Better foolish than dead.*

A mild groan greeted him. "Aw, Mighty Oaks, Dar. It isn't even light yet."

"We might have company."

Buck's eyes snapped open and he sat up, hand sliding out for his own sword. "Where?" he whispered.

"Outside," Dar looked to his left. Flickering lights from the street shone in faintly through the window curtains, illuminating the wood floor and two dark blotches against a darker background. He reached over and tapped Eric and Connor.

They awoke and Dar put a warning finger to his lips. The pair pulled out weapons. Connor crouched, his broadsword resting on one shoulder. Both Eric and Connor's eyes shone with a metallic-green glow. Dar wished he could see in the dark.

Dar eased himself up to stand. "I'll get the girls."

Another whisper of sound, this time from the back door. He froze.

When it wasn't repeated, he continued on. Clad only in underpants and a shirt, he tiptoed over to the inner door to his parents' old room.

And hesitated. Knocking was out of the question. It would alert whomever was out there. Knowing Brandi, just breaking into the room would likely get him killed.

He gritted his teeth. *Boy, I'm going to look like a minotaur's butt if it's only a raccoon.*

He pushed open the door but did not enter.

"Brandi?" he called.

A tiny click sounded from the front door to the house. He went cold.

The front and back doors burst open. He whirled, sword at the ready.

Dark figures swarmed into the room, hooded and bearing long weapons. They fell upon the dark forms on the floor, hacking. Dar's heart skipped in horror.

Suddenly, his companions surged forward from corners of the room. Pandemonium reigned in a chorus of clanging steel, screams and shouted curses.

Two of the intruders, realizing their mistake, broke away from the main knot of writhing forms and ran towards him.

Heart in his throat, Dar stepped aside and parried a sword slash from the leftmost attacker. Both shifted around to face him. He thrust at a dark form, was parried, then dodged a return thrust that came out of nowhere in the darkness.

Good thing none of us can see in the dark, he thought, heart pounding. *Someone might get hurt.*

Suddenly, a shadow with twin blades hurtled into the main room from Brandi and Megan's room. It slammed into Dar's rightmost opponent with bruising force, hurling them both into a pile.

Dar pointed his sword at his remaining enemy.

"Surrender," he said.

The reply was a slash. Dar parried it and then decapitated the figure with a left-right backhand.

He squinted at the rest of the room, trying to find friend or foe in the shadows. Crumpled heaps lay on the floor and a knot of struggling people thrashed about near his kitchen table. The tower of wrestling, shouting flesh toppled over, slammed on the table top and then fell off to crush one of his kitchen chairs.

Damn. There's another two weeks of carpentry to waste.

A person with long blond hair darted past him from Megan and Brandi's room, staff upraised. Dar dropped to guard position.

"Wait, wait, wait!" a voice called from the pile. "We got him! We got him! Don't kill me!"

Dar relaxed and grinned. That was Buck's voice.

Megan's voice sang out an arcane word. A ball of light flared over the table. Dar shielded his eyes. He picked his way over to the kitchen, careful to avoid the slick spots.

The rest of the group, looking rather bedraggled, stood blinking in the white glow. All had a weapon or two and were clad only in their underwear. Buck limped slightly and Connor looked he had been run through a sawmill, blood all over him, clothes ripped, and hair sticking out at all angles. Megan and Brandi were barefoot and clad only in knee-length tunics.

"Everyone okay?" Dar asked got a lot of nodding in response.

Brandi raised a shaking hand to her forehead, wiping a lock of hair away. "Who were they?"

Megan turned over one of the black-clad assailants. It was a young woman, about sixteen years old, with round, attractive features and dark hair. On the left breast of her leather jerkin, Dar saw the badge of a white, clawed hand, now splotched with blood.

Megan shook her head in disbelief, her eyes wide. "My God! She's just a child! What animal would send children after us?"

"The Whiteclaw recruit their agents young."

Dar looked up. Eric stood by the kitchen table, polishing his sword. The magical light from Brandi's spell cast deep shadows on his face, his eyes lit with a fading afterglow of metallic green.

Dar stared. Eric looked, well, sinister.

"Huh?" he asked.

"Whiteclaw assassins," repeated Eric. He sheathed his sword and came to join them, brushing at his short hair. "Based in Oakmoor. A very large band, hired by people all over the northlands. And I can tell you one thing. If she's a day over fifteen, she's not a child any longer. The Whiteclaw recruit from the streets at age twelve."

"How do you know all this?" Megan asked.

Eric grinned, looking a lot less menacing. "I'm not a Whiteclaw, if that's what you mean. I was in Oakmoor for a long time, remember? Taverns are great places for hearing all kinds of interesting stuff. And Melinor knows a *lot* of people in interesting jobs."

Dar watched Eric. *He must have visited some really great places.* Knowledge about assassins was hard to come by, even for agents and spies of the Royal Intelligence Service.

"I'll tell you one thing," Dar said, standing and stretching, "All this racket is sure to bring the city guard, if only to break up a noisy party. Let's at least be dressed when they get here."

They barely had enough time to put on some outer-clothes before fists pounded on the door. Ten soldiers and a stern-looking corporal stood in the lamplight outside. While the troops carted away the bodies, the corporal listened and took notes. Dar showed him their writs from the Baron establishing them as his agents and the corporal scratched his beard. Since Dar and his friends were baronial officers and equal to his rank, he could only order them to appear at the manor house at first light.

Dar sighed as he closed the front door.

First, Megan gets paralyzed and we have to use up almost all of our earnings to heal her. Then, we're called in by the Baron, given a tough assignment, and now these Whiteclaw jackasses are breathing down our necks. Plus, we've got to go to the manor to explain the battle in my living room.

The others tried to clean up. He squatted down next to Megan, scrubbing at a bloodstain out of the floorboards.

She looked up and brushed her hair back over her head with a smile. "Nice place you've got here."

He smiled back, his mood brightening a little. "Do you like the decor? It's the 'early battlefield' style."

Her eyes twinkled. His heart skipped a beat. She was so beautiful it hurt. *God, what's happening to me?*

"How long until dawn?" asked Brandi, walking out of her bedroom. She dumped her armor on the couch with a loud clink.

Dar shrugged. "Should be about two of the clock now. We've probably got another three hours before dawn. If we hurry, we can clean this place up, eat something, and make it to the manor at first light."

Brandi surveyed the wreckage and shook her head. "Somehow, I don't feel much like eating."

***

"Whiteclaw, in my town?"

Nolan turned to look out the window of his throne room at the gathering dawn, playing orange and red against the mountainsides.

"How many?"

Dar cast a look at the others.

"Five, milord."

Nolan's brow furrowed. Strong hands clenched and unclenched behind his back.

Dar knew Nolan had plenty of reason to be angry. Forester's remoteness and small size should have been reasons enough to avoid the attention of assassin's guilds.

The baron let out a sigh, all tension leaving his body, then turned back to the group. He gave a nervous smile of his own. "I beg your pardon if I am less than grateful for your assistance in removing these Whiteclaw from circulation. I have been trying to keep the peace here in Forester for twenty years. Assassins are the last thing I need, on top of the Westhaven tragedy."

He looked up. "You are getting close if the Whiteclaw are after you. Someone doesn't like the fact that you decimated the goblin stronghold. I'm sure they have spies in town, since the assassins were upon you less than a day after you came back from your mission."

He moved over to one of the small tables. "Let me see the map of the goblin caverns again."

Connor laid it out and they gathered around.

Nolan perused the map. When he was done, he strode over to one of the glass cabinets. He tapped the door once with a knuckle and whispered a word. The lock flared and he opened it, then returned to the group carrying a roll of parchment.

"This," he announced, "is a copy of the map I showed you yesterday. It isn't quite as large as the master but has been magically augmented and can take a lot of abuse."

He handed it to Dar. "There are three caverns near the place you investigated yesterday", he said, "I favor the closest one; it isn't like the Ja'al to leave an outpost without support. This nearest one is at the base of a high ridge, north by northwest of Forester. Dar, do you remember the area?"

The scout nodded. "Yes, Milord. Sir Tan took me near there several times. He told me about the caverns but we didn't go in. We had been in plenty of others and he said it was just like the ones I had seen."

The baron stepped to another side table and rang a small brass bell. In a few moments, a liveried servant stepped through a side door and bowed.

"Have Sir Colin attend me please."

As the servant left, he turned back to the free-lancers. "I will try to find out how the Ja'al knew about you and your recent success. In the meantime, I recommend you gather provisions and leave tomorrow morning. Examine the base you infiltrated yesterday and then make a concerted effort to find out if the Ja'al have any others nearby and what they are up to. I would lay money that it means trouble for Forester."

Chapter Nine- Something Old, Someone New

"Great Canon?"

Halkith the Grey opened his eyes and sighed. It was getting harder and harder to meditate these days with so many damned interruptions.

He altered his magic field and rotated around to face the door, careful to maintain both his levitation in lotus position and his calm exterior.

A beautiful elven woman stood in the doorway, golden hair falling down on her smooth shoulders. Her dress of midnight blue glittered as if hewn from precious stones, the cut of the neckline showing a hint of a small, well-rounded bosom. A single diagonal band of gold crossed her breast and abdomen and the tips of white boots peeked out from under the dress hem.

She turned a delicate, oval face to him, green eyes downcast.

"I bring news from the Borderlands, Great Canon."

Halkith's eyes wandered over every curve of her figure. He canceled the spell, floating down on his bed.

Gudarta's Nine Ways of Pain could wait.

"Yes, Lady Aalre."

She adopted an expression of regret and sympathy. Halkith knew she felt neither.

"My lord, I am saddened to inform you that the news initially brought by the survivors from Base One have been confirmed. The garrison has been almost completely wiped out. Strike Team Eight has begun the sealing operation. And Cleric Modron Derrig was just found near Base Two. He apparently survived."

Not for long, if I have anything to say about it, Halkith seethed. *That fat fool has failed me for the last time. No, second-to-last. I will make him suffer, then work twice as hard before I finish him off.*

He maintained his demeanor of outward calm. "As we suspected. I want you to send scouts to the other bases. Make sure the chieftains understand the nature of the threat, the rewards for success and the cost of failure."

She nodded.

Grey eyes met green ones full of fiery lust.

I can't wait for tonight, Aalre dear, thought Halkith.

He jerked himself back to the present. "And news of the Whiteclaw? We knew it was that band of freelancers from Forester who committed the crime. How did the assassins fare?"

Again she displayed an expression of regret. "Our informants indicated that the freelancers survived and that the Whiteclaw were wiped out. The squad leader perished as well, so we are not sure exactly what happened. All the freelancers were spotted heading to the manor house later that morning."

Surrounded by incompetent bunglers and worthless sons of she-goats! The 'mighty' Whiteclaw get their useless asses kicked in by a bunch of first-rank amateurs!

He let out a long slow breath.

"Well, it appears that the Whiteclaw have lost their talons for the time being." He rose from the bed in a swish of garish pink robes. "We must keep track of the nuisances from Forester and seek retribution when the opportunity presents itself. Are they being followed?"

Aalre was getting quite good at that remorseful expression. "Goblins from Strike Team Six followed them this morning when they left town, but had to hide from a patrol. Lord Nolan's suspicions have been roused. The strike team lost the trail and were unable to pick it up again. Apparently, there is at least one scout among the freelancers who knows how to pick a good trail and keep it hidden. In town, our contacts are trying the best they can without giving themselves away."

Just what I need.

"Interesting," he said. "We must keep this in mind. Send out four patrols in the region of Base Two. It's the closest and might be their next target."

She nodded acquiescence and bowed to leave.

"Incidentally, milady," he added as she straightened. "I must compliment you on your excellent execution of the Westhaven task. A thorough job."

She smiled, a weird fire flickering in her green eyes. "I am always happy to please my lord."

He smiled back. "And you may do so again at a later time. Would you give me the pleasure of your company here this evening?"

The smile never wavered, but the eyes flared. "As you command, my lord..."

***

This is great, thought Eric, kicking a rock. He looked down into the entrance to the goblin lair.

Well, there's plenty of them to kick now.

Boulders jammed the entrance. Smaller stones and earth filled in the gaps. He figured it would take a team of dwarven miners to clear it out again.

"Mighty Oaks," said Buck from his left. "Guess someone didn't want us to go back in."

Eric nodded. He shrugged to resettle his backpack, heavier with the meat from a boar he and Dar had shot that morning.

Dar unrolled Lord Nolan's map. "Well, since this one is out of the question...hmmm..." he mused, tracing a line on the map with a finger. "Looks like a trip of about a day from here to the nearest of the old mines."

"Are we sure they've gone?" called out Brandi from behind them.

"It's useless speculating," Eric answered over his shoulder. "Even if they're still down there, we'd need to find another way in and out. That could be anywhere."

Dar nodded, looking up at the sun. Eric did the same. It would be about two of the clock, if they had a clock to look at.

"Let's go then." Dar turned and headed north. "We'll have to follow the River to get to it, but it should be easy going."

Eric, Connor and Dar led the way, about fifteen feet ahead Buck, Megan and Brandi. They crossed a rise in the forest, following a dim trail. Many spruces, oaks, and banbans crowded around them, making it difficult to see more than a few score yards.

Eric scanned about, then topped the rise next to a tree. Nothing moved except a few yellow crickets that leapt up to whir away at his approach. In the distance, he heard the dim rush of the Whitehorse River.

He smiled, remembering Dar's questions about his date with Elaine.

I wonder why he's so curious. Maybe because they were schoolmates. But if he's got any sense, he'll start paying attention to Megan. She likes him, for some mysterious reason.

He found Elaine a bright girl with an active sense of humor and a no-nonsense air about her. He attributed this to her having to deal with such a rough and unwashed crowd at the Pit, not to mention that many in that same unwashed crowd were friends and neighbors.

Eric followed the downward side of the rise, next to a huge fallen tree. He skirted around roots raised to the sky like clawing hands. A slight movement caught his eye up ahead and he saw Connor wave the 'okay' sign. Shifting his spear, he nodded and continued.

His thoughts drifted back to his evening with Elaine. Her parents were very welcoming. After sharing dinner with her at the Pit, he accepted an invitation to meet her family. The Wards preferred living in their cabin about three hundred yards from the fort. Tom and Ella Ward were taken aback at their daughter bringing home a sell-sword, but Eric had set them at ease. He made sure to use his most polite manners, a tactic that worked so well that Tom had finally chuckled and asked to go on a first-name basis. Elaine's brother, a few years younger and a lumberjack, listened with the rest of the family to Eric's tales of his excursion against the goblins and life in the glittering capitol city of Oakmoor.

The evening ended quite well with a hearty farewell and return invitation from the family—and a kiss from Elaine. The guards at the town gate recognized him and let him in after only a cursory search.

Then Connor told him about the revelations by Dar, Megan and Brandi. He frowned.

Sad stories, and Eric knew a lot about sad stories.

Would the women's aunt and uncle arrive to take them away at a time when they were most needed? What about Dar? If he uncovered something about his grandparents, would he just leave them?

He stopped his musings when the trail led across a large meadow. He held up the formation at the edge of the glade while he and Dar slipped next to trees, eyeing the landscape. Connor's job was to scout ahead in the shadows while the rest of the group waited. Across the clearing, a large thicket blocked the way. The sound of the river was louder now. He glimpsed coarse grey rocks and an occasional flash of water between the trees, beyond the far side of the meadow. He relaxed a little, enjoying the bright spring sunshine and the warmth of the afternoon.

Connor waved from his right, made a fist and placed it on his head. He held up one finger.

Eric set his spear point-first in the ground and drew his bow, fitting an arrow to the string. He returned to the main party.

"Someone's coming," he said in a piercing whisper.

Connor trotted up the trail and stopped next to them. "There's a woman on the riverbank on our side. Her hair is wet so I'd say she swam across," the halfling spy said.

Dar's eyebrows rose so far they almost hit his hairline. "Swam the Whitehorse? Saint Ander! The river's two hundred yards across at that point and it's not moving slowly either."

Megan hefted her staff. "She's only one person, right? Why don't we go talk to her? Maybe Brandi and I could see what she's doing out here alone."

Eric tapped his chin. "Let's go have a look, but carefully."

The group made their way across the clearing and skirted the thicket at the other side. Eric took a peek as he walked past.

Just as Connor had said, a golden-haired woman sat on a large flat rock on the riverbank. A brown leather knapsack rested on the sand next to her and a cloak lay on another rock in the sunshine. Two steely, smooth-headed maces were propped up against the rock. She buttoned up the side of one boot.

Eric looked at Megan and motioned with his head. She nodded and went around the bushes.

Right into a pile of dry leaves.

At the rustling sound, the woman leapt up and whirled around, sweeping up the two maces in one motion. She held one weapon over her head and one in front of her midriff.

She was a half-elf, and as pretty as Brandi. Calf-high soft black boots covered her feet and shiny chain mail moved up the curve of her thigh. The symbol of a silver tree glimmered on her tunic. Honey-blonde hair in a single braid rested on one shoulder and penetrating amber eyes narrowed upon seeing Megan. Her face was heart-shaped and a trifle less finely carved than either of the Alenar sisters.

"Verian priestess," murmured Brandi from his left. Eric turned to her in surprise.

She returned his gaze with a smile. "Verian, the elven god of the forests and nature. Friendly to Christianity for the most part. Almost as persecuted in some places."

Eric turned his attention back to Megan, who smiled at the woman. "Er... sorry about that. I didn't mean to startle you."

The woman stood her ground. "Who are you?" she asked in a mellow soprano voice.

"Don't worry," Megan said, laying her staff against a tree and holding her hands out. "I'm not a bandit. My name is Megan Alenar of Saint Terenil's Order and I'm traveling in the forest with my friends. What's your name?"

The woman narrowed her eyes, then straightened. "Andyn Eleandir, mage and cleric of the Faith of Verian. Why are your friends hiding in the bushes? I'd like to see them."

Those were the magic words. Buck Bydecy tramped out of the brush and stood next to Megan.

He put a hand on his chest, drew himself up to his full height, and heroically announced, "I? I am Buck, Buck Bydecy. And these are my faithful companions."

Megan giggled and Buck looked hurt as he turned his head to see who was laughing.

Eric rolled his eyes and stepped forward. "Eric Indidarc of Oakmoor." He introduced the others in the group.

Andyn, more relaxed, smiled. "Pleased to meet all of you," she said, replacing her maces on hooks on her belt. "I haven't seen a soul since I left Wit's End yesterday. Actually, no friendly souls. I had to hide from an ogre yesterday or he would have had my head on a plate."

Dar grinned. "I looks much better on the top of your neck."

Eric chuckled as Andyn blushed. Dar certainly worked hard on his chivalry these days. He caught a look of confusion on Megan's face.

You better watch your step, Dar. More than one is trouble, believe me.

Connor took charge. "We just came from Forester. It is more than a half-day's hike from here."

"Any trouble?" Andyn asked, picking up her knapsack.

"Clear," Eric answered, "There's been a bit of goblin activity around there so the baron stepped up his patrols."

"I know," Andyn replied. "That's why I'm heading there. I'm answering a posting for a battle medic. I'll show you."

She rummaged in her bag and produced a sheet of paper.

Eric blinked and looked at Megan, who laughed.

Andyn looked confused. "What's so funny?"

"That's our advertisement," Dar said with a grin. "We're the ones who needed a cleric healer."

Andyn read the page, then smacked her forehead. "You're *that* Mister Cabot? Sorry. I should have been paying more attention."

Brandi chuckled. "The Lord works in mysterious ways, no doubt about it. Since you're our applicant, would you care to conduct the interview right here?"

Andyn considered this for a second. "Why don't we discuss it over a campfire tonight? I'll travel with you until then and if you decide you don't need me, I'll continue on to Forester."

"By yourself?" Dar looked alarmed. "I don't know if you should. It's not exactly safe around here."

Andyn shrugged. "I came as far as the river with a group of trappers and I'm sure I'll see someone along the way back if you and I decide to part ways. Verian will provide."

Is that faith or foolishness? thought Eric.

He looked at Andyn's calm eyes. *Faith.*

Dar replaced his bow. "We weren't planning on stopping here. If everyone's ready, I say we continue."

Together, he and Dar followed the Whitehorse River shoreline through the forest for much of the rest of the afternoon. They turned north as the sky turned to amber-red. Dappled sunlight streamed in through the trees with the majestic Dragonspine Range towering behind them. Small yellow and orange flowers stubbornly poked their blossoms up where the the undergrowth thinned.

Even though Eric was trained to view the forest as an ecological system, a battleground, and a storeroom, that didn't mean he couldn't appreciate it. Sometimes, it could be either a haven or a grave. Right now it was downright beautiful.

He located a good spot for a camp in a long hollow, hidden by lindus bushes and a few trees at one end and by overgrown slopes on two other sides. In between the vegetation was a large, inviting area, albeit a little damp and cold.

Andyn joined the rest of them in setting up the camp, even volunteering to cook, over Dar and Megan's protests. She and Dar soon had the boar roasting over a cheery fire.

They did an excellent job of it. With irony, Eric noted that the quality of their meals hadn't changed much from when they had left the town. He wondered if Dar could have a second career as a chef.

Their interview with Andyn took place during supper. The companions fired questions at her at random moments. Eric had to hide a smile several times. He could see what they were doing: trying to catch her off-guard, trying to trick her into revealing something hidden.

If she was really an agent of evil, they had no chance. She seemed perfectly normal and honest and answered their queries with composure and ease. At the end of it all, Connor finally stopped the questioning and declared that he, for one, saw no reason not to take her into the group.

Dar explained their mission to her and she shook her head, eyes blazing. "Wiped out an entire village?! Even if you hadn't sent the courier to Wit's End, I'd have joined you just to break the bastards."

Buck and Connor decided to keep watch while the others relaxed, an idea the others welcomed. It would give them a chance to get acquainted with their new partner.

Eric sat back and took a drink from his wineskin, listening to Andyn and the Alenars reminisce about Eleth-Anor, in Terenai. Andyn had been born and raised in that seaside metropolis and the Alenars had lived there for some time. Hearing them laugh and joke about mutual memories and social gossip brought out thoughts of his own home and family.

A dull ache started in his heart. *Melinor and Saren... when was the last time I saw them? Months ago?*

He looked up and saw Brandi's eyes, animated, laughing, and relaxed. She was a very different person now that he knew her better — less suspicious, more friendly and approachable. He admired the way firelight reflected in her hair.

He shook his head. *I can't tell them. Not Dar or Megan. And especially not Brandi. They wouldn't understand.*

Or would they?

Eric knew that the longer he waited, the more devastating it was going to be when he finally came clean. Melinor and Anne Indidarc had taken it well. Saren had taken it well. Why not they? They had a lot of the same qualities as Melinor. And after the Megan and Brandi's tale, maybe they would listen and not judge him.

A sliver of hope worked its way into his musings. *Well, Melinor took me in and he didn't care who I was before I met him. He's kind and funny and wise and accepting. Just like these people.*

He took another drink and watched his companions. Dar leaned forward, explaining a story to the three women. He made a gesture with his hands and then sat back and made a final comment, a rascally look on his face. The assembly dissolved in laughter. Connor added a comment over his shoulder, resulting in more chuckles.

These are good people. Just like Melinor.

Brandi caught his eye and smiled, motioning for him to come closer to the fire. His heart skipped a beat. He wanted to be closer to her, to them, to have friends. He longed for it, yet...

I'm going to tell them. The whole thing. Right here and now. His heart pounded in his chest and he wiped sweaty palms on his cloak. *I've got to do it. God help me.*

He took a deep breath and scooted forward. Brandi waved him to silence when he opened his mouth to speak, looking at Andyn.

"...And then," Andyn said in a dreamy voice, "he asked me to marry him."

Megan's mouth hung open.

"Well," asked Brandi, "what did you tell him?"

Andyn giggled. "I said yes, of course."

Great! I hear the middle of the story.

Dar shook his head. "Wait a minute. You mean you're married? What are you doing out here then? And where is your husband, Larad?"

Andyn's dreamy look faded. She dropped her gaze.

"He passed away to Verian about six years ago. He was murdered."

Oh God. He shot a glance at the others. The stunned silence spoke for them.

"What?" he managed in a raspy voice.

Andyn seemed to deflate. "Larad and I bought a small house in the city about a year after we were married. His carpentry trade was doing well, he'd taken on an apprentice, and I was earning good money as an apothecary."

"The house was in a very old neighborhood and people said that the property had been part of a sorcerer's compound in the days of the Esten Empire. I didn't think much about it."

Connor let out a low whistle. Eric nodded. That made the property very old indeed.

"One night," Andyn continued, twisting a green stick in her hands, "Larad came home in a fury. He muttered something about enemies who masqueraded as business partners. I tried to get him to talk about it but all he would say was that someone wanted our house and was going through some pretty underhanded tricks to get it. He said he would tell me when he wasn't mad anymore, so I let it go. He always told me things when he calmed down."

Shiny amber eyes looked off into the dark forest. "The very next night, he didn't come home from the shop. I looked everywhere for him. I went to my father's house and asked for his help, but even his soldiers couldn't find him. The night watch found him near the warehouses the next morning. Someone had shot him with a poisoned crossbow bolt."

Megan put a hand on Andyn's shoulder and Brandi took her hand.

Andyn blinked, two silvery tears running down her smooth cheeks. "I went home after that. I don't even know how I got there—it was on fire. On fire!" she repeated, voice breaking. "If they wanted it so bad why did they burn it down?! I think I fainted because the next thing I remember is waking up at my parents' house."

She wiped her eyes. "I didn't have the money to buy a new house, so I just sold the land to the city and went back home. Dad used every bit of influence he had to try to find out what happened, but there are even limits to what an army colonel can do."

"What did you do then?" asked Brandi.

Andyn sighed. "My grandmother talked to me for a while after the mourning period. I had been planned to go to the Four Winds Mages Academy before I met Larad, so now that I had the money from the land, I decided to give it a try. After that, I went to the Silver Tree College in Mil-Tereth. I was made a priestess five years later."

Connor nodded. "Did they ever find out who had killed your husband?"

Andyn's mouth settled in a firm line. "Yes."

"Really?" asked Dar, incredulous.

Eric blinked. "So who was it? Did they catch him?"

Fire replaced the tears in Andyn's eyes. "One of the city aldermen, Liander Tolin, suddenly left town about a week after Larad died. The police agents made a note of this and kept digging. It took them a while, so I was in college when I heard the news. Tolin had hired assassins of the Crossed Swords Guild to kill Larad. Apparently, Tolin had offered to buy the house, then threatened Larad when he refused to sell. Tolin then started several legal motions in court to declare our claim to the land null and void, but the judges threw out the cases."

Crossed Swords? Eric's mouth felt dry as paper.

Andyn looked up at the group. "On a hunch, I asked the police to examine the ruins of my house. A floorstone had been removed and replaced. It hid a hole in the ground about the size of a small box. The city guards said it looked as if someone had moved it after the house burned down."

Brandi's brow furrowed. "A box?"

Andyn glared furiously into the fire. "Yes. A stupid box. I don't even know what was in it! Treasure? Magic? Nothing was worth my Larad."

Eric could think of nothing to say. Only the crickets in the brush chirped, echoing in the hollow.

Andyn's jaw was tight. "I'm going to get that bastard if it's the last thing I do in this life. Verian help me..."

A single tear rolled down her cheek again and she closed her eyes. "I loved him so much. Why did they have to kill him?" She choked back a sob.

The companions sat in silence, not speaking.

Andyn let out a deep breath, opened her eyes and smiled shyly at them. She wiped her face. "Look at me. Carrying on like this, and the whole thing six years gone. And I hardly know you."

Dar smiled at her. "Forget about it. You're stuck with us for a while."

Andyn smiled through her tears. "I guess I am."

Connor walked over to her from his watchpost. "I know how you feel," he said, "We've all lost a loved one at some point or another. If this Liander Tolin ever comes anywhere near us, he'll regret the day he was born."

"Right?" he asked, turning to the others.

There was a chorus of emphatic agreement.

Eric wondered at Connor's words. *Now why did he say that?*

Andyn gave him a grateful smile. "Thank you."

The others came over to give her encouragement, decrying the evils of assassins and government officials who hired them. Dar, in particular, seemed more incensed than the others.

Eric gave Andyn's hand a squeeze and received a sad smile in return. He leaned back against a nearby rock and watched the fire.

Well, he thought, *that family story is going to have to wait a while longer. Now is not the time.*

Chapter Ten- Battalion of the High Ridge

All this and rain too, thought Connor Lomin.

Water dripped from the edges of the huge leaf over his head, providing a steady stream of jewel-like droplets in front of his face. He shifted his weight, eyeing the forest around him. The tanrin bush grew to a height of five feet or so. Its thick branches and two-foot wide leaves earned it the nickname of 'halfling canopy'.

Hurray for the little folk.

The night of Andyn's startling revelations about her husband, a light rain fell. This made their hollow colder and damper until the morning, when the precipitation turned into a cloying mist. The scouts stored up enough dry wood to last the night and figured out a way to protect it from the damp. Somehow, Dar and Eric kept the fire going until dawn broke through the trees. Everyone awakened with cold, tight muscles but for the most part, dry.

However, the heavier rain crept up on them during the day. It played dead amid a leaden sky until they started their trek towards the second of the old mines on Dar's map.

Connor peered out from under his natural umbrella, watching the others.

Buck and Dar stood behind maple trees. They watched a meadow just ahead, hair wet and cloaks dripping. Brandi, Megan and Andyn waited next to them, hoods covering their heads. They were almost dry, thanks to special cloaks treated with some substance that made the rain jump off the surface. Connor resolved to get one for himself.

He waited, eyes darting to the top of the sixty-foot cliff on the far side of a wide meadow beyond the trees ahead of him. Several figures moved about on the top of the bluff. Dar made sure that a healthy thirty-foot distance crowded with trees and bushes separated the companions from the edge of the meadow.

What's keeping Eric so long? the halfling wondered. According to the map, the next of the old dwarven mines should be hidden somewhere under the ridge.

The longer they waited to find out where to look, the worse their situation appeared. They had to hide twice from groups of goblins tramping through the wet woods, twelve strong and then some. Eric and Dar proved their woodcraft yet again, hiding all of them until the troops passed.

Hell if I've got any ideas. Storming cliff-fortresses wasn't part of my training.

Connor fished around in his shoulder bag for a dried apple. He watched Andyn fidget and felt a kinship with her, a common sorrow of loss of family.

He thought of his own loss. Would Janey have liked this kind of life?

Probably not. A comfortable soul, she had liked all the traditional things: hearth and home, children, good food, good friends, plentiful crops.

For you, Janey, I would have forgotten about the call of the wide, dark sky and the deep forests and grown old in the hills of Glen.

He felt a twinge of guilt. The others in the group knew nothing about Janey or the child. He consoled himself with the thought that it didn't matter now. They died two years ago and from nothing as sinister as Andyn's story. Just a disease, victims of an epidemic.

Bushes moved and he whipped up his bow. He relaxed as Eric Indidarc slipped up through the wet brush. Andyn heaved an exasperated sigh.

"What took you so long?" she asked in a low voice.

Eric wiped his brow and looked sheepish, ruffling the water out of his hair. "I saw what I thought was a way over to the cliff face, but it only ended in a thicket. Then I almost fell over a gang of our monkey-faced friends. It took me a while to get back without making a lot of noise. I did find a way around to the base of the cliff without exposing ourselves to the guards on the top. If we hurry, we can get there before the next patrol."

He pointed off to the right to a dense stand of trees huddled next to the sheer rock face, across the meadow from their current position. "It ends right there."

Dar looked at it dubiously. "What happens after that?"

Eric shrugged. "I don't know. But you said the map showed an entrance at the base of the cliff, right? And that's the only likely spot."

They divided their time and attention between following Eric and watching the cliff guards. Connor kept his head up at all times, alert and listening for any sign of trouble.

After skirting the edge of the meadow, Eric raised his hand and halted. Just ahead of them, the dripping stand of trees beckoned.

Kind of creeps up on you, Connor mused.

He slipped up next to Dar and tapped his arm. "Is that it?"

Dar nodded as he sized up the stand, chewing his lip. "The map says so, although I don't know how we're going to—" He broke off.

Connor looked all around. "What is it?"

Dar didn't answer but instead walked up to the trees and bushes. He grabbed a thick branch and pulled. A section of gnarled brush and a tree trunk pivoted away from their neighbors.

Connor blinked. A dim opening yawned at them from behind the vegetation, leading to a dark gash in the cliff face. Eric nodded slowly.

"They made a screen of bushes, branches, and this piece of tree trunk," Dar said, holding up the five-by-five section for them to see. Connor saw now the discolored leaves. He touched a leaf: dead. Wet, but dead.

"They left it out too long," Dar continued, looking pleased, "The plants died and the whole section changed color. At first, I thought it was the species, but that didn't make sense when I saw they were all the same type of tree. Then I noticed a few cords of rope and, there you go!"

Buck strode towards the opening. "Great. Now let's get down there and raise Hades. It's a wonder half the goblins in the area haven't come down around our ears by now."

Connor raised a hand and stopped him, shaking his head. *That big lug is going to get roasted by a trap one of these days.*

"There's no guards here and I think there's a reason for that," he noted, stepping towards the opening. "Either they consider their camouflage good enough or there's a trap. I'm a pessimist. Let me check it first."

"Your funeral," said Buck, favoring him with a smile.

Connor positioned himself next to the opening, examining the sides of the supporting trees and the ground, looking for trip cords. Finding none, he stepped through.

The space between the rock cliff and the trees measured not more than five feet across. He looked up at the branches overhead, saw nothing, then went to the crack in the rock. Triangular, about five feet wide at the bottom and narrowing to a point at the top, it reached up to a height of about a dozen feet. He searched again for cords and wires, inspected the rocks at the edge, and looked for magical sigils or glyphs on the stone walls. With a Ja'al cleric or two on the loose, looking for mere conventional traps didn't cut it.

Connor sniffed the air: musty and damp. A faint, familiar odor reached him.

Goblins, he concluded, screwing up his face in distaste.

He turned and beckoned to the others.

Dar joined him first. He peered into the dark crack, torch in one hand and a spark-snapper in the other. He flicked the two halves of the spark implement and the torch blazed to life.

"Here we go," he said.

***

Ellen Hanford looked up from the top of her library desk at the sound of boots clumping on the wooden floor. Colin Parker bowed.

"What of this Whiteclaw business?" she asked, settling back in her chair.

Colin made a face. "Well, milady, no one seems to remember much about any of the assassins. Workers at one of the sawmills recalled a couple of them to mind, but weren't sure how long ago they got to town. My guess is about four or five months. Mostly they were posing as day laborers or traveling craftsmen and their apprentices. We get many like them every spring."

Ellen sighed. "Typical Ja'al planning. I wouldn't be surprised if they decided to place the assassin team in town *last* spring. Dar Cabot and his friends have done us a favor. Now we won't have to worry about them causing trouble whenever the Ja'al make their final move, whatever that is."

Colin looked confused. "Milady?"

She had to smile. "You're going to learn more of this as you transition from Field Officer to Command. The Ja'al sometimes lay their plans a long time in advance," she explained, "and often what appears to be their true objective is a ruse to distract you from their real goal. They are very tricky, much more tricky than the church of Vardish or the Cla'agik."

The young knight grinned, looking like a boy. "I guess I have a lot to learn, milady."

"Do you have something for me?"

He handed her a dispatch. It was from one of her spies in the merchant yards. Usually, he was in the outlying villages, but in the spring and early summer he went where most of the new traffic gathered.

Her agent held the opinion that the Ja'al had sent the Whiteclaw assassins a month ago, blowing her theory of a long-laid plan. Or did it? Were they planning on something two weeks or two years from now? Why were they here in the first place? Dar and his friends had only just arrived this week so it couldn't have been for them. Were the Ja'al planning something big that required spies and assassins?

She chewed the end of a pen.

How is this connected to Clarissa's pottery, for God's sake? She had a nagging feeling they were missing something.

"What of the assassin leader?" asked Ellen, placing the dispatch back on the table.

"Well," Colin replied, "Her name is Calindra Pohlin. She's wanted for two counts of murder in Darlon. Her capture had a price of three hundred crowns, so someone wanted her pretty bad. She wasn't a high-ranking assassin, but by all accounts a very violent one. I took the liberty of depositing the reward in the city bank in Cabot's name."

Ellen nodded, eyes wandering to Clarissa's vase on top of this desk in her study. *Maybe by staring at it long enough I can figure all this out. Why it was worth the lives of a village?*

"Milady?"

She looked up with a start. "Oh, I'm sorry, Colin. You may go. Alert me if anything else comes up regarding this matter."

She picked up the vase as the door closed behind him, turning it over and over.

Clarissa, you're as sly as a Ja'al yourself. What were you up to?

***

Connor dropped the goblin helmet on the ground and wiped his hands. Filthy and smelly. *That just about sums up goblin society and goblins in general.*

He sheathed his broadsword and walked over to the others. Megan, Andyn, and Eric inspected goblin belt purses in the middle of the chamber.

Eight warriors lay on the rough dirt and stone in dark pools of their blood. On the left side of the room, Dar Cabot crouched next to an opening, his bow fitted with an arrow, a torch planted in a crack in the floor near him. On the opposite side of the room, Brandi watched a similar tunnel, the reflections from a nearby firepit making her armor golden-red. A heavy iron kettle lay on its side, charred on the bottom from countless meals. Its pungent contents puddled on the floor.

Connor wrinkled his nose again.

Eric shook his head at the corpses sprawled on the rocky floor. "Why do they always attack?" he asked.

Connor's mouth twisted in a wry, mirthless smile. "What do you expect them to do? We walk in here, charge them with a crime they know full well they committed, and then demand their surrender. It's either kill us or go to the gallows."

Eric looked resigned. "I guess I don't expect any different. But we have to try. It's what we've been charged to do. And maybe these goblins didn't have anything to do with Westhaven."

Connor shook his head. These people were so bent on doing the "right thing". Out here in the wilderness, "right" was whoever had the better weapons and greater skill. It was a simple and regrettable fact of life.

Connor said as much to the others.

Megan turned thoughtful eyes to him. "These goblins believed in might making right, and look what it got the people of Westhaven. If we start thinking like that, then we've given up and become just like the Ja'al."

Connor sighed. *Naive, just plain naive. These guys are going to get skewered by someone they let live out of mercy.*

He looked at Buck, who shrugged. The two of them tried to join forces and convince the others to attack right away instead of parlaying. However,

Andyn and Brandi, both well-versed in philosophy and their religions, only firmed the resolve of the others. They simply refused an all-out assault, at least until, in Brandi's words "we have enough dealings with them to realize when they want to surrender and when they don't."

Buck and I are outnumbered worse than by the goblins we keep running into.

Connor turned to Brandi and held out his hands. "I just think it's crazy to risk our lives trying to do things exactly right."

Andyn smiled. "And yet we are working for the side of the right, aren't we Connor? Shouldn't we try to do the right thing? The goblins do have a chance to surrender, and they won't go to the gallows for something they didn't do."

Connor suddenly realized how ridiculous it was for them to be arguing philosophy in the middle of a goblin stronghold.

He laughed. "There's no convincing you people. We'll probably all get killed while we're debating this."

"Hey!" came Dar's whisper from the left doorway. "We have visitors."

"Here too!" said Brandi.

Eric readied his bow and walked to Dar's position, beckoning to Megan. "Megan, come on with me and Connor. Buck, go with Andyn and help Brandi."

Connor nocked an arrow and slipped in next to Dar. He peered down the passageway. He blinked and shifted his concentration to pick up heat outlines, but only grey stone stared back at him.

Dar stood above him, arrow aimed. Connor looked up at him.

"Are you sure you saw something?"

Dar shook his head. "Heard, not saw."

Connor turned back to the passage just as an arrow hummed down it and shot past his right leg. Startled, he almost dropped his own bow. He recovered in time to get off a hasty shot at five hulking figures advancing down the corridor.

Where the hell did they come from?

Dar and Eric let fly. Connor heard Buck and Brandi's bows twanging from the other passage.

The figures down the hallway advanced in good order. They pressed against the stone walls to make smaller targets, waited for the arrows to sing past, then advanced again. Three of them provided cover fire as the other two marched forward.

An arrow clattered against the stone floor next to Connor. He fired his own shaft, missed, then watched as the front pair covered the other three.

Connor's mouth went dry. These had more discipline and order than goblins—and used their bows better.

He loosed another arrow, then heard a short word from Megan. Three glowing darts zipped out over his head. They tracked to their targets, striking the figures with sharp bangs. The creatures let out ululating hooting sounds.

The hair stood out on the back of Connor's neck. His father had told him of creatures that made that sound: *Gar-Hudu*, or Iron Brutes. Humans called them hobgoblins.

Eric muttered under his breath. "Okay everyone, hold your fire until they're really close."

"They're close enough to suit me, thanks," Connor muttered back. He put his bow away and drew his sword, stepping next to Dar's legs behind the covering stone of the wall. A pair of arrows skipped past him on the rocky floor.

He gritted his teeth. *Iron Ones. Great. Even grand-da had a lot to say about these bastards, and none of it good.*

He gripped his sword tighter and forced himself to remain calm. *Remember your training. Be silent, be wary.*

"Now!" shouted Eric and he and Dar fired. Connor heard a scream from the passage and another chorus of hooting, then the rush of booted feet. Megan leaped backward into the chamber, saying another word as she pointed the wand at the passageway. Two darts of fire shot out. There were two bangs and a large body fell into the room.

Gar-Hudu. Hill-breakers and Burners of Flesh.

Connor's heart leaped into his throat and he froze, staring at the body. It looked like a very large goblin, with more angular facial features than its smaller cousins and a head topped by longer white horns.

Dar and Eric jumped back as well, drawing sword and spear. Connor froze in place as three more Gar-Hudu burst into the room. They wielded large clubs and carried shields, short bows slung over their backs. With a flurry of blows, they drove Dar and Eric back and broke Eric's spear. He cursed and drew his sword.

As soon as the hobgoblins passed, Connor darted around behind them. He raised his sword two-handed and drove it into the back of the largest one.

The point of his blade ripped through scaled armor. The Gar-Hudu gave a rasping cough and fell forward, taking Connor with him. The halfling stumbled forward, almost losing his sword. He had to turn his lurch into a short hop to keep his grip.

His sword was stuck. Connor tugged at it, desperate to get it free before one of the others noticed him.

A motion on his left made him turn, grabbing for his boot dagger.

Hobgoblin eyes flared red. A warrior swung a club at him. Connor tried to dodge, but took the weapon full in the midsection. The wind shot from his lungs with a woof and colored lights burst in his brain. He had a sensation of falling, then hit stone with a bruising thud. He heard dim shouts and a loud clang, then a pair of bestial shrieks.

He sat up, trying to get his breath back, fighting for air.

Got to get the sword out. Why? Don't remember. Get the sword.

He locked his mind on the thought of getting his blade and regained some of his breath, coming up on one knee. The planet spun and he steadied himself against the floor with his free hand. His other hand, for some reason, held a dagger. He closed his eyes.

I have never been hit so hard in my life.

About ten years later in his woozy reckoning, a strong hand grasped his shoulder. He heard Buck's voice. With detachment, he noticed that the clanging and screaming had stopped.

"Wow! He really took a hit, didn't he?"

A gentler set of hands now lay on his head and he heard Andyn.

"Come on, you idiots, give him some room."

He tried to sit up but those gentle hands pressed him back and a pleasant warmth filled his head, chest, and torso. The warmth melted away pain, making him feel strong, healthy, and rested. Then it vanished and he blinked.

A sea of solicitous faces greeted him.

He felt like he had just had six hours of sleep. He nodded. "Much better, thanks. I'm okay now."

Andyn smiled.

"Damn!" called Buck's voice. "There's a whole army of them!"

Connor scrambled for his bow and slid next to Buck. Sure enough, he could hear the pounding of many booted feet. He concentrated his heat-vision down the passage and gasped. There were at least twenty Gar-Hudu pelting down at them. Even as he watched, half of them knelt, drawing back bows.

"Get down!" He jumped to the side. A hail of arrows sang down the passage, most clattering on the stone floor. Buck ducked behind his shield, two arrows quivering in the wood.

Connor dared another peek. One of the hobgoblins reached back and threw a glittering object.

He and Buck leaped out of the way. With a sharp crash, a flaming pool of oil burst through the opening, flames licking at them.

"Damn!" Buck said, beating out a small fire on his cloak. "They learn fast!"

Eric grabbed a flask of oil from his belt pouch and tossed it into the flames, causing a roaring conflagration.

"This way!" he called. "I bought us some time!" He headed down the other passage.

The others hustled after him. The tunnel twisted left and right, past other openings. Connor tried to commit the path to memory, wondering where they were going. Eric kept his eyes on the ground as they trotted along. Dar watched ahead, bow and arrow at the ready.

The walls became rougher and tighter. Connor felt his stomach tighten with them.

What the hell is he doing? We don't know our way around in here!

"Here!" Eric ducked through an opening at the end of the passage.

Connor followed and almost stumbled over a pile of skulls. He stepped to the side and waited for everyone else to enter, eyeing the leering crania.

Connor scanned the area. Smooth walls arched overhead, worn with age and decorated in places by faded carvings. About ten feet wide and three times as long, it led to a blank wall at the end.

No goblin hands fashioned this place, I'll bet my last copper.

"What the hell's the matter with you?" asked Buck, grabbing Eric by the arm. "We have no idea where we are!"

Eric waved him to silence, watching through the opening for pursuit. "I chose the pathways with the least amount of tracks. We can hide here until they pass us by. Those monkey men don't come here, I'm sure of it."

"You're guessing," said Buck.

Andyn pointed at the brace of shriveled heads attached to a wooden wheel. "I agree. See that pile of skulls and this amulet here? They're shamanistic warding totems. They're a warning to the tribe and supposed to keep danger away."

Megan cleared her throat. "Danger? What danger would the hobgoblins be afraid of?"

Connor stared at the totems and the pile of skulls, feeling his pulse thud in his chest. The shrunken heads seemed to mock him. Dead eyes beckoned him to join them. His skin crawled.

He tugged Buck's sleeve. "We've got to get out of here. What do you say we just head on back and try to go around them?"

"Great idea." Buck nodded, wide-eyed. Beads of sweat glistened on his forehead. "But those hobgoblins are probably right on top of us now."

Connor shot Eric an acid look. "This whole place is a trap," he said through gritted teeth.

They turned their attention to the exit, watching and listening. Still no Gar-Hudu assailed them. Dar wiped his forehead and glanced at Megan.

Then they heard it. A steady pounding noise, like that of many hammers striking rock, accompanied by low chanting. Connor felt the wall next to him.

It vibrated.

Andyn's pretty face turned the color of ash. "They're trying to cave in the passage."

"Follow me!" shouted Buck, lifting his shield up in front of him. "We can take them out while they're still pounding the walls!" He charged into the passage.

Dar and Eric quickly followed, Connor on their heels. The two bigger men in front of him suddenly halted. He heard Buck shouting and had to run back to the women to avoid getting trampled.

"Have you all gone mad?!" he screamed.

The sound of shattering glass echoed back at them and flame roared in the passage.

Connor gulped. "Oh," he said in a weak voice. *Why didn't we realize they'd do that?*

"Damn, damn, damn," muttered Buck, shielding his eyes from the inferno in the tunnel.

Then, a sound echoed through the tunnel: a low rumble building into a deafening roar. They scrambled back just as a cloud of suffocating dust billowed back at them. The thundering of rock faded, leaving only the dull thump of a few laggard stones.

Somehow, the fine-carved passage stood firm. The dust finally thinned.

Dar confirmed their unspoken fears with a quick foray into the passage.

"Well?" asked Eric. Dar shook his head. The companions sat in silence for a while, watching the dust motes sift down to the floor, sparkling in their torchlight.

Andyn looked down the passage at the end. "What about..."

"Dead end," said Connor. "Doesn't go anywhere."

He flicked a pebble.

Megan sighed, then stood, brushing off her robes and cloak. "Well, I know you guys think I'm crazy for always suggesting this, but I'm going down to see if there's a way out of here."

"You really think that leads anywhere?" Buck asked. "Besides, I'm not ready to go after anything that could scare the pants off all those hobgoblins."

Megan shook her head. "No other options, Buck. I, for one, don't want to just wait here until I starve or suffocate. I'd rather go out fighting."

Connor watched her stride down the passageway and stood. "Might as well," he told Buck. "One way or the other, it'll be decided for us pretty soon."

In a sour mood, he followed Megan to the dead end. A few seconds later, he heard the others following them. He and Megan stopped about ten feet from the end.

He inspected the walls with a critical eye. Worn bas-reliefs depicted a dwarven priest holding his hands out, eyes lowered to the ground. Faded carvings surrounded the figure.

So... dwarves built this place. Or, at least, this part of it.

Something on the floor caught his eye and he knelt down, brushing dirt off a crusty brown dust, caked on the floor near the bas-reliefs.

He showed it to the others. Andyn knelt down next to him and sifted the dirt and brown dust with her gloved hand, picking out a few blackened bits of hard material that showed up bone-white when she rubbed them a little. Her face a shade paler, she looked up at Brandi.

"Dried blood and scorched bone fragments," the priestess said, casting her eyes to the walls nearby. "And more than a little bit."

"Let's hope it's from goblins," added Dar, doing the same.

Connor straightened and turned his eyes to the letters etched around the priestly figures. The others joined him.

Megan pursed her lip. "Dwarven script?"

Brandi nodded. "Religious text. What do you think, Andyn?"

Andyn took some time to read the symbols. "I think it's a plea for protection addressed to Kurental. It also calls down a terrible fate for evildoers who dare disturb this place."

"Oh great," Connor muttered. "Well, we know why the hobgoblins didn't like it here. We can't go that way."

"Wait a minute," said Brandi, holding up a hand. "We're not evildoers. Kurental is a benevolent figure. Just after the Skyfire, when Christianity came to the Lands, they helped protect the first converts against some of the other religions. The church is friendly to both Christianity and Verian. I don't think there's any danger to us."

Andyn perused the faded runes again. "Well, the way it's worded, it could be translated as 'those who do evil disturbing this place'. In other words, it could mean that if we disturb the place, we're evildoers by definition."

The silence was more deafening than the recent cave-in.

Brandi shook her head. "I've met dwarven priests before," she said. "They've never been judgmental like that. I say it's okay."

She stepped forward before anyone could grab her. A pale blue light swept across her from three sides and she froze. With a last, bright flare, the light snapped off.

Connor didn't dare breathe. She stood frozen in place.

"Brandi?" asked Eric.

"I'm okay, I'm okay."

The group relaxed. Brandi turned around, eyes scanning the walls and ceiling. "Nothing happened to me."

Dar stepped next to her. The blue light appeared again with the same results. He shrugged and beckoned the rest of them closer.

"I don't know exactly why this would frighten hobgoblins, but at least it's benign to us."

Connor privately wondered about that. He watched as the others inspected the walls, running their fingers over the stone.

Finally, Andyn gasped and held up her hand, looking at a corner of the wall and moving her hand slowly in a circle. She pointed to a squarish protrusion of rock about two feet over her head.

"There," she said. "It's up so high, the goblins never would have found it. I can feel an air draft around the edges."

"Well, none of us can reach it either," noted Buck sourly.

Connor made a face. "Are you sure we even want to fool with it?"

Dar shrugged. "It's either that or wait here until we run out of food and water. Connor, why don't you go up and take a look?"

With a sigh of resignation, he clambered up the wall, using the rough little shelves and cracks as hand- and footholds.

He examined the protrusion. *A mechanism all right. Is it a gear, dial, cam, or lever? Hello, what's this?*

A tiny blue jewel glowed in the ceiling next to the square stone protrusion. He inspected it for a minute, puzzled. What did this mean? Was it the source of the blue light?

With a shrug, he finally turned back to the protrusion.

I'll have this figured out in a second. Simple little mechanical thing.

The second turned out to be several minutes. Even then, after much probing and poking, he managed to upgrade it from simple to diabolical. His leg muscles burned from having to stay on two narrow footholds. He tried pressing down, lifting, turning, rotating and every other combination.

Dar's voice floated up. "How's it coming?"

"Marvelous," he hissed through clenched teeth, trying once again to shift the stone upwards.

Now Megan's voice. "Is there anything we can do to help?"

"No," he grunted, pulling down on the protrusion. *Damn dwarves probably made this thing just to torment intruders. Can't do anything simple, can they?*

His vicious mood rapidly replaced the wonder of finding a dwarven contraption.

Andyn spoke, sounding disappointed and guilty. "Maybe this wasn't such

150

a great idea."

That's it!

"Look!" he snapped, "I didn't climb all the way up this stupid wall just to give up on the damn thing. Now be quiet and let me do my job!"

He punched the rock with the side of his fist.

With a groaning sound, the wall gave way and blackness yawned in front of him.

For the second time that day, Connor Lomin flew through the air.

Chapter Eleven- The Path of Peace

I hate the underground... Brandi griped.

"Are you sure about this?" she asked, ducking under a stalactite.

Connor shrugged, poring over his map. "We can't go back but I know the hobgoblins didn't get into this place. It's a sure bet they didn't find the secret door and this is a natural cave system. It probably was connected with the dwarves who built this place a long time ago."

He added a few lines to the map with a charcoal pencil, tapping the side of his jaw as he thought. Torchlight reflected off the lumpy stone walls, framing the profile of his face.

Brandi watched Eric examine a tall, sparkling rock formation. He ran a gloved hand over the surface. Dar knelt down next to him, eyes flickering over the slim, worn pathway through the center of the cave.

She leaned against a stalagmite. After reviving Connor from his fall through the secret passage, they paused to discuss their next move. They had no choice but to go forward and hope that they could find a way back to the surface. Any ideas of finding the leader of the goblin force vanished in favor of survival. Each of their backpacks held two full waterskins and about three days worth of rations so they didn't exactly have the luxury of time. Despite the fact that halflings lived at least part of their lives underground, Connor told them he only knew a minimum about how to survive in such a place as these natural caverns.

At least water isn't scarce... yet.

They found trickling little rivulets at intervals in the caverns.

Buck had opined sourly that this set of caverns probably led to an even worse place, but Brandi disagreed. Connor's discovery of the tiny blue gems near the Kurental carvings confirmed this place was special to whichever dwarves had originally crafted it. She suspected that hobgoblins had found the entrance, but were destroyed by a magic spell set to ward off intruders. Then the hobgoblin leaders, anxious to avoid losing more warriors, declared the area off-limits and set up the totems.

Brandi took a swig from her waterskin and capped it, letting it swing by her side.

But what is this place? And why was it guarded? She tried to ignore the knot in her stomach.

They couldn't afford mistakes. Already they had to backtrack three times due to dead ends and precipitous drop-offs. She was very glad Connor kept meticulous notes on his map. At least they weren't going to get lost.

She jerked her thoughts back to the present and sighed. *Escape from the dragon and meet the daemon. God, where is this all going to lead?*

Dar stood and brushed his hands together. "Let's get going," he announced, leading them towards a narrow passage.

"To where?" muttered Buck to no one in particular. Eric clapped him on the shoulder and tramped off after Dar.

Brandi picked up her bow and followed the others, joining the single-file line. If this really was part of the old dwarven mine, it sure was tiring and boring. So far, since Connor's fall through the secret door, they had trudged for what seemed like hours.

Her legs and arms ached. Dirt and dust covered her gloves and cloak from clambering over rocks and squeezing through tight spots.

She took her place behind Connor and in front of Megan, following a bobbing torch light. Soon, a rough, sloping rock tube closed in around her, wet with moisture and adorned with furry mold in places. Brandi eyed the walls with suspicion, very much aware they slipped through skinny little cracks in the earth with tons of rock suspended over their heads.

Ducking under a low roof, she emerged in a very tall passage, one so high that darkness swathed the ceiling. Dar's torchlight up ahead and Buck's from behind her cast capering, gamboling shadows around her.

She shuddered. In her classes at the Academy and the Seminary, Brandi had listened to tales of vile beasts that ambushed travelers underground. Some snared their victims with cords of silvery thread, pulling them to a horrible death. She had heard of pony-sized spiders that simply dropped down on their victims, slaying them with a single venomous bite, and of ravenous, acidic slime-creatures, and shadowy wraiths with glowing, raging eyes or—

Lord, I promise, if you get me out of this one, I'll never complain again about not having any money or having to travel all the time or not having nice things of my own.

With a mental sigh of relief, she followed the others into a narrower but shorter passage. It reached down at a steep angle after a while, making her and the others take careful steps down a natural "staircase". Eric looked back and up at her, flashing his trademark smile.

She smiled back and waved to show him everything was all right. She watched him turn down the passage, feeling a momentary pang of sadness and... jealousy? She had debated her feelings before, trying to figure out why she cared so much that Eric was courting Elaine.

She gave her head a vexed shake.

Hell, she thought a little glumly, *I don't even own a dress, for crying out loud. Eric probably sees what everyone else sees when they look at me. Next to Elaine, I'm kind of rough and unpolished.*

Even as she thought it, she smiled to herself. Daphne had even told her one time: don't be so serious. Life isn't meant to be grim or a drudgery.

Maybe if I asked Megan...

She smiled again, this time at the idea of Megan's help in attracting Eric's attention. Pretty dresses and courtly ways took second place to sword practice, archery, and healcraft. It was the price she paid.

Dar's torch carved a yellow arc of fire twice in the blackness, their signal for a chamber up ahead. Brandi lifted the bow off her back and selected an arrow.

I've got a few more important things to worry about right now, like how to keep something in this God-forsaken hole from making me into a wall trophy.

Dar's light darted forward, followed by a rush of footsteps. With long strides, she followed Connor into the chamber.

She gasped.

A towering ceiling spired up some fifty feet overhead to a cluster of delicate stalactites. Luminescent mold on the walls glowed light green. Crowds of small bats clung to the roof in dark galleries, like tiny spectators in a gargantuan theater. Crystalline formations along the walls met their torchlight, spraying rainbow fire in all directions.

Brandi stepped farther into the cavern, eyes wide. Sparkling dots of light sprinkled the stalagmites, making them seem like miniature towers with lighted rooms. At the far end of the chamber a large pool glimmered, fed by the gentle gurgling of a tiny waterfall. A veil of steam swathed the surface of the water.

A hot spring.

Scattered in random places in the cavern, mushrooms stood in clumps. Some of them towered over Connor, their spongy surfaces striped in purple, yellow, and orange or spotted with dark red. To the right of the pond, a ten-foot-high opening beckoned them onward.

"I was right," said Megan in an awed voice. "A Path of Peace."

"A what?" asked Dar. "What are you talking about?"

"*Kyliathuaten* in Dwarven," Connor answered. "Peaceful pathway, though I'm not sure how Megan knows about it."

"From the colleges," Andyn interjected, stepping over a delicate-looking stone formation. "I remember something about this from a lecture I heard. Dwarves use played-out sections of their mines as living quarters for the workers as they dig farther into the stone. Since they have to have recreational areas too, they also reserve paths through the most beautiful caverns. Workers, guards, and the clerics of Kurental take walks in the Kyliathuaten as a form of recreation or meditation when off-duty. It's a sacred place to them, from what I remember."

Megan nodded, eyes still wandering over the wonders in the cavern. "I figured that the Kurental carvings back at the secret passage meant that this was somewhere special. I'm not so sure all passages in a dwarf mine connect together, but this means we're on the right track. It'll come out in a more developed area soon, I'm sure of it. We can find our way out then."

"Not bad, eh?" Connor grinned at Brandi.

She nodded. Now she understood the hidden message from the dwarven patriarchs and matriarchs to their people: By toiling through adversity and tedium, one can arrive at a place of peace and beauty.

"It's beautiful," Brandi whispered, looking around the cavern with shining eyes. "How old is it?"

Connor shrugged. "Not sure. Dwarves live for about two hundred and fifty years or so, but this place could be many hundreds. It takes a bit of skill to find the right place and make it like this."

Brandi shook her head. It amazed her: this place of fantastic beauty, hidden in a long-lost dwarven mine, waiting for someone to enter with bright light and awaken its splendor.

Buck grunted. "This is great, but how do we know it's part of this path of peace thing? How do we know the dwarves didn't set up that magical trap at the door to keep something dangerous inside?"

Brandi shook her head again. "I can't believe that something this gorgeous is the hiding place of evil. I've got to believe it's part of the mines."

"Come on!" Eric said, waving. He spun around while walking, his face shining with wonder and curiosity. They followed him towards the pond.

"This is great!" he announced, his voice echoing in the chamber.

"Not so loud," warned Buck, his eyes watching the shadows. He paid particular attention to the dark opening by the pond. "We don't know what else is in here. Or out there."

"Geez Buck," said Eric, waving his hand. "We've been traveling for hours, right? Haven't run into anything yet."

He leaned his spear against an outcropping of rock next to the pond and held out his hand. "Here, Connor, let me see the map."

Connor handed the parchment to him, looking around all the while. "Buck's right. Don't you think we ought to give this place a closer look?"

Eric turned his eyes to the map. "There's no one here but us."

He looked up and smiled.

Two dark green clumps of four-legged flesh slammed into him and hurled him to the side.

The group gaped in shock. Frogs crouched on Eric's chest, each one two feet long and armed with teeth and claws. They opened their mouths and hissed.

Dear God! Brandi's mind screamed. *What are they?*

Eric yelled in delayed surprise, bucking, rolling and throwing the two frogs from his torso. They bounded into the pool with a splash and a shower of water, then just as quickly bounded out again. All hell broke loose as a swarm of fanged amphibians leaped at them from all directions.

Brandi raised her bow. A sharp pain struck her left arm and she yelped, dropping the weapon. An attacking frog landed in front of her, spitting and slobbering.

Brandi ducked a leaping frog from her left, whipping out her swords and slashing at the one in front of her. With amazing speed, it dodged, then attacked in a whirlwind of ivory needle-teeth and claws. She stepped back behind a stalactite.

Her amphibian assailant jumped again and bounced off the rocky surface. She took a long step to Eric's side. He held his longsword in front of him.

"You okay?" she called to him over the hissing, clanging of weapons and an occasional yell.

Eric's eyes locked on the four frogs crouched in front of them. They drooled and licked their lips, a weird intelligence evident in their glowing blue eyes. Thin limbs quivered in frenzied anticipation.

"Yeah," he answered, "what are they?"

In answer, their four opponents leaped. Brandi dodged one and impaled the second with her left-hand blade. The thing shrieked, flailing about spasmodically. She shook it free.

Before she could turn around, a sharp pain seared across her right calf and she cried out. A frog clung to her boot and leg armor, digging away with sharp talons.

Furious, Brandi plunged both swords into the beast. It gurgled and let go.

A sound made her whip her head around. Almost in slow motion, a frog hurtled at her face through the air. She started to duck, but a longsword blade swept across, cutting the frog in half and showering her with green ichor and steaming slime. Eric didn't even spare the corpse a second glance, turning away from her to guard the opposite direction.

She stumbled back and took a ready stance, looking for more of the things.

The waterfall gurgled gently.

"Dar?" she called out in a loud whisper. "Meg? Andyn?"

She heard a moan and a curse from a large rock in front of her and

Connor dragged himself out from behind it. He looked more irritated than hurt, untangling the remains of a frog from his cloak and casting them down with an oath. Buck stepped out from behind a stalactite. Brandi saw the others emerging from defense points.

Megan trembled as she sat down next to the pond. She had a slim red line along the base of her neck, just above her collarbone.

"What were those things?" she asked, wide-eyed. She felt her injury and stared at her bloodied hand.

"I don't know. How is everyone?" Brandi sheathed her left-hand sword. Still watching the shadows, she made her way to where the others clustered together next to Megan.

Dar eyed the room around him. "Demon frogs..." he said, his voice a little shaky.

Brandi put her other weapon away and got her healer's kit from her backpack, kneeling down in front of Megan and Buck, who seemed to have gotten the worst of it.

A little blindwort extract, I think.

Megan's wound wasn't serious, but it could have been. Brandi applied salve on her sister's injury. "You ninny," she chided, "an inch deeper and two up and you'd be in real trouble."

Megan winced as the medicine took effect. "Thanks. I'll remember to ask them not to attack me next time."

Brandi bit off a retort and pulled a bandage from her healer's kit. She wrapped the wound and asked a question to keep her mind busy. "Anyone know what were those things?"

Connor wiped frog-slime off his sword. "I think they're called *sluuthgha* in dwarven. I could be wrong, but it seems to fit. That means killing frog or assassin frog."

Megan shuddered and felt the bandage around her throat. "Whatever they are, they're horrible. Like little devil toads."

Brandi knelt down in front of Buck, rummaging in her healer's kit for a different salve.

Eric squatted next to her. "I should have been more careful," he said.

She stopped her searching to look up at him. "Nobody's perfect, Eric. We all should have been a lot more careful. Besides, we're okay now."

Eric nodded and sighed. "Still feel guilty."

She patted his arm. "Remember that when one of us does something wrong."

She examined Buck's face and arm injuries. The lanky warrior sighed in exasperation, but submitted to her attention.

Brandi smiled. *Healers are a nuisance until death knocks and then everyone loves us.*

From the pool's edge, Andyn gave an excited shout. "Look at that!"

"Shh!" Buck hissed. He lifted his arm, disrupting Brandi's attempt to wind a bandage on it. "That's how we got in trouble in the first...Ow!"

Brandi slapped his hand and gave him a look. "Don't fidget. I can't tie a bandage if you're waving it around like that."

He looked surly but only muttered to himself. She finished with Buck, then turned her attention to her right calf. The frog had gotten a couple of good licks in, but her chainmail extended down to her ankles.

Now if only they're not poisonous or diseased, we should come out of this just fine.

She joined the others near Andyn at the edge of the pond. Tiny pale fish swirled around twisted stone formations in the clear water. At the bottom, some twelve feet down, a collection of bones showed dirty white against the dark grey of the stones. In the midst of them, clearly visible, lay a box-shaped item.

"My swimming skills are mediocre at best," Dar said.

"What about you, Connor?" asked Eric.

The halfling shrugged. "I could, but I'm not that good."

Andyn knelt down, pulling off her gloves. She ran a hand into the water and tasted it, then smiled. "Don't worry about it. It's warm and tastes fine. I can go in there after it. I grew up in a seaport, remember?"

Megan cocked her head to one side. "Frogs swim too."

Andyn shrugged. "I'm sure we got all of them. Besides, there's nothing there except the bones and a few fish."

Brandi looked again. There didn't appear to be any hiding places, at least not the size that the frogs could have used. "Okay," she agreed.

Andyn smiled and undid her cloak, then reached for the straps on her armor. Brandi turned to an amused set of men behind her. They looked back at her in complete innocence, as if seeing a woman disrobe in front of them was the most normal thing in the world.

She made a circle in the air with her forefinger. "About face, gentlemen."

Dar's eyes were wide and guileless. "What for? We can ..."

"Now!" Brandi froze him with a look.

"Yes ma'am."

Eric grinned. "Oh, now, come on, Brandi. Surely you don't mean..."

She raised one eyebrow. He swallowed, then looked at Buck and Connor. The other men shrugged and they all turned around.

Just like adolescents, Brandi mused. Satisfied that none of the men could see Andyn, she turned around, ignoring their whispered wisecracks and muted laughter.

Andyn pulled her shift over her head, revealing a smooth, lightly-tanned body. Judging from her muscle tone, priestess training included physical conditioning.

Brandi blinked. *We hardly know the girl and already she's taken all her clothes off in front of us. I thought she would at least keep her shift on...*

Andyn winked at the sisters, stuck her tongue out at the men's backs, and slipped into the water with a small splash.

I know followers of Verian are a bit uninhibited, but...

Brandi looked at Megan, who shrugged.

The sisters watched her from the surface. Soon, Andyn swam back with the box, surfacing with a mere ripple. She treaded water, easily maintaining her position with powerful, smooth kicks.

Brandi took the box from her and inspected it as Megan handed Andyn a couple of cloaks and her clothing.

The box and its lock were both rusted, but Brandi left it alone. Traps, in particular magical ones, didn't care about their environment, so a little water might not matter.

"Okay," said Andyn, fitting the clasp on her cloak. Fully dressed in her armor, she acted as if a skinny-dip in a cave-pond was the most natural thing in the world. She stamped her feet in her boots and began wringing water out of her hair.

The men turned around and rejoined the women.

Brandi set the box down on the stone floor and Connor pounced on it. He turned it over, whispering to himself about retainers, spring coefficients, and properties of metals. Brandi thought he had forgotten about the rest of them. She was going to tap him on the shoulder when he spoke aloud.

"It's clean. I think."

He tinkered with the lock. A metallic clink echoed in the cavern. He opened it.

Brandi's eyes grew wider. Gems and a slim, ivory-colored tube lay on a pile of gold coins. In all, they counted up fifty gold crowns, three very good garnets, and the bone tube.

Holding the tube in her gloved hands, Brandi turned it over and over. She noted with interest and growing apprehension at the series of cursive script and angular, odd-shaped symbols etched in pink, red and purple on the surface. Two black tassels hung from the caps on either end, and whole thing seemed to shine with a translucent aura. She wagered it would glow in full darkness.

She felt a vague uneasiness. She would bet her swords the symbols were protective runes, and she wasn't powerful enough to erase them. She wouldn't even know where to begin. Judging from the whispered discussion between Eric, Andyn and Megan, neither did they.

"Well?" she asked.

Eric shook his head. "I don't have a clue. Those symbols make me nervous. Maybe we'd better hold onto it and see if Lady Ellen can help us out."

Brandi placed the tube in a sack and wrapped it, then put it in her backpack, cushioned by a coil of rope and an extra cloak.

"Let's get moving. There might be worse things in here," came Buck's impatient whisper. He crouched at the exit next to the pond. "Eric, give me the map."

Eric patted his tunic, looked in his belt purse, then blanched. "Where's the map?"

Andyn's eyes widened. "What happened to the map?"

"This," said Dar, making a disgusted face. He held up a tattered and muddy piece of what had once been parchment.

Brandi swallowed hard. The walls seemed to close in around her.

Buck brushed off his trousers. "Nice going, Eric. Maybe we'd better go back to where the hobgoblins penned us in and start digging, 'cause we're sure not finding our way out of here without a map."

"Buck!" said Megan.

Eric leaned back against a stalagmite and stared at the darkness above.

"Dar," said Megan, turning to the dark-haired scout. "It isn't that bad, is it?"

Dar ran a hand through his hair. "I don't know Megan. If this passage leads to a dead-end, I suppose Eric and I could find our tracks to go back to the place where we branched off. But I'm used to tracking outdoors in the daylight, not underground in the dark."

There was silence. Andyn put her hands on her hips. "You can't be serious. You mean we're lost?"

Dar nodded. Connor threw up his hands.

Brandi set her mouth in a firm line and walked up to Eric. She gripped his shoulder and turned to the others.

"All right everyone," she said in her most commanding voice. They all looked at her, even Eric.

"Eric," she continued, "I know you think this is all your fault, but you can't blame yourself. The area looked good to all of us and no one saw the frogs coming. We're all to blame. If it had been anyone else but you, you'd be here trying to cheer them up, wouldn't you?"

Eric looked at her for a long moment, then nodded. "Yes, I would. Still feels bad to be the reason we're lost."

She gave an exasperated sigh. "The reason we're lost is that we didn't take the time to check out the area, not because you happened to be holding the map."

Dar chuckled. She turned and looked at all of them. "I know we have no way to work our way back if we get lost, but we can start another map. Let's just keep going forward until we have to make a choice and take it from there. I know we have no idea what lies ahead. But we have each other, we have two trackers, and we're not dead yet."

"We also have no choice," noted Buck with a sour look.

She met his eyes. "Yes, we do. We can stick together. We can work together. And we can persevere. I know you don't believe in my God, but I do, and I know He won't let me down."

Buck looked down at Connor, who shrugged and gave a small smile.

"What the hell," Buck said, settling his backpack. "No one lives forever. Big wide unknown out there and here we stand arguing."

Dar stepped forward next to Brandi and clapped her on the shoulder. "I'm glad someone here still has their head on straight."

Brandi smiled her thanks and looked into Eric's eyes. "Okay? Let's do the best we can."

He nodded and joined the group, heading towards the exit.

She gave one final look at the cavern as they left, torchlight casting flickering shadows among the beautiful colors. It didn't seem quite so pretty any more.

The Path of Peace plunged into darkness behind her.

Chapter Twelve- Khelios

Kalar Cintos wrapped his cloak around him, feeling the wind ruffle his hair under the back of his helmet. He rested his black stallion and put gloved hands on the pommel. A thin ribbon of black figures moved in orderly fashion along the curve of the slope below him, heading south and east towards Forester. He counted three goblin tribal standards and about twenty horsemen.

Hanford was going to have his hands full. That column was part of a little "present" for him, and Kalar smirked.

And it isn't even their biggest problem. While he's dealing with our forces, we'll be securing the Black Legion.

Kalar shifted in the saddle with a creak of leather. Despite his feigned skepticism in Halkith's receiving chamber, he knew there was a very good chance the cleric would succeed. If he did, the Dark Rider would have the potent weapon she desired to use against Deran—and the Ja'al would have a powerful ally. She would aid them in further conquests along the frontier and, if she didn't, well there was more than one way to handle the Dark Rider..

Kalar frowned. It was a rosy outlook, except for recent trouble at the remote bases: attacks by free-lancers, maybe in the employ of Hanford, maybe on their own, but blank shields nonetheless. Soldiers were one thing, but the advanced training and magic-use of mercenary free-lances presented different problems altogether.

He knew that the High Command employed mercenaries, including Kalar himself. Fortunately for the Ja'al, there were many who took the free-lance who had no scruples about whoever paid them. Unfortunately, Deran's extensive universities produced many willing followers of the Irial, Verian, Kurental and Christian churches.

Kalar shrugged. An inexperienced group of newly-minted blank-shields, no doubt. They were Halkith's problem.

"Ready the troop," he said to his sergeant.

The hobgoblin at his side saluted, then growled an order. Among the trees, ten more hobgoblins stood at attention, awaiting his order to move out. They raised halberds to their shoulders and Kalar spurred his mount forward.

Time would tell. The next few days were going to be very amusing. And if Halkith could pull it off, they would also very profitable for the Ja'al.

***

Megan Alenar pressed herself against the rough wall, feeling the rock against her shoulder and trying to see ahead by the light of Dar's torch. Connor scouted the next chamber as the rest of the group crouched down in the tunnel.

I'd go completely insane if it was me out there, all by myself. What if something happened and we couldn't help?

She took a slow breath. *We've got to find a way out soon. We're running out of torches.*

Her mind spun a little at the thought. That meant they would soon need to use magic to create light for the humans to see. Just thinking of it made her tired. The longer she went without comfortable, uninterrupted sleep, the harder she found it to concentrate. That, in turn, made it more and more difficult to cast her spells or even remember the magical patterns that would loose the energy from within her—and it gave her a headache.

She felt the curious warmth of the little wand behind her belt, the prize of their battle with that mage.

I wonder how long I can keep using it? These things have a finite number of uses, after all. Maybe Lady Ellen knows.

She thought of the scroll she suspected belonged to the Ja'al. Andyn said the bones at the bottom of the pool were human and not goblin. While not certain about the cause of death, she had said that some of the bones appeared gnawed or chewed.

Maybe a Ja'al messenger who got too curious about the pool? The frogs had teeth. That could explain the gnawed bones, but how did a Ja'al get into the Path of Peace in the first place with the Kurental warding at the entrance?

She waited, trying to ignore the growl in her stomach. Ever since they had lost the map, Dar and Eric took stock of their supplies and decided to hold off eating until one of the party felt faint. Connor protested that he had been feeling faint for quite some time, but that had no effect on their strategy. Eric whispered to Megan that Connor would be standing long after the rest of them had passed out from hunger. The hardiness of halflings was as legendary as their impressive eating abilities.

They teased Connor about his alleged starvation, but despite the momentary light mood, a persistent fear tugged at her mind.

A figure moved up ahead. Megan grabbed for her wand and then realized it was only Connor returning. He joined Dar and Eric in the front and the three shadows melted into one for a while. Then, Dar motioned to the others. Megan stepped over a rough hump of rock and followed her sister.

She knew that they meant well by keeping her in the middle of the formation, where their armor could protect her. It made tactical sense. It didn't mean she had to like it.

A square of light beckoned ahead. The last chamber they entered turned out to be the abode of a large band of cat-sized rats, and aggressive ones at that. They fended them off with fire and burning oil long enough to exit through another passageway. Then they crept through another one with all the spiderwebs, but no spiders—thankfully.

She put aside her worries and followed Brandi into the room.

A circular cavern sloped downward away from them to a round opening. She saw the source of the light in the chamber: several patches of pale, glowing mold or lichens clinging to the rock. A ledge about three feet wide ran around the edges of the room at a height of about twelve feet. The whole area measured about thirty feet across and she could barely see the shadowed ceiling above them.

Bones and a few skulls littered the dirty floor: some, only shattered fragments, some looked like those of goblins, and others like those of dwarves. Several torn and mildewed backpacks, more than a few ragged strips of cloth, and a couple of pieces of what looked like rusted chainmail lay strewn about.

The group crept in, weapons drawn and watching the round opening.

Megan cast her eyes upward, watching the ledge, but nothing flew down to assail them. She stood on tiptoe, trying to look as high as she could, then gave up.

"Looks okay," whispered Connor, heading down to the round opening. Sliding up to the side of the passage, he got down on hands and knees and peeked around the corner.

He straightened, wiping his gloves against his breeches.

"Long tunnel, rough and curving to the right a bit, but nothing in it. I've got clear sight up to about twenty paces or so."

The others relaxed visibly. Dar snuffed his torch.

Brandi nodded. "Good idea. Save the torches. Let's use the light from those lichens while we can."

Connor and Andyn began rummaging around in the bits of armor and junk, tossing pieces out at random. They blithely ignored their comrades and comparing interesting bits of flotsam.

Dar went to inspect the phosphorescent plant life and Megan joined Buck in examining the ledge.

Funny, but none of the other chambers in here had ledges.

"Any ideas?" she asked Buck.

He nodded slowly. "That ledge up there is just big enough for a halfling to walk along. Or a gnome. Or a dwarf. I think there's something up there."

Eric stepped next to them. "What makes you think so?"

Buck shrugged. "It's the perfect place for hiding. And most people don't look up when they enter an area."

Megan eyed the ledge. "If you say so, but any dwarves would have to have wings," she offered.

Eric laughed. "Winged dwarves?"

A thought came to her and she snapped her fingers. "No, not winged dwarves. But imagine you're a dwarven warrior and you're pursued by goblins or worse. You throw a rope ladder up there, with hooks on one end. Then what would you do?"

"Climb up and pull the ladder after me," answered Connor. He and Andyn joined Megan.

"Great," said Brandi, placing her swords in their scabbards. "But we don't have a ladder."

Connor grinned. "But I have something almost as good."

He removed his backpack and pulled out an object that looked like a single iron hook. As Megan watched, he picked at one side of the hook with his fingers. Another hook rotated away from the first one, then another, and another. Soon, he was holding a five-pronged grapnel instead of a hook. He slipped a retainer ring on the assembly to hold it in place and then attached a length of knotted rope.

Megan whistled. "Where did you get that?"

He shrugged. "Hey, even spies go to school, you know. One of my professors gave it to me."

Connor made them clear a space around him, then swung the device and let it fly. It soared up to the ledge, landing with a clang. The halfling pulled on the rope until the heel of the grapnel appeared over the edge. With soft tugs, he coaxed it to fall just so that three of the prongs dug into the stone ledge. He leaned back on the rope, putting his full weight on it, but it didn't budge.

Connor swarmed up the rope, stopping just short of the ledge, hanging suspended about two feet below. "Okay," he called down in a soft voice. "Keep an eye open."

He started up the rope.

An arrow whizzed past his head and he flinched, almost losing his grip. With a hissing shriek, a dark thing plummeted past him and thudded into the stones below.

Buck lowered his bow. "Just saw its eyes over the edge."

Megan looked down and shuddered. A hairy spider writhed and curled on the stone floor. It was about two feet long and dirty brown and grey.

"Good shot," murmured Dar, his own bow aimed upwards.

Connor pulled himself up, waited for a heartbeat, then, with a startling motion, grabbed the stone ledge and heaved himself up over it. Lightning quick, he landed in a crouch, his broadsword flickering out. He froze there.

Then Connor relaxed and the group heaved a collective sigh.

Why can't anything be easy? thought Megan, feeling the butterflies in her stomach settle down.

Connor disappeared for a few heartbeats, then came back bearing a long object with a strap. He held it out to them.

"Here, Buck," he called out. "Catch."

He released the object and Buck caught a sword in a filthy scabbard. Turning it in his hands, he wiped it off. He saw something and grunted, then selected one of the cleaner rags from the many on the floor and began polishing in earnest.

Buck finished by the time Connor rejoined them. Bright blue gems winked at them from the tips of the guard. A twisting pattern in alternating black and white wood curled around the handle with short, blocky runes inscribed all along the white twist. Two tiny figures of sword-wielding dwarves stood en garde on either side of the guard. Buck turned the weapon upside down, eyes widening at the two red rubies set in the pommel.

And we haven't even seen the blade yet, thought Megan. She knew little of swordsmithing, but judging by the weapons she had seen, this one was uncommonly beautiful.

They regarded it for a while in the silence.

Buck licked his lips and shot a glance at his companions. "I should probably take it out of the scabbard, right?"

Saint Michael, the fool's going to get himself killed.

"Wait!" said Megan, holding out her hand. "This could be a magic weapon and that means it could be cursed. You might end up going berserk and attacking all of us. We've got to be careful with it."

Connor nodded. "Assuming it *is* enchanted. It might not be. Could just be a very finely made sword."

Brandi peered at the symbols on the hilt. "Well, these look like markings I've seen in Kurental temples before – holy symbols actually. Andyn, do the letters look familiar?"

Buck knelt down, offering the handle of the weapon to the halfling. Andyn, instead of touching it, peered at the runes.

"No, they don't," she said. "It's not written in common Dwarven, but the runes have a similar shape. Maybe a more ancient dialect?"

"I doubt if a cursed item could hold symbols of Kurental," Brandi stated.

"We could wait until we get back to town, but I think it's okay."

"Great," said Eric, reaching for the weapon. "Let's see the rest of it."

"Excuse me!" said Buck, yanking it out of his reach. "I had the idea to go get it in the first place. I should be the one to try it first."

Eric looked at the others. Megan nodded. "He's right. It was his idea to look up there in the first place. It's only right that he gets the spoils. The next sword we find will go to Eric, deal? Unless you want it, Connor."

Connor shook his head. "The blade's too long. I'd need to train with it for a while to get used to it and even then it might be too unwieldy for me. It's better off in his hands."

Eric and Buck looked at each other for a moment, then Eric grinned and clapped him on the shoulder. "Sounds okay to me. You'd better hope it's magic, Buck."

"Humph." Buck pulled the weapon free of its sheath.

A mirror-bright blade slid out of the scabbard with a silvery ping, flaring with a golden light.

Megan stared at it, dazzled. The metal glowed with a barely perceptible flame along the edge. As she watched, the flame died down to nothing.

"It's humming," Buck whispered. His eyes took on a faraway look and actually glimmered. Megan jumped.

"Did I just see—" she started.

"Wow..." Buck breathed. "I can see letters in the air... and I know what they mean."

"Letters?" asked Brandawyn, her hand edging toward her crucifix.

"Yes," said Buck, looking down at the sword. "They're the same runes on the sword hilt."

"What do they say?" asked Brandi, still sounding very suspicious.

"All praise to Kurental, Mighty King of Earth. All his loyal servants, serve ye the holy Creator. All praise Kurental," Buck recited. Megan noticed his eyes still glimmered.

No one spoke for a while.

"It's an augmented weapon," Megan said slowly. Her companions turned inquisitive eyes to her. "It gives its bearer special abilities."

"I'm not sure I like the glowing eyes part of this," said Brandi. "Buck, can you turn off your special vision?"

Buck looked at the blade and the light in his eyes winked out. He blinked. "I guess I can."

***

Later, Megan watched Buck sitting against the wall, polishing the magic sword's scabbard. "Amazing," she commented to her sister.

Brandi smiled. "Kind of incredible. Enchanted swords are rare and especially ones with augmented powers. Let's hope he knows how to use it."

Megan chewed her lip. She recommended that Buck just take some time to just sit with the weapon and become attuned to it, which he did. After a short space, he reported that he now knew several things about the sword.

First, it had a name: Khelios Giantbane. A dwarven lady named Aalyros had it forged protect her people from giants many hundreds of years ago. Neither Megan nor Andyn could remember any mention of a Lady Aalyros from their lessons and certainly hadn't heard of any weapon named Khelios Giantbane. Of course, it could be that both were lost in antiquity.

Second, Khelios provided Buck with some rather startling abilities. Not only did the blade strike giants with extra fervor and power, but it allowed him to read, speak and write several dialects of Dwarven, including the ecclesiastical tongue of Kurental and an ancient form. In addition, it could detect evil creatures to a radius of about ten feet and could communicate this to Buck with pulses and feelings.

Megan resolved to find out as much as she could about Khelios when she had the chance. If it was the Bane of Giants, that was wonderful, but not all giants were evil - and not all dwarves and magical swords were good.

At least it has the Kurental symbols on it, she thought, rising from her seat on the cold stone floor. *Remember what Brandi said. No evil can hold Kurental's name.*

After setting up her bedroll, Megan attempted to brush some order into her hair and gave up after a few half-hearted strokes. She regarded yet another rip in her dress.

Any more of this and most of my share of the earnings is going be used for a new wardrobe.

They decided to rest in the chamber since the lichens cast enough light and they could take turns watching the exits. The mages and healers would rest first to regain their strength for spells while the others watched. Then everyone would switch places.

Andyn tapped her on the shoulder. "Do you want to turn your bedroll this way or facing the entrance?"

Megan sighed. "I guess it really doesn't matter. I'll face that way."

She fluffed out her bedding and regarded the rocky floor. Despite the dryness in her throat, she didn't dare take a drink. Every drop counted.

That familiar apprehension rose in the pit of her stomach, vying with hunger. Trapped down here without a map and wandering in a dwarven mine, the momentary wonder of finding a magic sword started to fade. If they didn't find a way out of here soon, they were going to end up just like the sword's former owner.

Fear is useless. What is needed is trust, she reminded herself.

The last thing she saw before she fell asleep was Dar keeping a watch over the exit, a pile of bones gleaming next to him in the dim light.

Chapter Thirteen- The Battle Joined

They saw smooth walls, symmetrical design, and elegant stonework over the archways at entrance and exit. Empty stone rings for torches or lanterns dotted the walls at ten foot intervals.

"Is this what we've been looking for?" Megan asked, daring to hope.

"Yes, ma'am," Connor said, a new energy in his voice. "I do believe this is it. Definitely looks like dwarven handiwork."

"Finally," Buck breathed.

"But why does it smell like cows in here?" asked Andyn, sniffing the air.

Megan wrinkled her nose. She was right, and it seemed out of place.

The companions slipped into the room. Megan eyed the exit.

Some memory from her classes at the academy tickled her mind and she shook her head. This all seemed familiar for some reason and the more she tried to remember, the more she felt apprehensive.

"I think something's in here..." she whispered.

"We know, Meg," replied Brandi in a whisper of her own.

Her sister made a slow turn, both swords drawn. Buck stepped to the side of the room with deceptive casualness.

"What do you think it is?" he asked, drawing Khelios. The blade flared, adding to the light from Dar's torch.

"Dunno," answered Eric, eyes darting everywhere, spear held in front of him. "Whatever it is, it stinks to low Hades."

"Then the Ja'al must be close," quipped Dar, inserting his torch into a stone ring in the wall and pulling out his own blade.

The clack of rock on rock sounded from the exit and Megan froze. Her nervousness turned to wild fear when she heard a snort from the exit passageway. She jumped back, aiming the wand at the opening.

A bull's head emerged from the ebony darkness of the opening, white horns gleaming orange in the light from the torch flames. The eyes narrowed, taking in all the companions in an unhurried sweep around the room.

A huge body followed the head. A shirt of worn chain armor covered the broad, human-like chest and giant breeches covered the lower torso and legs of a goat. In its human hands, the creature held a massive flail, its wicked, flanged head dull and spotted with dark brown stains in places. It clumped into the room with giant, cloven hooves of dirty white. Its horns towered some seven feet from the stone floor.

Bull-satyr...

Dar, Brandi, Buck and Eric formed a protective arc in front of Megan and Andyn. Megan looked around, but somehow, Connor had vanished from the scene.

"Ohh, boy," Megan said.

The creature snorted again. "*Raghmlurt zsluugrabf goort mriff?*"

"Oh great," said Andyn. "Does anyone speak bull-man-goat-thing?"

"Failed that class in school," Dar remarked, keeping his sword pointed at the creature.

The bull-man pricked up its ears at this exchange. It regarded them for a moment, then shook its head and snorted. With alarming suddenness, it charged, swinging.

Megan darted to the side, firing a full brace of glowing bullets with the wand as she did so. The three missiles hit the thing dead-center and exploded, blowing a few chain links off. It didn't even slow down.

Another dart screamed in from her left, but this too exploded with little effect.

Buck stepped up to block the creature's path.

What the hell is he doing?

As if this weren't enough, Dar charged with gleaming sword.

Mary, Mother of God! Now he's trying to get himself killed.

The bull-man saw Dar and changed course to attack him. Buck darted forward, swinging with Khelios. The glowing blade flashed in the dimness and they all heard an angry grunt.

Megan moved over again, trying to get a clear shot.

Their opponent sidestepped, swinging its flail at Buck. It slammed into Buck's shield. With a mighty crack, the shield burst asunder. Buck staggered backward, pieces of the ruined shield falling from his arm.

Dar took the opportunity to stab at the creature, but missed. The bull satyr's head whipped around and Dar ducked to avoid the slashing horns.

Eric's dagger thudded into the bull-man's side and it grunted again. Megan, seeing her chance, fired two more firedarts. The missiles exploded and the beast stepped back under the onslaught.

Brandi stepped in, twin swords slashing, soon joined by Buck. Both scored hits, dark gashes appearing in the enemy's leggings and armor. The bull-man bellowed and swung its flail in a wide arc, forcing them to draw back.

A humming metal bullet glanced off the thing's forehead and Megan saw Andyn next to her, sling in hand.

Where the hell is Connor?

Eric joined the fight with drawn sword. The creature kept them at bay with wide sweeps of the flail-head and sporadic goring attempts with its horns. The chamber rang with the occasional sound of steel on steel.

Then Dar and Brandi leaped forward, trying to time the swing of the flail. They only got tangled up in the weapon chain instead. Brandi lost her footing and slammed into Dar. The bull-satyr whipped its head around.

"No!" screamed Megan, heart in her throat. She fired again.

Two little comets seared in and detonated on the creature's face. It jerked its head away with a snort. Then dark shadows flashed from its blind side as Eric and Buck leaped. A small figure hurtled from the shadows and landed on the bull-man's shoulders, broadsword stabbing.

Then they became a whirlwind of flashing blades, dirty white horns, and clanging metal. Someone cursed, the mass of struggling figures thrashed and the whole group of them tottered.

Megan barely noticed Andyn next to her as she ran forward, staff in hand. The struggling fighters and their horned adversary toppled backward, landing on the floor with a huge crash.

"Brandi!" Megan screamed. "Dar! Say something!"

The pile lay still save a few feeble movements, followed by a weak groan. Brandi flipped her cloak over her head and looked up at Megan.

"Where's my other sword?"

Weak with relief, Megan laughed.

"In its neck," Andyn offered.

The bull-satyr didn't move. Connor had managed to leap off its shoulders before it fell and thus avoided being crushed. He limped over to the others, beating dust from his clothing.

Megan found Dar and helped him stand, handing him his sword. "Ow," he said, feeling his side. "I'm one big bruise. Did we kill it?"

A wave of indignation swept over Megan and she stamped her foot.

Did he kill it? Is that all he can think about?

"Yes," she said, exasperated. "You killed it, you idiot, although I'm not sure how. Why did you have to charge it like that?"

Dar started stretching. He grinned at her. "Couldn't think of anything— ouch—better, I guess."

Hot fury surged through her for a split second.

How dare he stand there, making light of the whole thing when I was worried sick...

His eyes seemed to ask for forgiveness and understanding at the same time, playful but appealing. Then she saw the fear and anxiety in him and... something else. She realized he and Eric had taken all the responsibility of leading them to safety, without complaint.

He's probably as scared as I am, maybe more so. Instead of railing at him, she sighed and smiled back at him instead.

"Oh, you fool," she said, pushing him in the shoulder. "I can't stay mad at you. Just be more careful next time."

"Yes ma'am."

Her heart gave a funny little leap, catching the roguish twinkle in his eyes.

Eric waved at the dead bull-satyr. "Any ideas why he was in here?"

Dar looked down at it and shrugged. "Heavy hitter. Quiet and very dangerous, but they really prefer the forest to the underground. It would take quite a prize to get him to work down here. I'll bet you a keg of dwarven brandy he was the rear guard for someone."

Brandi and Andyn made the rounds, evaluating everyone's injuries. They counted many minor ones and no broken bones, although Buck's shield arm was heavily bruised. It took the two healers the better part of an hour to get him to the point where he could bend and flex it without major pain. The shield was a total loss.

Connor, meanwhile, searched the dead body. He disentangled a large sack and rummaged through the contents, lifting out a smaller sack with a grunt of satisfaction.

"Looks like someone paid him really well," he said, pouring gold and platinum coins into his hand.

Megan's eyes widened. That was a *lot* of money.

Buck grinned at Connor. "Finally."

"Ready?" asked Dar from his watch-point at the exit. They regrouped and followed Connor out and along the passageway.

Megan ran her hand over faint wall carvings as they proceeded, wondering. *How many years have passed since anyone's been in here? And who was here before them?*

They traveled on through the tunnel. They passed small wall sconces holding dusty statues of unknown dwarven heroes. Some of the alcoves had dwarven and goblin skeletons locked in a final, deadly embrace, covered with a thick coat of dust and cobwebs. The battle for this complex had made the Path of Peace into a Path of War.

The others stopped and she skidded to a halt, barely avoiding slamming into her sister's back.

Connor inspected an ancient, blocky door. He worked on the lock for a time, then popped it off with a deft twist. He turned back to the others and motioned for them to follow.

The passage beyond the door was smooth and, unlike the others, meant for someone without heat vision. Torches guttered in wall sconces every thirty feet or so. Megan's heart beat faster. She licked dry lips and swallowed. Unlike the previous passages, graffiti and odd symbols defaced the intricate carvings here. She eyed the walls, feeling a strange, paranoid sensation, as if the symbols inspected *her*. It reminded her of the Ja'al chapel and made her want to run.

When they came to a branch-off, they waited for a few tense moments while Connor scouted the passage. He returned and led them to a very new-looking door at the other end. He rubbed his hands together and took out a tiny metal tool, eyes on the lock. He moved towards it but started when a voice rang out from behind the door.

"I don't want to hear any more excuses, LeFond! Why do I give orders around here if those hobgoblin dolts are just going to ignore them? I said I wanted them captured alive for the sacrifice, not buried in some old dwarven passage!"

"But Your Excellency," answered a familiar man's voice, "I didn't even get your order until a few minutes ago and then it was too late to relay to the chieftain. At least you have to admit they are out of the way now."

James! thought Megan with a spark of anger. *He and that halfling, working for the Ja'al.*

They heard a thud of fist on wood and a grunt of surprise. "Lord Halkith is not going to be pleased with this display of incompetence. Would you like to explain to him how your hobgoblins let the intruders get in here in the first place? Or how they managed to find this complex?"

James' voice murmured and Connor drew his sword, looking back at the others. Dar, Buck, and Eric slid up to the door with only a mild clink.

Megan fidgeted, caressing the wand.

They heard unintelligible muttering and the Ja'al cleric's voice rose again. "I'm not interested in platitudes. I want results. Now get out there and tell those baboon-faced idiots I want them to get past the cave-in and bring me those sellswords!"

Dar, Buck and Eric hit the door and it crashed open.

"You called for us?" said Dar.

James LeFond whirled around, a stunned look on his face. A familiar rotund man in wild-colored robes turned with him, hands leaning on a round table. Behind the table and to the left, four burly hobgoblins gaped at them, open-snouted. A large chandelier hovered four feet from the ceiling, glowing balls of light suspended where the candles should have been. The carving of a woman-headed spider leered at them from the front of a double door across the room. Judging from the beds and furniture, the occupants certainly liked comfort.

"Surrender," said Brandi.

A tense silence followed. The Ja'al cleric slowly straightened, hooking both thumbs behind his belt. A screaming demon-head pendant hung around his neck, glowing coldly. His flail hung at his side and a large purple stone gleamed at them from the noseguard of a steel helm.

"Did you not have enough the first time?" he asked. Cold eyes bored into them.

Dar and Eric each took a step to the side, keeping a close eye on the hobgoblins. The burly creatures watched the party with baleful eyes. Armored in shirts of chainmail with metal plates and carrying swords and maces, they looked hard-bitten and tough.

Elite guards.

Brandi stepped forward a pace, a gentle smile on her lips. "We forgive you for your previous attack on us."

Buck looked at her in amazement. "No, we don't! We're going to smash their—" He gulped at Andyn's elbow in his ribs.

Brandi continued. "We once again extend to you the favor of a fair trial in Forester."

The Ja'al threw back his head and laughed.

"You must be mad, wench! I want none of your forgiveness or your trials. The gods of Ja'al will rule this world soon and you will be crushed to the dust. Do not trifle with us!"

Brandi shook her head. "I was afraid that would be your answer."

The cleric snorted, then saw Megan. A crooked smile crossed his face. "Ah, my little harlot. Have you come to taste the Ghoul's Kiss again?"

That arrogant son of a...!

Megan forced herself to remain calm. She feigned a yawn. "If it was as effective as the last one, no. I hope you have something more exciting to show us."

The rotund man's eyes narrowed. "Bitch! I'll—"

"Oh, shut up, you idiot!" Dar retorted. "We didn't come here to be tortured by your stupid insults. Either give up or fight."

"James," said the Ja'al priest, gripping his flail, "You will aid me in ridding ourselves of these vermin."

James LeFond smirked, flipping his long hair over his shoulder. "Not for the sacrifice any more, milord?"

The Ja'al priest smiled. "Keep the women. Kill the men."

James drew his bastard sword and pointed it at Dar. "You first."

In a slow, almost choreographed movement, the Ja'al began stalking.

Buck drew Khelios. The dwarven blade flared bright gold.

The Ja'al cohort froze at the sight of the holy weapon. LeFond's mouth worked but no sound came out.

With curse, the Ja'al cleric made a throwing motion with his right hand and a misty, glowing claw-like shape appeared in mid-air and spun out at Buck.

Buck tried to dodge, but it hit him in the chest. The ghostly claw disappeared with a sizzling crack and he staggered backwards.

All hell broke loose. Megan saw Eric flip a dagger at a hobgoblin, then kick a chair in its path. The hobgoblin leaped over and swung, but Eric drew his sword and banged the attack to the side.

"Your turn," said Megan. She pointed her wand at the Ja'al priest. A trio of magical missiles howled in, slamming into him. He reeled backwards, cursing as he stumbled against a chair, the plate armor under his robes smoking.

A figure with long blond hair and twin maces jumped in, blocking her line of fire. Megan almost screamed with exasperation and moved so that Andyn wasn't in the way.

She saw something to her right and turned. A hobgoblin charged with upraised mace. Suddenly, a short figure with a flashing blade slammed into the Ja'al soldier, hurling him sideways. The pair crunched into the stone floor. Connor jerked his sword free and tumbled away. He crouched, blade at the ready.

Megan turned her attention back to the Ja'al cleric. Andyn struck the Ja'al canon in the chest and he cursed her. He tried to take her head off with a powerful swing, but she ducked and Buck was there with her, Khelios ablaze.

I need a clear shot! Megan was forced to move yet again.

She saw Dar and James exchanging a series of ferocious blows out of the corner of her eye, but neither fighter appeared to be injured. They broke apart, panting.

The remaining hobgoblins charged at her. Brandi stepped next to Megan, blocking a strike with her left-hand weapon and evading a thrust from the second opponent. Her right-hand blade caught the second baboon-man in the throat and he dropped like a stone. Megan pointed her wand at one of the remaining warriors and spoke the keyword.

Nothing happened. Megan stared at the wand.

Brandi and two hobgoblins exchanged a series of thrusts and parries and Megan shoved the wand behind her belt and readied her staff.

It figures...

The Ja'al cleric took a glancing blow from Buck, his plate mail flaring golden as magic armor and magic sword contended. The Ja'al stepped around a chair to get away from Buck. He dodged two swings from Andyn, then weaved backwards. Suddenly, he moved forward. His fierce backhand caught Andyn in the left side. There was a clanging crunch as Andyn cried out in pain, dropping her left-hand weapon.

The Ja'al Canon shouted with triumph and moved in.

Buck took one long step and thrust the dwarven blade into the cleric's side with a shearing sound. The Ja'al leader gasped, staggering backward into a desk. Khelios was jerked free.

Buck hesitated, seeing the blood streaming down the man's armor and robes. He kept his sword up but did not move forward.

What is he doing? Megan wondered. *Maybe he thinks that guy has some kind of trick up his sleeve.*

"No!" screamed Brandi. "Don't let him use his magic!" She stepped towards the fray but her hobgoblin opponent intervened. Brandi blocked a mace strike.

The Ja'al cleric raised a hand to cover his wound and an orange light glowed. He grinned, then moved to the other side of the desk.

All right, if I can't use the wand... Megan relaxed and concentrated. The world slowed down to a crawl and she was able to feel the energy in the lights near the ceiling, from all the combatants, from Buck's guttering torch on the floor next to her, even from the small spider in the far corner. She gathered some of the power and formed her spell.

She turned to the warrior blocking Brandi's path. "*Khesar!*"

Two glowing darts shot from her hand at Brandi's opponent, blasting it dead.

"Thanks," said Brandi over her shoulder, then leaped to the attack.

Only one hobgoblin, James, and the Ja'al leader remained standing. Even as she watched, Megan saw Eric duck a ferocious swing and slash the hobgoblin's leg. It stumbled and he raised his hand.

"*Khesar!*" he cried, and a single dart blasted the creature in the chest. It jerked backward, crashed into a chair and thudded into the floor to lie still.

"Help Buck and Andyn!" yelled Brandi as she leaped over a dead Ja'al towards Dar, where he and James still clanged blades. Dar found an opening with a quick thrust and James leaped backward with a cry of rage, blood marking him on the right shoulder.

Megan climbed over a fallen chair. *Damn. This is the last time I'll wear a robe on one of these expeditions.*

The Ja'al cleric cast a quicksilver globule at Andyn. She whirled to her left. The missile splatted into the wall and disintegrated in a cloud of foul dust.

Buck swung overhead, trying to split the Ja'al's skull. The cleric sidestepped and Buck wedged Khelios into the desktop. Gleefully, the cleric brought down his flail, but Buck let go of the sword and dodged to the side. The Ja'al lunged over the desk and Buck obliged him with an elbow smash to the face. He staggered backward with a curse and Buck tugged his sword free.

Megan heard a loud, metallic snap from her right and she whirled in spite of the battle before her. Dar and James fell backwards in opposite directions, the long-haired Ja'al warrior thumping into the spider-woman door. The portal burst open. He tumbled head-over-heels into the passage beyond it.

LeFond stood and slammed his broken sword to the ground in disgust. His eyes widened, seeing Brandi coming to join Dar, who scrambled to his feet. With a curse, James leaped forward and slammed the doors shut. Megan heard the distinct thump of a cross-beam.

Dar spat a curse of his own. He started forwards but a voice halted him.

"Give up now," Eric called out. "It's hopeless."

Buck had backed the Ja'al cleric into a corner. Andyn pressed a hand to her injured side and a soft light glowed. She straightened with a wince and picked up her fallen mace.

Eric picked up a spear from a corner of the room and hefted it. Connor slid up next to an overturned chair and drew his bow, fitting an arrow to the string.

"You're finished," Brandi said. "Hasn't there been enough killing?"

The Ja'al canon looked up at them, helm askew and eyes wild with some kind of crazed light. "No! Never enough! Not for the Ja'al! I will slay you all!"

He pointed a finger at Buck and shouted, "Die!"

Horrified, Megan saw him freeze and then slump to the stone floor.

With a shriek of fury, Andyn slammed a mace into the cleric's side and then into his helm, hurling him backwards. Connor's arrow sped by and shattered on the wall.

A spear flew past Megan and she flinched.

There was a ripping clang and the cleric gasped.

Eric had pinned him to the wall.

"Just think of how those villagers felt, now. Isn't so nice, is it?" asked Connor.

The Ja'al looked down at the spear in disbelief, and then his eyes rolled back in his head and he slumped forward.

Megan joined the others at Buck's side in an instant. Brandi felt for a pulse and then sighed in relief. "He's fine. Unconscious. I should have guessed. As powerful as our little friend seems, he wasn't yet strong enough to use death-magic."

As she was speaking, Buck yawned and opened his eyes. "G'Morning."

The tension in the air dissipated.

Megan smiled at him. "You are nuts."

"Thank you," said Buck, sitting up.

Eric knelt down. "Don't do that again. You had us all scared."

"Ha!" retorted Buck, standing up. "Damn spell-caster couldn't hurt me if he tried."

Dar thumped Buck on the back. "Well, he sure did something to you." He turned towards the spider door. "Now we take care of unfinished business."

Brandi grabbed his arm. "He's long gone. We got the important one."

Dar made a face. After a long pause, he nodded. "I guess you're right. It's just that I had that daemon-spawn right where I wanted him."

Megan put a hand on his shoulder. "Don't worry, Dar. I have a feeling we'll see our Mister LeFond again."

"How's everyone feeling?" asked Andyn.

"I'll live," said Connor. He brushed his hair back into place.

"Good," Eric replied. "I wouldn't want to carry you back to town. You've gained weight."

Buck, in particular, seemed elated. He clapped his hands together. "Well! Do you know what we just did?"

Brandi and Dar looked up from inspecting the dead hobgoblins.

Buck spread his arms wide. "We just killed the head cleric. The Ja'al are finished. We've won! The bounty is ours!"

Connor nodded. "He's right."

Everyone except Brandi and Andyn began to smile. The two women exchanged a glance.

Megan frowned, watching them. She knew that look on her sister's face.

"I don't think we're done, gentlemen," she said.

"Oh, sure," said Eric, waving a hand. "We have to clean out this place, but the hard work is done."

Andy shook her head. "No. I have a funny feeling about him." She indicated the dead cleric with a nod of her head.

Connor rolled his eyes. "Oh, you religious people. Always getting funny feelings. What are you talking about? This guy was in charge, pure and simple."

Andyn raised an eyebrow at him. "Do you see any maps or charts here, sweetheart? Or anything dealing with pottery or crooked black lines? Don't you think the leader of this effort would at least have something like that lying around?"

Connor opened his mouth and then closed it. Buck stepped forward, looking to the others for support.

"Wait a minute! He could have hidden it all. Let's check the desk and the rest of this junk."

Brandi shrugged. "Fair enough. But you'll have to find something pretty convincing to satisfy me. This doesn't feel right."

The group sifted through every container and piece of furniture while Connor stood guard.

"Aha!" shouted Andyn. She walked over to Brandi, waving a sheet of vellum. The others crowded around.

She began to read. "It's addressed to Modron Derrig." She looked over at the cleric's corpse. "I guess that's him. Or was him. Anyway, it's addressed to the 'Commander, Fifth Ja'al Goblin Brigade', whatever that is." She peered at the parchment, pursing her lips.

"Fire In The Sky, Andyn!" said Dar, looking heavenward. "Will you get on with it?"

She smacked him in the arm. "Let me finish looking at it first. Here's the rest of it: 'Attend. By the rulership given me, you are commanded to find any and all artworks made by the sage known as Clarissa of Westhaven. The messengers with this letter carry with them silver as payment for your troops, but know you that my agents are in their midst, so keeping the money for yourself will only gain you a permanent position in Hell. The time grows short. Soon, the Golden One will take steps, as his kin are now in my hands. We must find the components of the map within a month or the entire project is in jeopardy."

Megan bit her lip, wondering. *What map? Did Clarissa have a map somewhere in her home? And who was the Golden One?*

Judging by the others' expressions, she wasn't the only one confused.

"Is that all?" asked Eric.

"Well," said Andyn, "It says at the end: 'I command. Halkith, High Priest of the Ja'al, Battalion Commander and Leader of the Blackwing Project.'"

Buck groaned. "Oh great. This thing gets more convoluted as we go on."

Dar's eyebrows rose. "Isn't that a rather big word, Buck?" That earned him a slug in the shoulder.

"I think," Megan began, tapping her finger on her chin, "we ought to let Lady Ellen and Lord Nolan have a look at this, as well as the scroll we found in the pond. One of them should be able to make sense of it."

Connor looked around at the mess in the room and then at the parchment. "I sure hope someone can."

Chapter Fourteen- Stories and Histories

Cortin the weaponsmith looked up at the commotion, frowning. It was hard enough to forge a blade without all this shouting in the street.

Leonard, his teenaged apprentice, looked up from wrapping the handle of a shortsword. He wiped his hands on a cloth and craned his neck to see the source of all the laughter and loud voices.

No one appeared on the avenue outside the shop and Cortin turned back to his work.

Time enough to see the parade later, he griped to himself.

"What do you think it is, Master Cortin?" Leonard asked, moving over to the open doorway and leaning on the frame.

Cortin snorted. "Probably some fur trappers with a great haul. Or maybe a new caravan with merchants and peddlers and trinkets for the ladies. Or a minstrel, or halfling actors on tour. Doesn't really matter, does it, boy? Finish that handle."

Leonard opened his mouth to protest, and seeing Cortin's face, turned away.

Then the commotion arrived, almost on their doorstep. A group of young people struggled through a growing crowd down the street towards the manor house.

"Humph. Free-lances and sell-swords. Blank-shields," Cortin grunted, joining Leonard at the doorway. *Two human males, four elves, and a halfling.*

All of them looked a little battered and tired. They also looked a bit embarrassed by the attention, except for the tallest human. He strode forward waving to the crowd like a conquering hero.

Cortin shook his head. *Bunch of fools. Just like the others that come blowing into Forester every year, fresh from the academies. They'll be gone just as fast too - dead, disbanded, or off more exciting places.*

A tall figure moved next to him and he looked up at the face of Hal Ersel, one of the teamsters for the Lervion Shipping Line.

Cortin peered up at Hal. "Who are they?"

Hal grinned down his hawkish nose. "Freelancers, of course. No one but the Guard has that much weaponry."

Cortin gave him a sour look. "I know that, you oaf. Which freelancers?"

Hal kept his self-satisfied grin and watched the scene in the street. "These are the ones Lord Nolan sent out to find the murderers of the Westhaven folks. Seems like they found 'em at that. Took out a Ja'al cleric and a platoon of hobgoblins."

Cortin spat on the ground and nodded, running a hand through graying hair. "And good riddance to 'em. Now if they'll just get out of town and go chase some other evil cults, I can finish my work."

Hal laughed. "Didn't you do that sort of thing a long time ago?"

Cortin nodded and shook a finger at the taller man. "The key there is 'a long time ago', and well done with it. Saw a lot of friends killed, all for glory or money or some high-browed lord's interests. I got out of it after a few years."

Hal stretched in the morning coolness, then nodded to Cortin. "Sure hope it turns out well for them. They seem like a decent bunch." He turned away.

Cortin's face relaxed, his eyes distant. "They all do, at first."

He stood there for a minute after Hal had gone, staring after the crowd.

***

"Halkith?" Ellen Hanford looked at her husband. "Where have I heard that name before? Wasn't he a minor cleric under Hollis Ironfist years ago?"

Nolan nodded, looking grim. "Hollis is dead now, but he was a mid-ranking cleric in the cult of the Ja'al. He had a string of brothels and drug-houses up here just inside the borders. I had them cleaned out by the

Company of the White Horn about ten years back. It looks like Halkith's career has seen new heights since then. Or new lows..."

Dar gave a soundless whistle and looked at a wide-eyed Megan. He had heard of Corowin Andor and his Company of the White Horn.

Too bad they're retired now. We could use a few pointers on this Halkith character.

Instead of looking impressed, Buck deflated. "You mean we haven't found the leaders yet?"

Ellen chuckled and took his arm. "No, Buck, you haven't. But you have scored a great victory. This other cleric, Modron Derrig, was probably an under-commander for Halkith. Stopping him is a big step. We are in your debt."

Looking somewhat mollified, Buck nodded.

Nolan picked up Halkith's letter from the small table and stood there for a moment. He pursed his lip, reading. Ellen came to look over his shoulder, her own brow furrowed.

She looked up, gazing out the tall windows at the mountains.

"Blackwing? Black wing?" She muttered, brow furrowed. "Why does that sound familiar?"

Her husband let the paper fall to the tabletop. "We'll have to figure it out later. What about that other scroll you found?"

Megan handed him the scrollcase with the strange, arcane symbols. "I can't make the language out, milord. I was hoping Lady Ellen could use a reading magic."

The Baron accepted the scrollcase and stared at it. Amazed, Dar watched as Nolan's eyes glowed a light silver. He blinked and it vanished.

"You're going to have to de-activate, milady," he said in a businesslike tone. "Evil spells, two of them, one on each cap. I think one of them is fire-based."

She nodded as if he had just asked her what was for dinner. "Understood, milord. If you please?"

She laid it on the table, spreading her hands over it and murmuring a singsong verse. Her eyes became dark slits against chocolate skin.

Two tongues of flame leaped from the ends of the scrollcase, accompanied by a cloud of white smoke. Dar stepped back, coughing a little. The air smelled sour, like sulphur.

"Not too bad," Lady Ellen said. "Standard warding spells."

She waved the smoke away and lifted the scrollcase. She turned it over in her hands, then picked up a letter-opener from the table and pried one of the endcaps off. She gently pulled out a roll of parchment, spreading it apart. Her eyes widened and she whistled.

"Is something wrong, milady?" asked Brandi.

The Baroness shook her head. "This is very old. It's made from pressed mandulla, a kind of mashed reed fiber. They stopped using it sometime during the late Paragon Age."

Megan and Andyn gasped and Eric looked a little dizzy. Buck and Connor shrugged at Dar.

Sir Tan would box my ears for not knowing this.

"Paragon Age?" Dar asked. "Er, A long time ago, right?"

Andyn nodded. "Very long ago. The Paragons were rulers of petty kingdoms just after the Skyfire, when the New Faith—that is, Christianity—appeared in the lands. Each Paragon started out as a blank-shield, or what passed for it in those days, and very highly ranked. The last of them died almost three thousand years ago."

Ellen turned her eyes back to the parchment. "I can't decipher this. It's in a very old tongue, probably one of the ecclesiastical ones. Maybe from a religion that doesn't exist anymore."

Buck rolled his eyes. "Great. Now we'll never know if it means anything."

Megan looked at Ellen. "Please, milady, might you try a spell of reading? I would do one myself, but I haven't learned it yet."

Ellen looked doubtful. "Spells of reading are useful in divining modern languages, both written and spoken, but not ancient ones. And languages of the churches are different still. But I might as well try."

Faster than it took to think of it, she snapped into a trance and passed her hand over the scroll. The pages glowed pale blue and her eyes became reflective, shining back the azure light. Then the glow faded and she shook her head, eyes normal again.

"I can't read it. We'd have to find a scholar who specializes in ancient languages. I know several at the Universities in Oakmoor, Darlon and Deorfast."

"Well," said Nolan, rolling up Modron Derrig's letter, "There is some reward due you for eliminating the Ja'al canon and clearing the outpost. There was a bounty on him." He reached into his belt purse, drawing out a handful of shiny items. He gave five to each of the companions.

Buck's eyes nearly popped out of their sockets. "They're platinum ingots!"

Nolan looked amused at the reaction. "Of course. You know what they're worth, don't you?"

Buck nodded. "Sure...platinum imperials are worth fifty gold crowns each, but I thought..."

Nolan nodded. "Consider it a bonus. Now," he continued, addressing the others. "Lady Ellen and I have other matters to attend to. Please meet with me in two days, here in the audience room when the town clock chimes eight, in the evening. I will send a letter to Count DeGrance in Hillton asking if knows any experts in ancient languages. We might not have to go to Darlon or Oakmoor."

The companions bowed their thanks and left.

Connor grinned at his fellows as they walked down the wide hallway to the front doors. "Quite a haul, eh? I haven't even seen two imperials together, let alone *five*!"

Andyn chewed her lip thoughtfully. "I wonder what the rest of that letter from Halkith means. You know, the part about the Golden One and all that."

She turned her pretty, oval face towards Dar and he smiled back at her. "I'm sure we'll find out soon, especially with Lord Nolan and Lady Ellen to help."

She gave him a wry grin. "Yes, but I have to know everything *now*. No delays in the slightest."

Dar had to chuckle at that. She sounded like the thoughts that ran through his own mind sometimes.

Buck shrugged and pushed open the double doors to the courtyard. "I don't really care right this minute. I'm for a round of ales and a hot meal. My armor needs repairing and we've got a few treasures to sell off to the merchants. And tonight..."

Dar gave him a sidelong glance. "Yes?"

Buck took a deep breath and adjusted his trousers. "Then I see if there's any women in this town who'd like to get personally acquainted with the slayer of the goblin chieftain."

Dar joined in the laughter as they left the manor grounds and entered the main street. "Well, then they certainly won't be talking to you. Besides, it was a grand sergeant, not a chieftain."

Buck waved a hand. "Whatever."

Brandi cast her eyes heavenward as they turned towards the Woodsman Inn and the Pit.

Brandi slowed her pace as they passed Saint Anne's church, looking thoughtful.

Megan also slowed down. "What, Brandi?"

Her elder sister motioned towards the church. "Tomorrow's Sunday. I want to see if they need any help with Mass in the morning."

"Sure," Dar answered, "Father Ander can always use a hand."

He grabbed Eric by the elbow.

"What, what, what?"

"Tomorrow's Sunday," Dar said, nodding towards the church.

"Ah." Eric smiled at Brandi. "Tell Father Ander if he needs any help I'd be glad to pitch in."

Megan looked exasperated. "We should all go in and ask, you ninny."

"Look," said Brandi, waving at them, "You go on. I'll talk to him and meet you at the Pit afterwards."

"Fine," Dar called out to her. "We'll save an ale in your honor. Don't be too late or Buck will drink it all."

He dodged Buck's backhanded swipe and then slipped in and clapped him on the shoulder. "Hey, chieftain-killer, what say I buy the first round..."

***

Father Ander tidied up the interior of the church as she walked in. A kaleidoscope of reds, blues, and greens shone from the stained-glass windows, casting patterns of apostles and angels on the dark stone floor. A cross glowed yellow on the priest's grey cassock as he carefully dusted off a statue of Saint Mary.

A brilliant painting, flanked by pairs of candles, depicted a small girl with a bright halo and two older people gazing at her, dimmer halos hovering over their own heads. The trio sat under the sheltering boughs of a tree, spire-like cypresses visible in the distance.

Saint Ann, Saint Joachim, and Mary...

Brandi genuflected and sat for a moment on a bench, enjoying the dark quiet of the place and the wonderful, painted lights. It reminded her of a church in Terenai, where she had prayed many times: sometimes in thanksgiving for her and her sisters' lives, sometimes in anger, asking why their parents had been allowed to die, sometimes in confusion, as she wondered what would become of them both. No matter how much turmoil followed her in, she left with a sense of peace and of being loved beyond all imagining.

The Lord is my Shepherd.

Ander turned and peered back at her. "Oh! Hello...miss... Alenar, isn't it?"

"Hello Father Ander," she said, a little abashed at not saying anything sooner.

He smiled in recognition. It was not a brilliant smile, but it made his entire countenance warmer. "How is your sister?"

Brandi found herself smiling back. "Very well, Father. Thank you again."

The smile turned a bit wry as he waved a hand. "All part of the Lord's work. Besides," here his eyes twinkled, "you gave quite a contribution for the poorbox for the service, did you not? It will help us in our ministry to the mountain areas."

Brandi had to chuckle. "Well, I thought I might want to contribute something to the Lord's work today or tomorrow if you have the need."

The priest's smile grew a shade brighter. "Well, what do you know! Just this morning, Liana's brother came to tell me she is ill. The children have no one to teach them their lessons this afternoon. Would you be willing to help? I understand you went to Saint Justin's Seminary in Alrihan and the Guardian Angels Academy in Mil-Tereth."

Brandi found herself blushing and wondering how he knew that. "Well, yes, Father, but I am no scholar."

The cleric put a hand on her shoulder and fixed her with a matter-of-fact gaze. "My dear girl, in a land where people are lucky to get ten years of education in their lives, anyone who has studied beyond that *is* a scholar. The children will be here this afternoon. I know you will want to get some rest and wash up in the meantime."

Teaching school? Well, she sighed, *why not?*

***

A small hand waved in the group of youngsters. Brandi frowned. What was that boy's name? Elric? Richard?

"Yes...er...Elric?"

The seven-year-old smiled broadly. "Richard, Miss Alenar."

Drat. "Do you have a question?"

"What's a Skyfire?"

Brandi leaned back against the tree trunk. The entire class sat in the warm afternoon sun in the grass next to the great maple tree. She figured they were probably tired of being cooped-up indoors during the recent rains so she brought the class outside.

"Now where did you hear about the Skyfire?" she asked.

Richard smiled wider. "My dad said he wasn't going to let a Skyfire-burned caravan master charge him fourteen silver discs for a shovel."

The other children giggled and Brandi shook her head, pursing her lip. There were about twenty town kids, ranging in age from six to thirteen. She wondered what other words they had learned from their parents.

"That's something from ancient history and you won't learn that until you're older. We have to go over your numbers and addition today."

They looked deflated. Miriam, the thirteen-year-old sitting next to her, tugged the sleeve of Brandi's tunic, brown eyes pleading below dark tresses.

"Miss Alenar," she said. "We don't get to hear any tales like that in the class. They only teach those things in colleges. Could you please tell us?"

Brandi looked down at her. Father Ander told her Miriam was a sort of unofficial classroom assistant. The girl wanted to be a teacher herself someday.

For a moment, Brandi considered refusing. Then she saw their faces, a mixture of hope and disappointment, and she relented.

"Very well," she said.

The kids' faces lit up with excitement.

"But you must promise to work extra hard for Miss Liana on Monday—and I'll find out if you don't," she finished with a warning tone.

They nodded vigorously and she sat back against the tree, bracing her hands on the ground. The children sat intent and quiet.

"Long ago, before any of the current lands were in existence, the world was a collection of little kingdoms. Each one had one major city, about the size of Hillton, and a castle, and some land—much smaller than Deran is nowadays."

"These kingdoms had, of course, kings and queens. These rulers did not worship the Father, Son, and Holy Ghost, as we do now. Instead they followed Irial Worldmaker or some people were druids, and others, like the elves, worshipped Verian, the god of the forests. The dwarves followed the ways of Kurental, Lord of Stone, and there were other, smaller religions too. Unfortunately, the evil churches were also in existence, like the cult of the many gods of Ja'al, or the Vardish, followers of the Death-god, or the Cla'Agik, the church of the Diseased One."

Her little audience gave a set of nervous looks at each other or at the surroundings.

Brandi forged on. She really didn't want to remind them of the world's dangers, but it had to be done in order to complete the story.

"Well, one day, legends say one of the wizard-kings looked out his palace window and saw an amazing sight: tongues of flame in the sky, descending to the earth like giant red and orange roses. Our scholars have very few writings left from that time. Some think there were Visitors in those flames. Some legends say that the Lord God Himself sent angels to bring knowledge to our world. Whatever happened, it became known as the Skyfire. The Bible appeared soon after, with words and ideas strange to the people of that time, but ones that mirrored some of the faiths already here. Soon, many of the people came to believe. And the way in which they believed also changed, because Those who brought the Word also insisted that it be accepted freely and not forced at the point of a sword."

"There were other things that arrived with the Skyfire, other knowledge that we take for granted today. Many magics were refined in the decades following, and great wizards rose to power. Soon, there came in the lands mighty kings and queens who were named the Paragons."

The children looked confused at the new word and she smiled. "A paragon is a person who is a shining example of the best of something. In this case they were excellent warriors and mages and priests. The Paragon Lords ruled for over two thousand years with relative peace. All was well. As time went on, agents of the evil churches worked their way into the courts of some of the kingdoms and convinced those Paragons that they should have more because it was their right. They became greedy and fought among themselves. Their kingdoms fell apart and the evil ones from the wilderness came. Then, the Fall of Night lasted for fifty-seven summers. Times were very hard and people did not know much of the outside world beyond their own villages."

"Finally, someone came to lead them. A man named Stephen Kalar of Esten established the First House of the Esten Empire. He united the many peoples under the banner of the Golden Unicorn. The Empire stood for more than a thousand and five years, but Stephen's descendants were not as good at ruling the Empire as he. The dukes and kings contended among themselves and the Empire fell to pieces. From what was left over from Esten, we have our current nations. There is Deran, where we live, and Astarel to the north. Rokon and Eldir and the elven Empire of Terenai joined with us and with Astarel to form the Northern Alliance three years ago. Then there is the Republic of Evendale, where the halflings live. Gorostol and Merdail are south of Terenai. The former is a multi-ethnic land and the latter is the homeland of the dwarves. All these were originally part of the Empire. Then far to the south are the evil Republic of Torosc and Morlan, land of the wizard-kings, and the Confederacy of Jered. Far across the sea are other lands, and the island nations of Derelia, but they are not often involved in our affairs here on the Continent."

Ten-year-old Elisa raised her hand. "Does anyone remember the Skyfire?"

Brandi chuckled. "Oh no, Elisa. This is 1086, Post-Imperial Year..." She did a few mental calculations. "...so that puts the Skyfire at more than four thousand years ago. Elves don't live that long. I don't even think the Elohir do."

Richard raised his hand again. "What are those?"

A male voice spoke from behind Brandi. "They are beings that live on Celestia."

Brandi turned to look. Eric Indidarc leaned against the tree behind her, slapping his gloves in one hand, eyes twinkling.

She gave him a look. "Come to join us for a little education, Mister Indidarc?"

He nodded and plopped down next to her with a clink of chain armor. She could see he had purchased a new, forest-and-sienna-dappled tunic and trousers of dark brown.

He looked out at the children and winked. "I am always on a quest for greater knowledge, Miss Alenar."

I'll bet. She turned to the class.

"Class, this is Mister Eric Indidarc of Oakmoor, one of my friends and traveling companions."

The children's eyes shone as they stood and gave Eric a series of little bows and curtseys.

"Are they always so formal?" he whispered out of the side of his mouth as they sat again.

"You're a famous free-lance, Eric," she whispered back. "Be glad they're respectful."

She addressed him in a louder voice. "We were just discussing a little ancient history."

He gave an innocent smile. "I know. I was listening."

"Did I leave anything out?" She raised an eyebrow.

He looked at her in mock surprise. "Brandawyn! I'm surprised at you. I would never question your knowledge."

The children smiled at their interplay. Two of the little girls whispered to each other and giggled. Brandi felt her cheeks growing warm.

She addressed the students again. "Now, where were we?"

"On Celestia," Eric volunteered.

"Ah yes," Brandi replied, leaning back against the tree and putting both hands behind her head, "Continue, professor."

Eric looked a bit surprised, then smiled. "Very well." He winked at the kids again.

"Celestia is a world far away from here," he began. "It has its own sun and three moons. If you were on Celestia, you could see all of them at night sometimes, just as you can see our own Kaliri and Diometrius here. There are many fantastic beings and creatures that live there, including dragons and alicorns. The land is beautiful and green, with towering mountains and lovely beaches, deep blue seas and tan deserts. Many good and wondrous plants grow there."

"There are no evil creatures on Celestia, and I will explain why in a minute," he continued. "The lords of that world are the Elohir. Each one is taller than I, about six feet and a few inches on average, even the women. Some have dark skin, like Lady Ellen, and others are more fair. And they look just like humans—except that they have wings! Just like an eagle's, or hawk's or peregrine falcon's. They dress in short robes of gentle colors and have sandals or low boots on their feet. Each one carries a mighty weapon to battle the forces of evil."

"Now," he continued, "all the Elohir are beautiful, the men and women and children alike. Many who have met them say it is a beauty shining from within that makes them so attractive. In any event, the Elohir are good and kind and brave and always seek to help other peoples."

"As I said, there are no bad people on Celestia, but on the world of Hades live the ones we call daemons, or the Fallen Ones. They are Elohir who turned to the Evil One out of pride or in their quest for knowledge or power. The *true* Elohir, who worship our God, pleaded with their kinfolk, but to no avail. There was a great war, with the evil ones contending with their brethren. The bad Celestials lost the war and were cast out. They traveled to their new, desolate homeland, from where they plot to destroy their former friends and family and anyone allied with the side of good."

The children looked on, wide-eyed and silent.

"And so," Eric finished, "The Elohir seek to thwart their evil cousins wherever the daemons try to destroy and spread misery. Sometimes, the Elohir come here to Damora, on special missions or when asked to come by a mighty patriarch or archbishop. They fly in through magical gates in secret, hidden places and can take the form of anyone or anything they please. So be watchful if you meet a feeble old person or a poor child, for they may be an Elohir in disguise."

He nodded at the children. "And yes, Miss Brandi is right. Elohir live for about a thousand years if left alone, but many die in war with the daemons. Elves, on the other hand, live for about three hundred, dwarves and gnomes two hundred, half-elves and halflings about the same and humans maybe a hundred. So, there are no persons alive who would remember the Skyfire, not even the lords of the Elohir."

A light wind ruffled the trees, bringing new-rain smells in the silence.

"Well, class," said Brandi, sitting up. "That's enough history for one day. Thank you, Mister Indidarc, for your assistance. Now, we will turn to our addition..."

"Miss Alenar!" called a voice from the church.

Everyone looked up to see Father Ander waving at them. The priest was standing on the back steps, a grey ghost against the ivory walls of the church.

"Class is over," he called out. "Their parents will be coming. Send them into the church for their prayer time."

They actually seem disappointed, thought Brandi as she stood with her students and brushed some of the leaves off her tunic. With a chorus of good-byes, the children scampered off to meet the waiting priest.

"Be good for Father Ander!" she called after them. "And remember what you promised me!"

"They're good kids," said Eric, pulling on his gloves.

Brandi smiled. "Yes, they are." She turned to face him. "And you're a good storyteller."

Eric stared after the children and let out a deep breath. His eyes were distant. "I'm good with stories. All except my own."

Something inside Brandi grew very quiet. She watched him for a long moment: Eric of the merry laugh and hidden thoughts. Without realizing why, she took his hand in hers.

"You can tell me," she said.

His eyes turned nervous and fearful, emotions she had never seen in him. Startled, she saw his hands were shaking.

"I don't know if I should say anything," he said, not meeting her eyes. He looked around to see if anyone else was in earshot. Only a few birds chattered in the trees nearby.

"Eric, after hearing my story, do you think anything can shock me?"

He looked down at the ground. "You may not like me very much when I'm done."

She set her mouth in a firm line.

"I don't care," she said, pulling him down on the grass to sit beside her. "And I won't let you go until you've told me."

He'll see how stubborn I can get.

He took a deep breath and let it out again. "Brandi, I'm not really from Oakmoor. Well, I am from Oakmoor originally, but I ran away when I was twenty-six. I lived with Melinor later in Whitepine, near Deorfast, up by the Astarel border."

Brandi nodded. *That would mean he was a young adolescent when he...ran away?*

"What do you mean, 'ran away'? I thought you said Melinor adopted you."

He cleared his throat. "He did...I...Brandi, my real last name is Hylar."

Brandi racked her brain but came up with nothing. She shook her head. "Am I supposed to know that name?"

Eric eyes shone like little violet gems, gauging her, measuring her. "Do you remember the assassins who killed Andyn's husband? The Crossed Swords Guild? Their chieftain is named Harkin Hylar. I'm his third son."

Brandi's heart skipped. She stared at him, eyes wide and mouth open. Finally, she realized she hadn't taken a breath and she gasped.

"Eric... this isn't funny."

"I'm not joking."

Oh sweet Jesus... Brandi's heart started racing frantically. *Oh my God. If Eric's an assassin...I...we...Wait a minute... he still hasn't killed any of us? Why is he telling me this?...*

His eyes still gauged her, except that now he was expectant and hopeful.

"You're not one of them," she breathed. "That's why you ran away."

He nodded. Some of his tension disappeared and he met her gaze. "I couldn't take it anymore. I'm no assassin and I could never be, no matter how much they tried to make me one. I decided I'd had enough when they killed one of my cousins because she tried to get out. I disguised myself as one of the servants, knocked out the guy I was impersonating, then left with a foraging party when their day ended."

Brandi swallowed. *And I thought Megan and I had a rough life! But is he telling the truth?*

As if he had read her thoughts, he took her hands in his. "You've got to believe me, Brandi! I had to leave. I'm not one of them. It was horrible in there. They would force us to train with them, and then, when we were old enough, they made us kill someone. If we disobeyed, we were tortured by Liselle, the Ja'al cleric, in her chapel. Or worse, the girls were raped by one of

199

the older assassins."

Brandi shuddered. *What kind of animals...?*

His eyes were wet and he spoke through clenched teeth. "I lost a brother and two sisters in that hell-hole. Mayarice was only fifteen. That's only eight in human years."

Brandi blinked, her mind reeling as she tried to come to grips with all this. She held his hands tight. "Okay... okay. Eric, this is bad, I admit that. But it's not the end of the world unless you let it be so. I mean, you're here, with us, not with them. And Melinor took you in, didn't he? What happened after you left Oakmoor?"

His jaw relaxed and he sighed. "I left on the next caravan out of Oakmoor the night I escaped. As soon as it stopped for a rest, I snatched some food and a dagger from a guard and headed out."

He surprised her by giving a short laugh. "I still don't know what I was expecting. Where the hell could I go? I didn't know anyone or anything except Oakmoor and the Hylar home and the Undercity."

"When did you meet Melinor?" she asked.

This time she got a real chuckle. "I was in Whitepine and I saw this old man sitting by himself at a cafe. He looked pretty harmless, except for the staff of white wood he had with him, and I was pretty sure I could outrun him. I took his beltpurse."

Brandi had to smile. Melinor Indidarc hadn't attained the name of Wizard of the North by accident.

"He caught you."

Eric grinned, looking like his old self. "His purse had a spell laid on it, one that would scream for help if it ever was stolen. As soon as I lifted it, the alarm went off and Melinor put a holding magic on me."

Eric picked up a twig and began rolling it between his palms. "I guess he saw something in me that told him I wasn't just an ordinary thief. Instead of turning me in to the guards, he took me with him, all the while telling me he would make my life easier if I told him everything."

"We got jumped by assassins on the way back. I told him who my father was and he decided to take me back to his home to hide me," he continued, tossing the twig onto the grass, "I told him the whole story later, with Anne and Saren there. I had been taught to trust no one, but he was so nice to me...

He used magic to hide me from my family."

"Wait a minute," Brandi held up a hand. "Yours is a family of assassins, not mages. How could they look for you with magic?"

He made a wry face. "My mother, Taramis, is multi-talented. She's where I get my elven half."

Her lips made a silent "oh" and he went on. "I heard later that my parents flew into a rage when they found out I escaped. They had the house searched for three days, certain I hadn't left. Then they expanded the search to the streets, and after that used magic, but by then, I was safe. They killed off about a half-dozen people trying to find me."

Brandi's heart melted at his expression. "But Eric, that wasn't your fault."

He sighed and smiled back. "I know that now. I had a lot of trouble with it originally, but I don't blame myself anymore. They killed people of their own free will. Melinor kept drumming that into me. 'A man can use a hammer to build a house or kill someone; it's what's in his soul that makes the decision'. Wise-old-man sayings like that. I learned a lot from him."

"And now?"

He took a deep breath. "That's it. They couldn't find me and just gave me up for dead, I guess. Melinor had a new apprentice and I was free for the first time in my life. I studied with Melinor exclusively for about three years. Later, I studied with Sir Tan Collins. Melinor knows him."

Brandi pressed her lips together and considered for a moment. "And no one else knows any of this outside of your family? Not even Elaine?"

Eric was aghast. "Are you crazy? I can't tell her this! She'd drop dead from shock."

"Well, then, how about us? And why tell me in the first place?"

He sighed. "I don't know Bran."

He met her eyes. "I guess I thought that since you were a cleric and clerics are counselors sometimes, and you've been really nice when you weren't being an uptight older sister. I thought I could trust you."

She blinked, taken aback at a receiving a criticism and a backhanded compliment all rolled into one.

"Well," she said, "I'm really glad you told me. And I won't say anything to anyone. But you really should tell the others."

He looked miserable. "Even Andyn?" he asked, eyes fixed on a spot in the grass.

"Yes, even Andyn."

"She's going to hate me."

Brandi moved her head down to meet his eyes. "She's going to hate your parents, not you. You didn't kill anyone."

He didn't answer.

She sighed. "You have to decide for yourself. Tell them all when you're ready, but please don't wait too long. It'll only get worse."

He nodded, looking like he would rather take a vacation on Hades. "Okay."

A voice called to them. "Oh, there you are!...Whoops!"

The pair looked up to see Buck, Megan and Dar coming around the corner of the church.

"Sorry!" said Megan, grabbing both men by the arm and turning to go. "Didn't mean to interrupt anything."

Eric chuckled. "Oh, hey, don't run off. Nothing earthshaking happening here."

Brandi smiled along with him. In her mind, she marveled. *Lord, he can change demeanors so fast! They say assassins are great actors.*

Nothing earthshaking. Well, that was an understatement.

Just a prince of an assassin's guild in our midst.

She looked up at the blue sky as she walked with him to join the others. *Jesus,* she prayed, *are there any more surprises I need to know about?*

Chapter Fifteen- Retaliation

The next night in The Pit, everybody wanted to thank "The Avengers of Forester" personally. The companions had to endure at least twenty toasts, five speeches of varying length and coherency, and three songs with heretofore unheard-of harmonies. However, Connor pointed out they didn't have to pay for their dinners or a single drink since arriving in the early evening.

Dar leaned back in his chair and stretched. The familiar sounds of clinking tableware and voices surrounded him, punctuated by occasional laughter or a call from one of the serving girls to the barkeep. The smell of roasting meats and cooking vegetables wafted in from the kitchen.

He sighed and relaxed. He felt something now he had never felt in all his time of training with Sir Tan and his original attempts to establish himself: respect. No one made any wry jokes, not even his old schoolmates who had teased him the week before. Everyone looked at him with something akin to … well, awe.

He enjoyed it but at the same time wondered if it would last. Sir Tan warned him it wouldn't.

For now, he was content. Their little team had been going non-stop for the last few days and it felt good to be able to stay in town, away from conniving Ja'al clerics and their minions. That morning, he and the other Christians had attended Mass, then spent the rest of the day tending to their gear, having armor repaired, or getting some much-needed rest.

At least Sir Tan's estimate of earnings rang true. The yield from Faedan's room as well as from the high ridge complex added up to a pretty good sum for each of them, good enough to keep Dar and his companions well-supplied for a while.

He smiled, seeing Brandi and Eric sitting side by side. Judging by the amount of time they had spent with each other in the last two days, Eric was going to have to make a choice between Elaine and Brandawyn someday, maybe soon.

The last strains of a song brought him back to the present, an ear-numbing chorus rendered by three inebriated woodcutters who leaned against each other like a human tripod.

He chuckled. "Pretty soon they'll have us go down in history as the rescuers of the world. I didn't throw a goblin chief into nine warriors!"

Megan's eyes twinkled as she watched the woodcutters give exaggerated, sloppy bows and stumble off, clapping each other on the back. "Let them have their fun. They need heroes right now and we're the next best thing. A more famous group of freelancers will make them forget all about us soon enough."

"Do you think so?" Andyn wondered, "Westhaven was full of their friends and relatives."

Dar nodded.

"So, what do we do next?" interrupted Buck, not noticing Connor filching an apple slice from his plate.

"We hurry up and wait, I guess," Dar replied. "Lord Nolan has to get word on that scroll before we do anything else."

Connor bit into the apple and shook his head. "Damned stupid," he said around the food. "We rush around like crazy to get break up those troll-turds before they disappear in the Wilderness and now we sit around watching the flea population increase."

The companions chuckled. Andyn flicked a bread crumb at Connor. "Hey, we need the rest and study time, you guys included. I can't meditate while dodging arrows and the underground isn't exactly the best place to pray to Verian. Enjoy it. I'm getting to like this dreamy little town."

"Dreamy?" asked Dar, eyebrows rising, "I guess it's dreamy compared to Eleth-Anor, but you can take that a little far. This place can put you to sleep.

There's some days in the off-season when a caravan of grain merchants or a bunch of carpenters coming through is an event. I'd much rather be out there in the woods, finding out what the Ja'al are up to."

"Yes, so would I," admitted Brandi, "But the scroll might be important. We've got to give the scholars a chance to figure things out."

"A scroll from the Paragons?" Connor looked incredulous. "Dolmide's Beard, Brandi! The height of the Paragon Age was over three thousand years ago. That scroll can't possibly mean anything to us now. The best we'll get out of it will be a bunch of gold from some scholar who likes rooting around in moldy libraries, and good riddance. I'd rather just get the cash and head back out."

Andyn shook her head, looked around the room and spoke more quietly. "You're missing the point. Remember, that skeleton that had the box was a human, not a goblin. That means that whoever sent the scroll sent it with an important messenger and don't forget that it was on the Path of Peace. Since the courier was from the Ja'al, that means he couldn't have gotten by the wards we passed after the cave-in... and that means there's more to those caverns than we thought."

Connor made no convenient retort to that. Dar heard a patron call to the bartender in the background.

"I agree," said Eric. "I think the scroll was something special."

The group digested this for a while. Finally, Buck threw up his hands. "Ancient scrolls be damned. I'm just glad we've got plenty of cash now. I can get a horse and not have to worry about hacking my way through the bushes."

Dar shook his head. "You wouldn't go much faster, Buck. After ten miles, it gets really thick in that forest."

Buck waved a hand. "I'm not worried. I need a horse for riding the highways, not the forests. I've got two hero scouts to help guide the way out there."

Connor guffawed but said nothing.

They sat without speaking for a while, listening to a crowd of people at the bar sing a rendition of "The Avengers".

Dar chuckled. *Sound like a bunch of drunken cats looking for a date...*

"Those songs are really stupid, but they're fun to listen to," he offered.

Megan giggled. "Even if I never cast a ball of fire at anyone in my life. I can't use that spell yet."

Dar leaned forward. "Now there's something I've been wanting to ask one of you magical-types ever since I was training with Sir Tan."

Eric looked at him. "And that is?"

Dar took a drink from his goblet of wine and gestured expansively. "This whole magic thing. How does it happen? Sir Collins could do it, and he said I would be able to use spells later in my career, when I got good enough. He said I had the potential but then he didn't teach me anything. Most of my training was woodcraft, ecology, tracking and weapons. You, Megan, Andyn and Brandi seem to use magic like breathing. I want to know what goes on."

The four began laughing. Dar looked at them in confusion.

Megan put a hand on his. "If you're comparing our magic use to breathing, it's more like gasping than anything else."

"Or wheezing," countered Eric. Andyn looked at him in surprised laughter.

Brandi smiled. "I think we put up a good facade, Dar. It's not as easy as it looks."

"Well," said Dar. "Easy or no, how does it work?"

The older Alenar sister looked at the others and shrugged. Megan turned to him, bright eyes thoughtful. "It's kind of hard to explain. It's a drawing or pulling energy from the world around me."

She looked up, searching for the right words. "There's a place deep inside in my head," she said, indicating a spot just under her ear, "where a part of my mind siphons off energy from all around me."

Connor's eyebrows rose and he smirked. "Kind of like a leech."

That got amused looks from Andyn and Eric.

"A leech?" asked Brandi with a wry look at the halfling, "Well, I've never heard it put in quite those terms, but it's accurate enough, I suppose. There are all kinds of energy around us. Mages and clerics draw a tiny bit from many sources and bundle it all up. We store it in our heads until we need it. Sometimes, we directly use energy from around us. As we get better at it, we're able to do more complicated and powerful spells. Then we have to rest."

"How come?" asked Buck, scratching his chin.

"Too much spell-casting gives you a headache," Eric said, shooting a look over at Brandi. "A really nasty one. Even just staying within your abilities is tiring."

Buck blinked. "Wait a minute. You mean you're sucking energy from the universe? How can you do that? Don't you know you can upset the balance of nature?"

Andyn smiled. "Our friends who follow the way of the Oak and the Mistletoe are a little alarmed at the comparison," she said mildly, "but, Buck, your druids use the same method. Remember, Brandi said 'a tiny bit from many sources'."

Buck looked unconvinced. "What happens to nature when you take all that energy away?"

Megan cast her eyes heavenward. "Buck, it doesn't disappear. When we cast spells we put it back into the environment. Besides, there are *lots* of forms of energy and not that many magic-using people."

Buck looked confused.

Andyn put a hand on Megan's shoulder. "Maybe if we take an example it'll become more clear."

"Okay," agreed Eric. He gestured at the room around them. "Take a good look at this tavern."

Buck, Connor and Dar did so.

"See the torches in the wall settings?" he continued. "They're giving off a lot of heat energy right now and they do it all the time they're burning. Megan and I and the others only need to snatch a tiny fraction of that energy once and then store it. See all the people walking around, drinking and laughing and telling jokes? They're giving off a tremendous amount of energy. The tiny bit that even all five of us are drawing from them won't even be felt because it'll be replaced almost immediately. Even the tables and chairs have their own energy, as do the spiders in the corners and the rats in the walls and the mold in the wine cellar. Though the range of the effect is only about fifty feet or so, mages and clerics take tiny amounts from everywhere and mix it up into magical energy. Imagine how much energy we can draw in the middle of the forest. Don't forget that our capacity is finite and grows with our ability, but we can't take in more than we can use, so after we're done, the process stops until we need to draw energy again. Even a convention of powerful wizards couldn't drain the energy in this room."

Brandi nodded. "And that's another thing. How many mages and clerics do you see besides us?"

Buck twisted in his chair, starting to count on his fingers. Andyn smacked his hand. "There aren't any, you oaf. All of us are pretty rare just because we're sellswords and the magic-using ones are more so."

"Remember," Eric added, "our brains do it without any control from us."

Dar made a face and leaned back in his chair. "But how? I don't see how you can change the light and heat from a torch into a firedart or the ability to read a foreign language or cast a healing spell."

The others shrugged at the exact same time. Dar suppressed the urge to laugh at the synchronization.

"I don't know," said Eric. "Melinor doesn't know. Even professors and masters of the arts and sciences don't know. I've heard of some mages, like Melinor, doing research on it, but most people just give up after a while. There's no good way to study it."

Buck looked unconvinced. "Well, doesn't your Church have something to say about that? I heard you guys have some kind of prohibition against sorcery."

Brandi nodded. "We do. But the Bible prohibits us from making deals with the forces of the Dark to gain special powers - that's how sorcery is defined. When Andyn and I use magic to cast a ball of light, for instance, is neither good nor evil. It's a gift, bestowed on us by God to help His people in whatever way we can, no matter how great or small. It's just like your talent with the sword, Buck. You can either use it to do good or evil. It's your response to the gift that matters."

Buck leaned back in his chair. Connor tapped the tabletop. "Fine, but how do you know you've got the skill?"

Andyn shrugged. "You don't. Either a mage comes through your town looking for an apprentice or you go to a university or college to get tested for it. When I was younger, I knew I was sensitive to certain things, but that was the extent of it. When I took a test at the University, I found out for sure. Don't forget, I'm pretty rare even among spell-casters. I can use healing and arcane magic, not just one or the other."

Buck finally screwed up his face in disgust. "Magic! I'd prefer a good sword in my hand to all this junk." He patted Khelios where the sword hung from his hip.

Brandi raised twinkling eyes to his, amused. "Even a magic sword, Buck?" She sipped from her mug.

Buck muttered something incomprehensible.

Dar leaned forward again. "So, what you're saying is it's something subconscious, you don't know if you have it until you get tested, and it operates in some way that wizards and scholars don't really understand."

Megan nodded firmly. "Yes, that's it."

Dar dropped his head to the table. "Great."

Megan laughed and Eric knocked Dar on the head with his fist.

"Get used to it," he said. "It's said that wizards and high clerics are the most mixed up of us all."

"Be sure to tell that to Melinor," offered Dar, raising his head.

Eric saluted him with his mug.

"What's that bell?" asked Connor.

Dar froze. A deep clanging sounded from out in the town. All conversation and commotion in the tavern vanished like a snuffed candle flame. The patrons and employees froze where they were, one man's tankard only inches from his open mouth.

God...no! Not now...

Dar stood, a knot growing in his stomach. The bell continued, compelling in its urgency.

"What is it?" asked Megan, alarmed at his expression.

Dar grabbed his belt purse from the tabletop, anxiety rising. "That's the general alarm bell. Come on!"

He headed for the exit in long strides, then broke into a run, heading for his cottage, his friends on his heels.

People scurried in all directions. Soldiers ran by, heading for the wall towers, and families rushed towards their homes, faces pale with fear in the light from street-lamps and torches.

"Wait a minute," called Buck as he caught up with Dar. "General alarm?"

Dar fumbled with the key, cursing his own clumsiness. Finally, he got the door open and darted inside.

Damn, damn, damn!

"Dar, what's going on?" asked Eric, running into the cottage.

Dar squirmed into his chainmail and began fastening the buckles. "The last time the general alarm sounded, four tribes of hobgoblins tried to burn the town. I was five years old."

Andyn and the others had just arrived. "What?" she asked.

Dar pulled his lower protections over his breeches. "When that alarm rings, it means the town is under attack."

He met their eyes. They all knew the one power in the Wilderness strong enough to attack a town—and they had just made that power very angry.

The others leaped into action. Faster than Dar thought it possible, they fastened on their armor, grabbed up weapons and raced out to the street again.

Dar led them at a trot to the main gate. He looked up, glaring at the red-orange glow visible from beyond the walls.

"Whoever it is," he said in a flat voice, "they sure know how to use the torch."

Eric suddenly blanched. "Oh my God! Elaine's family is out there!" He started for the main gate.

Brandi grabbed his arm and whirled him around. "Did she work in town tonight? It's Sunday. Doesn't her family come into town on weekend evenings?"

Eric looked around wildly. "I don't know...I..."

"Dar Cabot!"

The group turned at the shout to see Lord Nolan's aide-de-camp ride up on a dun war horse. Colin Parker's plated armor seemed red from the fire-glow and he carried a shield with Nolan's leaping-fish heraldry emblazoned on it.

Parker eyed them from under a raised visor. "You have clerics in your party?"

"Yes, Sir Colin," replied Dar. "What's happening?"

"There's goblin troops, about three hundred, with human mages, cavalry and some of those wild-haired Ja'al clerics leading the charge. They have undead with them, about seventy, mostly skeletons and walking corpses. The militia is holding them, but we've got to get spell-casters and our main troop out there, and now."

Dar nodded and Parker looked around. The knight's eyes scanned the milling tumult, then rested on Dar again.

"I need you over near Tower Two. I'll be back for you."

With that, he rode away towards a knot of woodsmen, trying to form a semblance of a unit, axes glinting in the torch- and fire-light. A more disciplined phalanx of infantry took up a position near the front gate.

Dar ran towards their positions with his companions, a frown creasing his brow. "Anybody know anything about fighting undead?"

Megan shook her head, knuckles white on her staff, but Andyn and Brandi exchanged a nervous look.

"I was trained to handle them," said Andyn, fingering the silver tree of Verian on a chain around her neck, "but I've never done it in combat before."

"Me either," said Brandi, "I know the techniques, but..."

"Cabot!"

It was Parker again, shouting at them from a few yards away. "Get ready! They're going to open the main gate now. You're to flank the enemy from Tower Two. Try to use your clerics on the undead and keep the goblin archers busy. We'll take care of the rest."

Dar saw a large body of Forester Guards arranged in orderly rows near the entrance, spears and shields at the ready. Behind them, a decidedly less orderly group of citizens stood fidgeting. Dar trotted over next to the tower's base, where a guard waited, sword drawn and hand on the wall.

The guard looked back towards Parker, awaiting a signal. Dar could smell wood smoke here, close to the action. Worse still were the sounds: the clanging of weapons, screams and shouts and an occasional sizzling that he cared not to identify.

What are we supposed to do? he wondered in impatient anxiety. *Jump the wall? God, what's happening out there?*

Suddenly, a great cheer rang out from the main gate. Dar looked and Lord Nolan reined in at Parker's side. Colin raised his sword in salute. The guardsman next to Dar pushed against the wall and a section of the construction swung away from them.

Dar gaped. *How come I never found this?*

They charged through the opening into a blast of heat from a burning building, near the walls. The screams, shouts, and ringing of steel doubled in intensity. Dar brought up his bow, blinking in the smoke and heat. He saw no targets.

A roar of voices from ahead of him and to the right drew his gaze. The Forester soldiery burst forth from the main gate, bristling with spearpoints like some massive, many-legged hedgehog, the citizens right behind them. Nolan rode at their head, shining bright in full armor. The force thundered out into the smoke and fire. A hail of arrows soared from the town walls overhead, arcing out at the unseen enemy.

A zipping noise near Dar's head made him turn. A shadowy pair of figures raced away, next to the burning building about sixty feet away. They stopped and let fly. Two more shafts sang past. He dropped to one knee and returned fire, hearing the bows of his companions twang.

A cloud of smoke blew in front of him and he paused, irritated. When it cleared, the figures had disappeared.

Buck leaped to the front of the group. "To the left!" he shouted above the din. "We'll hit the left flank while Nolan and the others are holding the center!" He charged off.

"Saint Kira, Buck!" shouted Dar. "If you get..." Buck was already rounding the corner of the burning building. With a muttered curse, he followed, the others on his heels.

They turned the corner and left the flaming structure behind them, careening around two intact houses. About a hundred yards ahead, they could see many struggling figures outlined against the flames consuming a barn.

Buck pressed against the side of one of the homes. "There's a bunch of hobgoblins with bows on the left," he shouted, "Let's take them out!"

With a loud yell, the group leaped out from behind the wall. Dar sighted on a shadowy, bow-wielding figure and let fly. His first shaft took the figure in the side and the second in the neck. Three other enemy archers dropped from a hail of arrows and Dar nodded in satisfaction, readying for another shot.

Megan's scream saved his life. He whirled, dropping his bow and ducking to avoid a scimitar blade that sliced the air where his head had been.

He grabbed for his bastard sword, growling in anger. *Whoever the hell that is...*

He froze.

A skeleton, armored in a rotting leather jerkin with rusted metal plates, grinned at him and drew its sword back for another strike.

Dar stumbled backward. The skeleton lurched and swung but Dar knocked the blade aside with his own. He cut from left to right without thinking.

The blade whistled below the skeleton's ribs, where vital organs would have been.

Damn! How do you fight one of these things?

He blocked the next strike and returned a swing that chipped off a small piece of thighbone.

His irritation turned to nervousness. Maybe if he went for the head instead...

As if in answer, a smooth-headed mace hummed in from his left and the skeleton's cranium exploded in a shower of bone chips. Dar blinked and stepped back as it clattered to the ground.

Andyn grabbed his arm, pointing at the larger melee straight ahead with her mace. "Form a circle around Brandi and Megan and I!" she shouted. "You guys can protect us while we work on the undead!"

Dar picked up his bow and located Buck, Eric, Connor and the three women. Together, the men formed a ring and advanced to within thirty yards of the main battle with the women in the center of the ring.

Dar took the point, breathing hard. They had a position just beyond another intact farmhouse. There was a large open area ahead, presumably for maneuvering wagons to the barn area.

Absolute chaos reigned. Wide-eyed, Dar saw three skeletons pull a Guard from his horse, rusted weapons hacking. Four goblins traded lusty blows with a trio of citizen levies, two falling to spears before downing one of the townsmen with a sword thrust. Three purple flashes seared the center of the fight somewhere, accompanied by several horrid shrieks.

Lord Nolan slashed about him with a sword lit by an angry blue flame, his crowned helm glittering. Every time Firesong struck, a dark figure dropped. As Dar watched, three whirling pinwheels of color streaked out from the Ja'al forces. Nolan barely got his shield up in time. Short bursts of colorful fire enveloped the baron, setting his cloak aflame. He reeled in the saddle. Colin and two other knights quickly pulled the burning fabric off him and tried to pull him away from the fight, but Nolan waved them off and urged his mount deeper into the fray. Angry Firesong rose and fell.

Dar swallowed hard and set an arrow to his bowstring.

"Ready!" he called, hoping Brandi could hear him above the shrieks and clanging of weaponry.

Then Brandi stood next to him, holding her little silver cross. He heard her say something in Ecclesia.

His first arrow broke on a goblin's armor and his second took it in the shoulder. The warrior spun around and crashed into a skeleton, bringing both down in a jumble of bones, limbs and armor.

He heard Megan speak arcane words and three tiny comets of flame blasted another goblin to the earth.

Well, let's see some anti-undead magic already... He looked up at Brandi. His eyes widened.

She stood perfectly still, a sparkling luminescence shining in her eyes. Her features were calm, peaceful and beautiful, relaxed. A network of tiny blue lightning bolts raced around the outline of the crucifix in her left hand. Dar gaped at Andyn as well, who stood with an identical expression and little green lights breaking out on the surface of her silver tree of Verian.

A loud moaning arose from the knot of undead in the enemy ranks. Four skeletons turned around and began rattling away from the battle. The zombies did likewise, hiding their faces and shuffling away.

Elated, Dar put an arrow into the back of a departing zombie.

Andyn's voice joined Brandi's and five more skeletons quit the field.

An arrow zipped by them. A dozen goblins turned away from the soldiers and raced in their direction, stopping to loose arrows on the way. Dar fired back in answer.

In the next few frantic seconds, arrows flew thick between them. One grazed the back of Dar's left arm and another glanced off his armor and cut his head, but neither injury was serious. Dar thought he took down two goblins, but wasn't sure through the smoke. When he could see clearly, the goblins had either retreated or been killed.

He heard a shout from his right and he aimed, then lowered his bow. Father Ander trotted toward them through the smoke and haze. The priest wore a coat of metal plates and wielded a flanged mace in one hand. Two howling goblins raced to intercept him and he turned to meet them, weapon flashing in the firelight.

Megan's voice rang out and a pair of glowing darts shot out at one of the goblins. The darts exploded with a twin crack and the goblin fell to the churned earth. The remaining enemy swung a club at Father Ander, who blocked it and crushed its skull with a return strike.

The priest stepped to their side in seconds. "Excellent work!" he shouted above the din. "If we can turn the undead from here, the infantry can drive the goblins from the center."

He hung his weapon on a belt hook and held out a gauntleted hand to Andyn and Brandi, smiling. "We do this together."

Dar whirled at a scream of rage from the battlefield.

A Ja'al cleric, tall and burly, loomed behind the retreating undead, huge and terrible on a dark horse. He held forth a symbol of his own, a writhing thing that throbbed with purple light.

The undead made a complete about-face and head back towards the battle.

Dar's heart skipped a beat.

Father Ander and the two women began chanting behind him.

This is madness, Dar thought, *what are they going to do, play skeleton-ball? Send the Skyfire-blasted things back and forth forever?*

The cleric talismans on both sides of the battle flared. Brandi, Andyn and Father Ander seemed to sing in an exotic harmony, then a brilliant flash lit up the night behind Dar and the ground jumped under his knee. The edge of a disk of blue-white energy expanded from behind him, about three feet off the ground, expanding with the speed of a galloping horse.

The undead froze, trapped in the light. Then they exploded in violent detonations, bone fragments spraying in all directions. Zombies burst into flames.

Dar turned his head, shielding his eyes from the light and fire. His pulse pounded in his ears.

What the hell have I got myself into?

The Ja'al cleric screamed a curse and pointed at them. Dar saw a greenish glow emanate from the Ja'al's finger and he quickly fired an arrow.

The shaft buried itself in his mount's shoulder. The horse screamed and reared, then lurched backwards, disappearing behind the goblin warriors.

Another cloud of smoke blew in front of Dar's view and when it cleared, there was no sign of the cleric. A large crowd of goblins and skeletons remained.

Dar reached back and his hand closed on nothing.

No more arrows. His mouth was dry.

Maybe Mom was right. Accounting is a nice safe profession after all.

One of the larger goblins bellowed an order. A score of his troops wheeled and charged towards Dar's little band. Dar stood and drew his sword. There was no way out of it this time.

Too many, he thought grimly.

As if in answer, he heard Father Ander's calm voice behind him. "Have faith and stand firm."

A glowing ball, trailing fire, arced from the castle walls to land about ten feet behind the charging Ja'al troops. It exploded in a blasting roar, the flash of fire so bright that Dar squeezed his eyes shut. He stumbled to one knee as the ground bucked and heaved. The wave of heat rushed over him.

He opened his eyes. Only a scattering of bones, smoking and melted pieces of armor, and piles of ash remained.

He gasped for breath. It seemed like there was no air nearby.

"Mother Earth!" called Buck's voice, unsteady. "What in the Mighty Oaks was that?"

"That," said Megan, her own voice shaky, "was a *real* fireball."

"Lady Ellen's work," said Father Ander firmly. "We had better not stay here," He stood next to Dar now, eyes peering out at the smoky, thrashing mess about a hundred feet from them. He bit his lip.

"Let us go over to the center a little bit. Perhaps we can..."

A titanic shout from the main battle cut off his sentence. Lord Nolan and the Ja'al cleric whirled on horseback in the center of the fight, weapons ringing against each other. The baron ducked a swing and wheeled his horse around, sweeping a backhand into the cleric. There was a loud clang and flare of magic and the Ja'al plunged from his horse. Another roar of voices greeted this and Nolan's forces surged forward. The Ja'al invaders surged to meet them, held for a while in the struggling, thrashing melee, then fell apart. The goblins retreated, stopping to loose arrows as they went, but the remaining undead stayed in place to slug it out with Lord Nolan's troops.

Dar felt a great weight lifted from him.

Megan let out a deep breath and smiled at him. "Let's leave the rest to the soldiers. I've fought enough this last week to last a lifetime."

Father Ander's hand was on Dar's shoulder. "She is right. Let us go back to the fortress, where we can be of some help to the injured."

The Ja'al retreated in good order, archers supporting the footmen and cavalry. Nolan's commanders took an equally disciplined approach and forced the invaders back until they disappeared into the forest. Only a few zombies stayed on the field, lashing out blindly in their last attempts to kill while the Forester infantry hacked them to pieces.

Dar shuddered.

"Elaine!"

Eric stood with eyes wide with sudden remembrance. He gave them all a stricken look, then turned and ran towards a section of cottages. Most were either on fire or smoldering. Dar turned startled eyes to his companions. They had forgotten about Elaine.

"Oh, Saint John and Saint Telric!" said Brandi, the fear in her eyes belying the exasperation in her voice. She took off at a run, the others pounding after her.

Dar leaped over a wrecked cart just to keep Eric in sight. He caught up with him next to a house with one side enveloped in flame.

Several townsmen unloaded a cart full of water barrels, passing buckets around with frantic haste.

Dar jumped forward to assist Eric in dumping water on the flames. Their companions joined them.

Father Ander's voice called out from behind them. "Stand back!"

Dar looked up. Father Ander stood with his eyes closed, hands extended before him. The priest spoke a couple of words in Ecclesia, then opened his eyes.

The air turned bone-dry. Dar shuddered. A silvery glimmer shone in the air above the flaming house and a veritable sheet of water crashed downwards.

Most of the flames disappeared in an immense cloud of steam. The water crew doused the last few stubborn fires.

Eric jumped forward, tearing away the ruins of the front door. Dar followed, heart in his throat.

God, not Elaine!

The remaining half of the house was a mess. Elaine's father lay under a fallen table, four arrows in his chest, a bloodied war hammer still clutched in his left hand. Two smaller figures, goblins, lay crushed under the wreckage.

Eric knelt in the rubble, clawing debris away. Dar saw Elaine's mother and brother lying together next to another pair of dead goblins. He knelt by them as Eric, not finding Elaine, forced open the back door and leaped outside again.

Ella Ward had a knife in her hand, the blade still buried in the chest of one of the dead humanoids. Her son Steven laid next to her, a quarterstaff across his chest and a goblin with a dented helmet at his feet. Mother and son had been shot with arrows.

Andyn knelt at his side. Dar looked up at her and shook his head, his vision growing misty. She closed her eyes, then opened them to look out the back door.

She stiffened.

"Dar..." She ran out.

Eric stood over a couple of dark forms on the ground.

Dar hurdled broken furniture and sprinted outside with her. As he arrived, Eric dropped to his knees next to one of the figures.

Elaine lay face down, her head turned to the side, hair thrown around her like a golden halo. The feathered shaft of a goblin arrow stood between her shoulder blades, her blouse stained dark. A goblin warrior, helmet some three feet away, lay next to her right arm, a knife handle protruding from his own back, a small bow still clutched in a dark paw. Somehow, with an arrow in her back, Elaine had managed to trip one of her murderers and kill him with a well-placed stab.

Dar's vision swam. An image of a rascally, pigtailed girl of nine danced in front of his mind. "Come play tag-the-wyvern, Dar..."

It can't be her. She can't die! I'll just wait until she comes back from work.

"I'm sorry Elaine," Eric was saying. "I came as soon as I could..." He reached out and took her hand.

Brandi arrived, knelt down next to him and put a hand on his shoulder, then worked the arrow out of Elaine's back and rolled her over.

Weren't we passing notes in class just yesterday? Dar wondered. He wiped at eyes. *How did this happen?*

"Oh wow," came Connor's voice from behind him. "Is she...?"

Brandi shook her head and closed Elaine's staring blue eyes with a gentle hand. "Too late this time, Connor," she said.

"Just like Westhaven!" Dar spat, not caring if anyone heard.

Eric looked up at him, tears streaking his smudged, dirty face. "Dar...I..."

Dar let out his anger in a sigh. "Eric, we did our best. If we had been here, we would have been killed too. The Ja'al just overran this place." His voice sounded calm and reasonable, almost as if it was another person speaking.

By now, Father Ander had joined them. He moved over to stand next to Brandi and Eric.

"Another young one," he said, shaking his head.

The priest put a hand on Eric's shoulder and sighed. For a moment, Dar was shocked to see how old and worn he looked.

How many times has he seen this? he wondered in a haze. *How does he keep his faith?*

"These were all people of my parish," the priest said. "I know they are in a place where they won't feel pain or suffering any longer, only happiness. I know it doesn't make the pain any less for us, but in time, it will."

Eric just nodded.

The cleric bowed his head and closed his eyes. "Let us pray, then, for these people and all the others who gave their lives tonight."

There was a snort of derision from Buck. "Pray." He shook his head, eyes blank. "That won't do them any good."

Andyn shot him a black look and he turned away.

A voice rang out from behind them. "You!"

The companions turned. A group of townsfolk strode in their direction, led by a stout, middle-aged teamster.

Their leader scowled at them. "You! Freelancers! You're the cause of all this!"

Dar blinked. "What?"

"What are you talking about?" demanded Megan, recovering her wits before anyone else.

One of the others in the crowd, a shopkeeper, gestured at the wreckage around them with a bandaged hand. "Look around you! If you hadn't gone out to the mountains and stirred up the Ja'al with your stupid quest for treasure and glory, you wouldn't have brought them down on our heads!"

Dar found his voice. "Are you suggesting we are the cause of all this?"

One in the crowd shook a fist at him. "They killed my boy!" Townsfolk near him began to shout imprecations at Dar and his friends.

"Right!" shouted Dar, silencing the crowd to angry murmurs. "*They* did the killing! *They* did the burning! Just like Westhaven. Or have you forgotten that the reason we went out was to bring justice, not 'loot and glory'?"

Unwilling to let it go, the teamster continued glaring at the freelancers. "These people died because you didn't get rid of the Ja'al when you had the chance."

"No," said Father Ander, stepping forward and laying a hand on Dar's shoulder. "All of these people beyond the walls died not because of failure, but because of success. They held off and confounded the Ja'al attack long enough for the guard to close the gates, then fought off the advance to save our town."

The crowd's angry mutter stilled. "You, William Dennis," the priest continued, pointing at a hostler in the mob, "would you have the crime of Westhaven go unpunished? Your friend Jack Miller died there. Weren't you just in the tavern, singing the praises of these people?"

Father Ander's eyes flashed. "You all talk as if the Ja'al were some lawful force, some group who we should be afraid of angering, as if they had just cause to punish us. Wrong! That thought is wrong and the Ja'al are in the wrong! They have no right to do what they do, plotting overthrow and mayhem and murder. They will have much to answer for in the days to come, and, indeed, on the Last Day. We are in the right, because it is our duty to prevent evil with the last drop of our blood and to bring justice to all peoples."

He surveyed the townsfolk. "Have you forgotten that it was our liege lord, Nolan, who commissioned these people to bring justice for Westhaven? Have you forgotten that Dar Cabot here is one of us, a citizen of Forester like you and I? A friend and classmate of this martyred girl, slain trying to hold up the invasion so that you all could live?" He swept his other hand to indicate Elaine.

The teamster at the head of the mob flushed and looked down.

The priest continued in a softer voice, encouraging. "We are all hurt by this evil, but we will not prevail over it by turning on one another. If we fight amongst ourselves, the Ja'al have already won."

The teamster's eyes dropped and he sighed. When he looked up again, it was with tears in his eyes.

"I'm sorry, Mister Cabot... the fighting and all..."

Dar gave him a tired smile. "Don't worry about it, Renton. I'm as angry as you are. More, even."

The crowd began to shuffle and disperse, many of them nodding in agreement. They headed away to where the soldiers picked through the wreckage.

Dar looked up at Father Ander. "Thanks."

The priest sighed. "Every word was true. Elaine, and these others, would be very sad if they saw discord on their account. I am sure of it. Come." He turned back to where Brandi and Andyn arranged Elaine's body so Buck and Eric could carry it.

Dar turned with his newest friends to say farewell to one of his oldest ones.

Chapter Sixteen —Revelations

"Megan, wait!"

Megan Alenar turned to look down the path behind her and smiled. Dar Cabot hurried to catch up.

He fell into step beside her. "Got tired of hanging around us?"

"Yes, I can't stand the sight of you..." She playfully shoved him in the shoulder. "Actually, it's a great day and Nolan's gardens are beautiful. It's the only place I can go, since he won't let anyone out of the town right now, not with all the Ja'al creeping around in the forest."

"Besides," she said, indicating Brandi and Eric walking about fifty feet ahead of them, "I've got to keep an eye on those two."

Dar gave her a sidelong look. "Chaperone or matchmaker?"

Megan gave him a sly wink. "Maybe both, maybe neither."

A neat, stone-lined path stretched ahead of them through the trees and shrubs. The garden burst with color every spring and this year was no exception. Brilliant yellow, red and white roses, colorful pansies of all shades, and tulips in blue, yellow and pink competed with each other in the sunlight. Bushes of all sorts, rare grasses, and unusual plants, like fairy feather reeds, grew in abundance. Nolan was justifiably proud of his garden, however small it might be in relation to the ones in the larger towns.

Gravel crunched under their boots as they strolled down the path, enjoying the peace and quiet.

Dar kicked at a rock. "Nolan's not really sure if the forest is safe. I hear he's declared it off-limits until he can determine the strength of the Ja'al force. One of the guards said he saw some goblins early this morning."

Megan nodded. "Andyn thinks that's the whole reason they attacked in the first place, and Lord Nolan agrees with her. The whole town is buttoned up until the Guard can figure out where the safe areas are."

In fact, Lord Nolan had asked them to appear in the grand hall of the manor house after lunch and it was almost noon now. The people of Forester had been besieging the Baron with pleas to do something about the Ja'al menace and, next to marching out with his army, the 'Avengers' were the best thing he had. Megan felt sure the baron would send them out as soon as possible.

We're a political solution, if nothing else.

Bright sunlight lit the garden, with shadows cast by the trees lining the trail. Insects darted off as they passed, indignant at the invasion of their playground.

Dar sneaked a look at Megan. She had opted for a rather boyish combination of brown trousers, white blouse and dark boots instead of her robes. Typical for her, the clothes were clean, neat and as stylish as her budget would allow. Even in such attire, she was just as trim and attractive as she had been in a dress or mage's robe. Her amber eyes were thoughtful, distant and very beautiful.

Dar gave himself a mental shake.

Despite the relative safety of the fortress and garden, she wore one dagger on each hip. Dar didn't blame her. He himself had decided to bring his sword and handaxe, although he had left his armor behind. He wondered if she, like Brandi, was ambidextrous.

"How's he holding up?" he asked, indicating Eric with a nod of his head.

Megan took a deep breath, the sunlight reflecting red-gold on her hair. "Better, I guess. Bran says he feels like he can talk to her, so she's been trying to get him to let his feelings out. I talked to him myself, too. He doesn't think he was in love with Elaine, but she was nice to him and took him into the family. Family is something very important to Eric."

An old, all-too-familiar pain gripped Dar's heart and he nodded, looking at the ground.

Megan stopped walking and took him by the arms. Her eyes were kind, soft. "What an idiot I am," she said quietly, "Here I am worrying about Eric and you are the one who knew her best of all of us."

He smiled thinly. "You're not an idiot. It's obvious Eric was quite taken with her and she was just my friend... and we'd grown apart in recent years. Being a sellsword does that to you, makes you different from everyone else."

She shook her head. "You grew up with her. She was your classmate. That counts for quite a bit."

He leaned against a tree. Emerald leaves swayed in the breeze above his head. "You know, some kids and Elaine and I sneaked in here once to play hide-and-seek. We were terrified we would get in trouble with Nolan's guards, until Lady Ellen came in. She pretended not to see us but we knew she did. She just smiled and went on picking roses. That was only a few months after she came here to marry Lord Nolan. It seems like so long ago. She was like some fairy creature, all dark skin and kind eyes and amazing magic."

Megan was silent. She picked at a corner of tree-bark. "I know you probably still feel guilty about Elaine, but please, Dar, don't blame yourself."

His jaw tightened. "I should have been able to do something!"

Megan resisted the urge to sigh in frustration. *Mary, Jesus and Joseph!*

"What did you say to Eric that night?" she asked. "Would you have fought off a hundred and fifty goblins? Changed the Ja'al to toads? You and I both know there's only so much you can do."

Dar stood very quiet for a few heartbeats, meeting her gaze.

Amber is a nice color for eyes, he thought.

"I know you're right." He looked past her, watching Brandi and Eric sitting next to a small fountain. "Everyone knows you're right. It just doesn't make it any easier."

She had to smile. "Who said it would be easy? Jesus Christ Himself didn't guarantee an easy life."

"Then why didn't He prevent all this?" he demanded before he could stop himself. He immediately regretted it. Here he was lecturing someone who had known far greater tragedy than he.

Megan ignored a twinge of pain in her heart and watched him with sad eyes. "Would you have Him blast with lightning everyone who does something cruel? Or has an evil thought? None of us would be alive, Dar. He gives us all the ability to choose because He wants loving friends, not slaves. I know you'll find this hard to believe—and it took a series of long discussions with Brandi for me to understand it—but God even gives goblins and ogres and trolls the chance to love Him, though very few do."

Dar looked down at the pathway, shaking his head. "Why? Why create us if we're just going to suffer, whether from disease or war?"

Megan watched him. *He's so angry, but still looking for the answers. Not that I have all of them.*

She lifted up his chin with her hand to look him in the eyes. "Dar, when you marry, do you want a willing spouse who chooses you freely or someone who is forced into it?"

Dar's heart skipped a beat at the word 'marry', looking at her eyes, tawny pools of light.

"You know which one I want."

She nodded. "God wants nothing less, from every creature who can recognize Him. And as for disease, He suffers with His people, all of them. His Son was subject to disease and pain just like everyone else. He knows what it's like. Besides, we have the means at our disposal to care for the sick and dying, and we can make it easier for them, if we choose."

Dar gave her a wry smile. "Are you sure your sister went to the Seminary and not you? How do you know so much?"

Her answering smile was sad. "Practice, Dar, practice."

Blast.

"Sorry."

"Don't be. I'm glad all that pain gives me a perspective to help someone else."

He snorted. "I need a lot of help."

She laughed. "Dar Cabot, you don't fool me. Behind all that bravado, you have a strong faith. You and I both know that Elaine and her family were good people and are in a much happier place. Their journey is done. Pray God we all end up where they are now."

She made sense, he knew, despite the turmoil and pain in his soul. Part of him still rebelled, but what he desired was peace. And, at that moment standing there with Megan, peace settled in him, the first he had felt in days.

"I'm just going to miss Elaine and her family. And I'm still angry about it all."

Megan nodded, taking his arm. "I understand. And if you want to be angry with God, do so, and keep on wrestling with it until you find the answer. He expects it and wants to hear about it. If you weren't, it would mean you didn't care, and it's obvious you do."

Dar put his hand over hers. *Well, then, I'm going to be mad at God for a while. I'm not ready to accept any of this just yet.*

They walked for a while in silence. He gave her a sidelong glance. "You think you're pretty smart, don't you?"

She gave him a roguish look. "As a matter of fact, yes."

They strolled in silence for a while, almost catching up to Brandi and Eric. A lark soared by in the blue sky, veering to a landing on a tree limb.

"Yes, family seems to be very important to Eric," said Megan watching the other couple.

Dar nodded. His own parents and brother were very important to him. "Melinor Indidarc must have been an exceptional father," he mused, "Where is Melinor's wife, anyway?"

"Oh, I hear she died about five years ago, from a sudden heart attack at her home while Melinor was away." Megan pursed her lip. "I think Eric has a special relationship with Saren DeMey, though she's been Countess of Tallemar for some time now now."

"Eric seems to get along well with Brandi," Dar offered.

Megan smiled. "Yes, he does at that. Brandi likes him a lot. She's told me so." She stopped to inspect a kalaca flower growing by the side of the road, cupping the purple and red blossom.

Dar stopped with her. "Eric thinks she's really pretty, and brave. He told me he admires her common sense and how much she cares about people."

She straightened. "He said that to you? He ought to tell her himself. Brandi doesn't get to hear things like that very often."

Please, God. Megan thought, daring to hope. *Send her someone good and kind. She deserves a man like that.*

Dar looked a little awkward.

"Men...sometimes have a hard time saying things like that."

She looked at him, wondering.

"Well," she said, "It isn't easy to do, I'll grant you that. But Brandi doesn't think she's very pretty. I'm the one men always notice first."

Dar gave her a roguish look. "I can see why."

Megan felt her face growing warm and looked at the ground. Why did he have to be so funny and easy to talk to and attractive and brave and...

Drat.

"Thanks," she replied, feeling very shy all of a sudden. *What do I say?*

"But Brandi's been the steady one," she continued, convinced she was prattling, "I'm always losing my temper or forgetting something or going off to buy something pretty I want but don't need."

She looked up to find him watching her. "I don't know where I'd be without her," she said. She watched Brandi, talking to Eric as she leaned against a tree.

Dar nodded. "You love her very much."

Megan felt a lump in her throat, remembering Brandi's face hovering over her bed, nursing her after a bout with some illness. Brandi, sticking up for her against town bullies who taunted them as traitors when they were very young.

"Brandi's the only family I have, aside from our aunt and uncle," she said in a low voice, then sighed. "She had to grow up fast after we left Torosc. She never complained. Not once. And believe me, I can be a lot of trouble."

Dar stepped closer to her. Megan looked up at his brown eyes, feeling herself go still and warm inside, almost as if Brandi had just used a healing magic on her. She felt fidgety and excited and at peace all at once.

He took her hand in his. "I know you can be, but I don't much care. I think you have some wonderful qualities yourself, Megan Alenar, and I'm glad to know you."

She smiled up at him, a sudden wild joy breaking out in her heart. "As I am glad to know you, Dar Cabot."

Is this what love feels like?

"Hey!" came a shout from behind them, towards the entrance to the garden. Megan and Dar both jumped in surprise, then hung their heads in exasperation. Connor stood under the ornate, carved stone archway, waving.

Dar ran a hand through his hair. *Blasted thieves,* he thought. *Can't they do anything so that we'd notice them before they did it? Or am I going to spend the next ten years jumping around like a damned grasshopper?*

The halfling called out to them. "If you guys want something to eat before we see Lord Nolan, you'd better do it now. We're supposed to be at the manor house when the watch cries one and we just heard him call out twelve noon."

The mood broken, Megan sighed.

Dar smiled suddenly. "No rest for the wicked, eh?"

She giggled. "That's why the Ja'al are so busy."

He laughed at that. Megan thought it a wonderful sound. He turned to go.

She shot a quick look at Connor to make sure he had turned away. Then, on an impulse, planted a quick kiss on Dar's cheek before he could get out of range.

He turned back in surprise.

She swallowed, feeling the color rising to her cheeks, and smiled. "Don't ask me why I did that."

He took her hand and kissed it. "I don't need to."

Megan's knees felt wobbly and weak. She didn't care.

He turned again to go, then shot her a rascally look over his shoulder. "Let's make Brandi and Eric run."

***

"Twenty-four dead, forty-one wounded, and eight homes and four barns destroyed," said Nolan Hanford, pacing next to one of the arched windows behind his baronial throne.

His wife stood next to the drawing table. She held a scroll in her hands, the same scroll the freelancers had brought out from Modron Derrig's complex.

Megan, standing with Dar and the others, looked at the baroness. "You didn't send that to the Count in Hillton after all, milady?"

Ellen shook her head. "No. We couldn't send it Sunday and then the attack came and we had more important things to do."

Megan made a silent "oh" with her mouth and nodded.

Buck cleared his throat from behind her. "Er...how many Ja'al did we get, milord?"

Nolan waved his hand. "There were forty-eight skeletons and zombies destroyed, plus about fifty-five goblins and a dozen or so human warriors. I killed seven goblins myself plus three Ja'al underclerics and one of their mages. But we can't afford a war of attrition. They have the advantage there: the Wilderness can provide them an almost endless supply of goblins, and worse, if the Ja'al give them enough incentive. We have to eliminate the source of these threats and do it quickly. The Ja'al are getting very bold if they think they can take Forester by force of arms."

Megan walked over to the drawing table and picked up the bowl from Clarissa's hut at Westhaven. Her eyes darted from the bowl to Lady Ellen's vase, also on the table.

What's so important about this that they have to kill to get it?

She hefted the pottery, examining the horizontal network of zigzag lines. They were raised surfaces on the fired clay, colored black to make them noticeable.

Her finger traced the pattern. *There's has to be something here. There has to. It doesn't make sense otherwise.*

"Megan."

She looked up. Lady Ellen regarded her with a queer look in her eyes.

"Do you have any paper?" the baroness asked.

Confused, Megan nodded. "Yes, milady."

"And a marker."

"I have a charcoal pencil, but..."

"Perfect," said Ellen, excited and absorbed all at once. "Get them please."

Megan produced the items from her shoulder bag. Ellen placed the paper over the designs on the bowl and began to gently rub the pencil on the paper.

A pattern emerged on the paper, a pattern that looked distinctly like mountains.

Oh my God. Why didn't we think of this before?

Andyn strode up to them. "What's she doing?"

"Tracing," said Megan, totally engrossed. "Those look like mountains."

But which mountains are they?

"Dear?" Ellen finished the tracing and turned to her husband.

Lord Nolan turned from gazing out at the Dragonspine Range and walked over to the table. His lady finished another tracing, this time using the vase with the tiny black flying horse.

Nolan picked up the first paper, then looked out the window. He turned towards the windows and held up the tracing.

"Clarissa," he said in a soft, admiring voice, shaking his head, "you sly old bat."

"What? What is it?" whispered Connor from Megan's side.

"This, Mister Lomin," said the Lord of Forester, "is a sketch of the Dragonspine Range, with Whitehorse Peak detailed. See the star?"

Ellen brought over the second tracing, a look of satisfaction on her face. "And I'm willing to bet the manor house that this is..."

She placed the second tracing over the first and matched up the black dots.

"... a map," Megan breathed.

The wavy vertical line from the vase tracing led from one dot to a second dot. Ellen had matched up this second dot with the dot on the tracing from the bowl. This was the dot next to the tallest 'mountain'. From where Megan stood, she could see a tiny black winged horse next to the dot and the 'mountain'.

"Which mountain is that?" asked Connor, pointing to the peak next to the horse.

"That's Whitehorse Peak," said Dar.

They all stood in silence for a long time.

Lord Nolan rested his hands on the smooth wood surface of the table. "Now the attack makes sense."

"Really, milord?" Megan looked at him in surprise.

"Of course," the baron answered, making a frustrated gesture. "They weren't trying to take over Forester. They'd need a force ten times that size to conquer us. No, their real intention was probably something else— probably to keep us in Forester while they go search for whatever that winged horse stands for."

Andyn looked doubtful. "How do we know these two tracings go together? And what could a pegasus represent?"

Nolan looked amused despite the seriousness of the situation. "First, we don't know they go together. But Clarissa was a very canny old bird. If she found out something while in the wilderness and wanted to keep it a secret until an emergency, this is exactly the way she would have done it. Secondly, a pegasus could mean anything: a real pegasus, a symbol for a military force, a magic item that can make people or horses fly, anything. Guessing won't help, I assure you."

He picked up both tracings and handed them to Dar. "Mister Cabot, these are your maps now. You and the other "Avengers" are going to Whitehorse Peak, Ja'al or no Ja'al. How long do you think it will take to reach it?"

Dar pursed his lip.

"Sir Tan and I got there in three days, but we were almost running all the way and we had to hide a couple of times from some of the beasts that roam around out there. We'll have to sneak out, probably at dawn. We'll also have to leave by the south gate, head west and then double back into the forest because of the Ja'al in the woods. I'd say at least six days one way."

"What about mounts?" queried Brandi. "Will horses help?"

Dar shook his head. "The woods get very thick after a day's ride, near a dwarven community out there named Dorn's Hall. Mules would be better."

"Er..." asked Buck, "shouldn't those sort of expenses be covered by the local government?"

"Buck!" Andyn scolded, but Nolan chuckled.

"Unfortunately, Mister Bydecy," the baron responded, "conditions have changed. I have a town to reconstruct and most of my people who lost their homes do not have the money to rebuild. I'm sure you'll understand."

"It was worth a try," said Buck.

"There's a caravan leaving at dawn," Nolan continued, "I've been putting heavy guards on every one that leaves town, so it won't be untoward when there are a lot of troops. When it departs the south gate, you'll be in one of the wagons. I'll send Colin out with you. When you get out to a spot far enough, you slip away from the main party and divert north. Agreed?"

Dar nodded.

"Now, get your provisions arranged, and Godspeed."

With a series of crisp bows, the companions left them.

They spent the rest of the afternoon at the general store and weaponer's shop, using their reward money and the remaining treasure from the Ja'al to buy enough supplies to last them for at least twelve days. Then Buck decided he was going to get his own personal animal companion, a pigeon.

"A what?" asked Brandi.

"A pigeon," said Buck with great dignity, patting the docile bird on the head. "Miners sometimes carry birds underground with them, don't they? Well, I think this pigeon will come in handy someday."

"Sure," said Connor, hefting a coil of rope from the store counter. "If we get hungry."

Megan had to laugh, but changed it to a chuckle when she saw Buck's reaction. "Don't worry, Buck. I'll protect your pigeon from the hands of evil halfling chefs."

What next? she wondered. *A jester?*

Buck shot the thief an acid look and Connor skipped behind a barrel of flour. Eric laughed and clapped Buck on the shoulder. "You might as well. Why not a pigeon?"

Dar paid the storekeeper for a set of waterskins and lifted them off the counter. He turned to Buck. "Got a name for your new friend?"

Buck stared into the bird's eyes with a very grave expression for a few heartbeats, then announced, "I will name him Puup."

Connor burst out laughing and Megan giggled. "What?"

Dar had a silly grin on his face. "Is this because of what he's going to provide for our party?"

Buck ignored them. "Don't you worry, Puup. They'll find out just how useful you are."

The pigeon cooed in response. Megan shook her head and petted the bird.

Chapter Seventeen- Iron Thunder

Andyn Eleandir crouched, listening to the faint drip-drip of water. She held her position as ordered, waiting in the shadows of a large oak.

So help me, if those idiots aren't dead by now, I'll kill them all for making us worry like this.

She looked down at her feet. Two goblin bodies lay in the grey, early morning light. Their blood mingled with the dew on the fern and blisterleaf. Nothing had gone right from the moment they hit the Forester-Darlon highway. First, rain fell, almost the moment the caravan left the south gate at dawn. Then, their wagon foundered in the mud and they had to wait inside while troopers and teamsters struggled to pull it out. Colin forbade them from leaving the vehicle, fearful that Ja'al spies near the road would see their duplicity before they could reach the drop-off point.

They never made it. Perhaps sensing something, a score of goblins ambushed them some two hundred yards before they reached their goal. None of the escort or teamsters had been killed, but several were injured. Worse yet, the companions were forced to defend themselves when goblins tried to clamber into their wagon, and several of the attackers got away.

Sensing their element of surprise gone, Colin shooed them into the forest.

"You've got the most out of this deception that you can," he had said, re-arranging his men to continue the escort. "I've got to see the rest of these wagons on their way to Wit's End. Now get going, and God watch over you."

Then of course, the alarm was raised. The goblins at her feet were just the

233

first. So far, none of the Ja'al soldiers had escaped to bring others. Dar, Eric and Connor skulked ahead in the dimness of the fog and misting rain to scout their way.

Megan Alenar looked up, almost prone next to a tanrin bush. "Anything?" she whispered.

Andyn shook her head. Buck and Brandi waited behind another giant oak to her left. Buck peeked between two boughs, then nodded and tapped Brandi on the shoulder.

"Come on," Andyn said, relieved.

The four slipped through the undergrowth, spying a shape moving ahead.

Connor Lomin flipped back the hood of his mottled camouflage cloak. In those green-and-brown colors, he was practically invisible. As one of their smarter moves, they had chosen to outfit each of their party with the water-resistant treated cloaks.

"Dar and Eric found another trio of those wart-asses about fifty paces that way," he jerked a thumb over his shoulder. "We took them out, but be careful. There's more around here, or I'm an ogre's lunch."

The Verian priestess nodded. "I just wish there was more we could do."

Connor looked at her in surprise. "Do what? We can't use arrows, slings or magic. There's a lot of trees out here and I don't think our luck will hold good enough to hit everything we aim at. They'd hear, and besides, if we miss, the little monkey-men will scream their lungs out for help. "

He motioned with his hand and led the way through the bushes and trees.

Andyn shook her head but followed. The forest had a strange, dream-like quality. Mist and rain made it difficult to see more than fifty yards. Scuttling sounds of small animals seemed amplified from all directions at once. Though she had an instinctive connection to the forest from her religion and elven blood, this was unsettling. The thought that a mass of goblins lurked in the undergrowth certainly didn't help matters.

Two figures rose out of the trees like specters and she muttered under her breath.

"Clear," said Dar. He held his hand-axe in one hand and a dagger in the other. Both were stained dark.

Eric nodded to Andyn. "Anything back there?"

She shook her head. The scouts turned and led the way without further comment. Andyn followed, eyes trying to discern out-of-place features that could signal an ambush. While Eric and Dar's talents lay in tracking and woodcraft, she had something they didn't: a feel for the life of the forest and now the forest was uneasy. She sensed an air of *un-rightness*, probably bred by the presence of goblins and worse, tramping through the woods looking for them. She felt the forest as a sacred place, a living thing, a cradle of good things designed by her beloved god. Creatures of Darkness prowling it seeking to slay the servants of the Light? Well, that bordered on sacrilege.

She suspected the fog between the trees to be unnatural as well, perhaps brought on by sorcery. Or maybe it had to do with the rain. Such a grey and dim day aided the goblins on the hunt and made travel difficult for her and her friends. Her uneasiness grew as they crept through the brush, slipping between trunks of maple, ironcore, and ban-ban.

Eric's hand shot up and she dropped to the earth, heart in her throat. She too saw the dull gleam of pole arms and spears to their right.

Despite the coolness and damp, sweat beaded on her forehead. Stifling the urge to move and wipe it away, she tried to listen and understand the goblin voices. Any advantage could help. The voices came closer.

"...not here, Sergeant."

A muttering. Then a snatch of something. "...turn towards the road, but by the Gnawer of Bones, stay hidden! You there, bring Lugarch to me."

A pause, then a set of heavier footsteps thudded towards the group of Ja'al. A rumbling, deeper voice broke the stillness.

Andyn froze, eyes wide in fear. She recognized the language - unmistakable, even though she could not translate.

Ogres! We are really in for it now.

She dared a peek. Over the leaves of the bushes, she caught a glimpse of a hook-toothed, blunt-faced horror with beady black eyes and prominent forehead. Light blue hair flowed down the sides of the face, over pointed ears. She estimated the creature was about nine feet tall and over three hundred and fifty pounds.

Oh Verian, we really need your help right now.

More discussion in the ogre tongue followed, then more in goblin.

"To the west, then. They must be turning back towards the road. The trailers will have to catch up as best they can. And watch every bush, you idiots! The Ghai-zhal have tracker-hunters among them. Laziness will earn you a fast trip to Hell!"

The clatter of weapons and armor and the dreaded thudding of ogre boots receded to her left and relief washed over her. With surprise, she saw her fingers buried in the earth from gripping so tightly.

Nothing moved for at least twenty heartbeats, then Connor rose next to her and nodded. The companions stood as one and headed to the right, away from the patrol.

She brushed off her gloves, sighed and looked at Megan. The younger Alenar sister shook her head, wide-eyed.

"That was close," she whispered.

They re-grouped and, after an admonition from Eric, turned right again. They moved over a rise. Andyn began to relax, feeling lucky to have slipped that trap.

A snap of a branch ahead of her made her look up from the ground and she froze, face-to-face with a team of ten goblins. For a split second, Andyn and her friends gaped at the warriors, who stared at them in shock. Then, the goblins howled and charged.

Andyn whipped out both maces and stepped in front of Megan. Three warriors attacked with hooked swords. She blocked two strikes, spun away from a third, and broke the skull of one of her attackers on the return.

The remaining two separated, one going to her and the other to Megan. Andyn's opponent tried to cut her legs out from under her. She leaped over the blade and swung with both weapons, but he twisted out of the way. Leaping up with a loud cry, he lunged. She let him go past, then whacked him in the back of the helmet, hurling him into a tree with a crunching thud.

Something whirred from her right, followed by a clang and two quick thumps. She turned to see Megan standing over a collapsing goblin guard, staff held before her.

"Damn!" Buck stepped over his fallen opponents, reaching for his bow. "How come we didn't see them?"

Andyn shook her head. It was only a matter of time, she knew. "They're thicker than spiders in a temple of Arachnia out here. "

Dar waved to them. "No more sneaking," he said, putting away his sword and reaching for his bow. "We're going to have to run for it."

As if in answer, shouts and a growling bellow reverberated from the forest around them.

"This way!" Eric shouted, racing off through the trees to his left.

"Eric!" Dar called out. "That's... Damn!"

Holy Tree! Running off again with Eric in the lead? Didn't we learn our lesson the last time?

She kept her maces in hand and ran alongside the others. Dar dropped back with her and Megan, pacing the young mage and looking behind them for pursuit.

They loped along at a good pace so they stayed together, dodging between trees and around bushes. Andyn stumbled once but caught herself on a sapling and continued. The mist grew thicker and the rain picked up, turning from a belligerent fog to a light spattering in a matter of seconds.

Sorcery? She wondered.

They broke into a meadow. Eric kept right on running, Buck, Brandi and Connor on his heels. By the time Dar, Andyn and Megan reached the clear, helmets and spears winked among the trees along the left edge of the meadow. With a roar, the goblins and their monstrous ally charged, at least twenty strong.

Andyn tried to remain calm though her breath came in gulps of air. The group veered to the right as one, heading for the opposite tree-line. Dar sped up, racing ahead, then drew bow and arrow and levered a shot at the pursuing Ja'al. One goblin spun to the earth but the others just came on. Eric, Buck and Brandi also turned and let fly, then continued to run.

They're herding us.

She broke through the trees at the other side. The spattering rain intensified, getting into her eyes despite the hood of her cloak. They ran full-tilt now, spurred on by the hoots and screams behind them. Andyn had to turn her head to keep from getting face-whipped by branches.

Eric made an abrupt right turn and stopped. Andyn skidded to a halt, barely missing Brandi. She was about to make an acidic comment when she saw why and gasped.

A steep, rocky slope awaited them. It wasn't vertical, but might as well have been, extending upward at an angle of at least forty degrees.

Oh Verian! We'll never make it up that thing in time.

Buck grabbed footholds and scrambled upslope. Connor grabbed Megan by the arm, pulling her with him. Dar and Eric turned towards their enemies, bows ready and faces pale. The goblin hoots and screams came louder.

There's got to be something we can do. Blast this rain...wait a minute! She gripped Dar's shoulder.

"We can't hold off twenty goblins and an ogre from here and those beasts are much better at climbing than we are. I've got an idea. Let's get upslope as far as we can."

"What are you going to do?" Dar asked, eyes darting to her.

She looked at the rocks and earth before them with a critical eye. "A little magic. Pray Verian that it works."

She clawed her way up the slope after the two scouts, heedless of dislodged rocks and stones behind her.

Halfway up, a tremendous shout told her the enemy had reached the bottom of the rise. She scooted over to her right, behind a boulder.

Arrows rattled in among the rocks and she heard the others return fire, then her shielding boulder trembled with a tremendous crack. She stared as two halves of a three-foot wide piece of stone thudded onto the muddy earth next to her.

She peeked around the boulder. The ogre reached for another large rock, its eyes flashing with eagerness.

The entire Ja'al force clustered down at the bottom. Some of the goblins climbed upwards, and at a much faster rate than she or her friends. She motioned Brandi forward.

"I'm going to try a spell, but I need your help," she told the elder Alenar. "If we combine energies, we may be able to pull it off."

Brandi hesitated, then put her bow away. "I hope you know what you're doing."

"Verian provides, Brandi."

They stood. Andyn took the other woman's hand and began chanting, heedless of a pair of arrows that thumped into the earth next to them.

She felt power surging in her, coming from her mind and body and the woman next to her. Her chant became stronger and she spoke the final word.

The skies opened up in a downpour. Despite knowing the effect of the spell, she gasped from the force of the water. Sheets of rain pummeled the slope, casting up small pebbles. She looked downslope. The goblins lost their grip, bouncing and thrashing down to crash into their fellows.

She tried to speak, had to spit out a mouthful of rain, then shouted to the others.

"Keep going, by all that's holy! We've got to get off this slope!"

She pushed Brandi upwards and gave a kick to a large rock, starting a landslide. Without waiting to see the effects, she clambered up after her companions.

The rain punished her, slamming into her back, head, shoulders and the ground with brutal force. It would have been an effective spell in any case, but on a day like this, the presence of so much water in the air tripled the effect. She kept moving.

Okay, so I miscalculated a little.

She looked up. Except for Brandi, all the others had reached the summit, their concerned faces peering down at her through the torrents. Even as she watched, Brandi hurled herself over the edge.

Andyn pushed herself faster. Then she felt what she dreaded.

The earth of the hillside slid under her and gave way. She scrambled upward, feeling herself slipping back again. Rocks tumbled past.

I'm not going to make it... Brandi's open hand beckoned her only a few feet away.

The hillside trembled, loosened, then broke. With a lunge, Andyn grabbed for Brandi's hand.

The woman's grip was amazingly strong. Andyn pulled back as Brandi lifted her and was rewarded by another set of strong hands, then another. Finally, she was among them, gasping and spitting water.

They looked down the ruined hillside. A massive pile of boulders, mud and rocks lay at the bottom, among bent and broken trees and the occasional goblin pole-arm poking above the earth.

Brandi clapped her on the shoulder and shook her head. "That was a nervy move, Andyn. Just tell us a little earlier next time."

She could only nod, staring down through the rain.

Buck's arm slipped under hers and they were up and moving.

***

"Well?" Megan asked.

Brandi looked up. She sat on a large rock, reading her Liturgy of the Hours. "Just relax. Dar and Eric should be back any time now."

Her sister sighed and sat back on the rock. Their camp nestled in a bend of the Whitehorse River where a large pool formed. While Dar and Eric explored the riverbank ahead, Connor lurked in the underbrush somewhere, watching their back trail. On another rock, Buck fed bits of bread to Puup while Andyn dozed on the shore nearby.

Megan cooled her heels. She tried to join her sister in devotions, but gave up after a while. Her thoughts kept flittering about, to the Ja'al, the scroll and the mysterious map.

She gazed into the pool. Thankfully, after the magic-induced landslide — which Dar had named "Hurricane Andyn" — the rain tapered off and ceased. Then it took a couple of days of exhausting travel through virgin forest to this place, traveling in full daylight to lessen the chance of goblin pursuit.

Megan watched her reflection. A strawberry blonde half-elf looked back at her with a bored expression. She noted a burr in her hair and picked it out, flicking it into the pool.

Even the local plants are unfriendly.

She sighed and looked up at the surroundings. Next to the pool, several large rocks and a couple of fallen trees provided convenient places to rest their backpacks and backsides. Farther upriver, the waterway curved to the left around a stand of huge trees on a knoll. Nearby trees and brush gave Megan a feeling of being comfortably hidden.

She didn't have any reason to be pouty. Divine Providence had even provided them with a couple of bonuses: black mules with deep brown eyes. Andyn found them munching grass in a thicket and enticed them to her side with soft, cooing words. Dar speculated they probably escaped from miners or trappers who had met with an evil fate out in the wilds. They patiently took large sacks slung over their backs, laden with game produced by the scouts' efforts at hunting.

Megan began to relax, watching the mules crop grass next to Andyn. They had to abandon with the caravan when the goblins had attacked. Now they had new ones for free.

God does understand.

Her gaze wandered to the ever-closer mountains. Never had she been so near such huge, towering peaks. Sure, some of the ones in Terenai were impressive, but not so gigantic. The biggest of these Deranese monsters, the Whitehorse, loomed ahead a couple of miles away. The light grey slopes soared upward, with a multitude of white patches near the top and clusters of trees farther down. Even in Aprilis, winter had not quite given up her grip.

Megan wondered why it was named the Whitehorse.

Something stirred in the bushes nearby and her eyes narrowed as she reached for her staff, an attack spell coming to mind.

She eyed the brush. Nothing moved.

"What's wrong?" asked Brandi.

"Something moved."

They watched the forest. Brandi reached for her bow and arrow.

"There!" Megan pointed.

They all stared at the spot. Megan peered intently, then made a face and let her hand drop. "Oh. Never mind. It's just a part of the tree that looks like a tiny dragon."

"Where?"

Megan pointed again. Brandi frowned. "Are you sure? I don't see anything. Oh, there it is."

Megan bit her lip. "I'm getting jumpy."

A splashing sound made them turn to look. Buck grabbed for weapons and Andyn jerked awake, but it was only Dar and Eric.

Dar grinned in a self-satisfied way. "Good news. There's a small waterfall about three hundred yards ahead, just like I remembered, not more than fifteen feet high. We can go up the rocks along the side of it, away from the forest. There's a log bridge extended over the rapids upstream. The river is very wide and shallow there. The dwarves over at Dorn's Hall must have made the bridge. We can use it to cross over to the other bank."

Megan looked at Brandi, who shrugged and went to join the others. She debated with herself whether to tell them about what she had heard, then decided to forget it. They had other things to worry about. Their greatest problem was how to get across the Whitehorse River. Deep, swift, and over one hundred yards wide in places, it barred their way to the peak, on the other side of the river. At least here, near the shallows, they had an easy way across.

Andyn stepped up next to her, leading the mules.

Brandi hefted her backpack. "What about the dwarves, Dar? Won't they mind us using their bridge?"

Dar shook his head. "They have a trade pact with Lord Nolan and have been on good terms with Forester for as long as I can remember. There's about eight hundred of them in an underground town, about a day or so east of the Peak. Clannish lot, but I hear they're hospitable and great help if you're in a pinch. We'll just wait for Connor to get back."

They had enough time to gather most of their gear before Connor reappeared. He nodded agreement when they related the information to him.

Megan brushed off her skirt and followed behind Brandi, trudging with one of the mules along the shore, thick with reeds. Once, when she looked up, she thought she saw a small shape with a long tail flying away from their former campsite, but it was gone quickly, lost in the trees nearby.

I'm starting to see things that aren't there. We need some rest.

The land followed the bend of the river around to the left and then began to climb upwards, gradually turning more and more rocky. The came upon the wide, rushing waterfall roared down into a pool, from there to follow a deep and swift pace towards Forester.

They clambered up the rocks. Megan helped as best she could. She held packs and weapons for people until they could move up to the next elevation, coaxing the mules all the way. Finally, tired and damp with spray from the falling water, they stood next to a very wide section of the river, nearly two hundred yards across. The water shot past them, only about a foot deep, but very swift, splashing over the many sizable rocks in the riverbed.

Dar shouted over the rush of the waterfall and pointed. A system of logs stretched over the waters, connected by stout ropes and extending from one riverbank to the other. The logs rested on top of a set of huge, flat stones, about three feet tall.

They arrived at the east side of the bridge. Dar, Eric and Connor kept an eye on the forest around them. Megan inspected the structure. It looked sturdy (which she expected from dwarves) and a little crude (again, expected since it was mostly made of wood and not stone).

Dar and Connor led the way. About halfway across, Megan's senses tingled with magic, and she looked around. The mule behind her snorted. Dar stopped their column, turning around to look at the animals. Their eyes rolled and they pulled at their lead ropes. Puup flapped frantically. Buck had to put a hand over his eyes.

A faint breeze started. That, in itself, didn't seem exceptional, except for the fact that all other sound besides the river stopped.

Only the water rushed by below them. They heard no more birdcalls, no more buzzing insects. It was as if nature held her breath.

Megan felt a chill.

God, what's going on?

"I don't like the feel of this," said Connor.

The wind intensified. The mules went wild, braying with a sudden terror. Megan tried to grab the rope of the closest one, but it jerked away, pulling her off balance. She slipped on the logs and half-slid off the bridge.

"Blast!" she muttered under her breath, striking her knee against a log.

Suddenly, a shadow covered them and the mules leaped away. Shouts and curses echoed over the riverbank. Megan tried to dodge the nearest animal, lost her grip and fell into the river, landing on gravel and small stones. The rushing current swept her up and she groped out, remembering the fifteen-foot drop downriver. Her fingers closed on a side of one of the large stone platforms and she pulled herself to it. She stood in a second, bracing her back against the stone support, sputtering and trying to wipe the water from her eyes.

The ground trembled with a heavy thud and water splashed on her from somewhere in front. The shock knocked her to her hands and knees. From behind her, she heard a gasp.

"Oh Jesus," came Dar's voice.

She cleared her eyes and blinked — and stared.

An immense, reptilian claw loomed up from the stones of the riverbed before her, about five feet long, covered with golden-brown, strangely metallic scales and tipped by talons as long as knives.

She followed the leg upward and her jaw dropped. The claw connected to a leg, which connected to a chest of immense size. Her eyes followed up a long neck and finally, to a head at an impossible height of thirty feet above her. Majestic wings spanned more than forty feet in either direction, glittering amber-gold in the afternoon sun.

She could barely breathe. The creature tilted its beautiful, reptilian head towards her. It was adorned with two major horns on top and a set of smaller ones forming a sort of ruff behind them. Megan dizzily estimated the longest tooth in the creature's mouth to be only a little shorter than Connor.

She looked into the creature's eyes: yellow with deep brown, cat-like pupils. Her fear stilled. She saw a vast intelligence therein, and wisdom, supreme confidence, curiosity and kindness.

It spoke in very pleasant, resonant tones.

"Well," the creature said, with a toothy smile. "Got a little wet, didn't we?"

Chapter Eighteen- Song of the Grey Riders

Andyn Eleandir plunged both hands deep into the pile of coins. She held the money in front of her eyes, watching copper, silver, gold and platinum rain down onto the slope of this immense mountain of wealth. She gazed at rings and bracelets and goblets and swords and staves and shields and armor and books and a thousand other, unfamiliar things around her. All of it glowed in the magical light of four bright balls hovering in the corners of the cavern.

She felt almost giddy. *Me, little Andyn from Eleth-Anor and I'm in a dragon's lair.*

A cooing sound echoed in the chamber from her right, where Buck Bydecy admired a mirror-bright silver shield. Puup fluttered his wings from atop the warrior's shoulder. The pigeon seemed to have recovered from his initial fright at the dragon's appearance.

"I can't believe we're here," Buck said. A metallic sliding sound rang out from her left followed by the ringing of many coins. Connor Lomin picked himself up from the rocky floor of the cavern.

"This is great!"

A movement from the entrance caught Andyn's eye. Brandi Alenar's face appeared. She shook her head and frowned in disapproval.

"Don't get too carried away with yourselves," she said, walking into the cave. "This isn't our treasure. And we won't be staying here for long. The dragon said he'd be back in a few minutes. I don't think he'd take too kindly to you playing on his treasure pile."

Andyn gave an exasperated sigh. "Brandi, he told us we could come in here. Don't you think he trusted us not to break anything?"

Honestly, she thought. *You'd think we were a bunch of drunken sprites. Brandi is a nice person, but she can be such a burr in the pants.*

Brandi looked somewhat chastened, but gave Connor a significant look. "Well, I wasn't worried about breaking."

The halfling spy grinned. "Oh, come on, Brandi. What harm can this be?" He spread his arms wide.

Andyn shot him a suspicious look. "Gained any weight in the last couple of days, Connor?" He looked a trifle fatter than when they had entered the cavern.

"Er..." he muttered as he stepped backwards. "...Uh, well, maybe it just seems that way in this light..." He gave a weak grin, then slid over to the other side of the pile.

They heard him cursing under his breath and the sound of coins dropping on the treasure pile. Andyn chuckled.

Brandi tried to hide a smile. "Just be ready to come out when the dragon returns."

Dar called out from the main cavern. "He's here!"

Andyn scrambled to her feet, brushing a few copper coins from her lap. Buck and Connor followed her out to an even larger cavern.

After the companions had recovered their wits on the bridge, the dragon, who would not give a name, offered them the hospitality of its home. In a whispered conference, Buck told them that he didn't feel the tell-tale vibration from Khelios that signaled the presence of evil. Brandi had noted that some dragons were well known for their sympathy for those fought on the side of good against the Dark. Connor had suggested that the dragon was probably their best bet to getting information about Whitehorse Peak and its secrets.

The dragon then produced an enormous reed basket from the woods nearby. This made Andyn wonder if he had planned to meet them at the bridge all along. The mules had already bolted into the forest and since it was getting late, they had elected to leave the animals on their own. Andyn hadn't liked that one bit, but she had no choice with night coming on. Asking Dar and Eric to track them down would have simply been a waste of time. Besides, as Brandi had pointed out, they seemed to have done just fine before the companions ever found them in the first place.

Then they climbed aboard the basket and the dragon gripped it in his foreclaws and leaped into air. Andyn remembered the feeling of soaring free and unfettered. It reminded her of when she was a young girl, diving off the rocks at the harbor in Eleth-Anor, slicing through the air with the wind whipping past her. This was a thousand times more enjoyable.

At the end of the voyage, the dragon alighted on a huge rock shelf outside an immense cave opening on one of the mountains. He invited them to make themselves at home in his caverns until he returned with "dinner". Dar gulped in amazement and told them that the dragon had just dropped them off at Whitehorse Peak itself. The more thoughtful of the group pondered this while Connor and Buck sprinted off into the lair to explore, soon finding the treasure room. Andyn followed them to forestall any foolishness.

She brought herself back to the present, straightening her tunic.

The main cavern towered above them tall and very wide. She cast her gaze around it again, taking in sparkling rock formations, stalactites, stalagmites, large table-like rocks, towering stone mushrooms and a tinkling waterfall. Multicolored lichens hung like furry tapestries on the walls. Four more balls of light hovered at strategic points in the room.

The group also noticed something else upon entering the caverns: a small, greenish, winged creature swooping about in the highest corners. Megan informed them it was not a baby dragon, as they had originally thought, but a peridragon, a species of intelligent creature that wizards and true dragons sometimes tamed as pets and assistants.

No wonder the dragon knew where to find them and what size basket to bring. According to Megan, peridragons had a talent for camouflage. At that, Buck had adopted a superior look and told everyone that he had been right— he had seen a little dragon at the treehouse after all.

Very good camouflage indeed.

A mild wind from the entrance ruffled her hair. She felt a heavy thud and fall of rocks on the ledge outside and the dragon entered, silhouetted in the entrance by the fading evening light over the mountains.

He snaked into the cavern, laying two dead elk on the stones before them.

Andyn marveled. She studied draconian anatomy in the university, but this was amazing. Dragons, as far as she could tell, were a peculiar mix of catlike movements, reptilian features and swanlike grace.

The dragon smiled at them, exposing its rows of sword teeth. "One for you, one for me," he rumbled. "Fair enough?"

Buck leaned far back to look at the creature's face. "Yes, Your...um... Dragonishness..." he finished. He, Eric and Dar set to the task of butchering the meat.

"Good," said the dragon, picking up his meal and depositing it on a clear spot in front of the waterfall.

Probably doesn't want to offend our sensibilities by ripping it to pieces in front of us, Andyn guessed.

The dragon sat on his haunches (and it definitely was a he) and smiled down at them. "What do you think of my home?" he asked.

"Wonderful!" exclaimed Megan, stepping a little closer to him and craning her neck to see his face. "I've never seen a cavern so well-decorated."

"Thank you," replied their host. "You are quite gracious."

Andyn rubbed the back of her neck, trying to ease the sore spot.

The dragon tilted his head down at her. "Is something wrong, Miss?"

Oh, he's talking to me. Andyn felt her face grow warm. "Really, Excellency, it is nothing. My neck is a little tired. Might you bring your face down to our level, so we may speak to you easier?"

"Oh, how rude of me!"

Instead of bending down, the dragon made a sweeping, circular motion with his claws. A sky-blue shimmering raced all over his body. The dragon-shape twisted, melted, and then shrank.

Andyn's jaw dropped. Instead of an immense creature, she stood before a tall old man in dark blue robes with a neat white beard. He stepped up to their little group, close enough to touch. His eyes gave him away: that same amber color with the catlike, brown pupil.

The man grinned. "Is this better, Miss?"

Andyn swallowed.

"Yes, Your Honor. And it's Mistress."

"Oh," said the dragon-man, bowing, "I apologize. And which of these fine gentlemen is your husband?"

Andyn blushed again. Dar, Eric and Buck grinned at her from where they were cutting up the elk carcass. *Just the kind of encouragement those jesters needed.*

"None of them, sir, thank Verian," she replied after first shooting a disapproving glance at the men. "My husband died years ago."

The old man's eyes turned sad. Her breath caught in her chest. She found herself unable to look away from the depths of his shiny eyes.

"I understand what it feels like to lose someone close. My own mate died many years ago, leaving me with a young one."

She swallowed with difficulty, seeing Larad's face for an instant.

No. I'll have no more tears. She smiled at him through misty vision.

"Thank you for your sympathy, Your Excellency."

He only smiled and gave a brief nod. "Well," he said, "May I know your names?"

Andyn blinked away the tears in her eyes. "I am Andyn Eleandir of the Faith of Verian. The other ladies are the sisters Megan and Brandawyn Alenar of the Christian Church, the halfling is Connor Lomin, a follower of the Old Faith," She waved a hand at the men butchering the elk. "Those are Eric Indidarc and Dar Cabot, Christians, and..."

She was interrupted by Buck, who sprang up and struck a heroic pose.

"And I? I am Buck, Buck Bydecy, and this is my faithful companion, Puup." The pigeon flapped its wings.

The old man bowed. "I am glad to meet all of you. Especially Puup."

Dar covered a guffaw with a cough and Megan giggled.

"I," continued the dragon-man, "am Donnervassilianelikilandra. But you can just call me Grandpa." The golden eyes sparkled with humor.

Donn...Donnerkasivall?...Oh hell. Andyn gave up.

"We are very glad to meet you, Grandpa. Your hospitality is much appreciated," she said aloud.

"Don't think of it further. I always treat new employees to a free meal," He winked at Andyn.

Uh oh. Andyn exchanged a glance with Megan, who shrugged. *How do we tell him we already have an assignment without insulting him?*

"Actually," Brandi began, "We are already employed by Lord Nolan of Forester...Grandpa."

Grandpa looked surprised. He turned those amber-yellow eyes to Brandi.

"Really? Tell me about it."

We're getting in deeper and deeper, thought Andyn. *What do we do now?*

Brandi looked hunted. She turned to the others for support.

The dragon bailed her out. "Oh," he said with a nod, "He has sworn you to secrecy then."

"Well," Brandi said, "Not in so many words. It's not that we don't trust you, but this is our first contract and we don't want to offend his Lordship."

Their host nodded again, seating himself on a large, flat rock. "I appreciate your candor and believe me, I understand. Why don't you tell me about what you have been doing in general, without being too specific? I would like to know what is going on in Forester."

Glad to keep Nolan's confidence without offending the dragon, Andyn told him about their recent expeditions. She included everything about Westhaven and the Ja'al but avoided mentioning the pottery and the map. She told him about the attacks by the Manipulator Church, the strange scrolls they had found, and all about the outposts in the Wilderness. When she finished, Grandpa stood.

"May I see the scroll you found in the iron box?"

Megan produced it from her scrollcase, eyes hopeful. "Do you think you can decipher it?"

Andyn's pulse quickened. Dragons lived for a long time, longer even than elves, and had vast knowledge. Maybe Grandpa would know something.

We'll need the blessedness of Tolan the First Prophet to be that lucky.

Their host shrugged as he took the scroll. "My grandfather was alive during the Esten Imperial days. Perhaps I'll recognize something."

He examined the scroll, then chuckled. "You said Lady Ellen tried to read it?"

Eric nodded. "Yes, but nothing came of it."

Grandpa gave a noncommittal shrug. He turned the page over. "It helps if you look on the right side."

Dar shook his head. "But that side is..."

Grandpa waved a hand over the parchment and it flared orange. Bright green runes leapt out on the page.

"...blank," finished Dar.

Their host smoothed the paper. "Ellen Hanford is an excellent mage, but she has no experience with the subtleties of the Esten Emperors."

Megan's eyes grew round. "Emperors?"

"Yes."

Andyn felt dizzy. A scroll from the Imperial Age! Historical value alone meant it was worth at five hundred gold crowns, minimum. If it was Imperial...

Grandpa resumed his seat. "The writing on the front of the page is sheer gibberish. Impressive-looking gibberish, but it means nothing. That was my first clue that it might be Imperial. The scribes sometimes wrote using invisible script on the back side of documents like this, then covered the front with a lot of false runes to mislead anyone who was not supposed to read it."

"What does it say?" asked Connor, leaning forward.

"It's a prophetic song," said Grandpa, placing his left hand on the rock behind him. "Written by a Great Cleric of the Faith of Irial. It's called the "Song of the Grey Riders". It goes like this."

He began to recite:

"Seven they are, the Riders Grey,
who come to serve the Holy Way.

Seven they are of varied flight,
on winged steeds of dark midnight.

The Riders Grey, the warriors brave,
who seek to stem the Evil Wave:

One with sword from dwarves of old
and one fair maiden with hair of gold.

To aid the ones who follow the Three
Comes another of the Silver Tree.

One with hawk of sharpened claw,
one forest guide of Christian law.

One small and swift, silent and light;
another the same with magic bright.

North they go to face Cold Fire
to battle the dragon and quench her ire.

When ogre's rage meets its end,
then does their true quest begin.

In tower cold and cavern deep,
the Diamond Eye they now must seek."

Andyn looked at her companions. To her amazement, Buck's mouth hung open. A rapid series of emotions raced across his face: shock, excitement and then guarded suspicion.

What was that all about?

Brandi let out her breath. "Well. That's very interesting, but I don't see how it's connected with anything we're doing right now."

Grandpa smiled. He seemed almost like a snake coiled up in a corner, waiting for the right moment. Andyn remembered that, despite his human-like appearance now, "Grandpa" was still an alien creature of great age and strange ways.

"I have a feeling," the dragon said, "that this has more to do with you than you realize. Much more. But you will see."

He rolled up the parchment and handed it to Megan. His eyes actually looked puzzled for a moment. "The truth is that the scroll isn't complete. Irial scribes always end prophetic writings with a special phrase and symbol and I don't see either on this page. There's still more to this Song than you have, so keep it well."

"Your mission from Nolan is to find out why the Ja'al have become so active recently and to bring justice for the slaughter at Westhaven. Very well. I have the answer to the first and the means for you to accomplish the second. But first you must hear my request."

Brandi exchanged a look with Megan and Eric, then Dar. Andyn nodded when Brandi looked at her, as did Buck and Connor. They had to find out as much as they could. If Grandpa knew something that would help, it behooved them to listen.

Dar spoke up. "I think we're agreed, Grandpa. We need information on the Ja'al and if you know how to help us break up their network, we'll hear you out."

Grandpa bowed. "I am honored. Follow me please."

Andyn stood and followed, anticipation and nervousness filling her.

Grandpa led them outside, crossing the broad rock shelf in front of the entrance until it ended. There, he traversed a hidden set of steps until he reached the rocky slope of the mountain itself. Small bushes and scrub growth were scattered about the slope, broken only by a small stand of trees a hundred yards from the rock ledge.

Along with her sense of foreboding, Andyn's pulse quickened, remembering the map from the pottery and its tiny black pegasus figure. *Maybe he does know something after all. Maybe this is it. What could it be? An enchanted weapon, mightier than Khelios Giantbane? A mountain of treasure? A magic fortress? Mystical warriors held frozen in time until we come to free them?*

Grandpa stopped at the stand of trees. "Now, no one follows me until I call, understand?"

They all nodded.

Grandpa turned to the stand of trees and raised both hands over his head. He spoke a long, rolling word.

Bright light flashed and the trees disappeared. Andyn's heart skipped and she gasped. A herd of winged black horses stood frozen in a shimmering, translucent globe.

Her mind reeled. *Pegasus. Correction, pegasi. There's more than one. How many? One, two...Verian's Breath! There must be more than forty of them! The entire air force of Eleth-Anor has that many.*

If trained, each one of them was worth more than forty-five thousand gold crowns. Only great lords or ladies could own more than a couple, if they even knew how to ride them. Their high price and expensive upkeep made them beyond the means of all but the most famous and wealthy of sellswords. Part of their expense lay in their genetics: a mix of raptor and horse, they not only ate grain and plants but also meat. Their feathers required special care and most ostlers knew only how to care for horses, not horse-falcon hybrids.

Only elite soldiery in each country trained in airborne combat, and only the best riders received the plum assignment of pegasi. They were the fastest mounts alive. No air cavalry short of dragon-riders was more prized.

Grandpa now held his hands out, palms down. He pronounced a series of short, sharp words. At each word, a section of the ground flared a bright color. Then, at his final syllable, the shimmering orb disappeared.

No one moved. Andyn stood breathless at the sight of the winged horses' shining coats, strong limbs, and gentle eyes. They began to move, milling about, blinking as if from a long sleep. Grandpa moved among them, speaking a calming word and patting their noses and necks.

He spoke to the freelancers over his shoulder. "You can step forward. They won't harm you."

Andyn took a deep breath. She held out a gloved hand to one of the stallions, a sleek, bright-eyed fellow. The pegasus snorted and backed away, then delicately sniffed her hand. It seemed to relax and stepped closer.

Tolan's Tears! I never expected this.

"They're tame," said Brandi in wonder.

"Better than that," said Grandpa, patting the biggest male on the neck. "Each adult is a fully trained fighting steed, males and females alike. Taught to maintain their riders safely even if wounded, capable of carrying barding and a fully armored human knight for a hundred miles a day."

Dar stood next to two foals and their mother, smoothing their backs. He shook his head. "Where...how did you get them?"

Grandpa stopped patting the stallion. "Actually, I didn't. My grandfather did. Near the end of the Imperial Age, the Emperor's General in this sector, Marcus Hartinell, realized the Empire was going to fall from internal struggles. He was insightful enough to realize that these mounts could be used against the Empire. Being a true Emperor's man, he decided to spirit them away from the various nobles he suspected of treason. He intended to hide them until the Empire began to put itself back together again, when he would present them to the new ruler, who he hoped would be wise and just. He picked these mountains because they were on the borders of a fiefdom ruled by a cousin of his who, though not as loyal as he himself, could be bribed to keep a secret. Hartinell also sought the services of a high cleric of Irial."

"The cleric was most helpful. He cast a spell of augury to determine if this course of action was the right one. Irial blessed him that day with a vision and he recommended to the general that the pegasi be placed with our family. The priest came to my grandfather. We, in exchange for a large payment of treasure, were to place the herd in suspended animation until a good king had arisen in the lands. My grandfather agreed to do so and entrusted my father with the same charge when he came of age, as my father did to me. We all knew that these war-horses could be used to wreak a great evil if they fell into the wrong hands."

Grandpa rejoined the group. "The conditions were these: We were to keep the pegasi safe until a just king ruled in Esten. Then we were to await the emissaries of the king, the Grey Riders. The Riders would come bearing a map made by a wise woman. They could prove they were the Riders by performing a great quest, after which we were to hand the pegasi over to them."

"Oh great," said Dar. "Now we've got to go find these Grey Riders. We don't even know where to start looking."

Grandpa gave him an enigmatic look and Andyn's heart sank.

I know what's coming. And I don't like it one bit.

"You don't have to look," Grandpa said. "They're right here."

"Oh no. No, no, no! Not us," said Buck, waving his hands. "We're not even wearing grey."

Eric winked. "Actually, only Buck looks a little grey after he has too much ale."

Grandpa smiled. "I am not joking."

"I knew it," muttered Andyn under her breath.

There was a pregnant silence, broken only by the sound of pegasus hooves on the rocky mountainside.

"Wait a minute," said Buck. "You've got to be kidding. We only just met each other a few weeks ago. Besides, we aren't the King's emissaries. We've never even met King Philip."

The dragon raised his eyebrows. "You most certainly are the Riders. Look. I can see your own sword is of dwarven design. One with sword from dwarves of old, correct? I see a small, silent thief, a pair of forest guides who follow the Christ-God, and no less than three maidens with golden hair. Andyn serves Verian and wears his Silver Tree on a pendant around her neck; she is aiding you and most of you are Christian, which means you serve the God who is Three in One. And you most certainly are emissaries. Lord Nolan is a vassal of King Philip; therefore, you serve the king if you work for Lord

Nolan."

"No, no, no," said Eric, shaking his head. "The song said there was only one of each. There's any number of people who could fit those descriptions."

Grandpa's eyebrows rose. "Really? How many groups do you think have managed to make it out here in the five hundred years with anyone remotely answering those descriptions? I can count them on one hand and I'd have fingers left over. Also, I will inform you that prophecies of any kind are more figurative and symbolic than literal. I have read texts where a single figure is used to describe an entire people. I am also willing to bet you have a map drawn by a wise woman or mage."

He nodded in satisfaction when their faces fell. "I thought so. May I see it?"

Megan showed him Clarissa's map. He nodded.

"This confirms it. Your appearance here during the reign of Philip is conclusive. I did not expect the Grey Riders to appear during his father's time nor his grandfather's. Both men, while capable, were not possessed of the high sense of justice and mercy that Philip embodies. He is the "just king". You are the Riders."

Skyfire blast it! Andyn moaned and put her forehead on the back of the pegasus' neck. She felt like she was being pulled down a steep slope. *Verian, this is not what I asked for! I wanted to learn slowly and gain my footing first, not a sudden launch into prophecies and ancient quests! Why can't anything be simple?*

A light wind rippled through the area, ruffling the pegasus' mane against her head, reminding her of the reality of the situation.

She sighed.

Well, screaming at the clouds never stopped rain from falling.

She raised her head and turned to Grandpa. "Let's assume for the moment we are the Grey Riders. Since we've found the reason for the Ja'al raids, half of our contract with Nolan is finished. What quest did you have in mind for us?"

Grandpa's eyes narrowed and his jaw set firmly. He turned a fiery gaze on a shorter mountain about five miles away from Whitehorse Peak.

"I was going to have you do something else until about a week ago. But now I have something much more important."

He turned back to them, dragon-eyes angry.

"I want you to rescue my grandchildren."

Andyn's eyes widened. She wasn't sure she had heard right.

"What...how...?"

Grandpa's eyes flashed in the dying afternoon light, making him seem even more alien. "My daughter and her husband had two children, Tholerios, a male, and Kindriana, a female. They all lived far from here, to the east, so I did not see them often. One day, my grandchildren flew into my cave, weeping and wounded. It seems that an undead prince, a vampire lord from Creator-knows-where, got wind of my daughter's home and decided to plunder it with his minions. There was a great battle and though the vampire and his army were destroyed utterly, my daughter and son-in-law died."

He sighed. "Kindri and Tholi were told how to get here if ever there was trouble. They have stayed with me for seventeen years, until a week ago."

He turned to look at a mountain across the valley from him, regarding it. The wind whipped his white hair around his face and his voice became icy. "Somehow, a Ja'al high priest named Halkith managed to lure my dragonlings within his grip, probably with promises of gold and jewels. My children are young yet and their heads turned by pretty baubles. In any case, he sent an ultimatum to me: turn over the pegasi to him or they die."

Andyn leaned against the pegasus in shock. "But..."

Buck spoke up. "Can't you go over there, tar their little asses and get your kids back? You're a dragon wizard!"

Grandpa shook his head. "The Ja'al have spies everywhere, looking for me. They would just kill Tholi and Kindri. Besides, if I leave the pegasi, the Ja'al have ample resources to find them and release them from their stasis. I am quite confident that they have several free-lancers of ill repute capable of airborne riding. If I went after Tholi and Kindri, the Ja'al would have the pegasi and they would ..."

He stopped speaking.

Megan nodded. "And you can't give them the pegasi, because, knowing the Ja'al, they would just probably kill both of the children anyway. So Halkith has created a stalemate without intending it, unless..." Now she turned to Andyn.

Andyn nodded, thoughtful. "Unless he's stalling to keep you here until he can do something with you..."

"You see my dilemma," Grandpa said, turning back to them. "I cannot give up my charge. The pegasi obey any who can control them, so the Manipulator Church would have a powerful tool with which to press its evil plans upon the world. I cannot negotiate, for my children's lives would be forfeit and I *will not* bargain with those offspring of The Serpent. Can you help me?"

Andyn met Brandi's and Megan's eyes, full of frustration and anger, Dar's eyes, cold and furious, and Eric's... just ice cold.

She shuddered. Sometimes, Eric looked sinister.

"We'll help, Grandpa," she said, putting a hand on his arm. "Just tell us where they're keeping them."

Grandpa pointed across the valley. "There, in Stonekeep Mountain."

Chapter Nineteen- Stonekeep Mountain

"Lord Halkith!"

Halkith turned a cold eye on the speaker, one of his human guards. The man bowed low, both hands held before his face.

The Ja'al priest let him sweat for a moment. The bowing and scraping would get old someday, he supposed, but watching them grovel was worth the entertainment value. "What is it?"

The warrior straightened, his features nervous. "A messenger, Sword of Ja'al. From Modron Derrig."

Derrig again? Halkith frowned, stroking his mustache absently. *What is it this time? Supply problems? Maybe news of those freelancers who've been giving us so much trouble.*

He eyed the guard for a moment, then shrugged. "Send in the messenger. And close the door. I am not to be disturbed."

He turned away as the soldier departed. If Derrig had somehow managed to foul up his assignment of preparing for the dwarves of Dorn's Hall, capturing that area was going to be a lot harder once the real fighting started.

Those little bearded bastards can be a chore.

The door opened behind him and he straightened to his full height and accepted the bows of the guard and a new visitor, a rangy human in banded armor.

"Greetings to Halkith the Grey, High Priest of the Mighty Cult of Ja'al," announced the newcomer as the door closed behind him.

"May Gudarta bring you power and blind your enemies," Halkith replied. "What news do you bring?"

The man raised his head. Halkith frowned. He looked familiar. What was his name? James Lefar? Something like that.

"Lord Derrig has been assailed by the freelancers."

Halkith nodded. "As I expected eventually. And...?"

The messenger swallowed but forged on. "The freelancers prevailed."

Halkith schooled his features to remain calm, though he felt a hot anger rise. He smoothed his colored red, purple and pink robes. "And what of Canon Derrig?"

The man shook his head. "I do not know, Great One. I was sent to you without knowing what had happened to him."

Oh, you know, all right, you stupid whoreson, thought Halkith, gliding in front of the man. *You're just too scared stiff to tell me.*

"What is your name?" he asked.

The warrior bowed. "James LeFond, Great One."

"Well, Mister LeFond. Is there anything you can tell me about these sellswords? My spy network only seems to be able to come up with a set of descriptions and nothing more." It was a lie, but Halkith needed to know what extra knowledge this man might have.

Always know the answer before you ask the question.

"Nothing more than what you already know, Sword of Ja'al," answered LeFond. "I know the chief scout for the group is a native of Forester and that a fighter of the group has ties to Astarel. There are two sisters among them, Brandawyn and Megan Alenar. One is a battle medic and the other a wizard. I know nothing more."

"Does anyone know where they went?" This Halkith also knew.

LeFond shrugged. "I did not see them leave Canon Derrig's outpost. I presume they went back to Forester."

Halkith thought for a moment. They were probably still in the town after the attack he had ordered a few days ago. His patrols in the forest surrounded the town to harass anyone who dared venture out, but the freelances were a different matter. With a good scout, they could slip away without being seen.

The Ja'al cleric pursed his lip. "You have a companion with you, do you not? A spy of the halfling persuasion, yes?"

The warrior nodded. Halkith turned away.

"Good. I am commissioning you and your associate to locate the freelancers. Once you find them, one is to report to me so we may set up an ambush and be rid of this scourge. Are these instructions clear?"

"Yes, my lord," was the answer as he sensed the man bow behind him.

"Good. Now get out."

The door closed behind the departing LeFond.

Halkith smiled to himself. Let the blank shields do what they will. His forces in the old bugbear mine in Stonekeep had a firm grip on the grandchildren of that accursed old lizard of Whitehorse Peak. Iron Thunder, as he was known in draconian circles, would have to deal or see them dead.

If the dragon decides to leave the mountain to rescue his little brats, I can move in and find the pegasi. Then the Dark Rider will have her air force.

He shuddered a bit at that, remembering his employer. Halkith wasn't sure why his superiors had agreed to contract him out to her, but it was his best opportunity to showcase his talents. Then, a few choice words to the right people, a judicious application of poison to the ones standing in the way of his well-deserved promotion to a Dark Bishopric somewhere...

For now, she had the upper hand. Halkith was more than willing to serve her until he had accumulated enough knowledge and power to move.

Then that bitch will feel the might of the Manipulator Church and rue the day she made demands.

He walked to a sideboard to pour himself a glass of gnomish bitters. He tossed back the heady liquid with one smooth motion, then grimaced and shook his head.

He picked up a dispatch from the table. Another note from his own Dark Bishop, demanding to know if he had received the scroll sent by courier two weeks ago.

Do they think I can't read?

This was the second such letter and he had already told them he didn't have it. It was supposed to be some nonsense about an Irial song.

He shrugged. The Irial were idiots anyway, and incompetent to boot. Their prattling on about songs and prophecies wouldn't do them any good.

He tossed the dispatch down and smirked, remembering reports of the battle outside the town and the role the freelancers played in it. They thought they had helped win the day.

Simpletons.

Of course, if he had Clarissa's map two weeks ago, he would also have the pegasi by now— instead of having to hunt all over the wilderness for them and get into this ridiculous chess-match with Iron Thunder.

Thoughts of the map brought his frustration to the fore again. He slammed the glass on the sideboard.

Incompetent. Fool goblins. Couldn't untie their own pants without their chieftains to help them. I'll bet a hundred platinum ingots the damn pottery was under their noses all the time.

He turned away and looked at the map again. As he pondered it, he relaxed.

We don't need Clarissa's pieces of junk, he thought, smiling. *We don't need to worry about Nolan or any of his amateur free-lance bastards. We've got the dragon over a barrel and he knows it.*

***

"I can't believe we're doing this," said Buck, hacking through a tangle of branches. Khelios glowed in his grip.

"Stop your moaning. Grey Riders don't whine," Eric said from up ahead with a wink. Early morning sunshine filtered in through the boughs overhead, shining through the mist in the air.

Buck gave him a sour look. "How the hell do you know what Grey Riders do and don't do?"

Eric only smiled, then continued forward on the path the party carved through the forest.

Buck shook his head. He knew what was making Eric so blasted cheerful all the time: Brandi. Buck recalled just how much he had seen them, together at meals, talking, or just marching next to each other when the situation permitted.

Buck looked down at the path and sighed. "I don't see why Grandpa doesn't just fly in there, pound the Ja'al, and grab his kids. If only he wasn't so damned honorable. Hang the pegasi anyway... what could the Ja'al do with them way out here in the wilderness?"

"Buck, what's the flying range of a pegasus with rider?" asked Megan from behind him. "A hundred miles or more. Easily enough to take them away from here and to a hiding place. Besides, there's no guarantee the children will still be alive when the Ja'al close the deal."

Buck gritted his teeth, then hopped over a large rock and ducked under a thick branch. "So why didn't Grandpa hand off his grandkids to the nearest dragon community years ago? It's been a long time, hasn't it?"

Megan sounded a little exasperated. "Grandpa couldn't give them up. He loves them too much. Not to change the subject, but where is your faithful winged companion?"

"I left Puup with Grandpa. Can't risk getting him injured in a fight underground."

"Smart move."

Brandi marched up next to him. "I hate to break up the discussion group, but could you keep it quiet," she asked, putting a hand on Buck's shoulder. "We're in enemy territory now."

Buck grunted and kept his thoughts to himself.

After they decided to help Grandpa, the dragon carried them in the immense basket to the southern face of this mountain under cover of darkness. His peridragon had scouted the area weeks ago, just after the dragonlings' disappearance. The north face, in particular, seemed an active place, with hobgoblin warriors predominating. Then the dragon flew off. He planned to divert the attention of the Ja'al early the next day, making sure he was seen in the morning light. It took the companions the rest of the night to get to this point at the base of the mountain nearest Whitehorse Peak.

Buck had a sinking feeling to go with his lack of sleep. Hobgoblins? Buck still had a couple of healing bruises and scars from his last run-in with them.

He trudged along the trail, trying to keep Brandi's back in sight (which, he had to admit, was quite a nice sight). He considered for about the fourth time mentioning to the others that these might not be the hobgoblins who captured the young dragons. For the fourth time, he kept his mouth shut. A repeat performance of their last debate would give him a headache and worsen his demeanor.

Come off it, Bydecy, he chided himself. *Going on to glory and riches in the Wilderness, just like you wanted all along, eh? Da' would be proud. And it's better than rotting in a Tyler prison, right?*

He remembered their latest escapades.

Yeah. Only in prison I don't have to sleep on rocks, no one's ever heard of the Grey Riders, and I don't have to deal with the Ja'al trying to split me like a melon.

It all started with those Alenar women. Or actually, with meeting Dar in the tavern. Or...he scratched his head. It all started when he met Eric.

Should have turned west instead of north, he concluded. *Prophecies. I can tell you more about the future with goat intestines.*

He saw a motion from up ahead and stopped short, grabbing his bow and putting an arrow to it.

Buck waited for the others to slip back to him.

"Well?" asked Andyn.

"We've picked up a trail." Dar whispered. "Eric thinks it's the hobgoblins. I'm not so sure, but we don't have anything else to go on."

"What do *you* think it is?" Megan asked, poking his arm with her finger.

Dar shrugged. "Hobgoblins usually wear boots. It can't be elves or halflings because there's too many broken branches and other disturbed things. The imprint is too heavy for dwarves."

Eric nodded. "It's either follow them or start searching every square foot of this north face."

They all looked at each other, then started up the slope towards the trail. Soon, Connor joined them. Eric explained what they had found and the halfling disappeared into the forest again.

Buck followed the others, his earlier bad mood fading. He wondered about telling the others about Derek and the frame-up and the Eye of Truth. He had no illusions: finding the Eye was going to be impossible without help. What if they refused? Or worse yet, what if they decided to try to find the Eye and take it for themselves?

Now the Irial song mentioned a "Diamond Eye". His pulse quickened. Did that mean the Eye of Truth? How did the Irial know about it?

A dark and sobering suspicion lurked in the back of his mind. The prophecy might be true since the Song mentioned something only he knew. He resolved not to think about it.

Buck caught up to Megan and Andyn, waiting for them to negotiate their way up a steep jumble of rocks that blocked their way. To his right, a small stream flowed in the center of a gully.

Dar's hand shot up and he motioned for them to get down. Buck ducked behind a boulder, then peeked out.

About a hundred and fifty feet away, just visible through the trees, he spied a half-dozen figures carrying spears. Their metal armor winked in the misty morning light. They moved in smooth, unhurried motions, turning to watch their surroundings as they clambered up a slight rise. Buck caught a glimpse of half-simian faces with white horns and his pulse quickened.

***

"You are sure you saw the dragon flying in towards us?" asked Halkith.

"Positive, my lord," answered Kili, looking up at him warily. "We're sure it was him. Not too many creatures shine golden like that in the morning. James and I were just about to ride out to find the Forester sellswords for you when we saw him coming in. He was flying from the north face towards the west, then turned north again."

Halkith's brow furrowed. *Now what was that crafty old bastard up to?*

"And how long ago was this?" he queried his minion.

"Only a few minutes," Kili said. He wondered how Halkith would take this latest news. "James and I had just made it back up to the west exit from the corral when we saw him."

Halkith stood lost in thought. He strode back to the bureau, looking into a shiny mirror.

Kili tried to relax, but failed. Of all his past employers, Halkith of the Ja'al made him the most edgy. He didn't know if he was going to be lauded for original thinking or punished for being distracted from his task. Kili and James decided to try to score some extra points with Halkith at the risk of the cleric's wrath. Now, that didn't look like the wisest choice.

Halkith turned abruptly and Kili, a seasoned freelancer, fought the urge to jump in surprise.

The dark-haired Ja'al cleric tapped a finger on his lips. "Is there anything else you can remember?"

"Nothing else, my lord."

Halkith looked puzzled, stroking his neat beard. "We've had his grandchildren prisoner for a week now and he's never left his lair, not even to receive our emissaries. Why leave now? Is he trying to get into the complex?" He shook his head and turned his eyes on Kili.

Kili fought down a feeling of revulsion as the cleric's grey eyes bored into him. The Ja'al leader had a way of looking at him that made Kili feel like he was going to be on the next dinner menu.

"Where did you see him last?"

Kili thought for a second. "He turned north and appeared to be heading to Wastrel's Peak, about five miles away."

Halkith digested this for a moment.

"He's probably going for help, or trying to distract us with something. Be that as it may, you and LeFond still have a job to do. I will send extra patrols down to the north base of the mountain, just in case. In the meantime, you two get yourselves down to the Forester Barony and bring me information on those freelancers."

Kili bowed, covering his face with his hands. *Stupid gesture of servility.*

"Yes, Mighty Sword of Ja'al," he answered instead. He turned to go.

"And Kili?" said Halkith.

Now Kili actually jumped. Halkith stood right next to him.

The halfling's skin crawled. *How did he get next to me so fast? And why didn't I hear him?* Sweat beaded on his forehead.

Halkith's gloved hand landed on the agent's shoulder. "You showed excellent initiative by alerting me about the dragon."

Kili relaxed.

Halkith's hand clamped down like a vise. Kili contorted, trying to lessen the intense pain by turning into the grip. Halkith's hand tingled with icy magical power.

"For the future," the Ja'al priest continued, "Don't try to grab glory for yourself by reporting to me personally unless I tell you to do so. That is what my chain of command is for. You had a job to do and let yourself get distracted. That is careless. I don't like careless. Understand?"

His face grimaced in pain, Kili managed to nod.

The grip relaxed. Kili let out a huge breath, then, schooling himself to walk slowly, left Halkith's chamber.

He stood for a moment, trembling against the doorjamb, then ran a shaking hand over his face to wipe off the perspiration. With disbelief he held his hand before his eyes, watching the shaking subside in the dim light. It had been many years since he had been that scared, and he had seen quite a bit in that time.

He set his jaw.

Understand? I understand all right. Understand when it's time to cut losses. James and I are going out, and getting out.

With a resolution in his step, he headed down the passage.

***

Halkith watched the door close, then turned to a corner of the room.

"Do you believe him?" he asked the thin air.

In a corner of the room, the air wrinkled and Aalre materialized. She walked towards him, midnight robes swishing about her elegant legs.

"I don't see any reason why he would make this up, Mighty One," she said.

"I guessed that, my dear Aalre," Halkith noted, "But is it possible that they just saw a wyvern or something. They are inexperienced."

The elven mage ran a finger up his sleeve and smiled at him. "No, my lord, although it isn't without the realm of possibility. It is unlikely that wyverns would be nesting so close to a dragon's lair. Iron Thunder would eat them for breakfast. Besides, wyverns are reddish, not amber."

Her hand ran up his shoulder and came to rest on the back of his neck. With admirable restraint, Halkith didn't obey his hormones and smiled back at her.

"Our draconian adversary is getting bolder or more desperate," he said. "I know he didn't come in here. If he had already penetrated the complex, we would have heard about it. I have magic sentry-spells at every entrance specifically to look for Iron Thunder in either dragon or human form."

Putting a hand on her neck, he continued. "This opportunity is perfect. We cannot let it pass. I will strike out with the retrieval team. If we hurry, we can get to his lair before nightfall. Then we can set an ambush for him and have the pegasi before tomorrow evening."

An elven eyebrow rose in a graceful arch. "Is my lord getting restless?

Why do we not simply wait him out?"

Halkith looked grim. "Because dragons are much more patient than we, and *especially* more than the Dark Rider. She appeared to me in a dream last night and threatened to send me a night hag if I didn't have the pegasi to her by spring's end. She wants to move this summer so as to allow for best travel conditions. If I delay too soon, she will petition the High Command to have me removed."

Aalre pouted, then smiled again. "And that wouldn't do for your career, would it, O Mighty Halkith?"

Halkith smirked down at her. "You talk too much. Have the team ready to go in five minutes. You will remain in command here until I return."

The smile remained, but a sudden tightness around the eyes gave her away. "Why can't I come? I am trained in airborne riding."

His smile turned more sardonic. "Because, my little kitten, you cannot advance in the hierarchy of Ja'al like I can. Any of my other commanders might be tempted to set a trap for me to advance their cause. So you are the logical choice for a loyal commander in my absence. And you are loyal, are you not, Lady Aalre?"

Violet eyes met grey ones in a struggle of wills, like an invisible arm-wrestling match. Then she kissed him on the lips.

"Loyal like no other," she breathed.

"Good," said Halkith, releasing her and feeling her do the same. He knew, as she did, that both had spell and counterspell ready in case one decided to press the issue.

He smiled in satisfaction. "The hunt is on..."

Chapter Twenty- Chamber of Fire

"Secure here," said Dar. Buck nodded at him, face shadowed in the flickering torch-light. He stood over the body of a hobgoblin guard.

Dar turned his gaze down the corridor, alert for the sound or smell that would give away attackers. Without thermal-sight, he had to rely on his other senses.

So far, so good.

Their first three encounters with Halkith's guards went very well. The companions dispatching fifteen enemies without so much as a scratch.

Must be getting better at this than I thought, he mused, shifting his bow from his right hand to his left. By now, he detected certain habits of training in the Ja'al warriors, habits he could exploit.

Having magic didn't hurt. Brandi shocked everyone by creating a silence spell on a small rock that she tossed into the first group of guards they met. After a soundless, eerie battle they heard no alarms and he thanked God for that.

"We're done," Megan said. She slid next to him and placed a slim hand on his shoulder. Amber eyes scanned the silent passageway ahead of him, her features tensed.

"Something wrong?" he asked.

She relaxed and gave him a little half-smile. "I guess I'm just a little scared. You know, taking on Halkith right where he lives."

"A little?" he asked with a grin.

"Okay, a lot." She forced a smile.

Dar felt a flutter of nervousness in his own middle but pushed it aside. "I know what you mean. I'm scared too."

He looked down the corridor again, not really seeing dark stone. An image hovered in his mind: a little blonde girl from the town school, teasing him.

"Dar, Dar, can't run far..."

And she was really good at ringball...

"I know the pegasi are important, but we have another purpose too," he said.

There must have been something different in his tone. Megan looked at him with concerned eyes.

No wisecracks to cover this situation, eh, Cabot? A sullen voice mocked him inside his head.

Megan gave his hand a squeeze and the voice disappeared.

"Anything?" Connor slipped up to them, an arrow ready on his bowstring.

"Not yet," Dar replied. "Is everyone ready? Which way?"

No one spoke. Dar ground his teeth. He hated this station-to-station groping around in the tunnels, trying to find a main corridor and get to the baby dragons before they were discovered. They couldn't keep it up for long. Sooner or later, Andyn, Megan and Brandi would run out of spells and then they would really be in trouble.

"Well, if it was up to me," he said, trying to sound calm, "The places with a lot of traffic probably lead to the barracks. We don't want to go there. Let's take this one while we're here. We can always backtrack if we think it's the wrong one."

Connor nodded, as did Brandi and Eric. Dar accepted a burning torch from Buck and led the way down the passage, keeping Eric next to him.

The flickering light brought into sharp relief many wall carvings and paintings decorating these halls. Dar shuddered. The Ja'al had been here for quite a while, as they had seen fit to embellish the passageways with testaments to their cult. He avoided looking at the positively nauseous ones, especially those of Torvu and his undead minions.

He found tracks here, far less in number, but very unsettling. He saw tracks of small booted feet, like those of a halfling, gnome or small elf, but also very large tracks, larger than even the hobgoblins. His spine tingled.

Ogres maybe, like the one that chased them in the forest? His palms became sweaty at the memory.

He pointed out the tracks to Eric, who nodded.

"Look alive," he whispered over his shoulder to the others. "The tracks are very different here and we may be getting close."

They headed down the left path, following another left turn after a long distance. They stopped. A large square opening stared back at them from the end of the passage about twenty paces farther down, with light shining in the chamber beyond. Dar motioned to the others, extinguished his torch and crept forward with Eric.

A thick stone doorframe carved with writhing centipedes supported the opening. Dar's attention locked on the creatures in the room. Five hobgoblins sat around a table, tossing small, clattering objects in a game of some kind. Copper and silver glinted on the table top. Two other warriors looked over the shoulders of their fellows, offering suggestions, insults and an occasional cuff to the head.

How many more of these do the Ja'al have? Dar wondered.

He pointed and Connor nodded. Eric motioned to their main group and the trio slipped back to their comrades.

Eric eyes were alive with intensity. "Maybe this is our chance to find out something. I have an idea."

Brandi gave him a questioning look and Eric winked.

"Trust me..."

***

"Hmm...interesting." Aalre gave her sergeant a once-over, as if to gauge his honesty by his appearance. "Do you think this could be our little group of sellswords?"

Grand Sergeant Gree shrugged. "Not sure. No patrols found in north entrance. I look, hobgoblin warriors all dead. They not killed by dwarves. Not killed by larger things. Arrows in bodies look like arrows from soldiers in town. You want us to sweep sector now?"

She considered his suggestion. An intelligent hobgoblin (as far as that went), he reminded her of Gorlak, her little goblin aide-de-camp. Gree's opinions were valued by the Ja'al command for their brutal honesty and accuracy. And he hadn't gotten the scars on one side of his snout from being ill-mannered at the dinner table.

"It could be the freelancers from the town," she murmured to herself. *But how did they get here? It would take at least...*

Something in her mind clicked and realization dawned. *Of course. The dragon, appearing on the north face! Now, infiltrators in the complex!*

She snapped her fingers. That had to be it.

That crafty old bastard! Iron Thunder had flown to Forester, hired the freelancers to do his dirty work, then flown them back over here to free the grandchildren. She didn't know exactly how he carried that many people, but that didn't matter. The dragon's unexplained flight to the north was just a ruse to distract Halkith and allow the free-lances some time to sneak in and take back the dragonlings.

Clever, but not clever enough.

"It has to be them," she said to Gree. A slow, wolfish smile crept over her lips, a germ of a plan growing in her brain.

And they've already shown their skill at polishing off hobgoblins, so a sweep is out of the question. We'll have to trap them.

"Grand Sergeant Gree, we will not annihilate them now. Gather two teams and come with me."

He looked at her, eyes narrowing. "Where we go?"

She smile widened. "To the dragon room. We are going to prepare a little surprise for our friends."

***

"Well," announced Brandi, slamming her sword blades into their scabbards, "It's your brilliant idea, Dar. You question him."

Dar held out his hands in protest. "It was Eric's. Besides, I can't speak hobgoblin, you know that."

Brandi favored Eric with a dubious look. "Well?"

Eric replaced his own sword, giving her a cheerful smile. "Don't worry. Everything is working according to plan." He walked over to where Buck crouched next to their trussed-up prisoner.

Dar rolled his eyes. Eric's plan worked, but not as intended. They sent Buck into the guardroom alone, although not without a whispered protest far back in the passageway by the party member in question and many promises of support. Buck then sauntered up to the gaming table, threw down a couple of silver pieces and blithely took a seat.

The looks of utter amazement on the Ja'al warriors' faces were almost worth the price. Buck gave them one of his homespun smiles and motioned for the dicing to continue. Then the rest of the Avengers of Forester had sneaked in.

Well, almost sneaked in. Dar winced and moved a sore shoulder.

Connor, of all people, had kicked a straw pallet and the hobgoblins had whirled, clawing for weapons.

However, the Ja'al forgot about Buck, who took the opportunity to punch one of them senseless. In the ensuing melee, the freelancers had to kill all of the hobgoblins except the one Buck had stunned.

Well, thought Dar, *I hope this works.*

His stomach tightened again. Every minute spent in a room that didn't have the baby dragons was a minute more for the Ja'al to find him and his friends. The botched 'hobgoblin-snatching' plan did nothing to settle his nerves.

Eric sat on his haunches talking to the captive, who glared at him with a baleful eye. Eric looked sympathetic, like a lawyer counseling a client in a heap of trouble. When the prisoner did not respond, Eric shrugged, jabbered at him and gestured at Dar.

What in hell is he doing?

Eric stood and came to join him. Andyn and Buck followed.

"I've told him you had relatives in the town that was burned," Eric said to Dar quietly, "That's not exactly true, but it's close enough. I said that you were very upset and might do something rash, but that I could protect him if he would cooperate. I need to convince him that you're a real danger. Make some threatening gestures or act crazy or something."

Dar's mood brightened at the opportunity for some creativity. He smiled. "I'll try to act like I'm out of my mind. Is that okay?"

Andyn snorted. "Shouldn't be any different from your normal behavior."

Dar blew her a kiss. "You're sweet too."

He motioned towards the captive. "Go ahead, mister Hobgoblin Lawyer. Protect your client."

Dar followed Eric, then picked up an overturned chair and sat about five feet from the trussed-up soldier.

And stared.

At first, the hobgoblin ignored him, instead answering Eric's questions with terse and surly answers. Then he shot a glance at Dar.

Dar continued staring. The Ja'al warrior fidgeted, its snout twitching.

Clearly nervous now, the prisoner stopped Eric in mid-question and nodded at Dar, eyes a little wider. Eric shook his head and spread his hands in a helpless gesture.

Dar continued staring. The prisoner grew more agitated. He even shifted his position to try to hide behind Eric, who obligingly moved to allow him a full view of Dar.

Dar finally moved, drawing his dagger.

The captive jerked as if stung. A steady stream of invective in the hobgoblin tongue echoed in the chamber. Eric shook his head in regret. The captive wiggled all over the floor now, trying to get away from Dar. For his part, Dar ran a hand along the blade of his weapon while still staring at the prisoner.

The hobgoblin shrieked an answer. Eric's hand shot out and covered his snout. He spoke in soothing tones. The creature's eyes became less wild and he stopped squirming.

Eric walked over to Dar, looking angry. "Follow my lead," he said. "I'm supposed to be your boss."

Dar stood, then was very surprised to get a fist in the stomach. It wasn't a hard punch, but he had no trouble doubling over and feigning injury. His dagger clanged to the stone floor.

Eric pointed towards a corner of the room. Dar, trying to keep a straight face and a contrite expression, slunk off to the corner.

Megan came over to him quickly. "What are you guys doing? Why did he hit you?"

"He didn't hit me hard," Dar muttered. He winked at her. "Doing a little theater play for our friend over there."

Megan pursed her lip, trying not to smile. "Are you jesters now?"

Dar just grinned.

Eric strode towards them, a satisfied smirk on his face.

Dar looked up at Megan. "Looks like our performance was a hit."

***

"The gold dragon's cave is just around this curve, Dread Lord," the warrior said. His cloak swirled around his black-enameled plate mail.

Halkith nodded. Perfect. Out of sight of the dragon, yet close enough for a quick move once he returned to his caverns.

The Ja'al leader turned to his group of six. "We will camp here. No fire. Move the horses downslope and hide them in the trees."

The team moved into action.

Halkith basked in both the late afternoon sun and satisfaction in his well-disciplined attack force. He hand-picked each Ja'al soldier for the rare skill of airborne riding. Each wore the finest armor available and was armed to the teeth with enchanted weapons.

He shaded his eyes, looking out to his own mountain, a few miles across the range. Shorter and broader than the Whitehorse, trees and vegetation crowded its slopes in a vast carpet of green. Halkith's specially-prepared and well-hidden path cut the travel time from Stonekeep to Whitehorse from two days to less than a half day. He ordered it constructed months ago. Almost invisible from the air, it wound down the slope from the west entrance of his command complex, across the small valley, and up the south face of Whitehorse Peak.

Let me see...Iron Thunder was sighted early this morning, it's now afternoon, no one has seen him for a while, although he was heading for Wastrel's Peak. How fast can he fly?

Halkith mulled over the situation. This was the best time to strike, while the dragon was away, and he knew he wouldn't stay away long. The team had been alert to anything resembling a gold dragon in flight, but so far, nothing.

And now what? Try to make a quick search for the Blackwing Legion or wait to ambush him?

It was a unique situation. This was the first time they'd had a chance to sneak up to his lair without being seen.

275

He decided to wait and ambush Iron Thunder. Getting caught on the clear rocky shelf outside the lair or even inside the caverns could be disastrous, so the best choice was to wait and then go after the dragon returned.

A rustling in the bushes alerted him and he spun, his black mace flicking out in a heartbeat. Two fighters near him also whirled, spears at the ready. Bushes and shrubs rustled in the breeze.

Halkith's eyes narrowed. He motioned the pair of warriors forward, following down the slope, careful to pick his way among the rocks and scrub brush.

Something caught his eye and he raised his mace, the flanged edges flaring crimson fire. Then he lowered it.

What he thought was a tiny green dragon crouching under a bush was just a bunch of leaves on a gnarly branch.

I'm getting jumpy, he thought with irritation. *Must be the proximity to the dragon's lair.*

"Let's get back up to the campsite," he said. "It must have been a bird or something. We'll do a perimeter check as soon as camp is set."

The Ja'al soldiers came back upslope and he relaxed. Once back at the wide rock shelf, Halkith breathed in the cool spring air. This was excellent: out in the wilderness, not cooped up in some dark underground hole, plan coming together.

Such musings made him wonder about Aalre and the two he had sent to find Cabot and the others. Aalre's assignment was simple: keep the hobgoblins and the ogres in line back at the complex and watch out for any subterfuge from the dragon. If she went off on wild-ass expedition of her own, there was going to be pain in her immediate future.

Of course, Aalre likes pain.

Now James and Kili were a different matter. Halkith frowned. They had something against Cabot and his group. It would do well to look into it later. Halkith didn't like subordinates with hidden agendas. They almost always reared up to bite him at a later date.

The thought of the heroes of Forester passed a cloud of anger through his musings. Not one, but two outposts smashed by those amateurs. Derrig gone, plus Faedan Delphin and Thulgoot the goblin grand sergeant, and the others.

I'll make them pay. My plans are too important to be tossed about by some low-grade swine who aren't fit to clean my chamber pot.

"Lord Halkith?"

He turned. A tall, lithe woman in black chainmail armor bowed low, red hair glowing even more red in the light of the setting sun.

"We are ready, Sword of Ja'al. Would Your Power care to join us for a ritual cup of wine and blood?"

Halkith smiled, anger fading. Now was the time. All the stupid machinations of those equally stupid freelancers were no match for the planning of the Ja'al.

"I believe I will partake with you, priestess," he said.

***

Dar crouched by the doorway. He licked dry lips, eyes darting around the chamber.

Smells like a trap. Actually, smells like hobgoblins.

The walls curved around in a wide circle, domed and supplemented by a shelf that ran around the perimeter, higher than Dar could reach with his hand. Various grotesque scenes from Ja'al mythology decorated the floors and walls.

In the center of the chamber, a circular channel cut the stone, filled with a brown fluid. It surrounded an island of cut stone. A low purple flame burned just above the surface of the liquid, casting an eerie, violet light.

Dar stared at the large cage in the center of the stone island. Two small, dark humps lay on the floor of the cage, rising and falling with rhythmic breathing.

Dragons. Our dragons. I should be jumping up and down for joy.

Eric hid on the other side of the doorway. He ran a hand through his hair and shook his head.

Eric knows something's not right. Damn! If we had brought the hobgoblin with us, we could at least threaten to make him go in first. But we tied him up and left him lying on the floor. And now we're so close, I don't think we want to go back to get him.

Their prisoner gave them directions to this chamber willingly, almost

277

eagerly. Then they sneaked for what seemed like hours through passageways with a minimum of fighting. Twice, Connor crept up on lone sentries to dispatch them. So far, none escaped to sound a general alarm.

A hand touched Dar's shoulder.

Connor nodded at the dragonlings in the cage, grey eyes intent. "Well?" he murmured. "There they are."

"I know," whispered Dar. "But it doesn't feel right."

Connor frowned. "Well, we can't sit here in the hall forever. Let me go in and have a look around."

Dar hesitated. He remembered Sir Tan's warnings about insidious Ja'al traps.

"I think we'd better have Andyn cast a spell of detecting," he suggested.

Connor snorted. "What would that do? I'm willing to bet all my gold there's magic in there. And we know there's evil."

Dar bit his lip.

Connor made a face. "The longer we sit here, the more chance we have of the Ja'al finding us. We've got to go in."

It made sense. Of course. It always made sense.

He nodded.

Connor slipped into the chamber. Dar followed with his eyes. Connor skirted the edge of the room and disappeared in the shadows.

They waited for what seemed like weeks.

Blasted spies. So quiet we can't hear them and too good at hiding. We have no idea whether he's alive, dead, polymorphed into a toad, or sitting in a corner playing cards.

Dar kept his eyes moving anyway. He saw a flicker of movement and Connor slipped to his side.

"No one's home," he said, eyes on the chamber.

Dar stood and motioned the others forward.

The chamber roof towered overhead. Darting color lit the plain grey chamber as the party's torch lights reflected off semiprecious stones imbedded in the ceiling. Along the walls, statues of warriors guarded with stone swords and equally stony stares.

Dar eyed these, but nothing happened. He felt a little sheepish to be so wary of mere carvings, but the Ja'al's devilry knew no bounds.

Andyn and Brandi faced outwards, towards the walls, eyes roaming the patterns. Buck waited, holding Khelios, and Eric stalked to the back side of the fiery little moat.

Dar took a good look at the figures in the little cage. Despite the seriousness of the situation, he relaxed and smiled. The dragonlings looked like miniatures of Grandpa, with the same golden-brown, strangely metallic scales. Their faces looked calm, peaceful and guileless.

Megan laid a hand on his shoulder. "Aren't they cute?" she asked, gazing at them.

He smirked at her. "Yes, they are, *mom*."

She cuffed him lightly in the head. "Oh hush up, you ruffian. I thought I'd never see any dragons in my lifetime."

"Hey!" Eric's whisper floated out to them. "There's a little bridge here."

Dar and the others joined him. Sure enough, a narrow strip of stone reached across the flaming moat. Andyn looked at Brandi, who nodded.

"You may as well do this one," Andyn said, "You've a little experience on me."

At her friends' mystified looks, Brandi gave a mischievous grin. "I've been studying."

She turned towards the cage and raised her hands. She closed her eyes and began to chant.

The air tingled for a few seconds and Dar shuddered. A little piece of the universe seemed to warp whenever any of the spell-casters used magic.

Brandi opened her eyes again. She appeared to be focused on something far away. "There's no trap on the bridge," she said, almost like someone trying to read a faded parchment, "But there's one on the floor in front of the cage door."

She blinked and shook her head. The faraway look in her eyes faded.

"That's pretty good, Bran," Megan whispered.

Her sister smiled. "Father Ander helped me a little."

"Great," said Connor from behind them. "Let's get to it."

Dar accompanied Andyn and the Alenar sisters to the stone island. Buck, Eric, and Connor remained to stand guard since the platform wouldn't hold them all.

Dar and the three women circled the cage, taking care not to get too close. When he neared the door, Dar peered at the floor stones. He squinted. A translucent etching of some kind, a symbol, hovered just under the surface like a seaweed in the surf.

"Well?" he asked. Andyn, Brandi, and Megan looked at each other.

Andyn's face was sheepish. "I don't know how to get rid of it. Brandi?"

Brandi blushed. "I'm afraid I can't either."

Dar's jaw dropped. "You mean you can see it but you can't get rid of it? What kind of magic is that?"

"Well," Brandi muttered. "Beginner's magic."

He turned back to the cage in disbelief and knelt in front of it. *If all this wool-gathering goes on when people start using spells, I think I might skip that part of my career.*

"Hi there," he called.

Two little amber eyes popped open, then widened. Dar kept still.

The larger of the two dragonlings slowly raised itself up, jaws open to reveal needle-sharp teeth.

"Who are you?" the creature asked in a light voice, eyes narrowing like an angry cat. The dragon's spoke Humana with no trace of an accent.

"My name is Dar," he answered. He nodded at the silent, amazed women. "These are my friends, Andyn, Megan and Brandi. What's your name?"

"Kindriana," the dragonling replied, eyes darting to Dar's companions. "This is my brother, Tholi. How did you get in here?"

"We sneaked in," he said with a wink. "Those old Ja'al are a bunch of cork-heads. Your grandpa sent us to get you."

"Really?" the little she-dragon stood up, her foreclaws gripping the bars. On two legs, she had to bend her long neck to avoid hitting the steel plate roof. "Is he here?"

"Well, no," answered Megan. She crouched down next to the scout. "He had to decoy the Ja'al away. He knew they would just kill you both if he tried to come with us. Besides, he has to stay somewhat close to the pegasi."

Kindriana looked dejected, her head drooping. "Oh. I understand." Then she brightened and looked up at them. "So you brought lots of soldiers with you, right?"

"Not exactly." Dar looked from side to side and then added in a conspiratorial tone, "That would have made a lot of noise. The Ja'al would have just killed you or moved you far away. We had to do it quiet."

"Hey!" came another high-pitched dragon voice from the cage. "You get away from my sister!"

Dar jerked his hand back just in time to avoid getting bitten by the second dragonling.

"Tholi!" snapped Kindriana, buffeting her smaller brother with a wing. "Stop that! These are friends! They came to help us get out of here."

"Aw, Kindri," muttered the little male, looking sullen. "I was just gonna nip him. Besides, I didn't know."

Brandi spoke up before the quarrel could escalate. "Do either of you know how to get that shiny symbol off the stone in front of the door?"

Kindri shook her head. "The big bad guy with the silly clothes always makes it with magic after he puts us back in here."

Dar grinned. *I'm beginning to like these two.*

The fellow with the snappy wardrobe was probably a Ja'al cleric, maybe even Halkith himself.

"There's a lock on the door," observed Andyn, hands on hips. "But it looks like you could probably break it with a solid blow. That must be a pretty good trap."

Dar set about inspecting the cage. Iron bolts secured it to the floor, so carrying it with them was out of the question. Another set of formidable-looking fasteners secured the top. As for the lock, it looked like he could break it with one sword swing, but he didn't want to make a move towards it with the trap nearby. Dar was willing to bet the weakness of the lock was another Ja'al deception to lure someone into the trap.

Eric called out to them. "Uh, ladies and sir? We haven't got all day."

Dar shook his head. This required drastic measures. He took his handaxe from his belt holder.

"Stand back from the door," he said to the ladies. "And you two," he instructed the dragons, "get as far away from it as possible."

"What are you going to do?" asked Megan in alarm. "Dar...!"

In answer, Dar hurled his axe at the symbol in the stone.

A bright light flashed and he heard a searing noise. A flat and metallic smell suffused the air. He stepped closer. Trying not to gag, he waved the smoke aside and looked.

Only a burning, smoking handle embedded in a large slug of molten metal in the floor remained of his axe. He saw nothing more of the symbol.

He shuddered. *If that had been one of us...*

"Well," said Megan with a grin, "It wasn't the most elegant solution, but it worked."

"We're free! We're free!" Kindri and Tholi squealed, despite Brandi's frantic attempts to hush them.

"How wonderful for you, my dears," said a sultry female voice from the chamber entrance.

The party whirled.

A tall female elf, clad in a black dress, leaned against the stone doorframe. She had two silver daggers in a belt of gold and carried a slim white staff with a red crystal on the top. She smiled.

"Too bad your string of success is about to end," she said with a negligent wave of her hand.

The stone statues and the wall shimmered and wavered, then disappeared. Instead of a forty-foot diameter room with ten statues in it, the freelancers stared at a fifty-foot diameter room with ten hobgoblin guards in chainmail, carrying bows and swords. In addition, two hulking ogres loomed behind them. They wore scaled armor with horned helms and each bore a mammoth flail. Dar felt a chill.

The elven woman snatched their attention back with a gliding step forward.

"Allow me to introduce myself," she said, smiling. "I am Aalre, Mistress of the Twelfth Circle of Sendatre and mage of Arachnia, Demonic Majesty of Assassins and Venom."

"Oh..." whispered Kindri, eyes wide. "She's a mean lady."

Dar's heart started beating again.

This is it. We're going to die right here, with Grandpa's kids in our hands. Well, Lord, if I'm going to go, I'm going to take a bunch of them with me and I'm going to do it in style.

"Is she really?" he replied. His heart felt light as he fit an arrow to his bow. "I was just going to bring her home to meet my parents."

Chapter Twenty-One- Love and War

Dar let fly, aiming for Aalre.

She dodged behind one of her guards. Dar's shaft skewered the hobgoblin neatly in the throat. The other Ja'al warriors knelt as one next to her, aiming at the freelancers. The elf said three sharp words.

Dar pulled Megan behind him. With a tremendous whoosh, the fire ring before them changed from a six-inch flame to a six-foot inferno, blinding him for a moment. Waves of heat seared at him, driving them towards the center of the stone island.

Multiple twangs rang out from behind the fire wall and flaming scraps of wood fluttered at their feet. A shriek of rage rose above the roar of the fire.

"No, you mindless fools! Not into the fire! Wait until I..."

The flames died down to a flicker and Dar seized the opportunity. He leaped forward, clearing the moat.

To his left and his right, Eric and Buck charged around to his side of the flame ring. He fired an arrow into the nearest guard and dropped the bow, grabbing for his sword.

Aalre materialized ahead and to his right. He had no idea how. She laughed and began a chant.

Dar leaped forward to disrupt her spell but a hobgoblin and one of the huge armored ogres cut him off. He squirmed away from a sword strike and got his blade up just in time to knock away a looping flail swing from the ogre. He staggered backwards, shocked by the power.

Then, a veritable storm of fiery darts flickered out from behind him and from Aalre. He heard Andyn and Megan cry out but was satisfied to see Aalre get rocked by a quartet of missiles herself.

He ducked under a swing from the hobgoblin's sword and retaliated with a thrust. His sword point burst through chain armor. Without pausing, Dar shifted his weight, then shoved the corpse forward, freeing his sword. The hobgoblin's corpse flew backwards, slamming into the legs of the ogre. The ogre kicked it aside.

Dar stepped to the side, trying to get a good angle on the eight-foot tall monster. Aalre shouted something and he heard a sizzling sound. Connor cried out and he heard Andyn's voice chanting something behind him.

His next attack clanged off the monster's armor. He dimly heard a roar from his right. Connor darted past him, sword slashing. The ogre moved backwards.

Trying to get us both in front of it.

Aalre, laughing wildly, disappeared from view. Dar, desperate to end the fight, lunged forward at the ogre. He feinted a leg cut, turning it into a head shot instead. The giant ignored the fake, blocking his second attack. It returned a blow two-handed, trying to crush Dar's skull from above.

Dar grinned wickedly, stepping to the right and swinging as hard as he could. His enemy's flail head crunched into the floor, pulverizing the tiles. Dar's blade sheared through the thing's armor, cutting into its ribs and side. Purple blood sprayed everywhere and Dar received an ear-shattering howl as a reward.

Connor's sword flickered behind the creature and it howled again, sweeping its flail backward to try to strike the dodging, darting halfling. Dar ducked a return backhand and stepped in under its wide-open guard. He drove upward with a vicious thrust. The blade ripped through the creature's armor, breastbone, and heart. It let out a huffing gasp and relaxed, falling forward.

Dar turned his weapon, using the giant's falling momentum to free his blade. He whirled back to the main fight, looking for Aalre.

Before he could even locate friend or foe, he heard a single word. A blinding flash of light exploded in front of him and a brutal blow struck him in the chest, hurling him back. He tripped over the edge of the fire circle and slammed into the tiles on the stone island.

Oh Jesus...

Everything hurt. A bitter smell filled the air. He wasn't too sure if he still had both arms attached. He moaned and tried to stand, but sat down. Only some ragged scraps of chainmail remained on his arms. His tunic had been blown off. He was amazed to find he still had an upper body left.

Got to get over there, he thought. *Got to help...where's Connor...Eric?*

He blinked.

Seven of the hobgoblins lay in pools of dark blood or sporting feathered shafts in their abdomens. The remaining three stood next to the doorway, swords at the ready. Both ogres lay dead.

Dar's heart sank. Connor, clutching his side and grimacing, crawled away from the doorway, his broken sword lying useless on the tiles. Andyn knelt next to him, an arrow shaft in her leg and a bloody mace held up before her, trying to shield him with her body. She wore only a few bits of charred leather and cloth clinging to hips and shoulders, leaving tanned and bleeding skin in full view.

He heard a grunt to his left. Brandawyn pulled her swords out of an ogre and staggered towards the elven sorceress. She leaned against the wall, a bloody patch growing on her right side. Next to her, on the floor, Buck sat on the reddened tiles, eyes glassy and a hand on his forehead. Blood ran down into his eyes. Khelios glowed in his other hand.

Eric stood off to Dar's right, leaning against the wall, panting. Two red lines showed in his midriff and left arm. The chainmail on his left side was gone and his arm looked painfully burned. He held his spear ready, eyes fixed on Lady Aalre.

The Ja'al mage stood tall and elegant. The red jewel on top of her white staff sizzled with tiny lightning bolts. A fiery light faded to a dull glow in the heart of the gemstone. Her clothing was ripped at mid-thigh and a couple of burn marks marked her arms. Other than that, she looked like someone who had unwisely decided to go hiking in a dress. With a contemptuous motion, she tore the dress, casting off the bottom section.

"Perfectly good dress," she said to herself, brushing her clothing.

"Surrender," said Eric through clenched teeth.

She began to chuckle. "Idiots," she commented, giving them a sympathetic smile, then shook her head. "Did you really think you could win?"

Brandi spoke to her in Elven, but the sorceress gave her a disgusted look.

"Please," she retorted with contempt, "Don't try to influence me with pleas of our common heritage. The Elder Children have too long put in their lot with the beggars, misfits and dirty masses of this world and what have we to show for it? Nothing but flimsy alliances with the unfit and unworthy. Now is the time to ally ourselves with the winning side, the side of power."

Dar felt a hand on his shoulder, pulling at him. He turned his head.

Megan used him as a brace to pull herself up to a sitting position. Holes in her trousers and blouse showed the curves of her body, marred by bloody, blackened circles where firedarts had struck. An arrow protruded from her side.

Dar's mind cleared. *No! Not her! Not like Elaine.*

He put out a hand to steady her, ignoring how much it hurt to do so.

She smiled up at him, her face pale. "Looks like we came up a little short."

He smiled back and stroked her face, wet with perspiration. "Don't worry about all this. We'll make it out."

She gave him a wry look, then closed her eyes. His heart sank. "It's okay, Dar. I'm just tired, and so cold. Dying won't be so bad."

The universe did a slow turn around him. He saw his parents' faces, proud on the day of his commissioning by Sir Tan. He saw his brother, his classmates, Lord Nolan, the townsfolk.

He took her hand and squeezed it, his next words amazing him even as he said them. "I love you."

Megan's eyes opened and she gazed at him for a long heartbeat. "Love?" she said. "Oh God. I love you too, Dar."

Shrill laughter forced them to look at Aalre.

"Love?! What are you talking about, you morons? There is no such thing, not here, not anywhere!"

Eric's voice echoed from his side of the room. "Brandi sweetheart, I'm ready whenever you are." He drew his arm back and aimed the spear.

Brandi smiled. *She looks so happy,* Dar thought. *How can she stand up, bleeding like that?*

Aalre's beautiful features twisted. "I said no more talk of love!" she shouted, slamming her staff butt into the tiles. "This is blasphemy! Folly and airy promises! There is no such thing, do you hear?"

She raised her staff, eyes glittering. Her next words came in an icy hiss. "I execute you in the name of the Ja'al."

Kindriana's voice whispered out to Dar. "Oh Mister Dar! We're so sorry. I wish we could help."

"You leave them alone!" screamed Tholi.

The gemstone on Aalre's staffed glowed with intense fire, and lightning arced through the air around it in a corona.

If only the dragons ... I am such an idiot!...

Dar hurled himself backwards to the dragon cage and shattered the lock with one swing of his sword. The door slammed open and he flopped down on the stones.

A pair of loud, high-pitched screeches nearly deafened him as a rush of air and golden wings swept over him. Aalre, her features frozen in terror, whipped her staff around to bear on the small dragons. Kindri and Tholi opened their mouths and hissed clouds of fire at the same time as lightning arced from the glowing jewel atop the staff.

Aalre tried to shriek as the fiery cloud consumed her. She writhed and convulsed in the flames, capering about in a bizarre dance. Whatever magic she had called forth in the staff expended itself, spraying sizzling bolts in all directions.

One stabbed through a hobgoblin's leather jerkin as if it were paper. Another burned into the stone island and Dar had to roll out of the way. The dragons got the worst of it. Tholi took one in the wing and veered off course, slamming into the body of the ogre Dar had killed. Kindriana was hit dead center and jerked back in the air, fluttering her wings to regain balance. She spiraled down to flop on the floor next to Eric, panting. Eric threw his spear and transfixed Aalre through the heart.

The burning pillar that had once been Aalre stopped its spasmodic, fiery jig and toppled over, thudding to the stones in a cloud of embers.

The remaining Ja'al warriors stared in horror, then raced out of the cavern, slamming into the walls in their haste to get away.

Only the gentle licking of flames and a horrid stench remained.

Dar let out a long breath, blinking in amazement.

I can't possibly be alive.

He stood and helped Megan up.

Brandi made the Sign of the Cross and sighed.

***

Halkith staggered into the copse of trees, leaning against a pine to catch his breath. What was left of his tunic and armor hung by a few blackened threads. This he ripped off his body with an angry jerk.

He ran a sweaty, shaking hand through his singed hair. Pain seared through him.

Damn that son of a bitch! He gritted his teeth.

He sank down to the cool earth, careful not to jostle his broken left arm.

How did he know where we were? He thought back over his actions of the previous days, seething. Unable to come up with any glaring errors, he sank back against the tree trunk, exhausted.

Iron Thunder had known exactly where to find them, even their hidden camp, halfway around the mountain and shielded from the air by a shelf of rock.

Halkith reached into his one remaining shoulder bag and carefully drew out pieces of a shattered bottle. He cursed, casting the shards to the rocky ground.

This is going to be a really bad day if that jar broke.

He relaxed upon finding a small, brown jar in the bottom of the bag. Twisting the top off with only one and a half hands was not easy, but he did it. He reached in to scoop out a blob of silvery, glowing ointment. He spread this on his injured arm and then the scrapes on his head.

The gel glowed brighter upon contact. He sighed and relaxed, feeling the healing warmth knit together his flesh and bone. When the warmth faded, he removed his armor and began to use the contents of the jar on his bruised and broken ribs.

And the old ox-fart had the audacity to "request" our surrender. As if a Ja'al would willingly surrender to a washed-up, ineffective, lazy...

The ointment depleted, he stopped his fulminations and let the gel do its work.

Where did I go wrong? he mused, thinking dark thoughts.

Even he had to admit the dragon was much more than the team could handle. Their first attacks had hurt old Iron Thunder, but the dragon had lived up to his name. Any delusions Halkith might have had about victory vanished in Grandpa's first fiery breath. Two warriors and a thief burned into clouds of ash in the blink of an eye.

Halkith used the last of the medicine on his leg and stood, naked except for a loincloth.

The dragon made mincemeat of the rest of the Ja'al force. Halkith himself managed to get off a darkness spell, which Iron Thunder had canceled with a counterspell, and get in a couple of hearty whacks with his mace before being hurled down the mountainside by a claw swipe. An abrupt encounter with a boulder near the trees stopped his tumbling, jolting ride down the slope of Whitehorse Peak. He lay there for a few seconds, gathering his wits and listening to the remainder of the battle, then used all of his healing spells to cure himself enough to hobble to the trees.

Halkith took inventory. His shield had taken the brunt of a blast of fire and lay ruined there on the slope somewhere.

He still had his magic mace, a war hammer, the contents of his shoulder bag, his boots, and a belt purse—not much, but better than nothing. He began to assemble something resembling clothing from the spares in his shoulder bag.

A rustle in the bushes made him whirl, mace at the ready. A small, brownish-green creature winged away, headed for the upper reaches of Whitehorse Peak.

He gazed at it, trying to figure out what it was, then went cold.

A peridragon.

Spying on us for Iron Thunder all this time!

In a furor, he slammed his weapon into the pine tree.

And that blasted Aalre and her spies! I'll...

A sudden thought cut like a blade through his curses. The peridragon flew up to its master, no doubt to report to the dragon—who would come down to finish the job.

Halkith began picking his way through the grove down the mountainside as fast as possible. Murderous thoughts of revenge gave way to a growing fear.

***

"Grandpa! Grandpa!"

Eric stood with the other freelancers in Iron Thunder's great entrance chamber, wishing he was invisible. He felt like an interloper, watching the reunion of the dragonlings and their grandfather.

The two little dragons writhed, wiggled, jumped and spun around in happiness, not standing still long enough for their grandparent to keep up with them. Finally, they calmed and stood there, clutching Grandpa.

The ancient dragon took his natural form, golden scales gleaming in the midmorning sunshine. He gathered his little ones up in a human-like hug.

"I thank the Great One you are safe," the giant dragon said, eyes closed.

Kindriana nodded, then looked up at him, eyes full of reproach. "Why didn't you come to get us, Grandpa?"

Iron Thunder looked so anguished Eric felt a lump in his throat. For an instant, Eric saw what an agonizing decision it had been for the old dragon to keep his promise instead of taking off after his grandchildren.

"Little Cloudchaser," Grandpa said, stroking her head with a great claw, "You know I couldn't. The evil ones who took you would have stolen the pegasi while I was gone and merely killed you or taken you farther away. I couldn't fit into the tunnels in the other mountain without changing to a smaller form and then I would be too slow and unable to use all my abilities."

Tholi looked up. "Couldn't you have used magic to find us?"

Grandpa placed a claw on his head as well. "I knew you were in the mountain, but that was all. The Ja'al have sorcerers and one of them was able to screen out my finding magic. All I could do was wait."

He hugged them again. "I knew that they valued the pegasi much more than you. You were their only means of bargaining. If I held the pegasi long enough and waited, they would grow impatient and make a mistake. Besides, Tholi, it was clan oath from my own grandfather's time. My ancestors gave blood to honor it."

Tholi nodded, as if that explained everything.

Grandpa smiled. "As it was, all worked out well in the end. The Creator

290

sent me these fine heroes to help find you."

Six admiring, draconian eyes turned to look at them and Eric looked down at his boots. *Now I'm really embarrassed.*

Blue light glowed in front of him. Eric jerked his head up to see an old human and two small dragons smiling at him.

His cat-eyes kind Grandpa held out his hands to Buck and Andyn. "I owe you more than my life, Grey Riders."

For once, no one protested the title.

"Uh, well, hey," said Buck, ducking his head. "A deal's a deal, right?"

Grandpa smiled again. "Yes. But you risked your lives for two beings you didn't even know. Two creatures who aren't even human."

Tholi flapped his wings and stuck out his chest. "You should have seen them, Grandpa! They really stuck it to them! And Kindri and I helped!"

Eric cleared his throat. "Actually, Grandpa, we couldn't have done it without your grandkids. They killed the Ja'al sorceress."

The old man clucked in mock-disapproval. "Ah, but they wouldn't have been able to do anything without you to free them. Besides, you all look fine. It mustn't have been such a hard fight."

Eric looked over at the others, all sporting sheepish grins. He shrugged.

Connor spoke for them all. "Actually, Grandpa, they kicked the snot out of us. The only reason we're alive is because Kindri remembered where Halkith's personal chamber was. We stole all his treasures."

The old man looked down at his granddaughter in surprise. "Really, and how did you know that?"

Kindri's snout wrinkled and she dragon-grinned at him. "Halkith tried to bribe me and Tholi with gold and magic when he first found us. He wanted us to fly away into the wilderness and lead you away from the pegasi so he could steal them, but we told him to stick it in his eye. The only way he could catch us then was to have all his hobgoblins tackle us. Today, after we killed the mean lady, I remembered how he hid his treasure under the floor stones in his bedchamber, so I took all of us there."

Now Grandpa really looked disapproving. "You went after treasure with hobgoblins still all over the place?"

Dar shook his head. "A couple of Ja'al soldiers escaped from the chamber where we found your kids. They lit out of there like they had daemons on their tails. I guess word spread about the dragons being loose in the compound and there were no other leaders strong enough to rally the force. By the time we got to Halkith's place, we didn't see any hobgoblins."

Grandpa appeared mollified. "As long as you thought it was safe. And what did you find in Halkith's chambers?"

Megan counted off on her fingers. "We found some suits of chainmail to replace the armor Aalre destroyed, plus another sword for Connor. There was a pile of gold, some jewels, and some bracelets and necklaces. We found some healing potions and a funny silver ointment in a tiny jar."

"That stuff was great," interjected Andyn. "I just wish we hadn't used all of it."

Eric felt his left arm and shook his head. "I don't."

"Did you have any trouble getting back?" asked Grandpa, releasing Andyn and Brandi's hands.

Megan spoke up. "Not a bit. It was a little slower going with all the loot, but we made it okay. We camped out at the base of Whitehorse Peak last night and made it up here this morning."

Grandpa looked satisfied. "I certainly hope we've seen the last of the Ja'al for a while. Now, come with me. I have something to show you."

Eric and the others tramped across the rock table, following the old man. The dragonlings still chattered on about their adventures in excited voices. Eric grinned. From the sound of it, the pair embellished the tale a bit.

Iron Thunder told the young dragons to fly into their chambers and get ready for bed and Kindri and Tholi complied. With a wink, the old dragon then led Eric and his friends into the entry chamber and bade them wait. He disappeared into a side alcove and returned afterwards bearing a sack. He sat on his large rock table and beckoned to the freelancers.

"Even though you have already acquired some valuables, I have decided to give you all a token of my appreciation."

"Oh no," gasped Brandi. "You mustn't, Grandpa. The deal was to find your grandchildren in exchange for the pegasi, nothing more. You've done so much for us already."

"But don't let that stop you," added Buck with a sidelong glance at the dragon's treasure room.

Brandi shot him a withering look. Iron Thunder chuckled.

"Now, now. The deal still stands. But an employer is still allowed to give his employees a little bonus for excellent performance, is he not?"

He set the sack in front of them. "What is in here is yours to keep. If you wish to distribute it among yourselves here, you are welcome to do so. Or, you can just take it all with you to town. In any case, please accept them with my thanks."

Brandi raised her hands. "Please, Your Excellency, we can't."

"You must."

Eric slipped up next to her and put an arm around her shoulders. "We will, Grandpa, and with great thanks. We're just glad your grandchildren are safe."

A peridragon's call skirled through the cavern. Grandpa's little spy floated in from the outside through the main entrance. The dragon-man held out an arm and the tiny winged creature alighted on it. It screeched and hissed at him.

Grandpa nodded. "I see. And where did he go?"

Another series of calls rang out.

The dragon-man looked grim, stroking his beard with his free hand. "While you were gone, a group of rather aggressive people of the Ja'al faith set up camp on the south side of Whitehorse Peak. My friend here spotted them and came back here to warn me. I confronted them and asked what was their business. Their response was a volley of arrows and a couple of lightning bolts."

Eric's eyes widened.

"You don't look hurt," noted Dar.

Grandpa winced and moved a shoulder. "I was, believe me, but I have a few tricks of my own. I destroyed most of them and swatted the leader down the side of the mountain. At any rate, the peridragon just spotted him in the valley between this mountain and Stonekeep. I thought no one could survive that tumble."

Eric's satisfaction at the Ja'al leader getting his comeuppance faded to a cold feeling. "You mean this Halkith is still alive?"

"Oh great!" exclaimed Buck, throwing his hands up. "No telling what he might be up to. And we haven't even got the pegasi back to Forester yet!"

Megan shook her head. "I don't think he'll try anything now. His army is probably scattered all over the forest."

Andyn agreed. "He doesn't have any soldiers. We have the pegasi, Kindri, Tholi, and Grandpa."

"Quite so," added Grandpa. "I believe he will slink back to the Ja'al High Command, wherever in the world that might be. We have seen the last of him."

"Now," he continued, standing and smiling. "We are ready for the next step, Grey Riders."

"And that is?" asked Andyn.

Grandpa's mouth curved in a sly grin. "Flying lessons."

***

Gorlak looked across the fire at his compatriots and grimaced. *Outfought and outwitted by two stupid Ghai-zhal, a gang of Urmum and a runty little Ghaizhal-ik.*

The goblin tossed another stick into the fire and considered his options.

They fled the complex when word reached them of the dragons' liberation and Aalre's death. They either could go out and look for Halkith and his hit team, wait here near the complex, or strike out into the wilderness and look for a tribe to attach themselves to. In Gorlak's opinion, the last option was the only one.

He looked at the rest of the squad of ten. Sergeant Grunda, one of Aalre's goblins, lounged against a tree about twelve feet away.

Ha! About the only thing good to come of this is the death of that elven bitch.

The whole, stupid, botched dragon hostage adventure stank to lowest Hell. The first reports from the panicked troops made them think that Iron Thunder himself had somehow made it inside the complex. They found out later it was the dragonlings, not their grandsire, who had crisped Lady Aalre. Worse yet, he and the other sergeants waited too long to return, giving the freelancers enough time to pillage Lord Halkith's personal treasure hoard and heal themselves. Now, Gree and Suboorgla were probably heading off into the forest somewhere, looking for more gainful employment.

As should we...

He shuddered, remembering the sight of the freelancers swinging down the path in the forest, two small gold dragons flying overhead. More than a match for him and the squad, especially with the dragonlings.

Oh, to get his hands on the Urmum! Visions of dark torture capered in his brain.

And yet, the freelancers and dragon could easily have destroyed him and the other goblins, but didn't. The idea mystified him. He bit his lip, trying to puzzle it out.

A sound from his right distracted him and he turned, seeing Jagida. A large female hobgoblin, Jagida's strength matched a stubbornness that could outwait the mountains. Too bad she was too dumb to know a spear haft from a tree in the woods.

He saw a glint of gold in her ear and his anger returned. "Private," he growled. "Where did you get earring?"

She eyed him. "Found it!" she retorted. "In the master's room. Mine now."

Gorlak stood. "Lord Halkith is not pleased when he sees that."

The female growled, showing her fangs. "He's dead. It's mine."

For a moment, Gorlak considered simply ripping it from her flesh, but discarded the idea. That would cost more in energy than he felt like sparing at the moment and he wasn't sure he wanted to take her on.

Huuvta looked up at him. "I think he's dead too."

Gorlak cuffed the bowman in the head. "Fool! He is not dead! And we are Ja'al, we are *Za'arak*. We will be victorious, you shall see. No bunch of cowardly surface-dwellers can beat us."

Huuvta rubbed his head and glared at him. "I think he is dead," he repeated. "We not see him for days and small dragons gone. How can he fight big gold dragon and live?"

Before Gorlak could fire off a rejoinder, a cold voice cut through the night air. "By using skills and intelligence that are obviously lacking in your feeble race."

The warriors scrambled for weapons, then froze in amazement and terror as Halkith the Grey strode into the camp. He wore a simple tunic and tattered boots. Some of his hair had been burned off, but his eyes still held that same icy glare the warriors had learned to respect and dread. He wore no cloak and he carried his deadly black mace.

He looked over the group, growing more irritated as the silence wore on. "What are you doing out here? You're from third platoon, first squad. Your duty station is in the complex. Has Aalre taken leave of her senses?"

Gorlak froze, then bowed, tensing for the inevitable blow. At times like this he wished he was a mere private. "Sorceress Lady Aalre is dead, High Priest. The freelancers sneaked in the complex while you away, freed dragons, and killed her."

The anticipated swat to the head did not materialize and he straightened. Halkith's jaw hung open and he wore an expression somewhere between shock and disbelief.

"What did you say?" Halkith leaned against a nearby tree.

Gorlak, confused, bowed again and repeated the news. He had never seen the mighty High Lord like this before.

Halkith looked around, blinked and rubbed a hand over his face. He looked lost. "Where did they come from? How did they...where is the rest of the battalion?"

"Dead, Great One," Gorlak whispered in terror. "Or fleeing for the hills. Chieftain Sanboor is dead as well."

Halkith stood for a moment, eyes far away. He stared into the darkness, a hand on his mouth. Then his eyes lighted on Jagida's earring and he went white.

"Where did you get that?" he asked in a tight voice.

Jagida ignored the obvious danger or she was too stupid to realize it. She grinned. "Freelancers drop when leaving. Jagida get. Belong to Jagida now."

The Ja'al cleric nodded. "I see."

Jagida beamed.

A black mace whickered out and smacked into her head with a sickening crunch. Jagida dropped like a stone.

Halkith ripped the earring from her corpse and turned to his troops, the runes on his mace glowing angry red.

"I trust," he said in a casual voice, "there has been no further looting of my personal effects."

Utter silence answered him.

"Good," he said, stepping over the dead body. "We can go back to the complex and gather our equipment."

"But Dread Lord," protested Huuvta, "The freelancers will come back, with the dragons."

This time, Halkith's fist lashed out, knocking the warrior to the ground.

"You ass!" he snapped. "If they have the dragons now, that means they're celebrating at Whitehorse Peak, not lying in wait to ambush us. Why should they care about the complex? They kicked the living crap out of you failures."

"Get up!" he ordered. He let his eyes roam over all of them and ran his free hand through what hair he had left.

"Besides," he continued in a more calm voice, "These types of freelancers have a concept called 'mercy', where they don't kick someone who's down, no matter how richly they deserve it. Not that they'd have that much of you to kick now anyway."

"What will we do?" asked Gorlak.

Halkith took a deep breath. "We gather supplies, move to another location, and wait. I will send a runner to the High Command for instructions. As for the freelancers, don't worry. They will make a mistake some time, and I'll be ready when they do."

Chapter Twenty-Two- Emissaries

Buck let out a whoop as he landed his pegasus. He waved a hand over his head and nearly knocked Puup out of the air. The pigeon dodged his flailing arm and landed on the pommel of Buck's saddle in a flurry of white wings.

Buck trotted his mount across the flat space outside the dragon-lair. Pegasus hooves clattered on the grey rock and Buck reached down to pat his mount. Late afternoon transformed into evening in the mountains, the light growing dimmer and redder.

He reined in the pegasus and turned to his friends, eyes afire with excitement. "This gets better every time!"

Brandi looked amused. "You'd think this was his first try the way he's carrying on."

Eric gave her a sly look and a light elbow in the ribs. "He's only been doing it for three weeks, Brandi. Maybe he still hasn't gotten the hang of it."

Buck gave Eric a regal look. "Fool. Just because you're too dull to enjoy it doesn't mean I have to be. Besides, you've been at it the same amount of time as I have."

Dar laughed. "Oh, Skyfire, Buck. He's just having fun with you."

"And for only three weeks," said a voice from Buck's side, "You are all doing quite well."

Grandpa, in human form, rode up behind him, sitting the saddle of the herd stallion.

"Really?" asked Megan.

"Yes. I've only had to rescue each of you from falling once so far. Plus prevent a couple of mid-air collisions."

Buck scoffed but had to agree. With each new day, the Riders found out new skills their host possessed, like airborne riding. Once in human form, Iron Thunder took to the saddle like he had been doing it all his life. By contrast, their own first attempts at riding the pegasi had resulted in some rather comical — but at the time, terrifying — incidents.

One time Connor ended up hanging half-on, half-off his pegasus because he forgot to buckle his waist strap. The saddles, which Grandpa brought from yet another cave in his lair, looked like normal riding saddles with two notable exceptions. First, the stirrups had straps with spring-loaded hooks that went around the rider's ankles and thighs. Then, another set of straps attached with a similar hook to a leather belt that went around the rider's waist. This second set of straps was then attached to the saddlebow and a spot just under the pommel. In addition, instead of one cinch at the bottom of the saddle, the special pegasus models had three. When all the attachments were complete, the rider had little chance of falling. The spring-loaded hooks, Buck found out, were for quick-release in emergencies.

It took the group a full day to get used to the blasted things. Grandpa insisted on something he called 'ground school', where the group each took turns attaching the straps and then riding around on the ground. More maddening still, the dragon offered no advice to them on how to install the gear. He maintained they would learn more by their mistakes than if he did everything for them. Judging from the bruises to bones and egos alike, Buck and his friends learned quite a bit.

Grandpa continued. "I certainly wouldn't try aerial combat anytime soon, but at least you can get from one place to another. Your king will have people in his employ who can train you further."

Megan stepped closer to Dar and slid an arm around his waist. "You mean we're almost done?"

The old man smiled and dismounted. "I think you are well-qualified to take the pegasi back to Deran."

Buck made a face, watching Dar kiss Megan on the cheek. Those two, as well as Eric and Brandi, had been all lovey-dovey for the past three weeks. Not that Buck had caught them in any trysts in the forest or anything like that. Quite the contrary. Both were scrupulous in avoiding even the appearance of impropriety.

That's an odd bunch of people and an odd religion, thought to himself. *By the Trees, if I had a woman like that at my side, I'd already have taken her out for a ...*

"Buck?"

"Eh?" Jerked from his thoughts, Buck looked over at Andyn. She petted the forehead of her mare, looking into the creature's eyes.

"What are you going to name your pegasus?" Andyn asked.

Buck wrinkled his brow in thought for a moment. "Shadowbane."

Andyn frowned. "I still haven't thought of a name for mine."

Buck unstrapped himself, dismounted and inspected the pegasus. The flying horse nickered and nosed at his belt sack for treats. Even though all of the pegasi looked uniform on first glance, each had a distinguishing mark. A white blaze marked the forehead of his mount.

Connor strode up next to them, leading his smaller pegasus. It took a while to find a one fit for Connor, finally settling on one of the younger mares.

Andyn asked his advice on a name for her mount.

"Why don't you use one of those languages you know?" the halfling offered.

Andyn frowned. "I want something different, something unique."

"Medianox."

Brandi walked up to Andyn, hand in hand with Eric. "Medianox means 'midnight' in Ecclesia, the language of the Church."

Andyn considered this, then smiled. "Medianox. I like that."

Grandpa led his stallion over to them. "You had better get your equipment organized. I'm sure the Baron and his people will be wondering what happened to you. Besides," he added with a twinkle in his eye, "I'm getting tired of playing innkeeper. Having the grandchildren around is bad enough."

They walked their mounts over to a makeshift corral of fallen logs and branches—not that a mere corral was going to deter animals that could simply fly over obstacles. It was a testament to the training of the pegasi that they remained where they were led, content to let their new owners take care of them.

Buck removed bit, bridle, saddle and blanket, then reached for a pile of old sacks lying on the ground. "Are we going to take all this gear with us? We'll need saddle bags," he noted as he started rubbing down Shadowbane.

Grandpa shook his head, leaning on Medianox. "I don't have any of those. What we'll do is use those sacks to store the brushes, special tools, and some of the food. When you get to Forester, you can buy standard saddlebags. The pegasi will take them, I'm sure. And you're going to need to feed them before you leave," he reminded them.

Buck rolled his eyes. The pegasi ate more food and drank more water than regular horses, even if they didn't seem to gain any weight because of it. Buck suspected they used up a lot of energy flying around. Hovering over the ground seemed to be the most taxing. Grandpa's stores contained a sizeable amount of oats and alfalfa in another of his caverns, protected from vermin and rot with a spell of preservation. Now even this ran low.

The Riders also witnessed an oddity: meat-eating equine animals. This astonished the Grey Riders but it was as Grandpa had originally explained it. As a hybrid of raptor and horse, they took on some of the characteristics of each. Thus, he supplemented their vegetarian diets with strips of meat, just like would be fed to a falcon. Buck found flying horses with incisors unnerving, but Grandpa assured him that these trained pegasi, at any rate, wouldn't bite.

Buck checked Shadowbane's hooves and cleaned them, although they didn't need it. Pegasus hooves didn't take nearly the pounding as those of normal horses, but he wanted to keep the habits he had been taught in riding school at the Academy.

Never know when it'll be a good idea to ride on the ground for a while instead of flying.

They fed and watered the pegasi in the corral and headed over towards the cavern entrance.

Kindri and Tholi hopped up and down in excitement, asking about the flying lesson. Andyn put her arms around the pair and walked into the cave with them, describing their latest 'class'. Grandpa made a rule that the two dragonlings stay inside the caverns during lessons. After a few complaints and much sulking, the pair obeyed. Andyn and Megan mollified them somewhat by offering to tell them stories each night as compensation, a proposition greeted with enthusiasm.

Buck walked into the giant central cavern with the others and began stowing his gear. Behind him, the women discussed their experiences with Tholi and Kindri in quiet tones, interrupted by excited questions and comments from the dragonlings. Plates clanked and he heard the sound of a whetstone, then Dar's voice.

Eric and Dar's turn to cook tonight, Buck remembered. *Just so long as it isn't me.*

He sighed. He immensely enjoyed their time here, learning to fly the pegasi, talking to Grandpa, and playing with the dragonlings. There were no goblins to worry about, no assassins creeping in on them in the middle of the night, and no Halkith the Grey. The thought of going back to civilization made his head hurt.

Buck walked to the cavern entrance and stood there quietly for a moment. He looked out over the valleys, feeling the cool air and gentle breeze. He breathed in deeply, enjoying the smell of roasting venison and watching the stars make their shy appearance in the darkening sky.

He cast a glance over towards Halkith's mountain. A small knot of apprehension remained with him despite the peaceful surroundings.

We've beaten him. So why do I feel like all hell is about to break loose?

"Buck, could you give me a hand over here?" Andyn called from the cavern.

He took one last look at the forest and sighed.

I know why. Because Halkith isn't dead.

*** *** ***

They left the very next morning.

"Now remember what I told you," said Grandpa, looking at Andyn in mock severity.

She smiled down at him from the saddle. "I won't forget. Let the herd stallion take the lead, guide him towards where we want to go, and try not to let any of them get out of formation. Keep an eye forward, backwards, up and down. And strap in tight. Did I get it all?"

Grandpa, in human form for their departure, smiled back. "If I didn't know any better, I'd have thought you were mocking me."

On impulse, Andyn bent down and kissed him on the forehead. "Now I wouldn't do that to such a dear, would I?"

To her surprise, Grandpa actually blushed. "Er, yes, well, just be careful—please?"

"Ready to go?" asked Dar.

She nodded. Kindri and Tholi stood behind their grandsire. The Riders had already said their farewells to them, a difficult thing considering what they had gone through together. Andyn smiled at them and waved.

"You be good now. And don't worry. We'll be back to visit someday."

"We will!" answered Kindri. "And watch out for the bad guys! Someday we'll come to help you!"

"Andyn," called Dar from her left. "We really have to get going."

Grandpa patted her hand. "Best of everything to you. And don't worry." He winked. "When you least expect me, I will be right there, keeping an eye on you."

A comforting warmth filled her, hearing those words. "Thank you for everything Grandpa. Verian keep you."

She turned her mount towards the herd. The morning turned out grey and misty, a low fog obscuring the bottoms and the sides of the mountains around the Whitehorse. She was glad for it—any enemies would have a hard time seeing them from the ground.

In lead position, Eric raised his hand, then dropped it.

"Go, Medianox!" Andyn whispered to her pegasus. Medianox nickered in response, then beat her wings and cantered forwards. A powerful gust of wind billowed up, blowing dust around Andyn and her mount. The earth held on to them like a miser parting with a coin. After a couple of strokes, the pegasus' strength overcame the swirling air seeking to hold her down. Andyn turned in her saddle and waved to the figures behind her, saying farewell one last time.

Up higher and higher they rose, the Riders bracketing the herd on all sides. Andyn felt her heart pounding with exhilaration.

I could learn to like this a lot, she decided.

***

"Which do you think looks better, the tan or the dark green?"

Nolan turned from the large window next to his bed at Ellen's voice. "Pardon?"

Ellen Hanford walked in from the bathroom, looking at two different dresses she held along one arm. Her dark skin contrasted with the delicate pink of her shift.

He pursed his lip for a second, then turned back to the window. "The dark green."

The Whitehorse Range loomed partly in shadow from the morning light. The dark verdant slopes, replete with spruce, alder, ironcore and aspen, showed the benefit of recent rains. The top of Whitehorse Peak, even at this great distance, towered behind the lesser mountains closer to the town.

Spring is my favorite time of year, he decided.

He felt, rather than saw, her look of exasperation from behind him, then a sigh.

"What is it dear?" she asked.

He turned away from the window, picking up his shirt from the back of a chair and slipping it on. "I was just thinking about Dar Cabot and the others."

Ellen gave him a sympathetic look. "You're still worried, aren't you?"

He nodded, buckling a belt around his hips, settling the dagger more comfortably. "I just wish I knew what happened. There's no sign of them at all. And the Ja'al have just backed off, without any explanation."

She frowned. "Nothing is decided, Nolan. Colin said they came away from the ambush just fine and he saw them go off into the woods. I know they've been gone more than a month already, but that doesn't mean anything, you know that. Some of our missions in the old days lasted over a month, remember?"

"Yes," he admitted, "but they aren't us. We had more experience when we went on those long expeditions. And Halkith is not a small order. Anything could have happened to them."

Ellen dropped the tan dress on the bed and slipped the dark green one over her head. "Button me up, please?"

He walked behind her and did as requested.

Come on, Hanford, he chided himself. *You know it could turn out like this every time you commission someone. It's part of the profession, both yours and theirs. They know the risks and so do you.*

He remembered the intent, eager gleam in their eyes, especially Dar's: hometown boy hoping to make good against the bad guys from the badlands.

He heard the thud of running feet outside their bedchamber door, followed by a clattering halt and much whispering, then a tentative knock.

"Yes?"

"Milord, Milady," announced a teenaged voice, tremulous with excitement and nervousness. "Winged creatures have been sighted coming in from the North."

Nolan's heart skipped.

"Winged creatures?" he asked.

"Yes, milord. Pegasi. It looks like a whole herd."

Ellen's eyes widened. She joined him at the window.

Coming in low, just emerging from one of the near passes, a great herd of winged forms soared towards the town, about a hundred feet above the treetops. Their dark black pinions beat in steady rhythm.

Nolan's jaw dropped. Seven of the creatures had riders.

"Tell Sir Colin I need him here on the double!" he called out towards the door. "And get the stablemaster!"

***

Dar leaned back in the chair, setting his winecup down on the table. "And Grandpa, er, Iron Thunder said that was the end of it. Halkith went tumbling down the mountainside into a stand of trees. Grandpa sent the peridragon back later, but Halkith fled."

Nolan stared into his goblet, watching the wine swirling as he spun the cup in his fingers. He shook his head.

"A dragon..."

He leaned back in his chair, nodding for Dar to continue. It was the morning of the fourth day since the freelancers had returned in triumph from Whitehorse Peak with the pegasi, bearing treasure and many tales. Loathe to expose them to a retaliatory strike by more Ja'al assassin, he decided to let them stay in guest rooms in the manor house.

Forty pegasi held suspended in time by magic from the waning days of the Empire.

And all battle-trained. A prize that could tip the balance of power in many regions.

Nolan scratched his chin. *No wonder Halkith was so bent on finding them. But why? The Ja'al don't have any nearby installations where they could be based and as for getting them down to Morlan or Torosc...well, that's a long way and a lot of things could happen.*

"And that's it," finished Dar, bringing Nolan out of his reverie. The baron stood up from the dinner table.

"If I may have a moment," he said.

Everyone quieted. Ellen put her arms around their ten-year-old boy, Timothy, and his six-year-old sister Alice. The children looked up at their father.

"As you know," he began, "I sent a rider to Hillton immediately upon your arrival here. It has been three days already, more than enough time for Lord DeGrance to send word to the capitol via magical means about your discovery. Also more than enough time for a representative from Oakmoor to arrive. I think you should get acquainted with a little etiquette and protocol before anyone of importance arrives."

Ellen stood. "Timmy, Alice, come with me. You've already had lessons in this."

Alice tugged on Dar's sleeve. "Mister Dar, didn't you have this lesson already?"

He leaned towards her and winked. "No," he said in a loud whisper, "Never had much use for it."

The children giggled as Ellen took them off to the playroom.

"Now then," the baron began, "This will be a formal reception of the King's representatives."

Nolan stifled a grin at their expressions. Dar looked like he had swallowed a lemon and Bydecy scratched his head. Only the Alenars and Andyn nodded in affirmation.

"His Highness," he began, "will probably send his Master of Steeds and a military officer. The proper address for the Master is simply that, as in "Master Hollis". Officers are addressed chiefly by their rank, unless he or she is also nobility, in which case the honorific for the noble title is used. Knights, whether male or female, are addressed as Sir. I had hoped you already know how to speak to a Baron, but, judging from past experience, I'll have to remind you again."

Grins and chuckles at this last barb.

"Counts and earls are addressed as 'Your Excellency'. On the off-chance that a duke is sent, which I highly doubt, your address would be 'Your Grace'. If the royal Steward arrives, it is 'Master Steward'. If it is anyone else, look to me for your cue."

Dar still looked sour. Nolan raised an eyebrow.

"Something wrong, Mister Cabot?"

Embarrassed at being noticed, Dar forged on anyway. "I still don't see why this is necessary."

"Though some people put far too much stake in titles, there is a purpose for them," Nolan said, "They are a sign of respect for the responsibilities of a person's office, a concept which I admit might be lost on you."

The freelancers caught the twinkle in Nolan's eye. Eric poked Dar in the ribs.

"Just get it right," he admonished. "We want to make a deal, remember?"

Nolan raised an eyebrow. None of the companions offered anything further and he didn't pursue it. He would find out soon enough.

He continued. "In any case, bows and curtseys at the introductions will be sufficient. I will speak first as the liege of this fiefdom. After that, all will adjourn to the receiving room."

He looked them over. All dressed in their finest, their faces showed more than a little apprehension.

A stunning dress of dark lavender graced Megan's slender form, new golden bracers shiny on her wrists. Brandawyn looked every inch the battle medic, a clean new tunic of smoke grey covering her chainmail, a crucifix of silver lying against it. A shiny new sword in an ornate scabbard hung from her left hip and she wore new boots and a cloak of snow white.

Eric wore a dark green cloak, a tan shirt, and dark brown leggings. A new silver-chased sword hung from his belt in a turquoise-studded scabbard. Buck's brand new suit of banded armor clanked at every step, the dwarven sword Khelios at his side. Dar looked as he always did, his bastard sword hanging on the chair behind him, polished armor winking from underneath a clean tunic of dark green. He put his hand on his newest item, a handaxe of dwarvish design with a curved blade.

Andyn looked a vision in dark blue tabard and silver chainmail, the golden braid of her hair glowing all the more against the deep azure of her tunic. The Baron noted a new mace when she arrived, made of dull-blue metal with a mother-of-pearl handle. Connor, dressed in black leather, wore black pants and a new cloak of grey, a strange white ring on his right hand.

Presents from the dragon or prizes of battle? Nolan wondered.

Eric raised his hand. "Are you sure the pegasi are ours to deal with? I mean, Grandpa said they belonged to the King."

"It is difficult to say," Ellen answered, closing the door behind her. She swept in and took her seat.

"When pegasi were left with the dragons, the Esten Empire still existed," she continued, "and there was no such thing as Deran. Also, since Grandpa gave them to you as the heirs of the prophecy, they are yours to do with as you please. However, the 'new king in Esten' was the original reason he decided to reveal them to you and his charge was to bring the pegasi to this 'new king' but since Esten doesn't exist and King Philip is not of the Kalar line, it makes things a bit murky."

Nolan chuckled at their confused expressions. "Don't worry about it. I think there's room for negotiations. Now on to other matters. How is your training coming along?"

Andyn, Megan and Eric exchanged pleased grins. Andyn spoke first. "Excellent, Milord. Lady Ellen is a most gracious and patient teacher."

Ellen nodded. "Would that I had forty students like you. We could conquer Torosc itself."

"And our warriors?" Nolan asked, looking at Dar, Eric and Buck. "How are the practice sessions going?"

All three men's hands went to sore spots on their shoulders, arms, or chests. All three simultaneously noticed it and put their hands down.

"Fine," said Dar, giving a weak smile. "Just fine. Sir Colin is a very, um, capable instructor."

Ellen shot him an amused glance. Nolan turned to the smallest member of the group.

"Miss Ila has been helping you with your study of the arts of espionage? I am glad Lord DeGrance saw fit to send us his chief spy."

"She's been very helpful, Your Lordship," answered Connor.

"Good." Nolan picked up his goblet and took a sip. "They were all very gracious in accepting the assignments to train you, but I think they wanted to know more about the free-lances who brought the pegasi to Forester."

In fact, Ila Belarus, Degrance's chief spy, had made a point of asking to train Connor. Ellen even pulled rank on John Warhite, her assistant, upon whom the task of training would have usually fallen.

Of course, word of the return of the "Avengers" spread through the town like the wind once they landed in the town square. The unenviable task of keeping the townsfolk away from the corral fell on Sergeant Roldan, who executed it with the same hard-bitten efficiency he used on all his assignments.

Indeed, trade and production in the workshops and stores ceased the day the Riders came back from Whitehorse Peak.

Now? Well, the group found themselves to be quite the celebrities. They couldn't walk fifty feet before someone approached them. Everyone in Forester had seven extra places at the table or a daughter who wanted to meet them or a son who was dying to hear their latest exploits. Looking at the group now, he could see why. Any of the three ladies could turn heads and he figured that the village girls were quite taken with Eric and Buck.

Yes, they were quite the heroes, all except Dar. No one in Forester, save Nolan, his family and manor staff, knew quite what to make of Dar Cabot any longer. The prettiest and most confident town girls turned to wide-eyed, stammering statues. Even his old school friends didn't know what to say to him. Nolan could see that it didn't sit well with Dar, who tried to act as if nothing was amiss.

He shook his head. Dar would find out soon that fame had its price, even if that fame was confined to a small barony on the borderlands of Deran.

"Lord Nolan," Megan asked, "Have you learned anything more about the prophecy?"

Nolan opened his mouth to speak, but a knock on the door interrupted him.

"Enter," he called.

Colin bowed at the door. "Visitors from Oakmoor to see Your Lordship. Shall I bring them to the audience chamber?"

"Yes, please." Nolan turned to the group as Colin exited.

Nolan saw a little apprehension among the Riders and knew it for what it was. He nodded. "Ready enough. Let us see whom our King has sent."

Ellen stood with the Riders, her dark green dress a cloud of forest-colored fabric. Gold edging and embroidery made the garment seem to glitter. She glided to Nolan's hand and smiled. He smoothed his red-and-blue tabard and led the way out by the side door. They entered the audience chamber.

Three men and two women awaited them with Colin in attendance.

At seeing them, Nolan's knight came to attention.

"My Lord of Tallemar, Lady Ellingson, Master Ward, Sir McKay, and Sir Cullen, I present to you Lord Nolan Hanford and Lady Ellen Hanford of Forester and the Grey Riders: Dar Cabot, Buckminster Bydecy, Andyn Eleandir, Megan Alenar, Connor Lomin, Brandawyn Alenar and Eric Indidarc."

Their guests bowed in unison with Nolan and his party.

A slender brown-haired half-elf with a simple, seven-pointed gold crown straightened first. Sea-grey eyes looked over Nolan and his party. He wore a slim longsword with a golden handle and a matching dagger. Fine silvery chain armor glinted under his blue tunic up to the top of his neck. His tunic bore a silver unicorn's head embroidered in the center and a red soaring falcon above the right breast. Nolan's heart beat a little quicker. This was Terenil DeMey, Earl of Tallemar.

Husband of the White Demon.

He remembered stammering in amazement on meeting Countess Saren in Oakmoor with Terenil, years ago. Despite her fame and appearance, she put him at ease immediately by asking about Ellen and the children. After a while, Nolan found himself laughing at her quick wit and gentle manner, the strangeness of her ivory bat-wings and tiny white horns forgotten.

Terenil spoke first, as was his right by rank. "Milord, milady. I am pleased to see you both. It has been a while since Lord Hanford visited our capitol."

A quickly stifled gasp from Andyn behind him confirmed that at least one of the Grey Riders recognized him.

Nolan shot a look at Eric – Terenil's brother-in-law. Terenil gave a short nod. Eric bowed low, trying without success to hide a smile.

Terenil gestured to the first person on his left, a middle-aged human woman with greying hair and a no-nonsense air.

310

"This is Lady Mary Ellingson, the Vice-Mistress of Steeds from the Royal household. Lord Bannister, the Master of Steeds, is ill so His Majesty bade her come instead."

She wore blue and silver as well, her dress hem ending at the knee just above dark black riding boots. She held a silver riding crop in her hands and a short sword handle stuck out horizontally behind her lower back.

Nolan and Ellen nodded to Lady Mary, who nodded back.

Terenil held out a hand towards one of the men, a stout human of middle age with a mustache and beard and amused blue eyes. Dressed in blue and silver like the rest, he carried a locked iron box and had a slim dagger behind his belt.

"This is Thomas Ward, the Assistant Royal Treasurer. He is commissioned by His Majesty to negotiate for the pegasi."

Terenil indicated the other man and woman. They were young, not past their mid-twenties. "Sir Alfred McKay, Lieutenant Major of the Royal Guards and Sir Marian Cullen, Major of the Fifth Royal Legion. Both are riding instructors to His Majesty's armies."

"Shall we sit here for the discussion?" Lady Ellen asked, leading them to the long oak table. She smiled and chatted pleasantries with the visitors, asking how was their journey and inquiring after their needs.

Nolan sat, not at the head of the table, but to the right of it, next to Ellen. As highest ranking, it was Terenil's place to sit at the head of the table.

Terenil looked at the chair in surprise. "My Lord. Please. This is your fief. And thank you for the honor."

Nolan smiled back and took his place. Once everyone was settled, he nodded to the Earl. "Your Excellency, if you would care to say anything."

Terenil looked across the table at the crowd of adventurers and Ellen. "There is not much to say. I believe Lord Nolan's excellent letter explained everything in detail. You have in your possession a herd of trained war-pegasi, given to you by one Iron Thunder, Gold Dragon and arch-mage. According to what he told you, they are in fulfillment of a prophecy and should be given to the King of the land. Master Ward?"

The official nodded, placing the box on the table. "I have here," he said in a deep, rich voice, "funds to compensate you for the entire herd. I am sure you will find it satisfactory and more than enough to retire in comfort."

"Can we see it?" asked Buck.

All eyes pivoted over to him. Andyn frowned at him.

Buck made a face at his companions. "We should see it, shouldn't we?"

Terenil nodded. "Certainly. Master Ward?"

The treasurer nodded and brought out a glass key from under his tunic. Instead of using it to unlock the box, he merely tapped the lock three times. With an audible click, the lock sprang open.

Ward opened the box. "I think you will find this adequate."

Diamonds, sapphires and rubies showered colored light in all directions, reflecting a thousand times over the lights of the hovering chandelier overhead.

Nolan suppressed a reflex to gape at the gems. Not a poor man, Nolan set considerable reserves aside for both his family and for the welfare of the town. This was a princely sum. His entire fortune would only make up a fifth of the box contents and he figured all the jewels could be used to buy most of Forester. And that didn't count the coins.

The freelancers gasped.

Buck looked like he was going to faint and Connor's eyes opened wide. Dar Cabot bit his lip then looked over at Eric. Eric eyed Brandawyn, on his right, and Megan, on his left. The women gave almost imperceptible shakes of their heads.

"Your Excellency, my lords," said Dar. "This is an amazing price. It is truly generous."

Thomas Ward smiled. "More than fair market price."

"However," Dar continued as if to get the words out before he lost heart, "we were wondering if we could strike a bargain with His Majesty."

Thomas Ward, Terenil and Lady Ellingson exchanged glances. The Earl shrugged.

"And your counteroffer?"

Dar cleared his throat. "Purchase rights to the pegasi of our choice, from any in the herd. Fair market value, no profit margin, and payable in installments as we get the funds. Full use of the pegasi in the meantime and training in riding techniques. Starting right away."

Thomas Ward chuckled.

Terenil looked at Eric. "Is this your doing?"

Eric's eyes twinkled. "No, it was actually the brainchild of Mister Cabot. I don't think I could have come up with something like this—I'm not enough of a merchant."

Terenil chuckled. "Your sister would disagree."

Lady Ellingson leaned back in her seat. "Well, you cannot mark them down for lacking initiative."

Ward turned to Dar with a smile. "Mister Cabot, that is a fine counteroffer. It would leave the Crown in the profits from the entire venture, but first, two questions. One, what is to say that you just put a down payment on them, mount up and ride away. Second, why? You could retire with what the Crown has offered, wealthy beyond your dreams."

Dar, looking a little relieved, smiled back. "Well, as to the first, you've got me there. You don't know us from a giant's hind end and we could just take off if we wanted to."

The visitors laughed. Nolan joined in the merriment.

"Lord Nolan and Lady Ellen can vouch for us, though," Dar continued. "We did bring the pegasi all the way to Forester, instead of leaving with them for sale to the highest bidder."

Nolan turned to Terenil. "Your Excellency, I can vouch for the character of Mister Cabot and his friends. If they refuse to pay the balance, I will find a way to pay it for them and deal with them myself. Agreed?"

Terenil nodded. "And the second question, Mister Cabot?"

Dar shrugged. "We really don't want to retire, Excellency. We have many things to do and there's a lot to be made right in the world."

An eyebrow rose under the seven-pointed crown. "Such as?"

Dar looked embarrassed. "We'd rather not say. We wouldn't dream of doing anything illegal with them, if that's what you're worried about."

"No," said Terenil, relaxing back in his seat. "The word of Nolan of Forester is as good as his life. I ask out of curiosity, but as long as there is no danger to the people of Deran, I won't pry. Well, milords, miladies?"

"I would have to stay here for a few more weeks to train them," offered the Mistress of Steeds. "However, I could keep one pegasus for myself and send Sir Alfred and Sir Marian on with the balance of the herd. Master Ward?"

The treasurer looked pleased. "The market value of a trained pegasus is about forty thousand gold pieces, leaving the total at three hundred twenty thousands for the eight of them. We have much more value in the box in gems alone. I am in favor."

Terenil looked askance at his two young officers. Sir Alfred deferred to the lady. She smiled at him and turned to the Earl of Tallemar.

"It would help to have a wing of air cavalry here on the borderlands, as we've never had a rover-patrol available before. These free-lances could act as His Majesty's agents. We have enough left from the herd to create an entire new air battalion in Oakmoor or Eastbluff. Besides, the extra eight pegasi would have had to be made part of another platoon anyway."

Sir Alfred nodded. "With Lord Nolan up here, there would be little risk. Even if the freelancers prove to be untrue, a message sent to Darlon or North Corner could catch them in a matter of days. They could be restricted to flying only in Northern Alliance air-space until the debt is paid off. In the meantime, perhaps the Crown could make use of their services?" He raised an eyebrow.

Terenil nodded. Dar and the other freelancers leaned forward in their seats, intent with anticipation.

The Earl held out his hand to Dar Cabot. "We have a deal."

You'd think they just became kings, Nolan thought, watching the young people smile and laugh and clap each other on the back.

Chapter Twenty-Three- To Serve the Holy Way

They spent the next four weeks with Mary Ellingson, Mistress of Steeds of the Deranese Army. Each day, she introduced them to a new way of mounting, riding, controlling, and landing the pegasi. She gave them daily training missions near Forester.

She took one look at them on that first day and shook her head. "I don't think I can make you air cavalry. Hobilars is more like it."

Megan scratched her head. "Hobilars?"

Buck explained. "Hobilars are mobile or mounted infantry. They really don't spend most of their time in the saddle, just to travel to the site of the mission. They fight on foot."

"Very good," Ellingson noted with a sardonic smile. "Sky Knights are a totally different matter. I don't have time to train you for that, even if I was sure you could do it. I have to be back in Oakmoor as soon as I can to take care of the rest of the herd."

At their chagrined looks, her expression softened. "Oh, come now. I know you've heard fantastic tales of Sky Knights, but you have to be realistic. We just don't have six months to do this. Make the best of the opportunity. Besides, I'll teach you a few cavalry tactics when I'm satisfied with your progress."

With that, they embarked on a series of intense (and, in Andyn's words, 'intensely painful') training sessions. They learned how to make the winged horses hover over the ground. Lady Ellingson taught them to land and take off from small knolls, among trees and bushes, on sloping surfaces, and even in water (an interesting episode in the Whitehorse River that left everyone drenched). She showed them the fine art of quick-mounting, a process by which she and her pegasus were in the air in a matter of a few seconds. Buck was the only one of the Grey Riders who managed to look halfway competent at that trick.

As far as aerial maneuvers were concerned, they were in the hands of a master. Ellingson could induce her mount to spin, loop, dive, corkscrew, shoot straight up, stop into a hover, and fly upside down. Even though Dar could sense she knew more maneuvers than that, she spent her time trying to get the Riders to learn just those. They did well, although Dar couldn't tell from Mary Ellingson's sarcastic comments, prayers to heaven for deliverance from cloddish students and constant urging to work harder.

The most difficult tasks turned out to be mounted combat. Not only did Dar have to ignore the great height at which they practiced, but he had to keep a weather eye out for other riders in the sky, both above and below him. Gusts of wind and sudden changes of direction made it difficult to hold a weapon. It was like trying to thread a needle while sliding down a hillside. With practice, he became competent in firing his bow and wielding his sword from the saddle. He even got a grade of 'passing fair' from Mary in throwing his hand-axe at targets while flying. The special saddle was a big help, despite the troublesome straps and belts.

As promised, she taught the Riders how to charge in formation, wheel in groups and pairs, and set up wave attacks at both air and ground targets. These were the vaunted air cavalry tactics she had promised, and, as Dar found out, it took incredible skill. They stopped after learning the basics. Dar could see why Sky Knights took so long to get trained.

Amazingly enough, Buck's pet pigeon was the calmest participant in the training. The pigeon simply sat on his master's shoulder or in the hood of his cloak during training flights.

The Mistress of Steeds also taught them one of her own personal tricks. Since they were going to be hobilars, she decided they would need to send their mounts to safety and call them back when needed. One by one, they trained their pegasi to fly up and away at a command and return when they saw a signal from a special arrow or spell fired up into the air. Dar asked about the wisdom of sending the pegasi to possible danger, but Lady Ellingson waved a hand.

"Pegasi are the fastest mounts flying," she explained, "If they're healthy and in decent weather, nothing can catch them if they don't want to be caught, not even dragons. You'd have more to worry about if you left them on the ground. These are Imperial war steeds. They'd wait on the ground for you until the sun burned out if you commanded them. They're far better off flying to a place they sense is safe. Besides, they won't go more than five miles from you. Not only do they have an exceptional sense of smell but they also have attributes common in raptors, such as extremely sharp eyes. They can tell when you leave an area. You won't lose them."

Of all of them, Connor proved to be the best archer, drawing rare praise from Mary upon hitting a target with an arrow while executing a turn. Eric bought a new spear and this turned out to be his favorite mode of combat.

Dar sometimes asked Megan about spellcasting from the saddle and she grimaced in response. Their practice sessions in that area did not go well. Mary Ellingson was a warrior by trade, and she knew little of the intricacies of spellcasting. She watched with sympathy as Andyn, Megan, Eric, and Brandi tried their best at magic while flying. Finally, after their riding instructor got them to the point where they could at least complete the spell four times out of five (never mind the effectiveness), she declared them "passable" and let it go at that.

Their graduation day came on a bright summer afternoon in mid-Junio. Mary lined them up in the town square of Forester, with most of the town watching, and handed them scrolls that declared them "Graduates of Basic Flight Training". As an officer of the Royal Guards, she gave them ranks of brevet sergeant and charged them to serve well the King and people of Deran. Then, with a twinkle in her eye, she announced to Lord Nolan that she considered them to be 'no danger to the people of Deran' and that he would be one of the few barons to have an entire air squadron at his disposal.

Dar wondered at that. Did that mean they were at Nolan's beck and call, or that he would leave them free to do what they wanted? He didn't want to be tied down doing patrol duty when he could be scouring the wilderness, looking for clues to his grandparents. That was the real reason he wanted to keep his pegasus. He sensed that he was going to have to do a fair amount of searching before he found out what had happened to them so many years ago.

That night, at the farewell feast for Mary Ellingson, Lord Nolan took Dar aside and whispered that he had 'precious few ideas on what to do with an air squadron' and if he came up with any suggestions, he was open to them. Dar grinned and promised to tell him if he did.

In other respects, the weeks after their return to Forester with the pegasi were idyllic, despite the demanding training. The freelancers went to the market square, ate meals, practiced their skills, and talked and argued together. It was their first real chance to take a breath since the discovery of the Westhaven massacre.

True to Dar's initial assessment of them, Buck and Connor were dependable, funny, and straightforward. Despite Connor's profession as a spy and thief, he avoided the appearance that he even thought of stealing from the party. Buck, with a big grin, told everyone that he would try it, but that the women would probably skin him alive if he succeeded. Considering Buck's lack of manual dexterity, Dar didn't consider this a threat. In addition, even though both Buck and Connor followed the Old Path and the others followed Christianity or Verian, they never made religion an issue and tried to sidestep theological arguments when they saw them coming.

Dar found he liked Brandi, Andyn and Eric. Megan's sister proved to be quiet, approachable, and non-judgmental, even though he had felt her a little too controlled and aloof at first. She had a kind, gentle heart and he found, to his surprise, that she detested violence. From the way she handled herself in combat, he would have come to a different conclusion.

"I had other options in the seminary, you know," she had told him, relaxing outside the general store one sunny afternoon. "I could have chosen to be a normal healer or even a cloistered nun instead of a combat medic."

He gave her a quizzical look. "What changed your mind?"

She looked down at the dusty porch with a rueful little smile. "A cloistered nun. She told me it would be a waste and a shame if someone so capable of protecting others and standing up to evil gave up that talent and hid it in a convent. Strange, isn't it?"

After a while, he understood her worries and ambitions better, but wished she would relax some more.

Dar suspected that something had gone on between Eric and Brandi beyond their mutual attraction, but he couldn't quite put his finger on it. Inquiries into Eric's life with Melinor's family got him detailed and often humorous stories, but only vague descriptions of his life before that. Dar suspected there was something else going on behind the merry smile and fun-loving demeanor. He resolved to be patient.

Andyn Eleandir was another matter. She was quick-witted, smart, and very open about herself. She lost her temper easily and could curse like a lumberjack. She was easy to talk to, listening without judgment to most points of view. Her somewhat casual attitude towards the unclothed body caused him some consternation when she suggested going swimming in the Whitehorse River, men and women both, in the 'natural state'. Andyn gave him and Eric a look of exasperation at their polite refusals.

"What's the big deal?" she asked, raising her hands. "We're all friends here and I'm sure we know what we're going to see. Nothing's going to happen."

Then she sighed and agreed to go upstream with the other women when Megan suggested it.

The weeks of training had also provided the couples some extra time to learn more about each other. The more Dar found out about Megan, the more apprehensive he became — and not because of some character flaw. On the contrary, he could find absolutely nothing wrong with her. The timing was terrible.

He talked to Father Ander about it, who listened with a grave expression and a twinkle in his eye. Dar didn't tell him anything about his own quest for his grandparents and the Helm of Shadows, but mentioned that romantic entanglements could keep him from an important family matter.

"Dar," the priest told him, "Think of this: Will this family matter disappear if this relationship bears fruit and you and the young lady marry? And will she eventually tire of waiting for you to make your mind? It has to do with what you are willing to give up in order to gain what you truly want."

That was the crux of the matter. Dar didn't know what he wanted. He found his affection for Megan growing every day but didn't want to get distracted from his goal of finding out what happened those many years ago. She could be very distracting.

Her merry, positive outlook on life energized him and inspired him to try new things. Of course, trying to stand on his head on a log in the Whitehorse River wasn't Megan's idea of the height of inspiration, but her peals of laughter when he plunged into the water more than made up for her exasperation at his attempt. Behind her disapproving looks at his wisecracks and puns she kept a laughing, roguish spirit. He wondered at how she managed to maintain it, considering all she had been through in her life.

He also found her completely beyond him intellectually. Megan's grasp of the subjects from her Academy days was amazing and her memory phenomenal. She learned faster than any of the other Riders, proven by the fact that she had been the first of the group to get a spell off in mid-flight. She spent more than a few late nights trying to get him to work the simplest magic. She clapped her hands in glee when he was finally able to make a tiny blue light hover over his hand for about five seconds.

He grew to love her laugh, the way the sun brought out the red highlights in her hair, and her smile, so joyful that it seemed to light up any room. She completely captivated the townspeople of Forester. They took every opportunity to wave and call to her whenever she went about in the town.

All of this worked havoc with his hormones. This was very difficult to deal with when she kissed him. Her slender body, all smooth curves, seemed to fit into his embrace as if the two of them had been created with just this in mind.

But something always held them back or interrupted at an opportune time. Sometimes it was someone walking up nearby, or the trusting look in her eyes, or a careless phrase or word that seemed like a warning. Some of his contemporaries, he was sure, thought him a fool. He knew some of the town lads were more apt to jump beds than he, but that had never been his way. For one thing, his parents' attitude towards sex had always been respectful but serious. To give in now would make his relationship with Megan sullied and cheap.

He even talked to Father Ander about this, in general terms, of course. With a straight face, the priest offered his advice, in general terms, of course. Instead of quoting Scriptures, he asked Dar to think of his friends who allowed their passions to take control of their judgment. Thinking back, Dar couldn't remember a single dalliance where anyone had ended up happy. Only misery seemed to come of it.

Besides, Father Ander pointed out that holding back on the physical side of the relationship let Dar see Megan's true person, with all her faults and qualities.

Ah yes! The faults: Megan had a temper, was charmed by baubles and pretty clothes, and was sometimes as impetuous as the wind. She got into a snit one night because he refused to fly up to the Whitehorse to watch the stars.

"Going off with an entire party of seven to hunt the Ja'al is one thing, Meg," he had told her as she turned away from him. "But taking a spur-of-the-moment ride into the Wilderness? I've lived here all my life and the old-timers in town aren't just spinning yarns. They know what it's like. We've been really lucky up until now."

"Ha!" she retorted. "Lucky? We traipsed all over that forest and if the Ja'al weren't there, we wouldn't have seen anything but some wildlife."

He took her by the shoulder and turned her to look at him. "I mean it, Megan. Meeting up with Grandpa saved us a lot of grief. Eric and I both know how dangerous it is. Even Lord Nolan won't try something like that and he's a retired paladin free-lance with fourteen years of experience."

She met his eyes, then dropped them and sighed, looking ashamed. "I know, and I'm sorry. I just feel the need to get away sometimes, you know? I feel trapped having to stay here training. I know it's for the best—"

He hugged her to stop her from talking.

Brandi changed as well from her relationship with Eric. She seemed to relax, smile more, and take part in their joking and camaraderie. The mantle of being "responsible big sister Brandi" fell from her shoulders, both from Eric's influence and from seeing how Megan handled herself.

Eric and Dar talked sometimes about the sisters when one or the other did something incomprehensible. Still subject to the hereditary Alenar temper, Brandi didn't indulge in emotional outbursts like Megan. Instead, the older Alenar sister resorted to sarcasm, black looks, and indignant silence. Eric's more easygoing nature managed to cajole Brandi out of her bad mood whenever she was miffed.

Despite enjoying the relative peace, two things nagged Dar. First, the sisters always had the specter of their aunt and uncle in the back of their minds. Despite all their talk about leading their own lives and trusting in

Divine Providence, he could tell it bothered them.

Maybe if they weren't in Forester when and if Aunt Daphne arrived, there would be no way for her to take the sisters away. Then they could stay with him and help him find the Helm of Shadows. That idea held merit. He resolved to begin asking around for tasks, starting with Lord Nolan himself.

More unsettling, Halkith the Grey had disappeared from the face of the earth. Nolan had sent troops to every village east, west and north of Forester to no avail. No one had seen any Ja'al clerics, singed or otherwise. For some reason, this bothered Dar more than the idea of Megan's Aunt Daphne.

What was Halkith up to? Did he even care about the freelancers and the pegasi any more? From what he had heard about the Ja'al, Halkith probably cared quite a bit—he cared to part Dar's hair with a scimitar for thwarting him.

Of course, Halkith could be dead. The evil religions were not known for their forgiving natures. Or he could have been sent to another country, or kept at the Ja'al High Council, wherever that was.

Despite all his rationalizing, Dar worried.

Three days after their graduation, Dar's scheme about finding something to take them away from Forester was solved for him. Dar and the Riders received a summons and arrived at the manor house to meet with Colin Parker.

"We have heard," the knight announced, "that a group of ogres have been harassing commerce along the road between Forester and Athor." He indicated an eastward road on the map of Northern Deran on the table in front of him.

Dar nodded. "There's several spots on that road that make ambushes very easy."

Colin fixed him with a keen eye. "Ever fought ogres before?"

Dar nodded again. "We buried one in the forest and fought some when we killed Lady Aalre. They're nasty."

Colin smiled at that. "Indeed. Lord Nolan is willing to pay bounty if the ogres are captured. One hundred gold pieces each."

Buck looked shrewd. "And how many are there?"

Colin shrugged. "Only about a half dozen or so. And they have a tribe of goblins to support them."

Connor paled. "A half dozen? We only fought two with Aalre and almost got torn to pieces."

Dar agreed.

Buck waved a hand. "We can take them two at a time then."

Dar snorted. "If they'll cooperate! I can see us now."

He struck an imperious pose, like a schoolteacher mediating a class argument. "'Excuse us, Mister Ogre sir, but you are the third ogre in this group. It is against the rules to send more than two at a time. You will have to stand back there among the trees while we knock the stuffing out of your buddies here. And put that boulder down.'"

The three women giggled and Eric guffawed.

Colin coughed and continued. "Let's get serious. These are tough customers. They have killed fourteen people, including three guards from Athor. We think they're striking from the north side of the road most often, nearest the wilderness. Your pegasi will give you a significant advantage."

Colin indicated a section of the map between Forester and Athor. Dar inspected it. The map showed a series of low hills, heavily forested, just north of the road. The entire section stretched parallel to the highway, about fifty miles long and thirty deep.

Colin noted his expression. "I know it's a lot of territory, but we didn't order this assignment from the general store. You'd better get going as soon as you can."

After making a copy of the map with the locations of the known strike points marked in red, they left.

"This should keep us busy for a while," noted Andyn with satisfaction as they walked down the main street.

"You said it," replied Eric. "Ogres. Not as easy as the hobgoblins."

Dar looked at him. "As if the hobgoblins were easy."

Megan stopped in her tracks. "Wait a minute."

"What?" asked Connor, perplexed.

She turned to the bag slung over her shoulder and rummaged in it for a moment, coming up with a bone tube. She removed the caps and pulled out a parchment, unrolling it for them to see.

"Look here," she said, pointing.

Dar and the others crowded around her. She held a copy of the Song of the Grey Riders— at least, the portion they had found so far.

"So?" he said. "It's the copy of the Song you made while we were at Grandpa's."

"No, you ninny. Read the passage."

Brandi read aloud. "...When Ogre's breath at last does end, then does their true Quest begin..." She looked up.

Dar felt a cold chill.

"Oh, now wait a minute," said Buck, holding his hands up. "Just because we have an assignment to take out some ogres doesn't mean anything."

Damn! Dar fumed, trying to fight the feeling of helplessness. *This prophecy dogs us wherever we go.*

"Let's calm down for a second," said Andyn. "I know it looks like the Song of the Grey Riders is dictating our lives again, but this could be significant or it might not. After all, even though we *think* we might be the Riders and Grandpa is sure we are, it's far from certain."

"Yeah," said Buck, petting Puup's head. "We're not sure."

"Right," agreed Connor. "Prophecies aren't that accurate anyway."

The others nodded in agreement. Dar looked at them. They avoided his gaze.

God help us, he thought.

***

This looks like a good spot, thought Dar. He pulled on the reins to halt Virasi. He cast a careful eye around the knoll, patting his pegasus on the neck as he did so.

Megan suggested the name. *Virasi* meant "White Star" in Elven. Looking at the star-shaped white mark on the animal's forehead, Dar knew he couldn't have picked a better name.

The knoll stretched about seventy yards or so on its longest side. A small clearing of sorts occupied the center, surrounded by elms, aspens, hartberry bushes, and ferns. Two giant ghostwood trees towered some eighty feet overhead, providing a covering canopy, broken by gaps large enough to allow two pegasi to fly in side by side. The smooth white trunks were bare up to a height of about thirty feet.

Dar waved a gloved hand to the others hovering overhead. Eric waved in response and the Riders glided down to join him.

Buck and Shadowbane cantered up next to him. "Look okay?"

Dar nodded. "So far, so good."

Buck petted Puup on the head, then tossed the pigeon up. Puup fluttered off into the hartberry bushes.

Dar shot a glance at Buck. "Aren't you afraid he'll get lost or eaten?"

Buck looked hurt. "Are you kidding? I've been training him. He's a battle pigeon now."

Dar shook his head.

"Is this one of the strike points?" asked Andyn as she unbuckled herself.

Dar nodded and unbuckled in a matter of seconds. "It's the farthest one from Forester. Eric and I can start tracking from here. If we don't find anything, we can work our way back towards town. We've been searching from the air for a while now and haven't seen anything."

Andyn took her saddlebags off Medianox's back, kissed the pegasus on the forehead, and made a circular motion with her free hand. When she finished the circle, she pointed straight upwards.

Medianox snorted, prancing backward and extending her wings. With a few powerful beats, she leaped up and through the gap in the trees. Dar watched her go, then sent up Virasi. Soon, the Riders stood alone in the clearing.

Brandi walked up next to Andyn, squinting up at the bright sunshine. "Think Eric can get an arrow up through that?"

Andyn looked at her in mock surprise. "What? Are you doubting the archery abilities of your one true love?"

Brandi blushed. "I...no, I didn't mean that...Oh, forget it!" She grinned sheepishly at the other woman.

Andyn laughed merrily. "Oh honestly, Brandi! You are so easy to tease!"

"Just one big happy gang of sellswords, aren't we?"

Dar chuckled, then froze. That was not Buck's voice—or Eric's.

He dropped his saddlebags and whirled.

Six figures in black and silver emerged from the trees at their left. Two dark-haired human women sidled out. One wore shiny scale mail, carrying a broadsword and shield while other carried a metal wand and wore dark grey trousers and blouse.

With them strode three men, all armored. One wore shiny plate mail, hefting a war hammer in each gauntleted hand. Black-enameled chainmail glittered on the other two. One carried a massive two-handed sword, the other a spiked morning star. Everyone in the group wore a multicolored patch of pink, red and purple on one shoulder of their cloaks—a symbol exactly like the ones worn by the Ja'al warriors Dar and his friends vanquished months ago.

Dar's heart froze when he saw the last one. Without ever having met Halkith the Grey, he knew the tall, handsome figure in jet-black armor, wielding a black mace that glowed with red runes. Brown-haired, blue-eyed, and with a smirk on his face, he glided into the clearing with his companions like a vile black panther.

Dar sneaked a look at his friends. Connor stood apart from the main group, trying to slide over towards the bushes. The halfling's sword blade reflected the dappled sunlight. His eyes glittered but he showed no expression.

The same was true of Megan, standing just to Dar's right, hands on her daggers. Buck looked calm, but Dar could see his hand gripping Khelios' hilt, white-knuckled. Eric stood with his spear pointed at the Ja'al.

Andyn and Brandi, the two clerics, one Christian and the other Verian, stood defiant, eyes glaring at the Ja'al force. Dar's fear stilled.

Have more faith, Dar Cabot, a voice whispered in his head.

"One thing about pegasi," Halkith said, breaking the silence. "They're quite noticeable when they fly down into the forest bearing riders and even more noticeable when they fly up without them."

When they didn't respond, he continued. "You must be those amateur bastard sellswords we keep hearing about."

"I don't know," said Eric with a merry smile, "There are many sellswords out here on the Frontier this time of year. Who did you have in mind?"

Halkith laughed and his troops joined in.

"Let me see," he said, "I had in mind a particularly stupid bunch of asses from that second-rate, backwater hovel they call Forester. Mindless little panty-waist cowards who couldn't piss in a bucket without their mothers to help them."

Buck looked at Dar. Fear in the warrior's eyes mirrored his own, but Dar also saw defiance.

"That can't be us," said Dar. "I don't use a bucket."

Buck grinned and Dar could feel his own fear receding. He took a good look at Halkith. Here stood the man who masterminded the massacre at Westhaven, the one who had attacked Forester. His troops killed innocent women, children, and men without remorse, then slew Elaine in the prime of her life. Halkith kidnapped the dragonlings, conspired to steal the pegasi, and made life miserable for everyone on the Borderlands.

"Ah," Dar said, relaxing and moving a hand towards the sword on his back, "I know who you are. You must be Halkith. I could tell from the stench."

Halkith's eyes narrowed. "Just what I expected from a country dullard. But I see you have lovely companions. I doubt if you'd know what to do with these women here if I drew you a picture."

Brandi's eyes flared. "Enough insults," she snapped. "Are you here to torture us with your foul manners and poor humor?"

Halkith brightened and smiled. "Not exactly, my little slut. Tortures first, the like of which you have never imagined, until you are almost dead. *Then* I will kill you."

The bushes behind Halkith rustling wildly. With a curse, the Ja'al leader and his party whirled. A white pigeon fluttered up towards the branches of the nearest ghostwood tree.

Thank you God!

Dar whipped his sword out.

With a tremendous shout, the Grey Riders charged.

Halkith realized his danger and turned back. Dar raced at him, sword raised. Megan's fire-darts beat him to it, detonating with sharp cracks on Halkith's black armor. The Ja'al cleric laughed out loud and pointed a hand at Megan, fingers crackling with magic. Dar tried to cut it off. Halkith jerked his hand away and stepped backward, white with fury.

The loud ringing of steel on steel and a magical sizzling resounded in the little glade, but Dar saw only the high priest in front of him. He took another swing. Halkith blocked it with his ebony mace. Red light flared from the magical discharge.

Behind him, Dar heard the dull thud of a magical detonation and felt a blast of heat. He resisted the overwhelming urge to turn and look.

"So, little man," hissed the cleric. "You first."

He spat a short, sharp syllable. The world went dark, darker than the blackest moonless night. Remembering his training, Dar dropped on one knee and whipped his sword left and right. A clang resounded as he deflected a mace strike. Suddenly the blackness vanished and a bright ball of light hovered over his head, illuminating a wide-eyed Halkith.

Andyn stood next to him, fingers pointed at the ball of light. In a second, the light winked out.

Dar leapt to his feet. Halkith pointed a hand at Andyn and cursed. A bright green flame arced out at her just as Dar reached him. Dar heard her scream as he swung. His blade slammed into the cleric's armor, producing a blinding purple flare. Halkith staggered backwards, a grimace of pain on his face, his plate mail dented.

Dar stepped back a pace and shot a glance at Andyn.

She knelt down, holding her side. The green flame had struck there, burning through her armor. One of her maces lay on the ground.

Dar turned as Halkith stepped up, muttering in rage. A head strike came whistling in from his left and Dar blocked it. He spun right, slashing out with his blade as he turned. His opponent spat an oath and blocked, then kicked Dar in the chest.

He tumbled backwards. Turning the fall into a roll, he popped up kneeling in guard position. The black mace clanged off his blade once, twice. Dar swept his right leg out and lifted Halkith off his feet. With a crash of armor, the cleric landed on his back.

Dar's overhand strike ended up cutting into the earth instead.

Quick. Got to give him that.

The Ja'al leader rolled to his feet just as Dar drew his blade out of the ground.

Dar attacked twice, using a downwards cut followed by a right-left slash at Halkith's shoulder. The cleric stepped out of the way of the first one, then blocked the second, gritting his teeth to hold back the force of Dar's blow.

Dar grinned.

The Ja'al priest saw the grin and snarled in rage, lashing out. Dar ducked

328

the first blow, but guessed wrong on the follow-up leg-strike. He blocked some of the impact, receiving a brutal shock to his right thigh. The black mace glowed and smoked when it hit his chain armor. He gasped in pain and stepped back.

Another swing hummed in at his head and he ducked, feeling a flange ruffle his hair. Dar turned but was met by a fist to the face. His vision grew spotty and he staggered backwards and rolled. He stood.

Halkith stalked forwards. "Now, you little..."

Andyn darted in from the side and Halkith cut off his oath. A blue-metal mace slammed into his right shoulder, eliciting a flash of purple fire. He cried out and whirled to attack her but was rocked by a silver mace in the midsection. He doubled over.

The Verian priestess stood over him, gasping. She raised her new mace over his head. "Take this, you son of a..."

Halkith's mace snaked out and whipped upwards. The head of the weapon caught Andyn just behind the ankle. Halkith jerked up and Andyn flipped up into the air to thud on the grassy earth.

Dar shook his head to clear it, then stalked forward. Halkith turned and Dar greeted him with a slash on the arm. This time the blade cut through the armor with a purple flash, drawing blood. Halkith cursed and stepped to the side.

I've got to keep him busy, Dar thought, panting with his efforts. *If he gets off another spell...*

He unleashed another tremendous swing. The rage in Halkith's eyes turned to desperation as he repulsed it, staggering backward.

Halkith took a breath, pointing a hand at Dar and beginning a spell. Dar's heart leapt in his throat and he lunged forward. His enemy suddenly screamed in fury when ball of light popped into being in front of his face. He ducked and stepped out of the way, muttering and blinking.

Dar heard Brandi's voice from behind him. "Hang on, Dar! I'm coming!"

Halkith pointed a fist at Dar, calling forth another arc of green fire. Dar tried to dodge, but the flame caught him in the left shoulder. The mail burst apart. He gasped in agony from the searing pain but somehow kept his weapon up, blinking away sudden tears.

Without warning, the Ja'al leader uncorked a hideous scream and charged straight at him, swinging. Dar stepped right and deflected the blow downwards. He turned his sword point towards the Ja'al cleric and thrust with all his might.

There was a ripping clang and a gurgle.

Slowly, a black mace slipped from nerveless fingers. Halkith turned amazed eyes first to the bastard sword in his midsection, then at Dar.

"Not bad, little man," he gasped, blood running out of his mouth.

Dar brought up his foot and pushed, jerking the blade out. Halkith fell backwards and thudded onto the churned sward.

The other Riders joined Dar him. He leaned on his blade, gasping from pain and exertion.

Buck limped up to his side, the mirror-bright surface of his new steel shield scratched and nicked. Khelios glowed in his right hand. Eric had a long rip in his chainmail along the middle, blood showing through the rent armor. Brandi walked up to Eric, slipping an arm around him. Of all of them, she seemed the least damaged, her new sword blade red.

Connor was so covered with leaves, grass, and blood that Dar couldn't tell where the injuries started. Andyn arose from the ground, grimacing.

An arm slipped around his waist and he turned to Megan. She had a cut above one eye, a bleeding right forearm and her clothes had burn marks, but she nodded to him.

"I'm okay," she said, looking at Halkith.

"Hey!" said Connor in awe, "He's still alive!"

They crowded around. Sure enough, Halkith stared at all of them in a mixture of amazement and black rage. Brandi knelt down.

Her voice turned gentle, almost tender. "Accept the True God, Halkith, and he will save you from your sins."

A hideous rasping sound came from bloody lips. It took Dar a second to figure out that Halkith was laughing.

"You...think...I want mercy from your puny god...? Don't make me..." Suddenly the blue eyes locked on something the Riders could not see. His features froze in horror.

"No! Not you...! I have been faithf..." His gasp of fear turned into a gurgle.

A dark, icy wave swept the glade, filling Dar with pure terror. He shut his eyes and forced himself to stand still. Megan's grip tightened and she shuddered against him.

Brandi and Andyn raised their holy symbols, praying out loud. Women's voices in the languages of Christianity and Verian filled the clearing. The chill faded and vanished.

Brandi sighed then, a sound that seemed to come from her shoes, and made the sign of the cross. Dar, Megan and Eric did the same as Andyn held her hand over the corpse. The two clerics whispered benedictions, each in the language of her religion, then Brandi rose.

Eric put his arm around her and she leaned her head on his shoulder.

Puup fluttered down to land on Buck's shoulder and preen himself.

Dar hand still trembled as he wiped his sword in Halkith's cloak and sheathed it. Megan smiled at him, her grip on his hand steady.

"See," said Buck in a shaky but self-satisfied voice. "I told you Puup would come in handy."

Chapter Twenty-Four- The Lost Verses

Ellen Hanford made a face, setting the jar of healing ointment down on the arm of the chair. "Megan, if you don't sit still, I'm going to call the guard in here to hold you down. Let the others talk about Halkith. You sit back."

Megan blushed and did as she was told. "Yes, milady. I'm sorry."

Ellen tried to look severe. A smile crept onto her face as she finished applying medicine to Megan's wounds. "You are either the luckiest freelancers alive or you have extra guardian angels."

Father Ander looked up from where he tended Buck's broken leg. His somber, long face creased in a smile. "I favor the latter, milady."

How much will they need those angels in the future, thought Ellen.

Even Lord Nolan worked on them. Andyn lay on the couch in the baronial library, her chainmail pulled up away from her midsection. Kneeling next to her, he placed his hands on the cruel burn in her side. Andyn bit her lip but said nothing. Blue light glowed from Nolan's hands as he concentrated, lips moving. Then he pulled his hands away.

Andyn's wound vanished. She sat up, feeling her ribcage and flat stomach. "Thank you, milord."

Nolan gave her a smile and stroked her hair like a father. "You're welcome, Andyn. It is a good thing you got back here quickly. The spell of the Scalding Tongue comes with a wasting disease. I think I got it in time. You and Mister Cabot are blessed indeed."

Dar grinned at him from his seat and held up a goblet in a salute. "I thank

Your Lordship. I hope I can return the favor someday."

Andyn smiled and pulled her armor down, then frowned at the hole in the chainmail.

"Blast!" she muttered under her breath, putting her fingers through the rent. "I just bought this damn thing."

Ellen finished treating Megan and stood with a sigh. "Well, I hope you are all satisfied now. We're finally rid of Halkith the Grey and you managed to get yourselves beaten to a pulp in the bargain."

Nolan's eyes twinkled at her. "It makes you wonder if I should even pay the bounty or just take the whole sum in charge as payment for our services."

Father Ander looked disapproving until he realized the nobles were not serious. "I would say they have more than merited their reward," offered the priest.

"Er..." asked Buck, rubbing his leg, which now looked perfectly normal, "What exactly is the reward?"

Andyn and Brandi rolled their eyes. Ellen chuckled.

"For Halkith, one thousand gold crowns," she said, picking up a piece of paper marked with calculations. "For the members of his attack team, a total of one thousand."

Buck's eyebrows rose and he grinned at Connor.

Megan looked up at Ellen. "Halkith had something in a scrollcase. I was wondering if you might have a look at it for us."

Ellen and Nolan made eye contact. The baroness turned to Megan, arranging her hands with deliberate calm on her lap.

"Did you open it?" the baroness asked, keeping her voice neutral.

Megan shook her head. She fired an exasperated look at Andyn and Brandi. "No, we didn't have the time. Besides, it might have had a curse or something on it. Those two over there convinced me to bring it to you."

Thank God for Brandi and Andyn.

Ellen patted her on the arm. "Prudence is always the better choice when dealing with the Servants of the Dark Ones. May I see it?"

The dead black, purple-inscribed surface of the tube glowed with a deep red fire, decorated with orange and red tassels hanging from metal caps. She motioned to Nolan. He came over, joined by Father Ander.

Her husband frowned. "Warded?" he whispered.

She nodded. "Heavily. Three independent seals, see there? I'll need your help. Father Ander's too, if you don't mind."

The priest nodded and Ellen set the scrollcase down on the table, motioning for the Riders to step back.

"Please. A little room."

She closed her eyes, centering her energy, then opened her eyes. The purple sigils weaved like drunken sailors. A red glow on the end-caps and a shimmering on the tassels confirmed her suspicions. Above it all hovered a ball of light only her eyes could see.

She bit her lip. *Binding and charming spells... illusion and obscuring as well. Someone has gone through a lot of trouble to protect this thing.*

With a rapid succession of thoughts, she sent spears of light into the sigils. They writhed but her light ate them up, like a runner bird after snakes. Father Ander and Nolan worked alongside her. Her husband's magic operated on brute force. Powerful and straightforward, it blasted through the arcane protections on the caps. Father Ander's was more subtle and gentle. He teased out the magic in the colored tassels like a parent coaxing a child to eat a hated vegetable, stretching it thin until a blade of light slashed through.

Ellen closed her eyes, then opened them, blinking.

The Riders stared. The baroness looked down at the scrollcase, now smoking along its entire length.

Eric Indidarc's mouth hung open. "Wow."

She smiled, feeling a bit drained after the effort. With a shake of her head, she touched the tube and found it cool. She popped off one of the caps and pulled out a roll of vellum.

Spidery runes in dark green crawled across the page. She concentrated for a split second and waved her free hand over the symbols in a Spell of Reading.

Her stomach tightened with every sentence. She finished and dropped the pages on the tabletop, feeling like she had just gone swimming in the castle cesspool.

"Ugh..." she said before she could stop herself, shuddering and wiping her hands on her dress.

Everyone gaped at her, even Nolan.

"Are you okay, milady?" he whispered in her ear.

She relaxed and let out a long breath. "Yes, milord. Thank you."

She read it for them all. "Halkith The Grey of the Ja'al, Former Commander, 7th Goblin Brigade. Attend and Obey. I have determined that your talents and skills make you, for the time being, useful to Our Cause. Rest assured, your failure to produce the pegasi of Whitehorse Peak will not go unpunished. However, your plan of action to rectify your error has merit and it is thus Our decree that you be allowed to accomplish it. May the Wand and the Flail strengthen your arm and give you victory. Crush the blank shields of Forester into the dust and bring Us their hearts in a leather sack, that We may eat of their flesh. Thus is the fate of those who seek to naysay the rise of Kher Mardil.

Enclosed with this letter is a requisition for an attack team. Choose well. Know that We do not have trained riders to waste on ill-executed plans. Succeed in bringing to Us at least a remnant of the pegasus herd and We will be merciful. Fail and you shall wish you had not been born.

The time is fast approaching and the armament goes well. Make no mistake. We will be victorious, with or without the Darkwing Legion. Kher Mardil will rise again. Signed, Zhinia Margoth, Princess of Kher Mardil, Lady of the Nightshade, Priestess of Garon-zith."

Buck Bydecy groaned. "Oh, great! What does all that mean?"

"Be quiet, Buck," scolded Andyn. "We don't even know what this Sangor Margith thing is."

"It's Zhinia Margoth," Megan corrected her. "What does it mean?"

Ellen shook her head. "I must confess I don't know. Kher Mardil sounds like a place."

Father Ander picked up the second page that had fallen out with the letter to Halkith. "I presume this is the requisition for the free lances?"

Ellen nodded. "Whoever she is," she said, "she sounds like she's arranging some kind of attack force. The fact that she's a princess isn't very comforting."

"What do you mean?" asked Andyn.

Nolan spoke up. "If she is truly a princess, she could raise a significant army. The fact that she has her eyes on this part of the world makes me nervous. The only problem is that I've never heard of Kher Mardil and I know of no place like that in the world. I'll have to send a message to Count DeGrance in Hillton and let him know. I'll probably alert Count Dellingdale in North Corner and the Duke of Darlon as well."

Ellen pursed her lip, narrowing her eyes.

"You aren't going to like what I have to tell you now, either," she said, reaching into a bag slung from the back of her chair. "Before the Earl of Tallemar left, I asked him to find out all he could about a Song of the Grey Riders when he got to the University in Oakmoor. Lady Saren came up with the rest of the verses. That's quite a feat, considering the age of the document."

Buck looked sour. "So, what's in the rest of the stupid thing? We're supposed to save the world? And go out in a blaze of glory?"

"Oh, come on," said Eric, smacking him in the shoulder. "It isn't that bad."

Buck dropped his head on the table. "Oh, yes it is," came his muffled voice, "I know we're going to get sent on some wild-troll chase. We won't have any time to enjoy our booty."

"Never mind him," said Connor. "Let's hear what it says."

Ellen smiled a little and unrolled a parchment. "This is a copy of a text Terenil and Saren found at the University archives. It's more than a thousand years old. Part is the same as what you found already, so I'll just read the parts you don't have.

It continues:

For good or evil all must choose
or choosing none, their lives to lose.

When gold to red at passage end,
then halfling toy upward must send.

Golden sorrow, heart's true Love,
pray to God in Heaven above.

That she may see, and all may learn,
what Truthful Eye cannot discern.

Holy relic, giver of life,
meant for tresses of carpenter's wife.

Ancient Evil, Good to slay,
seeks to thwart the Holy Way.

Relic's might of love is wrought,
so evil's will avails it naught.

One Dark Rider fights seven of Grey,
yet Queenly Crown shall win the day.

Seven they were, from varied flight,
on winged steeds of dark midnight.

Seven they were, the Riders Grey,
who came to serve the Holy Way.

Irial Nus Chor'drim."

There was utter silence. Ellen rolled up the parchment.

Buck's abject stare fairly screamed "I-told-you-so". Dar scratched his chin and looked at Eric, who shook his head, eyes narrowed. Megan Alenar chewed her lip.

Nolan let out a long breath. "Well. It looks like we are going to have to think about this one for a while."

***

They met the next day to discuss Halkith's letter from the Margoth princess. Ellen and Nolan greeted them in their study.

Dar sneaked a look at Megan. She gazed at the library, eyes flickering over the rows and rows of books lying on shelves set into the walls. She walked over to a scroll-rack and touched one of the papers.

He suppressed a grin. The Hanfords had quite a library, complete with some very old and valuable records from the late Imperial times. He knew from his few previous visits to the manor that the study was off-limits to anyone but the baronial couple and special guests. He suspected ample and potent magical protections prevented the more curious from getting into things they shouldn't.

"I know book-learning may be a little foreign to the warriors," Ellen said, turning towards the oak table in the middle of the room, "but if you'd like, some of us can look through texts and the others can go to the practice yard."

She slid several thick, leather-bound tomes on the table.

Dar waved a hand. "Don't worry, milady. Sir Tan made me study plenty of books and scrolls so I'm used to it."

Buck and Connor exchanged a look, then shrugged.

"Haven't got anything better to do," Buck said. "Besides, I'm still a little stiff from yesterday."

Nolan beamed and handed the largest book to him. "Then let's get started."

The morning crept by. Only the gentle chirping of sparrows in the trees outside the window and the occasional turning of a page broke the silence. Dar himself pored through several scrolls and a book of Esten Imperial history.

He decided to take a break and looked out the nearby window, surprised to discover it was full mid-day already. He stretched in his chair and yawned. *Haven't read this much since Sir Tan gave me a botany test. Almost failed that one, too.*

"Um, Lady Ellen?" Buck asked.

Dar turned in his seat.

Buck held a book in his hands, leaning against a bookshelf. "What was the name of that place that this Margooth character was from?"

Megan looked up. "Kher Mardil. Why?"

Buck swallowed, eyes round. "I think I found it." He handed the book to Ellen.

She read for a while, then wiped a hand over her mouth and chin. "This is not good."

She sat in one of the chairs as they all gathered around. "It says here that Kher Mardil was a Principality in the late Paragon Age, just before the start of the Wars. There were only three princes and one princess in its history. Guess who the last ruler was."

Dar felt a chill.

She shook her head. "Listen. 'Then arose by means divers and foul to the throne of Mardil, Zhinia, daughter of Romeon. Rumor and hearsay maintained that she had thus attained the power by means of assassination of her father but any who said such soon vanished into the night. Zhinia, mage and priestess of the cult of Garon-zith, now held sway with a more iron grip than had her father. All were subject to her edicts, even the high priest of Garon-zith, though he did not naysay her, as she provided him with steady and plentiful sacrifices. For all children, born and unborn, were subject to her approval and whim. Those who were found wanting, either in health or mind or heritage, were handed to the cult for the sacrifice. Kher Mardil became strong in armies and in wealth, headed by the servants of the cult and Princess Zhinia's own advisors. The Princess made it known that she sought to purify the people of her land, to wean out the rabble and the unfit, and thus make her realm mightier than all others.'"

"Nice lady," said Eric wryly. "Good thing she's dead."

Ellen shook her head. "There's more. 'When Clarissa, Queen of Tanamoor, assailed the Emperor of the Elves, Caelin by name, Zhinia sought her advantage, joining with Clarissa's armies. Then Caelin, a ruler both evil and foul, brought in his allies of the dark elves. But lo, there arose other armies to contend with them and with each other. From the south, an Alliance arose to oppose Zhinia, from Tor Haldin and from Laemin, led by Queen Alyssa, of the faith of the Christ. Zhinia marched out with her armies to war upon the Alliance and did not return. Records of her demise are none, nor is there mention of her after the Wars. A Saint of the Christ's Church became Alyssa of Tor Haldin and it is presumed that she caused the downfall of Zhinia, Princess of Kher Mardil.'"

She closed the book. "That's all. This is from the late Esten Period so it's probably pretty accurate."

Dar let out a deep breath. "Well, that's not so bad. Like Eric said, she's very dead by now. The Paragon Wars were over four thousand years ago."

Ellen looked grim.

"No, Dar. That isn't all." Nolan put his hand on Ellen's shoulder and gave her a squeeze.

"What do you mean?" asked Brandi.

Ellen turned to the freelancers, eyes intent. Dar started. He had never seen her like this.

"Listen to me, all of you," she said, voice filled with the timbre of command. "Zhinia was a mage, probably a wizard if she could rule a nation, and certainly a powerful one if she could control an entire cult by herself. Either someone else is using her name to instill fear in us or..."

She looked up at Nolan, her brow furrowed.

Nolan nodded. "She became a lich."

Dar's chill decided to run down his spine at that moment. "A what?" he breathed.

Brandi looked out the window. "A lich," she said in a hollow voice. "An undead wizard, one of the most powerful of the minions of the Dark. Created by magic and their own willpower, possessing spells that can kill at a glance. They do not die, but continue to exist in a state of non-life. They cannot be banished or driven away and can only be destroyed. They never repent."

Dar's stomach tightened. Connor stepped up to Ellen with disbelieving eyes. His hand gripped the pommel of his sword so hard the knuckles showed white. "And one of these things is hunting us?"

Nolan shook his head. "She's hunting all of us. And I think she's raising an army."

***

The shock and alarm of the discovery about Zhinia Margoth remained with them days later. They spent the rest of the time in the library but found nothing further. Ellen finally sent them home on the fourth day after Halkith's demise. She told them that Nolan would alert King Phillip and his Court about the possible danger on the Borderlands.

Dar mused about the situation all the way to his house, ignoring the idle chatter of the others behind him. The idea of a lich on the loose in the Borderlands made his skin crawl. He stepped up to his front door in the fading sunlight, fumbling with the keys.

Megan sighed behind him. "Dar, there's no rush."

He relaxed, found the key, and inserted it in the lock. "I know. I'm just edgy, I suppose."

Eric stepped up next to him, a wry look on his face. "Oh really? I wonder why."

Dar pushed the door open and led the group inside.

"I have to run down to the general store to get a few things," he said, reaching for one of the lamps in the main room. He snapped the striker and the lamp flared to life. "I want to make sure we don't need anything else."

"You don't," called a gentle alto from the kitchen.

A hooded silhouette stepped forward, a dark outline against the red sky of the setting sun in the kitchen window. Dar and his friends drew their weapons and spread out. Connor scuttled away from them into the darkness.

The figure held out a hand. "Don't be alarmed. I am not an enemy."

The hood fell back. A tall woman in plate mail armor brushed at dark auburn hair, tied in a warrior's braid. She stood taller than Lady Ellen, with steel-grey eyes and a pretty, oval face. A well-worn longsword and a military pick of ornate design hung from her leather belt. Her tunic, a deep brown, was emblazoned with a white cross on the left breast.

Dar looked at her face again and his heart skipped a beat.

I know her for some reason. She looks like—

The woman bowed. "I am honored to meet all of you. My name is Daphne Alenar. I believe my nieces and I have something to discuss."

Chapter Twenty-Five- Farewells

The afternoon sun reflected off Daphne Alenar's hair. Dar watched as she spoke with her nieces outside the main gate at Forester. A physical pain gnawed at his midsection.

If only she was a complete witch. If only she could give me some reason to dislike her.

He leaned against the side of the tree. Eric stood next to him, snapping twigs into little pieces and tossing them onto the nearby road.

Dar sighed. *Whatever I'm feeling, Eric must be feeling too.*

Megan, her eyes downcast, adjusted the saddlebags on her pegasus. Daphne said something to her, a hand on Megan's shoulder. Megan nodded but didn't raise her head.

God, I thought she could be the one.

The discussion in Dar's home the night before was brief and decisive. After taking the two sisters aside for an animated, whispered discussion in Dar's parents' old room, Daphne had emerged with two very subdued young women. She was sympathetic as she listened to Dar's protests and suggestions.

"I know, I know. I am truly sorry, Dar," she told him. She had sat in the living room, surrounded by the somewhat stunned Riders. She toyed with a fraying thread on Dar's couch, eyes distracted. "My brother Steven and I have arrived at an impasse in our quest. It is more tangled than we thought. We need Megan and Brandi's help. Involving you would just endanger you for no reason. Where we're going, a small group is best."

"I like you," she added, looking up and giving a dazzling, friendly smile. Despite his agitation at the time, it completely disarmed him. "Megan and Brandi have told me a lot about you and Eric, and will doubtless tell me more during our trip to the south. I am very glad that they met such fine men as you and the other Riders. Were the circumstances different, I would go my way and leave you with only my blessing."

He shook his head in exasperation then. "I still don't understand."

Daphne sighed. "I can see you and Megan have become close, and I'm glad. I want her and Brandi to meet good, kind men. I truly hate having to do this, but we have found critical information. It is critical not only to us, but to all of Torosc—and by that I mean the ones who don't follow the Evil One. There is the possibility that at long last, the people of those lands may yet be free. However, the fewer who know the details right now, the better. Besides, if Megan and Brandi are with us, our enemies can't use them against us."

Dar thought of protesting that the Riders could help protect the sisters. But then, the dark badge Daphne's tunic proclaimed her to be a Knight of the Kestrel. He and Eric both knew of the clandestine order of Christian warriors affiliated with the Order of the Falcon. They were charged with helping the faithful in the 'dark lands'. Anything that could overpower her and Stephen would certainly be able to destroy the Grey Riders.

At least Daphne showed no lack of funds. Pleased to find the sisters trained in airborne riding, Daphne paid off the remaining debt for Megan's and Brandi's pegasi that morning.

Dar brought his thoughts back to the present.

But, God, why now? Everything was going so well. Maybe I shouldn't ever have gotten involved...

A thousand brooding, conflicting thoughts echoed back and forth in his head.

A pair of brown boots stepped next to the tree roots, interrupting his musings. Daphne Alenar hefted a pair of odd-shaped saddlebags and smiled. He thought she looked shy, almost apologetic.

"I suppose this is it, Dar," she said.

He nodded.

Dar's mouth dried up, just like all his clever phrases.

Daphne gave his shoulder a squeeze and went to meet her nieces. After a couple of words, she put her arms around them and gave them a warm hug. Then she turned and walked about twenty feet away, far enough to give them privacy but close enough to remind them time marched on.

Megan led her pegasus to the tree and looped the reins on a low branch. Her eyes shone with tears, but she smiled. "I've picked a name for my pegasus. It took me long enough. I'll call him Larinor. It means Ranger in elven."

Dar tried to smile back. "Good name. Maybe someday I'll actually be a ranger so I'll be allowed to speak to him."

Megan laughed, then broke down crying, almost hurling herself into his arms. Dar just held her, unable to talk because of the lump in his throat.

Finally, Megan pulled herself away and stamped her foot in exasperation. "Blast it!" she brushed at her eyes. "I promised I wouldn't do this. We aren't leaving you forever, just long enough to be able to send for you. I'm such a fool."

Dar's own vision got blurry and he tried to blink the tears away. The red highlights in her hair glowed in the sunlight. He watched her gentle hands wipe away tears and straighten those beautiful tresses.

"Yes, you are a fool," he answered, feeling a swell of emotion, "But you're my fool."

Megan looked up into his eyes. He met her fierce shiny-eyed gaze, surprised at the intensity there.

"And you're *mine!*" she whispered almost angrily. "I promise you, Dar Cabot, I will come back for you! No force of evil or dark secrets can keep me away. No matter where you are I *will find you*. I promise it! Our God Who loves us will make it come true."

Dar found he could breathe again. A quiet fire burned in those amber eyes, constant and powerful. Something stilled his knotted emotions and the sick feeling in his stomach eased.

He nodded. "I will wait and watch for you, Megan Alenar. We will see each other again."

Won't we, God? Please...

He kissed her. Her lips, warm and yielding, met his and she pulled him close, melting into the embrace. Then, after far too short a time, he pulled back and she released him.

"Remember. It's a promise, Dar Cabot," Megan said as Brandi and Eric approached them from the other side of the tree.

From the looks of it, Brandi and Eric had a similar conversation. Brandi set her jaw and came up to Dar as Megan went over to Eric. The elder Alenar sister put both hands on his shoulders, tears in her clear violet eyes.

"Goodbye, Dar. We will meet again."

"I know," he said. He waited.

She leaned forward and kissed him three times, once on each cheek and once on the forehead. "In the name of the Father, Son and Holy Ghost I mark you, Darius, son of Stephen. The Lord will watch over you and guide you all your days."

He swallowed and nodded. The damned lump was back in his throat.

She saw his emotion and gripped his forearm in a warrior's clasp, strong and steady as her gaze. "We will be back."

Dar relaxed again and returned the grip. "I know you can't tell us where you're going to be, but write to us when you're able. You can always reach us through Lord Nolan. We still have to catch that ogre gang and he'll have other things for us to do, I'm sure. We'll be here for a while."

Brandi smiled. "Bet on it. I'll let Meg do it. She was always the better writer."

Megan returned from her conversation with Eric. The Alenar sisters gave them one last hug and swung into their saddles. Buck, Andyn and Connor came over to join them. Megan and Brandi exchanged a few quiet words with each one of their companions, giving a kiss and a hug to each one of them. Buck looked awkward at the affection but gave them his trademark smile.

Daphne Alenar stood at their side. She carried a small, silvery medallion of an owl in her hand.

Dar wondered. *What the hell is that for?*

Then he realized that she saddlebags but no mount. How had she traveled to Forester?

Daphne placed the medal on the ground and held her hands over it.

"Paractus!"

The medallion flashed light blue and expanded at an impossible rate. Before Dar could even blink, an enormous owl stood before them, its great

345

brown eyes peering at them.

It's magic, he thought in awe.

The creature towered over them, eight feet tall at the crown of its snowy head. A coat of leather armor inlaid with dull metal studs covered its body with ample holes for the wings. On its back, between the wings, sat a large, high-backed saddle. Daphne swung her saddlebags over the back of the seat and lashed them down with a few deft tugs on leather straps.

She whistled. The owl turned its head around and then pivoted forward and down. Daphne climbed into the seat and patted the bird on the head, saying something soft and gentle.

They must have all been standing there with their mouths open because the three Alenar women smiled.

"You should have told them," Megan said to her aunt. Daphne shrugged, a crooked smile on her face. She tapped the owl on the side of the head and it turned away from them, pointed southwards. Daphne raised a gloved hand.

"Farewell Grey Riders. God's peace."

The owl gave two beats of its huge wings and leapt up from the ground. Dar shielded his face from the dust and debris and the stiff wind.

Brandi and Megan raised their hands in farewell and soared into the sky in a flurry of black pegasus wings and blown leaves.

Dar watched the receding figures until they were dark specks against the ochre and crimson evening sky.

Goodbye, Megan.

He felt empty.

A hand clapped him on the shoulder. Buck stood between him and Eric. Andyn and Connor joined him.

Eric's eyes still held tears. He set his jaw firmly as he looked off to the south. He cleared his throat and blinked. "They said they'd be back," he said, "I wouldn't want to bet against them."

Dar nodded. "Especially Megan."

A light breeze scattered a few leaves past them in the dusty road.

"I told them to write," Dar said.

"Good," Connor nodded. "We'll be pretty busy for a while. It'll be good to hear from them."

Andyn's eyes narrowed. "Now what happens to the Song of the Grey

Riders? Not that we ever fit into it perfectly to begin with, but now we've lost two of us. What can that mean?"

Dar sighed, tired. "Right now, I don't much care. I don't feel like anything."

Andyn took his hand and Eric's and gave them a squeeze. "I know what you're going through."

And she's lost someone who's never coming back, Dar realized. He tried to smile his thanks, but he knew it looked tired and thin.

Buck Bydecy laid his arms around their shoulders. "Come on over to the Pit, you guys. I'm buying this time..."

The End

Appendix - Glossary

Aalre Sendatre - A beautiful, evil elven wizard, a follower of the cult of the Ja'al and mistress to Halkith the Grey, a commander of Dark forces on the northern border of Deran. Sadistic and controlling, conniving and treacherous, Aalre was tasked with finding a clue to an ancient Imperial secret by Halkith and ended up destroying the hamlet of Westhaven.

Agent - A spy, bounty hunter or thief, depending on context and the particular agent's morals and ethics. Connor Lomin, an agent, tended more towards the "spy" variety. Most agents provide a stealthy component to the groups they support. In military terms an agent would be part of a reconnaissance unit.

Alenar, Brandawyn (Brandi) - One of the original Grey Riders, a half-elven female, trained as a soldier and combat medic/corpsman. The older sister of Megan and fellow refugee from Torosc, she and her family were persecuted for their Christian faith and eventually fled under tragic circumstances. Originally suspicious of Dar Cabot and his companions, she eventually becomes friends with all of them. Reserved but kind and devoutly religious, Brandi is quite pretty, with red-gold hair and violet eyes, but doesn't see herself as attractive.

Alenar, Daphne - Ranger knight and agent of the forces of good in the Realms. The sister of Megan and Brandi's human father, she spirited her nieces northward away from Torosc to safety.

Alenar, Megan - Another of the original Grey Riders and sister of Brandawyn Alenar, she attended college in Terenai and graduated as a wizard and scholar. Possessing red-gold hair like her sibling, Megan is friendly and outgoing, somewhat vain and impetuous, yet fiercely loyal and brave. She is also very attractive, with strawberry blonde hair and amber eyes, and is fond of baubles and fancy clothes. With her sister, she fled persecution in Torosc to arrive in Deran.

Arachnia - Evil elven goddess of poison and assassination. One of the gods of the cult of the Ja'al, Arachnia is worshipped by dark elves (q.v.).

Astarel - Kingdom to the north of Deran, along the coast. The homeland of Buck Bydecy, it is a seafaring nation with a robust navy and an eclectic society comprised equally of elves, humans, dwarves and halflings.

<u>Blank Shield</u> - Another name for a mercenary or free-lance. Sell-sword.

<u>Bydecy, Buckminster (Buck)</u> - Another of the original Grey Riders, he traveled south in search of employment as a caravan guard and met Eric Indidarc, Dar Cabot and the rest of the Grey Riders. A tall, rangy, sandy-haired human male warrior and free-lance, Buck is a native of Tyler, Astarel. His easygoing nature is often mistaken for boredom.

<u>Cabot, Darius (Dar)</u> - An original Grey Rider and native of the town of Forester on the northern border of the kingdom of Deran, Dar ran afoul of Ja'al goblin troops in the wilds and headed back to town for help, setting the events of *Whitehorse Peak* in motion. A young, dark-haired human male, he is a ranger/scout and adept in the woods. As someone skilled in woodcraft, Dar seeks to determine the fate of his grandparents, who disappeared while searching for an ancient relic in the Wilderness.

<u>Cla'Agik</u> - Evil god of disease and suffering, allied with the Ja'al cult in its pursuit of darkness and domination of the world.

<u>Collins, Tanner (Sir)</u> - Aged, curmudgeonly and demanding ranger knight. Collins trained both Eric Indidarc and Dar Cabot in forestry and wilderness skills.

<u>Crossed Swords</u> - Guild of assassins based in Deran and Terenai. Founded and ruled by the Hylar family, the Crossed Swords are often used by evil forces to eliminate opposition.

<u>Daemon</u> - Evil to the core, the otherworldly race of daemons spends most of their time trying to overthrow the Elohir (q.v.) or conquer various regions of Damora. They are known as the Fallen because legend has it that they were originally Elohir who turned to the side of evil and worship of themselves (and the Dark One). While many Daemons look like nightmarish beasts, some are very attractive and almost human-like or elven in appearance. The overriding philosophy of the Daemons is that Damora is a free zone, ripe for the picking. Daemons are also known as the Fallen Ones.

<u>Damora</u> - Imaginary world setting for the Grey Riders novels. The fourth planet orbiting the star 82 Eridani, it is roughly 1.15 times the size of Earth and possesses climate regions and flora/fauna similar to Earth. The parent star is a G5V spectral class, main-sequence yellow star approximately 20 light years from Earth. It has two moons, Kaliri and Diometrius, which provide both tidal forces and substantial moonlight for the planet's surface. The

technology level of Damora approximates the High Middle Ages of real life, with significant differences due to the use of magic and scientific advancement.

Darlon - Major city in Northern Deran, pop ~ 170,000. Home to people of many races, creeds and professions, it is a trading center and university town. Ruled by a duke, it controls trade, borders and access between Deran and the northernmost nations of Astarel, Elder and Rokon.

Dark Elf - General term used for elves who have left the religion of the Elven god Verian (q.v) to throw in their lot with evil, usually in the cult of Arachnia. Dark elves have all the magical talents, beauty and intelligence of their brethren but no morals.

Deran - Constitutional monarchy in the northern lands of the Western continent of Damora. A nation built from the remnants of the Esten Empire, Deran is also a meritocracy, where nobles are elected by their peers and the legislature based on merit and ability more than noble connections. Deran has an advanced network of roads, potent military, and several universities. The seat of the Christian Church, Saint Martin's Town (St. Martin's), is in Deran.

Dragon - Everything one would expect in a fantasy environment, the reptilian race of dragons falls into the sub-races of sarkany, balar, drakes and true dragons. Some dragonkind are terrible and evil while others are noble and kind. An adult true dragon is massive, typically at least a hundred feet long and weighing many tons. Various subspecies can be winged or wingless and span an amazing array of colors. Dragons live for extremely long times (1000 years or more) if left alone.

Dwarf - One of the major races of Damora. The term "Dwarf" comes from the ancient elvish word, *duarfae* (Elv. *duar* = 'stone' + *fae/ fey/ fej* - = 'magic', literally "those of stone-magic"). A typical dwarf male is about four feet six inches tall. Dwarves tend to be burly, sturdy or muscular for their size and can live for almost two hundred years. Males are often bearded (though not all are). They are generally honorable and appreciate strength and resolve in others. Their main talent, as indicated by the name bestowed on them by the Elves, is in stonework and metallurgy.

Eleandir, Andyn - One of the Grey Riders, Andyn was added to the group while on her way to Forester. A priestess of the Elven god Verian and a wizard, Andyn has honey-blonde hair and amber eyes, a trim figure and a marvelous singing voice. Rather impatient and quick-tempered, she nonetheless displays unwavering faith, mercy, warmth and a nimble mind. She is a widow and seeks her husband's murderer with fierce resolution.

Elder Children - Colloquial name for an elf, used by humans, to denote their relatively long life spans.

Elf - One of the major races of Damora. The term "Elf" comes from the ancient word for their race, *Ellfae* (Elv. *ell* = 'life' + *fae/ fey/ fej* -= 'magic', literally "those of life-magic"). Elves are more slender than humans and possess intriguing eye colors, such as aqua, amber or violet; they also have a slight point to top of the ear, though this is not usually pronounced or even noted if the ears are concealed under hair, hat or helm. Elves tend to be a bit more reserved than the other races and have more of an affinity for magic of all kinds. They possess skills for getting along well with animals and have a remarkable talent for healing trees and plants. They dislike the underground but will tolerate it for short time periods if need arises. An elf can reach the age of almost 300 years. Elves are not particularly fertile; an average elven family will have 4-6 children, a remarkably low number considering their life span. For this reason, elves prize children highly and many seek to marry humans, since the humans' higher fertility rate and shorter life span virtually guarantees an elf at least two spouses and 8-14 children.

Elohir - Denizen of the planet of Celestia (the 5th planet of the 61 Virginis star, a single G6 spectral class, main-sequence yellow star approximately 28 light years from Earth). Sometimes called "Celestials", they appear to be winged humans. Skin color covers the range of typical shades seen in humans (porcelain, tanned, brown, yellow, dark brown) and their eyes are often compared to jewels. Their beauty is described as 'unearthly'. All possess potent magical and martial skills but are usually reluctant to meddle in the affairs of Damorans. They are uniformly kind, wise, honest and just. Elohir live extremely long lives (~ 2500 years) if not killed in warfare with their evil kindred.

Esten Empire - An empire formed of various kingdoms controlling much of the known world during the second age of Damora (known as the Imperial Age and denoted in calendars by the letters IY (for Imperial Year)). It fell after over a thousand years of rule due to infighting, a breakdown in the social fabric and the influence of evil.

Evendale - Small halfling nation south east of Deran and northeast of Terenai (q.v.). A republic, Evendale consists of seven districts or counties, each of which have a prescribed number of representatives (aldermen) and senators who draft laws that are approved by the High Minister, another elected position. A land with mild climate and productive farmland, Evendale nonetheless has a border with the Wilderness, which means the halflings are always on vigilant watch, having been invaded by evil tribes from the wild lands multiple times.

Forester - Town along the northern border highway of Deran. Forester is ruled by a baron and controls trade along the borderlands. Its defining feature is the central town proper, which is surrounded by a tall, well-built palisade with giant, living trees as its guard towers. Forester is the hometown of Dar Cabot (q.v.).

Ghai-zhal (Gobl. "Surface slug") - Goblin term for human.

Ghai-zhal-ik (Gobl. "Surface slug snack") - Goblin term for a halfling.

Gnome - Half-breed race resulting from the marriage of halfling and dwarf, gnomes possess features from each parent: natural affinity for stone and the underground from the dwarves and a cheerful disposition and natural talent with all things organic. Somewhat taller than halflings but shorter than dwarves, gnomes are industrious and found in all the known lands. They usually have dark hair, tan-to-dark complexions, and brown, amber or grey eyes. A typical gnome lives about 180 years or so.

Goblin - Short, half-simian creatures who often serve as foot-soldiers for the forces of evil, looking somewhat like horned chimpanzees. Extremely agile and able to use any available weapon that is sized for them, they are also good at hiding in shadows. They dislike sunlight. Their social structure is usually in a hierarchical monarchy, with the chieftain or king of a particular tribe wielding absolute authority. Goblins particularly hate dwarves since the two races compete for underground areas and resources. They are capable miners and are about the size of a gnome or tall halfling (a few inches short of four feet tall).

Gorlak - A goblin sergeant and aide to the Ja'al (q.v.) forces in *Whitehorse Peak*. Originally attached to Lady Aalre Sendatre (q.v.), he is more mentally adept than the average goblin and an original thinker.

Half-Elf - The offspring of a union between an elf (q.v.) and human, half-elves are a mix of their parents' heritage: magically talented, strong, adaptable and capable of learning new skills quickly. If it were not for the fact that they are noticeably larger than elves by a couple of inches in height, they would be indistinguishable from elves due to their predilection to inherit their elven parent's eye color, hair color and ear shape. Half-elves live to between 100 and 150 years.

Halfling - The smallest of the races, halflings (from the elven for "those of hearth magic" - *haliv-fae*) prefer pastoral villages and countrysides to large cities, though they are at home in any setting. As adaptable as humans, halflings have a talent for craftsmanship (with things other than stone) and farming. They are known for their skill in the kitchen and the durability of their finished goods. Halflings sometimes intermarry with dwarves, producing gnomes (q.v.) among their children. Their hair color (blonde, brown or black), skin color (porcelain to dark brown) and eye color (blue, green, black or grey) remind the other races of miniature humans. They live about 100 years or so.

Halkith - A human cleric of the Ja'al cult (q.v.), Halkith is a commander of troops in a set of bases in the Wilderness near Forester, Deran and is charged with a secret mission by his church hierarchy. Arrogant, controlling and cruel, Halkith tends to use people and things to further his ends without caring what happens to them. He is a violent individual and skilled in various types of evil magic.

Human - Humans on Damora (q.v) are much like real-life people of the planet Earth, with the exception that they can use magic in the same manner as elves, dwarves, halflings and other denizens of the fourth planet of 82 Eridani. Humans are energetic, adaptable, learn quickly and are endlessly curious about Damora and its people, flora and fauna. They live in all climates and places that will welcome them. They have the same coloring (skin, eyes and hair) as people of Earth. Humans can live to the age of 100. The origin of the word "human" has no Damoran equivalent as it does not translate from any Elven or Dwarven syntax.

Humana - Language of the human race on Damora (q.v).

Indidarc, Eric - One of the original Grey Riders, Eric is the adopted son of Melinor Indidarc (q.v.) a famous wizard. He meets Buck Bydecy (q.v.) on his way to Forester, Deran to seek his fortune as a blank-shield freelance mercenary guard. Able to use magic and martial weapons with equal proficiency, Eric is cheerful, optimistic and friendly. He treats everyone he meets with the same courtesy and kindness, whether a beggar or noble. Eric has violet eyes and blond hair and is a half-elf (q.v.)

Indidarc, Melinor - High Wizard of the northern kingdom of Deran, nobleman and confidante of royalty in the Kingdoms of the Northern Alliance (q.v.). He adopted both Eric and Saren (q.v) after his own children were grown. A formidable ally and genius with knowledge of magic, science, medicine, literature and history, Melinor is fluent in several languages. A kind but somewhat absent-minded man, he is singularly focused on thwarting evil plots in the known lands.

Irial - The halfling god of harvests, craftsmen and home, Irial is a benevolent deity who sometimes counts elves and humans among his adherents. The precepts of Irial are hospitality, kindness, courtesy, respect for people, animals and nature, and steadfastness in the face of hardship, whether caused by nature or evil designs.

Iron Thunder - Rough Humana translation of the name of a dragon who lives near the Deran borderlands and the town of Forester.

Ja'al - Also known as the Manipulator Church (for their penchant for twisting words, lying and otherwise using others callously for their own ends) the Ja'al are one of the evil religions on Damora. The cult is a polytheistic religion worshiping a number of harsh and cruel deities. The precepts of the Ja'al are world domination, rule of the strong over the weak, eugenics, personal gain at the cost of other people, and treachery.

Kaftu - Bipedal hyena-folk based on the hyena-men of African legend, the Kaftu resemble spotted hyenas with paws that can grasp weapons and have sufficient dexterity to cast magic spells. Ruled by queens, their tribes retain male Kaftu for specific roles (magical research, mating, manual labor, elite units) while the bulk of their warriors are female.

Kelematris - The dwarven name for Whitehorse Peak (Dw. "Mountain - Horse").

Lomin, Connor - Another of the original Grey Riders, Connor is a halfling who hails from Evendale (q.v.). Serious, but with a somewhat ribald sense of humor, Connor appears stoic and sober most of the time. He is knowledgeable about traps, curious about ancient ruins and secrets, and wields a broadsword, a rather heavy weapon for a halfling. Dark-eyed and dark-haired, he has a muscular build and an almost uncanny skill for moving unseen.

Northern Alliance - A multinational alliance similar to NATO in the real world, the Alliance is composed of Deran, Astarel, Rokon, Eldir, Evendale and Terenai.

Oakmoor - The capital city of Deran, home to over 300,000 people, Oakmoor is based on three large hills at the confluence of the East River and Lonmar Rivers. It has several suburbs in addition to the main city proper.

Ogre - Large, human-like creatures with fangs and odd-colored hair, ogres are brutish, violent, and not particularly smart. Their leaders are usually the more intelligent members of a particular tribe. Some of their number are smart enough to use magic. They are usually over seven feet tall and three hundred and fifty pounds. Used as shock troops by the forces of evil, ogres are also greedy and fearless.

Paladin - A holy warrior. Paladins are highly-trained fighters proficient with most weapons and heavy armor and adhere to a strict code of conduct and morals. Most of the good religions of Damora have paladins serving as free-lancers or special guards for high officials. Their reputation for faithfulness, bravery and skill along with the ability to use various forms of magic make them formidable agents of Light in the war against Darkness.

Peridragon - Small, dragon-like flying lizards, peridragons are not true dragons in the sense of being able to use magic and having long lives. Some are used as familiars by true dragons or wizards and have the equivalent intelligence of an eight-year-old human. They are skilled at camouflage.

Puup - Buck Bydecy's pet pigeon who somehow manages to avoid getting killed despite being in or near several battles.

Saren DeMey - The half-sister of Eric Indidarc by adoption, Saren DeMey was found by Melinor Indidarc as an infant and raised by him and his wife, Anne. A devout Christian, Saren appears to be a complete contradiction in terms as she is half-daemon but fights for the forces of good. Dark-haired and dark-eyed, she transforms to a bat-winged, horned half-daemon at will. As the wife of Terenil, the Earl of the Oakmoor (q.v.) suburb of Tallemar, she is ranked as a Countess of Deran.

Skyfire - A mysterious event from antiquity that changed the face of Damora. Legends say that visitors from another place arrived on disks or globes of fire and brought with them the Christian faith. The location of the actual arrival and the details of the event are lost in history. As a point of reference, it is rumored to have taken place more than 5000 years before the events of *Whitehorse Peak*.

Terenai (Elv. "Realm of the Elves") - The hereditary homeland of the Elven people, Terenai lies due south of Deran and also shares borders with Evendale (q.v.), Gorostol and Merdail. A verdant and fruitful land, it is heavily forested in places. It is ruled by an Emperor (or Empress) and is the oldest of the nations on Deran. Its capital city is Mil-Tereth (Elv. "King's Palace").

Troll - Large, brutish bipedal creatures similar to ogres but taller and heavier. Trolls are hairless and can have four arms rather than two. Somewhat related to giants, they are considerably less sophisticated. They prefer mountains and forests and will kill and eat anything edible. Cruel, greedy and selfish, they can nonetheless be outwitted by smarter creatures. Some more intelligent of their species can learn to use rudimentary magic. Trolls have the unnerving talent of being able to blend in with trees and rocks by merely holding still and often use this ability to ambush the unwary.

Tyler - A major city of Astarel (q.v.) located on the coast just north of the border with Deran (q.v.). It is known for its large harbor, excellent fishing fleet and naval base. It is the hometown of Buck Bydecy (q.v.).

Urmum - Goblin word for "Elf", used both in the singular and plural sense. Translated literally as "Glowing Thing", probably due to the fact that elves live in sunlight and are adept at magic.

Verian - Elven god of forests and nature (from the Elven "Veri" meaning "Lord" and Verian meaning "Highest Lord".) Followers of Verian worship in open structures usually in groves or copses of trees. The organizational structure is somewhat loose, with a council of high priests and priestesses making decisions of doctrine and teachings every year. Andyn Eleandir (q.v.) is a priestess of Verian.

Ward, Elaine - Childhood friend of Dar Cabot and waitress at a tavern in Forester named "The Pit". She has an attraction to Eric Indidarc during his stay in Forester.

Westhaven - A small town near Forester, Deran specializing in the hand-crafting of unique items of pottery (due to clay deposits nearby). Clarissa Eventide, a retired sage, is the de-facto leader of the community, which numbers slightly more than two dozen souls.

Za'Arak - Goblin word for their race, loosely translated as "The Rulers".

ABOUT THE AUTHOR

A route to fantasy fiction through the aerospace industry may seem an odd one to take, but PG Badzey has been writing stories since grammar school and has never stopped even though his path took an unconventional turn for someone interesting in writing. A trained systems engineer, he kept up with creative writing and coursework throughout a career working on the C-17 airlifter, the International Space Station, the Delta IV Rocket and the James Webb Space Telescope. He has enjoyed and been influenced by JRR Tolkien, C.S. Lewis, Katherine Kurtz, Christopher Stasheff, Terry Brooks and C. Dale Brittain, to name a few. Previous publications include short stories published in *Dragonlaugh*, an online fantasy humor magazine, and in January 2014, the publication of the first in the *Grey Riders* series of novels, the critically acclaimed *Whitehorse Peak*. PG Badzey has studied martial arts for many years, mentors a world-class high school robotics team, and is active in his parish community. He lives in California.

Find out more about the World of the Grey Riders at
https://pgbadzey.wordpress.com!

www.ingramcontent.com/pod-product-compliance
Lightning Source LLC
Chambersburg PA
CBHW072013110726
47910CB00005B/1743